W9-CEG-497

RESISTANCE
REBORN

BY REBECCA ROANHORSE

Trail of Lightning

Storm of Locusts

Race to the Sun

Del Rey books are available at special discounts for bulk purchases for sales promotions or corporate use. Special editions, including personalized covers, excerpts of existing books, or books with corporate logos, can be created in large quantities for special needs. For more information, contact Premium Sales at (212) 572-2232 or email specialmarkets@penguinrandomhouse.com.

RESISTANCE REBORN

REBECCA ROANHORSE

NEW YORK

Sale of this book without a front cover may be unauthorized.
If this book is coverless, it may have been reported to
the publisher as "unsold or destroyed" and neither the author
nor the publisher may have received payment for it.

Star Wars: Resistance Reborn is a work of fiction.
Names, places, and incidents either are products of
the author's imagination or are used fictitiously.
Any resemblance to actual persons, living or dead,
events, or locales is entirely coincidental.

2020 Del Rey Mass Market Edition

Copyright © 2019 by Lucasfilm Ltd. & ® or ™ where indicated.
All rights reserved.
Excerpt from *Star Wars: Galaxy's Edge: Black Spire*
by Delilah S. Dawson copyright © 2019 by Lucasfilm Ltd. & ®
or ™ where indicated. All rights reserved.

Published in the United States by Del Rey,
an imprint of Random House, a division of
Penguin Random House LLC, New York.

DEL REY and the HOUSE colophon are registered trademarks of
Penguin Random House LLC.

Originally published in hardcover in the United States
by Del Rey, an imprint of Random House,
a division of Penguin Random House LLC, in 2019.

ISBN 978-0-593-13013-1
Ebook ISBN 978-0-593-12843-5

Printed in the United States of America

randomhousebooks.com

2 4 6 8 9 7 5 3 1

Del Rey mass market edition: September 2020

To my big brother, Tony, who let his annoying
little sister play with his action figures
(even Boba Fett) and rarely complained.
Look what you started!

THE DEL REY
STAR WARS
TIMELINE

THE DEL REY

STAR WARS

TIMELINE

A long time ago in a galaxy far, far away. . . .

RESISTANCE
REBORN

PROLOGUE

THE TIE FIGHTER STREAKED across the Corellian sky, flames licking the sides of the ship and thick smoke billowing from its burning hull. The ship screamed loudly as it threatened to come apart midair, the dying cries of a metal bird. Below, the citizens of Coronet City paused in their evening commute to stare at the doomed ship. These days it was not so unusual to see a First Order fighter speeding above the city. The First Order had commandeered the shipyards of the capital to build its war machines, and sometimes those machines failed in a fiery mess. But this ship was different; it was being pursued by one of its own.

If the denizens of the capital city had looked more closely at the dying TIE, some of them might have noticed that the distressed ship was of an older model than its attackers, which meant it couldn't have been a prototype out on a test run. What they could not have seen was that the pilot of the doomed TIE fighter was a native daughter, a Corellian who grew up in the mountain town of Doaba Guerfel, not so far from the capital. A pilot who had dreamed under a New Republic flag as a child and when the First Order had arrived—and most of Corellia had balked but eventually bent to First Order occupation—the pilot had fought back. Only now her fighting days were quickly ending.

"Mayday, mayday, can you hear me?" the pilot cried into her comm. She blinked frustrated tears from her eyes, tasted blood in her mouth. Her head throbbed from where she had taken an earlier blow on the head in the firefight.

"Can anyone hear me?" she cried, again.

The pilot cycled desperately through the secured channels that the Resistance had provided her when she'd taken the mission, but no one answered. She tried the *Raddus* again, certain someone there would hear her, but nothing. Either the attack on her ship had severed the communications module, or the channels were being blocked.

She let out a small sob as the stolen TIE shuddered and rocked beneath her. She could feel the heat at her back, smell the acrid scent of the engine smoke as it filled the cockpit. She knew she had only seconds left to live, and she didn't want her mission to have failed.

Her assignment after the Hosnian cataclysm had been to help make sure the construction of a planet killer never happened in secret again, and the pilot was certain she had found something that would help defeat the First Order in the stolen encryption key she now had in her possession. But the precious code breaker would die with her if she couldn't pass it along. With a shaking hand, she quickly shoved the small datachip into the port just below her ruined holo display and held her breath until the console acknowledged it had read and uploaded the file.

She smiled, small and grim. She would not fail. If she couldn't get through to her Resistance contacts, perhaps there was another way. Another way from her past. She briefly clutched the small snake pendant she always wore around her neck, muttered a plea to her gods, and then, from memory, she punched in the illegal radio signal that would call the only person she still trusted on her homeworld.

She held her breath and waited.

But no one answered, and it was too late. She couldn't wait to confirm the connection. She would just have to hope.

She hit the command to transmit, knowing that sending the key put her friend in danger. If anyone found out, they would have a First Order target on their backs. But she had no choice.

A bright blinking green light told her that the transfer was complete just as a blinding brightness surrounded her. She opened her mouth, but she didn't have time to scream before her world disintegrated around her.

The citizens of Coronet City watched the TIE explode into nothingness. Some curious, most apathetic. And then they continued on home to waiting

families and household pets, or to the cantina to
meet with friends, or to a thousand other places
under the setting sun. The exploding TIE didn't
even make the evening newsfeeds, and by the next
morning, it was all but forgotten.

CHAPTER 1

LEIA JERKED AWAKE, HER head snapping back against the rough fabric of the headrest. Her hands grasped for purchase in the armless chair as she tried to keep herself from falling. She cried out, a small startled breath in the otherwise empty room, as her fingers clasped around the edge of the console table. It took her a moment for her senses to come back to her and for her to remember where she was. The low hum of machinery and the distant clank of someone doing repairs, even at this odd hour, told her she was on the *Millennium Falcon*. Not on the *Raddus*, during the First Order's attack, when she had felt the presence of her son nearby. Not in the cold darkness of space into which she had been flung immediately after.

She had been dreaming just now. The same dream that had plagued her since it happened. She was alone, cold, her body failing, her spirit lost, surrounded by the vast emptiness of space. In real life she had woken, and the Force had flared hot and alive in her. And it had brought her back, guided her to safety. But in the dream, she stayed suspended in the void. Failing her friends, her family, and the people she had vowed to lead. Failing her son most of all. Everyone she loved, dead.

"When did I get so morbid?" she muttered to herself, pushing her aching body upright in her chair. She knew when. Since she had died. Well, almost died. She'd had plenty of close calls in her life. The bombing during her senatorial days back on Hosnian Prime. The torture session with Vader that even now, decades later, spiked her adrenaline and set her on edge when even the barest hint of that memory surfaced. A million narrow escapes with Han back in the days of the Rebellion. But nothing quite like being blasted out of that ship, drifting through space alone.

She rubbed a tired hand over her face, looking around. It had been a long few days since Chewie and Rey had shown up on Crait to rescue them from the First Order. Since she had seen her brother again and lost him just as quickly. She wondered how much she was supposed to suffer in a single lifetime, how much exactly one person could take. But then she put that indulgent self-pitying moment away. She had work to do.

The communications console of the *Millennium Falcon* was laid out before her, silent as space itself. When she had called for aid on Crait, sending out her distress signal to her allies, she was sure someone would respond. But they had not, and that fact still shook her. Were they alive? Was her signal being blocked? Or—the answer she least wanted to contemplate—did they just not care?

No, she wouldn't believe that. Couldn't. Something had happened that prevented her calls from reaching friendly ears. That made more sense than believing she and the Resistance had been so thoroughly abandoned. She would figure out what went wrong, and until then, she would keep trying.

She reached for the communications rig just as the speaker in her headphones buzzed to life and a green light blinked, signaling that a transmission was waiting. Her heart ticked up in anticipation. Someone was trying to reach the *Millennium Falcon*. She slid the headphones on, adjusting the mike as static rained through the connection. Without the sensor dish, the *Falcon*'s subspace radio signal was scratchy at best.

She punched in the encryption code, opening the channel to whoever was on the other end and had known the code as well.

"Hello?" she whispered anxiously into the mike. "Who is this?"

At first, all she got was more static, but then the voice resolved, faint but getting stronger. ". . . Zay with Shriv . . . mission . . . remember me?"

A small flutter of defeat flickered in Leia's stomach. She had hoped it would be one of the Resistance allies, a powerful government offering refuge or ships or other aid. But it was the girl she had met directly after the destruction of Starkiller Base, the daughter of Iden Versio and Del Meeko. She remembered Zay well. Her parents had both been

Imperials-turned-rebels, her grandfather the notorious Admiral Garrick Versio. The girl had lost both parents, had already been through so much at so young an age. Well, hadn't they all? Leia certainly had. It was the nature of war, to put its children through hell, to murder their parents.

"Stop!" she told herself loudly, her voice echoing around the room.

"What?" Zay asked, through the static.

"Not you," Leia said hastily. "I didn't mean you." How embarrassing. Leia shook off her malaise and pressed the headphone to her ear, leaning into the mike. "Say it again, Zay. I'm having trouble hearing you. You're breaking up."

"Oh." And then louder and slower. "SHRIV AND I . . . HAVE GOTTEN . . . SOME PROMISING LEADS . . . ?"

Leia smiled good-naturedly at the girl's exaggerated overcorrection. "I can hear you fine now. Speak normally."

"Oh yeah? So, we tracked down some old friends of my mother who were Imperials but have renounced and have no love for the First Order. We're going to pay them a visit, if that's okay with you. It will take another three or four standard days, at least."

"What happened to the Resistance allies I asked you to find?"

"That's the distressing thing," Zay said. "They're all gone."

"Gone?"

"Or at least they're not where they should be.

We've hit over half the names you gave us and found nothing. In some cases, whole homes just abandoned."

"Maybe they've gone into hiding." Or worse.

"Whatever it is, General, something bad is happening."

Leia rubbed her neck, feeling the tension locked in her muscles. More allies out of reach. Zay was right. Something was happening, and it scared Leia, too.

"Zay, I want you to keep looking. Find out what you can."

"Copy. And the ex-Imperials?"

Leia hadn't imagined ex-Imperials would be the allies she needed, but it looked like their options were thinning. And who knew? Zay's mother proved that some of the fiercest rebel fighters out there had once been on the other side. People were complicated, and if there was one thing the Empire had been good at it was offering people what they thought they needed—only for them to find out that the peace and order they desired came at too high a price. Leia would never hold someone's past against them. She had enough demons in her family tree to guarantee she was not one to judge.

On the other end, Leia heard muttering and muffled arguing, as if someone had placed their hand over the mike. After a moment, Zay came back.

"Shriv says you should trust us. After all, what could go wrong?"

What, indeed? "All right, if Shriv agrees that the ex-Imperial leads are solid, go ahead and extend your mission. But be careful. There's . . . it's not safe to go up against the First Order." Like the girl with the dead mother didn't know that.

"Not a problem, General. We'll use caution."

More muffled muttering. "Oh, and Shriv says 'Careful' is his middle name. Plus, he's not dead yet, so somebody or something out there must be looking out for us."

"Yes," Leia said quietly to herself, and then into the mike, "May the Force be with you, Inferno Squad."

"Same to you. Over and out!"

Leia pressed the button to end her connection and leaned back. She hoped she hadn't given the girl too much responsibility too soon. Zay couldn't be many years older than sixteen, but at sixteen Leia was already fomenting the Rebellion. If anyone knew that youth could be underestimated, it was her. No, Zay was strong, smart. Capable. And with Shriv as a steadying force, she trusted they'd complete the mission.

A sharp pain in her temple brought Leia's thoughts up short. She squeezed her eyes shut in sudden agony. These headaches were a side effect of the healing process, the medical droid had said. She was to expect them to last for a few weeks, but between the headaches, the nightmares of being lost in space, and the grief of losing her friends and family, Leia was exhausted. What she wouldn't give for just a moment of relaxation, of safety; a few days or even a handful of hours of knowing everything would be all right.

"General Organa?"

The voice came from behind her and Leia turned to find Rey standing in the doorway. The girl wore a version of the same scavenger garb style Leia had first seen her in the previous day, only now Leia recognized touches of Jedi influence in her ensemble. *She's changing,* Leia thought, *but there's still some Jakku there that she hasn't let go.* But perhaps that wasn't fair. Perhaps Rey simply clung to the simple things she knew in a sea of chaos, the way they all did. Speaking of simple, Rey held a steaming cup of something in her hands and when she saw Leia notice, she proffered it forward.

"I brought you a cup of Gatalentan tea," Rey said.

Leia smiled. "Do you read minds?"

"What, like a Jedi? I . . . I'm not—"

"I was just thinking about how much I would love a cup of tea," Leia said, saving Rey from her awkward scramble. "Nothing Jedi about it. Just"— she motioned Rey forward—"a welcome surprise. Thank you. And please, call me Leia."

Rey nodded, looking relieved, and hurried forward. Leia took the tea from her. The fragrance immediately filled her nose, and she could feel the muscles in her shoulders loosen.

"I could get you something stronger if you like," Rey said, pointing back toward the galley from which she'd obviously come. "I think Chewbacca keeps some caf in there."

Leia blew across the hot beverage, sending small tendrils of steam floating through the air. "I'm surprised he had this." Ah, but it probably wasn't Chewbacca that kept a stash of Gatalentan tea on the *Millennium Falcon,* but Han. Oh, Han. Gone, too.

"And I've made you sad," Rey said, noticing the look on Leia's face.

"Not you," Leia corrected her. "Life. This war. You are a light in the darkness." She gestured to the seat across from her.

"I didn't mean to stay. I just heard your voice in here and thought you might need the tea."

"Well, you were right, and I insist you stay. I could use the company, and you're making me nervous standing there. Please." She gestured toward the seat again and this time Rey sat, sliding her hands under her thighs and smiling awkwardly. "There," Leia said, patiently, hoping to put the girl at ease, "isn't that better?"

Rey nodded. The two sat in silence as Leia sipped her tea and Rey made a show of looking around the room, gaze floating across the communications board. Leia followed her wandering regard.

"Why aren't you asleep like everyone else?" Leia asked.

"Oh, me? I haven't slept much these past few days," Rey said quietly. "Too much on my mind."

"I know the feeling."

Rey shifted in her seat, eyes on everything but Leia. My, but this girl was nervous. She hadn't seemed this nervous when they'd met earlier. But so much had happened since then, or maybe she just had something on her mind.

"Rey—" she started.

"I heard you talking to someone," Rey said hastily. "Did you finally get through to our allies?"

"Not yet," Leia confessed. "That call was from a couple of pilots I have scouting, but, and I hope this doesn't come out wrong, we need more than pilots. We need leadership. Pilots are crucial, but the First Order took Holdo, Ackbar, others." She sighed, the grief heavy in her bones. Leaders she had called them, yes, but also friends. People she had known most of her life, now gone. "We need strategists, thinkers, those with the means and will to lead us forward. To inspire others to do the same."

"I didn't know them," Rey admitted. "I'm sorry for your loss."

Leia nodded. "We've all experienced loss."

Finally Rey met her gaze, a question lurking there. *Perhaps she wants to talk about Luke,* Leia thought. *We spoke of him, but briefly. Just an acknowledgment that he was at peace in the end.* But then Rey said . . .

"Kylo Ren. He's your son . . ."

Ah. Leia nodded and drank from her now cooling cup. Rey squirmed uncomfortably in her seat.

"What happened to him?" she finally asked. "I mean, how did he turn to the dark side? He started in the light, didn't he? He told me a story about Luke, about his training." She exhaled. "I guess I just want to understand."

"I do, too."

"So you don't know?"

"I think you would have to ask Ben what happened to him."

"He wanted me to join him, but I couldn't. I thought I could help him, but he only wanted me to become like him."

Rey's face fell, and Leia could see the pain etched there. The girl cared about Ben, and he had disappointed her. "Ben has made his choices," Leia said. "No one can save Ben but himself. And I don't know if that is what he wants."

Rey nodded, a sharp dip of her chin. "I know that. I mean, rationally I know, but I guess I held out hope."

"Hope is good," Leia said, her voice gentle with understanding. "Hope is important, and sometimes it is all we have. But," she said, smiling, "what does hope have to do with being rational?" She held out her hand and Rey leaned forward and took it, pressing her palm to Leia's and squeezing.

"I don't know how I'm going to do this," Rey whispered quietly.

"But you will do it," Leia said, her voice a little louder, filled with a little more steel. "And you won't be alone. We will be here with you."

Rey seemed to steady, and a smile blossomed briefly, her first since she'd arrived.

A buzzing on the console and Leia answered. "Hello?" she called into the mike. "Identify yourself."

"General Organa! It's Poe!"

"Poe." She turned slightly away from Rey. "Where are you? What's your status?"

"Ikkrukk. It was close, but Black Squadron pulled through. Zero casualties although Jess and Sura-linda were pretty banged up. But I can report that Grail City is secured. We sent the First Order running."

Finally a small bit of good news. "Wonderful, Poe. And the prime minister, Grist? Is she well?"

A moment of static and then Poe was back. "Can confirm that yes, Prime Minister Grist survived. And she's invited us to a party."

Leia exchanged a look with Rey, who gave her a small grin.

"Poe, can you do something for me?"

"Anything, General."

"Go to Grist's party and tell me what the attitude is there among the guests about the First Order."

"Well, considering the First Order attacked them, I imagine they're none too happy right now."

"Maybe not publicly. You will need to look past their words, Poe. Be alert for the subtler things. Note who still won't criticize the First Order, or who criticizes too loudly, as if to prove their loyalties. Notice who's not at the party. Did anyone declare themselves openly with the separatist faction?"

A moment when Poe was clearly talking to someone else and then, "Cannot confirm. But I'll keep an eye out."

"You do that. And see what Grist is willing to commit to the Resistance. That was the reason Black Squadron was there to begin with. Your timing ended up being fortuitous, so let's see if that buys us anything."

"Okay. Anything else, General?"

"Yes. Have fun. You survived the battle and you're all still alive for another day. Make sure to enjoy it."

"Flying's all the joy I need, but I hear you, General. Copy that."

"And let me know where Black Squadron will head next. Grail City is a good win, but we have so much farther to go."

"Copy that," he repeated. "Okay, Poe out."

The transmission clicked off and Leia leaned back, the worn chair creaking under her weight.

"Well, that's good," Rey said, startling Leia. She'd forgotten the girl was there, she was so quiet.

"Yes, it is," Leia agreed. "But it's barely a drop in the bucket of what we need."

"But every drop counts, right? A drop here and there and before you know it, you have an ocean."

An ocean. What did a girl who'd grown up on Jakku know about oceans? But Leia said, "I like the way you think, Rey. Yes, you're right. No need to minimize what Poe and his Black Squadron accomplished. Now, why don't you get some rest?"

As if on cue, Rey's jaw cracked in a yawn. "Yeah, maybe I should. I was working on the compressor. The humidity on Ahch-To caused the condensation to build up in the casing. I need to clean it out, find the leak, and seal . . ." She pressed her lips together. "I'm sure you don't care." She stood.

"On the contrary, I'm glad you're taking such good care of Han's ship." Leia lifted the cup. "Thank you again for the tea."

Rey gave her a quick nod and left.

Ahch-To. Of course. That was where Rey had found Luke. Maybe the girl did know something about oceans after all. And perhaps there was a lesson in there for Leia, too.

She shook her head, rueful, and turned back to the communications console. One more attempt, she told herself, and then she'd follow her own advice to Rey and try to get some sleep. Today it was droplets, she thought, and tomorrow it would be a river. And perhaps, eventually, a mighty sea that could stand against the First Order. It seemed improbable, but improbable was all she had.

She ran through her list of allies again, starting at the beginning.

CHAPTER 2

SURALINDA JAVOS WAS DRUNK. Or at least Poe was fairly certain that Black Squadron's Squamatan pilot was drunk. Why else would she be up on that stage doing . . . well, he wasn't exactly sure what she was doing. Poe shook his head. He loved Black Squadron. Would die for any one of his pilots. But sometimes he wondered.

When Prime Minister Grist had invited Black Squadron for a celebratory drink to toast their victory in securing Grail City against the First Order, it had been politic to accept. He knew his job here was part pilot and part diplomat, and anything he could do to secure Ikkrukk's support of the Resistance was something he had to do.

"Shouldn't they be happy enough that we saved their butts from the bad guys?" Jess Pava grumbled when Poe told Black Squadron that they'd be going to a party.

"Don't you like a party, Jess?" Suralinda asked, laughing. "I mean, I can't think of a better reason to have a drink than survival. Besides, I'd love to get a quote or something from the prime minister, something I can use to really make the story sing."

"You're writing a story?" Poe asked, surprised.

"Of course I'm writing a story," the pilot-turned-journalist-turned-back-to-pilot said. She shook her head, her brown eyes set in mock disappointment. "When are you going to get the hang of this public relations thing, Poe? My journalistic skills are an asset to the Resistance, but only if we get our story out there. And what a story it will be with Grist praising our ragtag group of heroes saving her and the planet from the evil First Order!"

Ragtag? After Crait, that was closer to reality than Poe cared to admit.

"That's not a story. That's just the truth," Jess said. Poe looked at her sharply, wondering if she knew how bad things were for the Resistance, but his fellow pilot was guileless.

"Of course it's the truth," Suralinda said, sounding annoyed. "I don't lie, Jess. I just"—Suralinda waved a hand, as if conjuring something out of thin air—"embellish."

Jess folded her arms across her chest and let her long black hair fall across her face, unimpressed. Poe had noticed that her and Suralinda's relationship was often strained, but if he thought about it, it was no more contentious than anyone else's relationship with Suralinda. She was an old friend of Poe's from his navy days, but she was hard to pin down even at the best of times. Her loyalties seemed to shift and eventually land right back on Suralinda alone, but he couldn't deny that she had been there for him and Black Squadron when they most needed her, including right here at Grail City. Jess wouldn't have gotten the defense system back up without Suralinda's help, and it was good for everyone to remember that. Even if Suralinda sounded selfish now, Poe knew she would have their backs when push came to shove, and that's what mattered.

"So," Suralinda said, hands on her hips. "Who's up for a party?"

"Pass," Jess said, turning away. "I want to check on my astromech. After what I put the little guy through . . ."

Suralinda grunted disapprovingly. "Poe? Surely you're coming."

"I kind of have to. It would be rude not to . . ."

"Exactly!" She slid her arm around Poe's and pulled him along before she looked over her shoulder at the other two members of Black Squadron. "Karé? Snap? Care to join us?"

Temmin Wexley, whom everyone called Snap, took the hand of his wife, Karé Kun, and motioned Poe and Suralinda forward. "Lead the way. I wouldn't mind a drink. And I hear Ikkrukk makes a great ale."

"It's fine to have a drink," Poe said, "but I need everyone to keep your eyes and ears open, too. Anything you find out may prove useful." He paused, looking over his shoulder. "Beebee-Ate, you coming or staying?"

The little droid beeped his reply, and Poe nodded. "Keep an eye on the ships for us, then. And help Jess out if she asks."

BB-8 whirled, sounding distressed.

"I'm not going to hurt you," Jess protested, clearly offended. Poe kept the grin from his face. He knew the droids called Jess the Great Destroyer because of how many astromechs she sent to the scrapyard, but he trusted her with BB-8. As long as they stayed on the ground.

"Have fun," Jess said, sighing, her hands on her hips and her eyes on the astromechs who all were now conferring with BB-8.

"We will!" Suralinda said, smiling big enough to show her needle-sharp teeth, which were as much a part of her Squamatan heritage as her blue skin and taloned nails. "We'll have fun and we'll get some information. Win-win."

Jess waved them away over her shoulder, already focused on the droids, and the four of them headed to the palace where Prime Minister Grist of Ikkrukk waited for them.

That had been an hour ago.

Poe had politely nursed an Ikkrukk ale for that hour. He'd taken a single sip under the prime minister's watchful eye. The dark bitter brew had sat like engine fuel on his tongue, but he'd managed to swallow it down without a telltale grimace. He'd then proceeded to circulate through the party, engaging in small talk with the guests, looking for the signs Leia had told him would reveal loyalties and uncover motivations. He made mental notes as he moved among the civic leaders and politicians, and what he saw worried him. There was doubt here, fear that perhaps fighting back had only doomed Ikkrukk to a more brutal invasion in the future. That perhaps First Order occupation wouldn't be so terrible, that cooperation was a more viable strategy than war, and that maybe there was even financial profit in joining the First Order.

Poe held his tongue through it all, but inside he wanted to scream. Black Squadron had risked their lives to save this city, this planet, and now Grail City was questioning whether it had been the right thing to do. He wanted to shout that they were cowards, all of them, ready to bow down to the First Order to save their own tails and line their already well-lined pockets without a concern for what occupation would do to the average citizen on the street. He wanted to warn them that occupation might seem reasonable now, but if they allowed the First Order to establish itself on the planet, the grip that began as loose would inevitably tighten until Ikkrukk was choking.

But he didn't. Instead, he circled back around to the prime minister.

"Are you enjoying the party?" Prime Minister Grist asked politely, a dour eye on Poe's almost untouched ale.

Poe gave up all pretenses of drinking, handing the glass off to a passing server. "I was hoping we could talk about Ikkrukk's promise to aid the Resistance."

"Promise?" Grist said, voice fluttering in distress. "I don't recall a promise."

Poe pressed his lips together. When he had first talked to Grist fresh off Black Squadron bringing down the First Order ship that had threatened to obliterate Grail City, she had indeed made promises about doing whatever she could to aid the Resistance. But now, a few hours later and her city out of immediate danger, it appeared her memory was conveniently failing her.

"It's not that we don't want to help," Grist said, sounding regretful. "We are grateful, and we wish we could do more to show our appreciation for your cause. But my engineers have reported substantial damage not only to our defense system but also within the city itself. It seems the First Order sympathizers tried to destroy as many cultural centers as they could before they were defeated. It's imperative we rebuild immediately, so that people understand the First Order cannot beat us. You understand."

"I don't think I do," Poe said, a touch of anger in his voice. He wondered if he should mention that the routing of First Order sympathizers might need to continue within her own cabinet but decided that wouldn't win him any points. He was trying to be diplomatic. Well, as close to diplomatic as he could manage. He had never been known for his tact.

The prime minister's golden eyes faded around the edges. "Oh dear."

"It's not that I don't appreciate your situation," Poe said, doing his best to rein in his irritation. "But you have to understand the urgency of *our* situation."

"Of course I understand, and I can promise you that the First Order will find no purchase here."

"Are you sure of that?" It was out of his mouth before he could stop himself.

Grist blinked. She took a moment, as if to reset her own temper, before she said, "Yes, I am certain. But we simply cannot actively support the Resistance. We are already a target for First Order occupation. I don't dare give them more cause to return. However, in appreciation for your efforts on our behalf, I am happy to provide you with fuel and food, enough to see you on your way." Grist's well-managed smile was brittle.

And there it was. The dismissal. Poe knew a lost cause when he saw one, and while he usually took on more than his share of lost causes, Ikkrukk didn't feel like one he was interested in fighting for. He made noises about being grateful and excused himself from the hopeless conversation, more disturbed than he let show. He couldn't help but worry. If a planet fresh from a First Order attack was this reluctant to take a chance to aid Leia's Resistance, what would a planet that hadn't seen the violence up close think? Maybe Suralinda and her ragtag-hero story did have a point beyond embarrassing them all. He'd have to talk to her about it more, see how maybe they could get the news out on the holofeeds, past the political gatekeepers and into the eyes and hearts of the common people. But first, he had his own news to share with his squad. He'd been putting it off long enough.

He found Snap and Karé huddled in a corner, their heads so close they almost touched as they talked, Karé's darkly tanned skin contrasted against

Snap's paler shade, her blond hair against his brown. They might be physical opposites in a lot of ways, but they were one of the most well-suited couples Poe knew. Their relationship always impressed him.

"Am I interrupting?" he asked.

"Of course not," Karé said, easily making space for him. "Join us."

Poe sat on the low bench across from the couple, sinking into the deep cushions. He shifted his weight back and forth in an effort to get comfortable but only succeeded in working his way deeper into the doughy seating.

"They do like a good pillow here," Snap said, laughing. All the furniture in the prime minister's cave palace was carved from the same rock as the walls that surrounded them, from the low flat benches to the equally low tables. It seemed to be the fashion here to soften all that hardness with rich fabrics, so the palace was adorned with wide swaths of embroidered shimmersilks and wildly colorful paintings on the rock walls themselves. Cushions in a riot of colors were piled two or more deep on every seat.

"No kidding," Poe said. "I feel like I'm sinking."

"It's kind of nice after sitting in a pilot's seat all the time," Karé countered. "Nobody designed an X-wing for comfort, that's for sure."

Frustrated, Poe pulled the cushion off the bench and dumped it on the floor at his feet, revealing the hard stone beneath. He sat on the bare rock. "That's better."

Snap and Karé laughed and Poe grinned back. He

looked at his friends with a deep fondness. "I'm glad you both are here," he said, his voice earnest. "I mean it. It was close up there . . ."

"It's always close," Karé said.

"How'd the talk with the prime minister go?" Snap asked.

"Worse than expected," he admitted. "I don't think the Resistance is going to find support here."

"After we saved them?"

Poe shrugged, a wave of resignation rolling over him. "Not everyone sees it that way."

"They're scared," Karé said, "of the First Order."

"We're all scared," Snap said, softly. "But we fight anyway."

Poe pressed his palms together, suddenly feeling anxious. He knew he had to tell Snap, Karé, and the rest of Black Squadron what had happened on Crait, what was left of the Resistance, and the part he had played in it all, but he wasn't looking forward to it.

"There's something we need to tell you, Poe," Snap said before Poe could speak. He glanced at his wife, Karé, who gave him an encouraging nod. "It didn't go so well back on Pastoria, that first planet in our mission brief. I don't want to say we were duped into doing the dirty work for some unscrupulous jerk, but . . ." He spread his hands, a gesture of helplessness.

"We thought we were doing the right thing." Karé rested a hand on her husband's knee, her voice gentle.

"Yeah," Poe said, "Jess sent a transmission out

when she and Suralinda were trying to restore the planetary defense system here. She was afraid she wouldn't make it and she wanted someone to know what had happened, just in case."

Snap's shoulders tensed. "We were lied to, sure, but that doesn't change the fact that we picked the wrong side in a civil war. Hell, we shouldn't have been picking sides to begin with."

"We thought we were protecting the government, but instead we only helped take out the opposition party," Karé further explained. "It was a disaster."

"It was a screwup of epic proportions," Snap agreed.

"Trust me, I've got my own screwup to tell you about that makes yours look reasonable." He took a deep breath and exhaled slowly. He looked each of his friends in the eye, not sure how they were going to take the news, but knowing it was more important than ever that they understood what they were up against. What they were all up against.

"You know who Vice Admiral Holdo is, right? Well—"

A screech that rattled the walls pulled him up short. The three turned to see Suralinda front and center on a raised dais that functioned as a stage. The prime minister had given a reasonably laudatory speech about Black Squadron's rescue of Grail City from the dais when they'd first arrived and then ceded the spot to a three-piece band. They'd been playing some kind of innocuous background party music all night, until now. A deep thumping bass emanated from a flat drumlike instrument that the musician stomped with a foot, and a sonorous wind instrument of some kind joined in, lacing the melody around the heavy beat. And then . . . Suralinda.

"What in the world is that noise?" Snap asked.

Karé had instinctively clapped her hands over her ears. "I-I think she's . . . singing?"

They listened a bit longer and sure enough, Poe could make out words in between the shrill trills and warbles. Poe had visited a lot of worlds and seen a lot of unsavory things, even done a few himself, but seeing Suralinda belting out a tune had to rank up there with the worst.

"Is she drunk?" he asked anyone who was listening. "I mean, she has to be drunk."

Karé shook her head. "No, I think that's just her singing voice. Squamatans aren't known for their musicality."

Suralinda raised her hands over her head and kicked out a long leg. She swayed her hips to one side and then the next and then came up on her toes.

"Or their dancing," Karé added drily.

"And that's our cue." Poe stood up. "Time for Black Squadron to make our exit. We've got another mission, and it doesn't involve attending this party or, mercifully, Suralinda singing and dancing. You both ready to get out of here?"

Snap and Karé were on their feet immediately.

"Seriously, Poe," Snap said. "I thought you'd never ask."

———

They waited until Suralinda had finished her mercifully short rendition of whatever song she was crooning to leave. Black Squadron departed to a round of surprisingly enthusiastic applause, for their heroism or for removing Suralinda from the stage, Poe wasn't sure, but he took a deep and refreshing breath of fresh air once they were out of the palace.

"Not your scene?" Snap asked, standing next to his commanding officer.

Poe shivered. It was colder out here in the rocky mountains after the sun set. Beyond them was a wide expanse of starry sky. Somewhere out there was Leia and what was left of the Resistance, and they were counting on him.

"I love a party," Poe said, slapping Snap on the shoulder, "but we've got work to do. Let's get back to Jess and the ships and I'll fill everyone in."

Snap nodded and they all retraced their steps down the winding mountain path to their ships. Suralinda was in a fine mood and kept the chatter up with Karé, who seemed to be taking the whole night in stride. Around them Grail City was celebrating, and music and laughter filled the night. Colorful lights spilled from windows, and the smell of roasting meats wafted down to make their mouths water.

"It's a nice place," Snap said quietly. "I'm glad we could help them out."

"Yeah," Poe said, but he wondered how long Grail City would remain a nice place and how long it would take the First Order to try again. And if they did, whether Grail City would fight them or welcome them in. He thought about pressing his case, even trying to force Grist's hand for the sake of her city. But he knew where that path probably led, and he wouldn't do that again. He shivered involuntarily. Well, it was Prime Minister Grist's problem now. He just hoped she was up to the challenge.

The X-wings, Suralinda's A-wing, and Poe's loaner from Grakkus the Hutt huddled together on the open landing strip, shadowy masses in the growing darkness. Poe's keen eyes scanned the area, looking for Jess. He caught sight of her, apparently napping between the boxes of food rations and fuel cells that Grist's people had already delivered. *Well, at least Ikkrukk kept their word about that,* he thought, *and quickly.* Grist really did want them gone.

"Hey, Jess," he called, as he approached.

No answer, and he tapped a nearby box with a toe. "Wake up, Pava, we got a mission brief."

Jess's eyes popped open and for a moment, she looked terrified. Poe stepped back, surprised. "You okay?"

"Oh." She sat up, shaking off what was left of her sleep. "Yeah, bad dreams is all. I-I thought for a minute I was back on . . . well, never mind."

Poe squatted down beside her. "You having nightmares? Something I should know about?"

"What? No." She flushed and rubbed self-consciously at her neck. "I mean, no more than usual."

"Right." Poe held out a hand and helped her to

her feet. "I'd tell you to report to medbay for an eval, but . . ."

She grimaced. "Kind of impossible. Besides, I'm fine."

"I need you whole and healthy, Pava. Truth is, it's only going to get harder from here."

She frowned. "What do you mean?"

"Come on. Let's gather the others."

He motioned the rest of Black Squadron over, and they gathered by their ships under the stretch of the night sky. And he told them. Everything. Of the D'Qar evacuation and his decisions that led to the loss of the Resistance bomber squadron, of the slow chase across space, of Rose Tico and Finn's mission to Canto Bight, of his own insubordination and demotion, and, finally, of the Battle of Crait and all they had lost. And what little they had left.

"I don't understand," Jess said, her voice an octave too high. "They're gone? The fleet is gone?"

"They can't be all gone," Karé countered. "Can they, Poe?"

"I'm sorry," he said, head lowered.

"Oh . . ." she covered her mouth with her hands and turned away. Snap gathered her to his chest. Poe could see tears in his eyes.

"The people, too?" Jess asked. "Are you sure?"

"Jess," Poe said gently. "I was there. The Resistance . . ." He spread his hands. "It's pretty much the *Falcon*, and us."

Silence, as Poe let it sink in. Just how bad it all was, just how desperate they were. And how much of their situation was his fault.

"I understand if you want to leave. I mean, if you want to leave without me. Black Squadron seemed to be doing fine without my presence. But if you stay and allow me to lead you, I will do everything in my power to make it up to you. That, I promise."

He closed his mouth and waited. For their confusion, for their judgment, for their disavowals. When all he got was silence, he looked up.

Snap was the first to speak. "That's some heavy stuff, Poe," he said, voice serious. "And I'd be lying if I said it didn't bother me."

"I underst—"

"But," Snap continued before he could finish. "Didn't I just tell you about our massive disaster on Pastoria? People died because we let ourselves get played. We have to live with that, too."

"The droids call me the Great Destroyer," Jess added. "Still. I mean, it's not like I'm trying to get them killed, but they end up scrap all the same."

"Well—"

"And I'm pretty sure my middle name is *Insubordination*," Suralinda added, "but that's because I'm misunderstood."

"I'm not making excuses for—"

"You're going to have to face your mistakes, Poe," Karé said, "and make amends where you can. But you'll do it with Black Squadron at your side. You're not getting rid of us that easily. Besides, it sounds like all we've got is one another, screwups and all."

The heaviness that Poe had been carrying lifted a bit. They weren't saying what he did was okay, but they weren't going to abandon him, either. "I'll work to make it better," he said, quietly, head down, shame heavy on his shoulders. "I swear it."

And then there were arms around him and faces too close and steady words of encouragement. Poe soaked it all in like a dying man given an impossible reprieve. He had hoped that Black Squadron would forgive him, if only enough to let him stay on as their leader, but he had never dared to dream they might actually understand him. After the group hug broke up and the camaraderie settled, Poe took a step back, raising a hand.

"Now it's time to talk about what's next."

"Revenge?" Jess asked, voice rough with emotion. Poe knew that she had been friends with many of the people lost when the First Order shot down their escape pods over Crait.

"Eventually," Poe said, "but not quite yet. Leia has given us a mission. Well, a continuation of the mission she first assigned Black Squadron. The Resistance needs not just allies, but leaders. So we're to narrow our search to specific people—strategists, thinkers, elders—that we think can help us rebuild and quickly."

"Makes sense," Karé said, thoughtfully. "Any ideas where we start?"

"Yeah, and Snap, you might not like this one."

Snap frowned, thick arms crossing his chest. "Why is that?"

"I want you and Karé to go talk to Wedge Antilles."

Snap's eyes widened almost theatrically. He shook

his head, one sharp no. "Negatory, Poe. Wedge is retired. Settled down with my mother on Akiva. The last thing they need is me showing up and dragging them back into a war. They earned their rest."

"I know," Poe said, sympathetically. "And I wouldn't ask if we weren't desperate."

"No way Mom is going to want him to go."

"I know that, too. And I'm counting on it. I want Norra to join us, too."

Snap Wexley made a deep guttural sound in his broad chest. "My mom? She's nuts, you know that, right?"

"She's a damn good pilot."

"She's great! But she's also nuts."

"All the best pilots are," Suralinda murmured, loud enough for everyone to hear.

"You don't get it," he pressed. "She has no self-preservation instinct. Did you know she once jettisoned herself in an escape pod over Jakku, all to chase an Imperial admiral through a blockade?"

Poe held back a grin. It wasn't *that* crazy. "We need her, Snap."

"She's going to get herself killed!"

Karé rested a hand on Snap's arm. "She's survived this long. And Wedge will be by her side. He'll keep her grounded. They could be a real asset to the Resistance."

Snap looked helplessly at his wife. "They're the only family I've got."

"You've got me," his wife said, soothingly.

"You've got all of us," Poe added. "We're in this together. Isn't that what you said to me?"

Snap closed his eyes, exhaling. He dropped his head back, face tilted to the stars. "Okay. Karé and I will go to Akiva and talk to them. Let them know what's going on with the Resistance. But I'm not going to force them. They're old . . ."

No older than Leia, Poe thought, but he kept his opinion to himself. No need to push Snap any harder than he already was.

"What about me?" Jess asked. "I don't have any notorious rebel leaders in my family."

Poe spread his hands. "I'm open to ideas."

"Actually, I think I have a lead," Suralinda offered, "but it's kind of weird."

"Go on," Poe said.

"Back at the party, I heard Grist and some others talking—well, complaining—about rumors coming out of Rattatak that some old Imperial had claimed power over one of the warlord factions there. They were thinking someone should put an end to that, but that's because they lack vision."

"What are you suggesting?"

"I'm saying that this old Imperial, whoever they are, has the leadership skills to unite a war clan. I mean, Rattatak's no joke, right? You have to be willing to do violence, sure, but you also have to be smart."

"Okay."

"So, doesn't that sound like someone who could be an asset to the Resistance?"

"They're an Imperial," Jess protested.

"Former Imperial," Suralinda countered. "And

you know a lot of those have no love for the upstart First Order. Maybe we can make them an offer."

"We're not bribing people to—"

"No, no." Suralinda cut him off. "I'm talking about a good story. A chance at redemption, to make up for the evils the Empire committed."

"They're likely a sympathizer," Jess complained, but her voice had softened a bit.

"Or it's just as likely they're horrified by what happened to the Hosnian system and worried about anyone having something like Starkiller Base at their disposal ever again. Some of these Imperials were just caught up in the machinery, you know. They're not all evil."

Jess rolled her eyes. "Are you kidding me?"

"Jess," Poe said, gently. "Suralinda might have a point. Not that these people aren't responsible for their crimes, but they might have something to offer the Resistance, and something the Resistance can offer them in turn." Even as he said it, the words struck close to home. Was he talking about former Imperials, or was he talking about himself?

"Redemption?" she said, eyes cutting to Suralinda. "As if they deserve it."

"Not redemption," Poe said. "Penance."

Jess quieted. They all did, likely wondering what it would take to atone for crimes as dark and horrifying as those the Empire had committed, wondering if they could judge when none of them had spotless hands.

"Well," Suralinda said brightly, breaking the silence, "you never know until you ask. So let me go ask."

"You can go to Rattatak," Poe said, and Suralinda beamed, "but you have to take Jess with you."

"What?" both women said at the same time.

"Makes sense," Snap said, grinning.

The two women started to protest, but Poe held up a hand and they fell silent. "It's the only way I'm saying yes. It's too dangerous to send only one of you. You go as a pair, or you don't go at all."

Suralinda pursed her lips, considering. It was Jess who held out her hand first. "I'm in. Are we going to do this?"

Suralinda, never one to hold a bad mood, broke. She shook Jess's hand. "You bet."

"Good," Poe said, relieved. He wasn't sure if the two of them would go for it, but it hadn't been so difficult. Despite their differences, their success at Grail City showed that the two women made good partners, and if there was something positive to find at Rattatak, they would uncover it. And hopefully keep each other alive along the way.

"So we know where we're headed," Snap said. "Where are you going, Poe? It's not too late for you to go see Wedge yourself. He trained you at the academy, after all."

"Can't, Snap. BB-8 and I are going to find an old friend and ask a favor."

CHAPTER 3

POE DROPPED OUT OF lightspeed above the planet Ephemera and marveled. BB-8, secured behind him, beeped and hummed.

"It is beautiful," Poe agreed.

BB-8 asked a question.

"No, I've never been here," Poe answered. In fact, he couldn't recall visiting any gas worlds that weren't already giants. He half remembered some lesson from the academy, now gone vague, about required size and distance from any system's primary sun for a gas planet to form, but Ephemera didn't quite fit the description. It was an anomaly, something in part occurring naturally, but also something aggressively engineered by its inhabitants, if what he had heard was accurate.

The droid beeped and Poe replied. "It was once a mining planet, like Bespin. You know Bespin, right? But here they mined the tibanna gas to extinction. After it was all gone, the Empire abandoned its colonies and most of the settlers ran with them. Good riddance, from what I hear. It left the planet back in the hands of its original inhabitants and a few hold-outs who weren't there just to cash in but had grown to love the place. And then, surprise, they discovered tuusah."

BB-8 whirled loudly, curious.

"Tuusah is the residue from the mine runoff. Turns out tuusah has medicinal properties, so a new industry was born. Maybe it wasn't as lucrative as the Empire's strip mining, but it was a heck of a lot kinder to the planet's flora and fauna."

BB-8 whirled again, and Poe laughed.

"You're right," he said. "The Empire has never been kind. But the planet is a resort destination now, and the capital is called Wish. What a name, right? It used to be Outpost 665 or something boring like that. But now?" He waved his hand. "Wish.

"It's one of the largest spas in the galaxy. All kinds of mineral baths and healing treatments and some kind of legendary oxide therapy that's supposed to make you look younger."

The little droid sounded distressed.

"You look pretty good yourself, my friend. But we're not here to get pampered. We're here to find Maz Kanata, remember?"

When Maz Kanata had sent him Ephemera's coordinates, she had also told him the planet's history. "A bit remote," she had said, "way off any useful trade routes, but there's plenty of rest and relaxation to be found if you like drifting in a cloud. And the population is a hoot." And then she'd cackled and cut off the communication with a *See you soon.*

So here he was, maneuvering his way through a

gaseous sea of pale pinks and greens and blues to a landing pad that seemed no more substantial than the heavy atmosphere through which his starfighter flew.

A transmission came in, and BB-8 opened the channel without Poe having to ask.

"Welcome to Ephemera airspace," came a strangely wispy voice, almost like the soft exhale of a child. "Please identify yourself so that we can grant you landing clearance."

"This is . . ." Poe hesitated. He was known to the First Order. Known and despised. He didn't think the First Order was lurking on this anonymous Outer Rim resort world, but he had been wrong about that kind of thing before, and it paid to be cautious, even when he was flying a ship that no one would mistake for an X-wing. But he didn't get a chance to answer before another voice replaced the first one, this one not wispy or soft at all.

"Poe Dameron, is that you?" This voice was crankily familiar. There was muffled protest on the other end and then, "Oh, give me that mike, dear, I can take it from here." Poe heard sounds of struggle. "I didn't hire you to . . ." More struggle, and then a heavy thump.

Poe waited a moment before asking, "Maz?"

"What? Of course it's me, you fool. Who else would have asked you to this backwater?"

"Is . . . is everything all right?"

"What? Oh yes, of course. Why wouldn't it be?"

"It sounds like you're having problems."

"Bah. Just some people getting a little possessive

with the equipment. Nothing to concern yourself with. I've handled it. Now hurry up. I haven't got all day."

Poe's brow creased. "Uh, I'd be happy to land, but I don't see anything that looks like it'll hold the ship up. Am I in the right place?"

Silence, and then, "Oh, you're right. Isn't that funny? Some kind of security measure, the locals assure me, but really I think they're just partial to the undulation."

"The undulation?"

"You'll see. Everything here sways a bit. Now . . . let me . . ." He could hear her shuffling things around and the decided click of something heavy engaging, and just like that, the thing that had borne only the suggestion of a landing pad gathered and appeared to solidify until it looked like a normal place to put his ship down.

"What in the . . . ?" Poe muttered.

"It's perfectly safe, Dameron. Now are you going to land or not? I thought you were on urgent Resistance business."

Poe shook his head. No use arguing with Maz when she was right. Whatever it had been before, the landing pad was now the real deal.

"Copy," he said. "Coming in now."

"Good, good. See you soon. Oh, are you hungry? Have you eaten? I should have food brought up, shouldn't I? I'll have to ask them to prepare something special unless . . . you don't have time for a psychedelic experience do you, Dameron?"

He chuckled in disbelief. "Not today, Maz. Like you said, urgent business."

"Of course. Okay then. Tah." And with that the transmission ended.

Maz Kanata was a legend. No one could deny that. Rumors ran rampant anyplace pilots gathered about wild nights spent back at Maz's castle on Takodana or of some fortuitous run-ins with "the pirate queen" that made everyone a bit wealthier. But she was hard to pin down, harder still to understand. She always seemed to know who was doing what even in the most remote corners of the galaxy, and she was an uncanny judge of character. Poe had no idea how she did it, or how vast her network was, but it was impressive. And now he hoped that she would muster her impressive powers to help the Resistance regroup and find its footing.

"I'm not helping you with anything," Maz said, adjusting her spectacles to get a better look at Poe's astonished face. "If you recall, last time I stuck my neck out for the Resistance, the First Order destroyed my castle. Do you know how much I loved that castle?"

"It was a great castle," Poe admitted.

"The best. Do you know how long I had had it?"

"A thousand years?"

"A thou . . ." She paused, giving Poe a suspicious look. He grinned, playfully. "Longer than you've been around, flyboy, that's for sure. So don't sniff at me like I'm being unreasonable."

She dipped her hand in the gelatinous goop that

filled the bowl next to her and brought back a handful of something pink and smooth that smelled distinctly of sulfur. She leaned out of her recliner, offering some to Poe. "You want?"

"No, I'm fine."

They were both sitting on long sinuous loungers in one of Wish's ubiquitous day spas. Poe was still in his uniform, small mercy, but Maz was wrapped in a thick fluffy white towel, a second white towel wrapped tightly around her head. Her bare feet soaked in a mix of muddy chemicals Poe couldn't identify, and willowy attendants fluttered in and out of the room, proffering teas and colonics and other concoctions Poe politely refused. Maz was now smearing the sulfur-scented goop she had offered Poe on her broad cheeks and humming merrily.

"What is that stuff?" he asked, sniffing. "It smells terrible." The sulfur odor had been replaced with an ammonia one.

"Feline poop. From some species that's lived here so long that it's practically native to the planet. Imagine. A planet with no solid ground but plenty of cats. The story is that the founder of Ephemera was a Rothkahar philosopher. He domesticated this species because he thought them of advanced intelligence . . . or maybe they domesticated him. I forget. Anyway, later on, he found that their excrement had healing properties. High concentrations of tibanna gas, naturally processed into tuusah." She laughed again. "Does wonders for the skin."

"That's great, Maz," Poe said, thinking it was not

great at all, "but can we get back to the topic at hand? The Resistance needs your help."

"Yes, you told me."

But you didn't seem to hear me, he thought. He needed to get through to her, and he decided brutal honesty was his best bet. "We need a place to hide and regroup. It needs to be outside of prying First Order eyes but able to handle our needs for housing, supplies, communications . . ."

"Didn't you say there were only a handful of you left on a single ship? What needs could you have?"

Poe bristled at her callousness. Maybe she had heard him, and she just didn't care. He hadn't expected that. "There will be more," he said hastily. "We've got people all over the galaxy, and we're making new allies all the time. We were hoping you could provide shelter. And more than that. Leadership. Leia can't do it alone. We need you to help lead the Resistance."

"Lead the Resistance? I thought that was your job."

"I . . ." Poe frowned, feeling unsettled.

"Expecting me to do your job for you?" she grumbled, now dutifully applying the cream to her neck. "You're the commander in the room. Or has that changed?"

"Nothing's changed," Poe said automatically, but it was a lie, wasn't it? After the *Raddus,* everything had changed.

Maz finished shellacking her throat and sat back in her chair, eyes closed. The last attendant had left a steaming pot of tea on the side table, and Maz blindly reached a hand out, found her cup, and lifted it to her lips to take a sip. She set the teacup down. Poe waited patiently for her to speak, but after a moment he could hear light snoring. Had she fallen asleep?

Poe stood up, exasperated. "This was a waste of time. I should go."

"No!" Her hand closed around his wrist like a vise, all the whimsy fled from her voice as if it had never been there. She cocked one eye open, fixing it on him. He froze.

"Listen closely to me, Poe Dameron," she said. "You see me like this, and you think me a fool. Good for me, because when an enemy perceives you as foolish or weak, that is when they are most vulnerable in their arrogance. That is when you strike." She twisted her hand, pulling hard, and his feet flew out from under him. He went down on his back, hard enough that a bellowing breath escaped from his lungs and pain radiated from his tailbone.

Maz was up off her recliner and standing on his chest in seconds. Her eyes, surrounded by the sulfurous skin treatment, were centimeters from his own. She narrowed her gaze, taking him in. Judging. "I see arrogance in you. And that is what gets you in trouble, causes pain."

He flushed, still thinking of the *Raddus*. "I learned my lesson," he spit through gritted teeth.

"Have you?"

"I . . ." Poe collapsed back, resting his head on the floor. He thought about lying, or at least not telling Maz any more than necessary, but she looked at him like she could see right through him, like she already knew the ugly truth.

"You asked me if I was still a leader," he started, eyes focused on the ceiling. "The truth is that I don't know. I-I made some mistakes . . ."

"Mistakes?" Maz's tone was scalpel-sharp.

"I led a mutiny," he confessed. He hadn't meant to tell her, but there it was. And now that he had begun, he wanted her to know everything. "I didn't understand what was happening. All I knew was that we were running, when we should have been fighting. I had to do something!"

"Did you? Have to do something?"

He blinked, taken off guard. A moment ago he had wanted to defend himself, to make her see reason or at least understand his reasoning. But suddenly all that fight was gone and reality hit him like a punch to the gut.

"No," he admitted. "I'm a soldier and she was my commanding officer. All I had to do was trust." He exhaled, instinctively wanting to sink farther into the floor, to hide from his own dishonor. He looked at her, eyes pleading for . . . not sympathy. Not even understanding. But something else. A second chance.

Maz made a humming sound. She leaned her head away from him and sat back. She didn't get off his chest, but at least there was some distance between their faces.

"And now what, Poe Dameron?"

"What?"

"Let's say you're right. That your actions, your

arrogance, got many people killed. Led the Resistance to where they are now: broken, on the run, destitute, and begging for help."

He flinched. Opened his mouth to protest her words, but what was there to say besides "I fix it."

"How will you do that?" she asked. "You can't bring the dead back. You can't single-handedly rebuild the Resistance, although—" She snorted, sounding amused. "—if anyone was going to try it would be you."

"I can bring down the First Order."

"Alone?"

"If I have to."

She shook her head. "Arrogance. Still." She rose up on her knees, looming over him. "You know who else is arrogant? The First Order."

"The First Order is evil."

Maz stared at him, lips pursed. She fine-tuned her spectacles, her eyes growing larger behind the magnifying glass. When she spoke, her voice was soft, almost reverent. "I've seen evil in many forms, Dameron. The First Order is no worse than the Sith, or the Empire, or countless others who would use the dark side. As always, they must be countered with the light. But . . ." She climbed off his chest and into the chaise lounge. She removed her glasses and leaned back, covering her eyes with a masque of something slightly furry that had been soaking in a pale-blue liquid on the side table. "I have my own way of fighting. Not everything is about armadas and starfighters, you know."

Poe sat up, rubbing his lower back. He stared at Maz, thinking how easy it was for her to dismiss him, to not care about the fate of his friends and the people he loved. To her, they were nothing. Is that what happened when you lived a thousand years?

She grunted, as if she could read his thoughts.

"You think I'm callous, but I'm not. You will be fine without me."

"I sure hope you're right, lady," he said, unable to keep the bitterness from his voice. "Because if you're not, me and mine are going to die. And you can sit with that for a thousand more years for all I care."

His confession had left him scraped raw, feeling exposed but no closer to finding a way to close the wound. And now he had failed again by not convincing Maz to join them. It was all he could do to get to his feet.

Silently, he gathered his things and left. If he had bothered to look back, he might have seen Maz Kanata lifting the corner of her masque to stare intently in his direction, a small smile leaking from her lips.

Poe sat in the cockpit of his borrowed starfighter, primed for takeoff. He'd asked for clearance to depart twice now, and each time the wispy voice on the other side of the communications link had denied him, claiming the airspace was occupied and he needed to stand by. He suspected it was a ruse, but he wasn't about to go charging blindly forward into the stew-thick atmosphere without clearance. Exasperated, he flipped the transmission switch one more time and asked for clearance to depart.

"Negative, pilot," said the breathy voice a third time. "You have company."

Poe looked up through the clear canopy of the cockpit and saw nothing. But then what would he see in this atmosphere? It was like living inside a pastel cloud.

A sudden tap at the viewport to his left and his heart was in his throat. He was fumbling at his belt for a blaster before he realized what he was doing. Big eyes peered at him, and he exhaled slowly, forcing himself to breathe so his heart would stop racing.

"Open up," Maz said, tapping on the transparisteel again.

Against his better judgment, Poe released the air lock, and the cockpit parted between them.

"There's something I meant to tell you before you ran off like that," Maz said, leaning in. "But first, where did you get this ship? It's a relic."

"It's a loaner. I told you we're down to scrap metal, everything else destroyed. Now what do you want?"

Maz looked around, unperturbed, examining the display console. "It's a relic, but it's also a collectible. When you're done with it, come see me. I might buy it."

He thought to explain that he had to return it to a very particular Hutt, but decided it wasn't worth it.

"Maz, what do you want? I've got to go."

She waved his protests away. "We've long suspected that the First Order has been taking children and disappearing people on the margins of the galaxy. But things are escalating now: arresting people on phony trumped-up charges. Small crimes that they've blown up into capital offenses, or charges simply fabricated out of nothing. People going missing in the dead of night, their families having no idea what happened to them. Nighttime raids or picked up off the streets and"—Maz made a gesture, spreading her fingers wide—"vanished. And the people most likely to disappear? People with ties to the old rebellion. And interestingly enough, we're seeing it with some old Imperials, as well. Those who have been outspoken about their distaste for the First Order, but also those who have remained neutral. Anyone who might pose a threat, now or down the line."

Poe frowned. It was disturbing but didn't surprise him. The First Order thrived on abusing power. "Do you think that's what's happened to Leia's allies? They're not answering because they can't? They've been arrested?"

Maz shrugged. "Maybe. Possibly. But the First Order used to do it in secret. Now they don't bother. They snatch people off the streets and don't even pretend to have whatever planet they've infiltrated hold a sham trial. Just death or labor camps."

"Labor camps?"

"Someone has to build all those fancy new ships, eh?"

Poe chewed the inside of his cheek, thoughtful. "Thanks, Maz. Leia will want to know about this."

"Yes, I thought she might. Rumor has it that there's a list somewhere of all the people they've taken. A big list. No one's seen it, but I've got people chasing it down. I hear something definitive, I'll call you."

Poe nodded. "Do that."

"You sure you don't want to sell this ship?"

"Not mine to sell."

"A shame."

He started to lower the cockpit transparisteel when Maz called his name. "Poe!"

He turned.

"Be the light, Poe."

CHAPTER 4

WINSHUR BRATT HELD UP his Corellian work identification card for the First Order guard's inspection. It was the third checkpoint that he had passed through that morning on his relatively short walk from his apartment in the newer part of Coronet City to the offices of the Corellian Engineering Corporation where he worked, but he didn't mind. He always enjoyed the inevitable moment when the guard's expression changed from mild superiority to chagrined humility as he belatedly realized that Winshur was An Important Person. The way the guard would straighten from his bored slouch, the sudden anxiety that would pale his face as he wondered if Winshur would find fault in his performance and report him to his supervisors. Today Winshur found that kind of elicited fear particularly soothing, a balm on what had otherwise been a less-than-ideal morning.

Winshur had spent the early hours of the day sitting at his breakfast table and contemplating whether he should listen to the communication that had been waiting for him when he woke that morning. It had come from his hometown of Bela Vistal, which meant it could be from only one person—his mother. He had done his best to sever all ties to the town and people of his birth, but his mother still managed to find him, again and again. This time it had taken her six months, and in that six months he had accomplished so much. He'd secured a respectable job with the Corellian Engineering Corporation in middle management as head clerk in the Records Department, and he'd been able to keep that job when the First Order had come in and taken over the company, recommissioning it to build warships for the burgeoning power. So many of his co-workers had been eliminated after their re-employment interviews, but Winshur had not. In fact, his interviewer, a relentlessly ordered woman from Alsakan, had told him he was exactly the kind of citizen the First Order was looking for. He had felt immense pleasure at that. He had always known he was destined for more than Corellia, but to have someone like her tell him so? He had floated happily around the nearly deserted office for days.

And then it had happened. Winshur had been called out of Records and moved into a position of prestige, as he so rightly deserved. He was now the First Order's executive records officer on Corellia. Which, if he was honest, was essentially the same job he had before, but it did come with a new title, two assistants, and, eventually, a raise. At least he thought it might, once his superiors realized that he was a man of quality. And he did have his own office with a view into the massive ship bay that was part of the larger complex. No one could deny that meant something. He had wanted a window that overlooked the city, but had been told that was only for those of higher title. Rather than be disappointed, he had told himself that it was something to strive for, the next step on his climb to the top. Executive records officer was great, truly, but it was just the beginning. There was so much more to accomplish. He merely needed to find a way to impress his peers in the First Order, as he had done in his interview, and then, truly, there was nothing in the galaxy that could hold him back.

Except, perhaps, his mother.

He had finally deleted the communication from her, unopened. It was for the best. The sooner she realized he wanted nothing to do with her or anyone else in his past, the better. Besides, the First Order was the only family he needed now. He would prove himself worthy of their high regard soon enough.

"Bratty?" came a voice from behind him.

Winshur froze, horrified. His eyes met those of the guard who still held his ID, and the guard smirked slightly. Winshur felt his stomach drop and his face redden in humiliation, but he held his composure as he turned to face the person who had called him by the old nickname that he loathed.

It was a woman, pale, short, and dark-haired, like himself. Blue-gray eyes crinkled in a friendly hello. "I thought I recognized you," she said, voice bright. "I wasn't sure in that fancy uniform but wow . . ." Her eyes traveled over him, no doubt noticing his fresh, well-oiled haircut and the precise creases in his trousers and jacket. Finally, her eyes rested on the badge on the left side of his chest.

"You working for the First Order, Bratty?" she asked, a hint of both revulsion and admiration in her voice. Or at least he thought it was admiration. What else could it be? Jealousy, perhaps.

He took in her dirty gray jumpsuit and heavy boots, the loop of her tool belt slung around her hips, the grease stains under her nails. A mechanic, surely. Someone working in the shipyards as so many Corellians did now. Which meant she, too, worked for the First Order, or more likely as a contractor under some mandatory contract. He had seen those contracts. Received and verified and filed them, as he did so many documents for the First Order. The terms were usually heavily biased toward the First Order, but it wasn't like the Corellian contractors had much of a choice. These days they either worked for the First Order or they starved. The smart ones knew the future when they saw it and the rest fell along the way, like so many weeds to be pruned.

But how did she know him, and by that abominable nickname? It was something the children had called him at the religious center in Bela Vistal, the one his mother had insisted he attend for most of his life until he was old enough to leave to find work in Coronet City. He had vivid memories of wanting to burn the low-slung whitewashed building down, all his classmates still inside. Including this mechanic, no doubt.

"The name is Winshur," he said crisply, letting his disdain hide some of his embarrassment. "It has always been Winshur."

"Sure, sure," she said, shrugging like it wasn't a big deal to her either way. "I'm Navah. Remember me?"

He did now, placing that dark mass of curls and the impish face as one of his former classmates, but he'd never give her the satisfaction. "I cannot say that I do remember you, Navah. Bela Vistal was so long ago."

"Ah, but you knew I was from Bela Vistal," she said, slyly.

He pressed his lips together, annoyed. A small mistake he should not have made.

The checkpoint guard cleared his throat.

"Is there a problem?" Winshur asked, irritated, as he whipped back around to face the man. He expected more smirking, but the guard had a serious look on his face and his tone was respectful.

"No problem, sir," the guard said, sliding Winshur's ID free from his handheld datapad. "Your security clearance is in order for entry into Building Two. You may pass at your convenience."

"Oh?" Winshur stood straighter. "Well, of course it is. Why wouldn't it be?"

The guard gave him a quizzical look as he handed his card back. Winshur had said too much, acted like a novice instead of an executive records officer. And in front of this Navah person. He was ashamed. He slipped his identification into the pocket of his neatly pressed jacket, that bore the symbol of the

First Order on his chest where his Corellian Engineering Corporation logo had once been, and gave
the guard a curt nod. But before he could walk away
the woman leaned in close.

"Deeper into the creature's maw, eh, Bratty?"
Navah whispered. "Well, I guess we do what we
must to survive the occupation. Just remember
who's got your back." She squeezed his arm through
his jacket, and he flinched. Who had his back? It
certainly wasn't anyone from Bela Vistal.

He thought about reporting Navah to someone,
but what would be the charge? She had squeezed his
arm, so perhaps he could claim she assaulted him.
But if he did, no doubt she would say she knew him,
perhaps even that they were childhood friends. He
shuddered at the thought.

The guard cleared his throat meaningfully. Winshur could hear the checkpoint line behind him getting restless. Someone wondered loudly what was
taking so long.

"Do you need an escort to Building Two, sir?"
the guard asked. The question was polite enough—
but was that a hint of mockery in his voice? Winshur thought it was.

"No need," Winshur said dismissively. "I know
the way."

He stepped around the guard with a tight smile
and hurried on his way. He didn't bother to say
goodbye to that woman Navah, but then why would
he? She was no one.

———

The rest of the walk to his office was uneventful. The halls were busy but everyone was focused on their own work and paid Winshur no mind. He did make brief eye contact with a tall gray-haired man who strode by surrounded by a deployment of stormtroopers in their thrillingly intimidating armor. The man looked very important and Winshur had given him a sharp nod as he passed, as one would to a peer. The man must not have seen him, though, because he did not return the gesture. Well, Winshur would have to make more of an effort next time.

He opened the heavy door to his office with another swipe of his identification card and entered. Once through, he tapped the control button that held the door open. His office itself was not very large, but it was better than the cubicle he had occupied before his promotion. One wall contained a long, high window out into the ship bay. If he stood on his toes, he could see the busy production floor below, but he rarely did that. He had no interests in ships or the people and droids who built them. The other walls of his office were taken up by filing shelves holding magnetic tapes and holographic recordings. They crowded his office like expectant ladies waiting for his particular attention. Each record had to be reviewed, approved, assigned a location, and ultimately signed off on by him. He had thought to delegate some of the work, and he still might, but for now he liked to remain hands-on. He dared not leave anything to his current staff, of which he had exactly two. One was a First Order cadet named Monti Calay, fresh from some Corellian town Winshur had never heard of. He was competent enough but strange. He kept his dark curly hair cut appropriately short and his uniform was impeccable, much like Winshur's, but he kept asking Winshur to come to lunch or to join him for a drink at one of the local cantinas after work, as if he didn't understand that there should be a deep and unassailable separation between management and staff. Winshur had not made up his mind about Monti Calay yet.

His other employee, well, he definitely had an opinion about her.

First of all, Yama was young. Winshur wasn't exactly old by Corellian standards, or any standards really. He had been born the year after the Battle of Yavin, a child of a prosperous if overly devout Bela Vistal middle class family. But this one, this girl, was a decade younger than him, at least. She had obviously been plucked from the streets of Coronet City for some reason beyond Winshur's ken. A secret talent or political connection was dubious, so perhaps she had captured the merciful attention of some officer and been given a future with the First Order that would have otherwise been beyond her grasp. However, such kindness had clearly been a mistake. It wasn't just the girl's appearance that made her unsuitable, but also her behavior. Her manners were rough and often nonexistent, she fidgeted relentlessly while waiting for orders, and she frequently gave him incredulous looks when he asked her to simply do her job. He wasn't sure why she had been assigned to him by his superiors, but he was not in a position to have her removed from his service. However, he kept copious notes on her every fault so that if the opportunity to review her record ever arose, he would be prepared. Still, he found it difficult to spend any time around her without getting annoyed.

Winshur removed his outer jacket and hung it from the hook on the wall closest to the door. Next, he removed his gloves, taking a moment to brush a naked hand across the fabric, straightening any wrinkles that might have attempted to form since his last grooming. He hung his cap on the hook next to it and placed his gloves on the small shelf below. He tugged his black tunic smooth and, removing a white cloth from his flared pocket, wiped his high boots to a shine. He slipped the cloth back in his pocket. Only then did he turn to face the work of the day.

Two new boxes of records had been placed on his desk that had not been there yesterday when he'd left. He approached the boxes warily and peered inside. Each one held a disorganized pile of what looked like palm-sized black metal boxes. He reached in, turning a few over with careful fingers. No labels. He looked more closely at the storage boxes themselves. No labels on those, either. He could feel a small scream rising in his throat. Who would dare dump these here without any identifying features? As if he didn't know.

"Yama," he called, and then a little louder, "Yama!"

A scurrying sound from the outer office and then,

breathless, as if she had been running, Yama entered through his open office door.

"Yeah?" she asked. "I mean, yes, Executive Records Officer Bratt, sir! What do you want?"

Winshur's anger flared, but he made himself take three deep breaths, just as he had learned at the religious center of his youth, before he turned and spoke. "Did you leave these boxes on my desk?" he asked, admiring how calm his voice sounded.

The girl was wearing her black cadet uniform, but the buckle on her belt was clearly tarnished, and she had slung it too low. It sat at a jaunty angle across her hips instead of tightly at her waist. Was she attempting to make her uniform fashionable? Surely not. And her hair! Regulation required her tight curls to be oiled and slicked back against her head, but today her orange hair was parted down the middle and tied back in two identical puffs.

"Your hair is not regulation," Winshur said.

"What?" The girl raised a hand to her hair. "Oh yeah, sorry. Was running a bit late this morning and didn't have time to change it up. But it's neat and off my face, right, so it will do."

"It will *not* do."

Yama opened her mouth as if to protest, but she must have caught the censure in Winshur's stare and thought better.

"Sorry," she said, lowering her head.

Winshur smiled slightly. He took a step forward and rested a heavy hand on the girl's shoulder. She flinched slightly, which made him smile a bit more.

"Look around you, Yama," he said. "Do you understand where you are?"

She didn't meet his eyes, but she nodded morosely.

"I don't think you do." He lifted his hand off her shoulder and paced around his desk, gearing up for his favorite speech. It had been a few weeks since he'd had to lecture the girl on the importance of order, on the vital role each and every one of them played in maintaining the impeccable reputation of the First Order here on Corellia, on how their presentation must be above reproach at all times. Clearly it had been too long.

"All creatures are ruled by the strongest among them," he said, settling in his chair. "It is the way of nature. The strong survive and the weak are crushed. Now, how do we identify the strong among us? Is it only the largest? The most muscular? No, Yama. It is the ones with the most discipline. The ones that can master their own base instincts and project"—he slammed a hand down on his desk, and she jumped—"power." He sat back and adjusted his cuff. "Do you want to be one of the powerful or do you want to be crushed by your weakness?"

She mumbled something he couldn't quite hear.

"Speak up," he said, exasperated. "You certainly won't project power by muttering to yourself."

"I want to be powerful," she said, her voice just a fraction higher than before.

"Yes. As you should. But you won't do it by breaking the rules. Now, tighten your belt. That's right. And pull your hair back."

Yama finished tightening her belt and smoothed a hand over her hair. "I-I'll need a brush."

Winshur sighed. "I suppose you will. Well, it can't be helped today, then, but please don't leave the offices and let anyone see you."

"It won't happen again," she promised.

"I should hope not." He folded his hands across his desk in a way that he thought looked benevolently paternal. "I can't always waste my time trying to teach you, Yama. I have important work to do."

She nodded again, still not meeting his eyes. Well, good that she feared him. She should. But he'd thought she would have a bit more backbone than this. Another layer of disappointment.

"You're dismissed," he said, torn between disgust and a mild admiration at how effectively he had handled the situation. He really was leadership material. If his superiors could see how he had taken this wayward girl in hand, surely they would be impressed.

"Oh, and take these boxes with you, Yama. Find out where they came from and organize the tapes within. I want them labeled—origin, date, and they all need a provenance. I won't have people saying I am not doing my job," he said, emphasizing the "my" just enough to make her hunch her shoulders in shame. He clapped his hands together. "Go!"

The girl scurried forward to take the boxes. She balanced one on top of the other and slid her arms under the bottom box to pick them both up at the same time. The load was clearly too bulky to carry all at once, but Winshur just watched her struggle.

He could have suggested she make two trips or even, stars forbid, help her. But he did not.

He watched her take one awkward step, and then another, toward the door. And then, with a bitter flash of unsurprise, he watched the girl shriek as she dropped both boxes on the floor. Black tapes skidded across the polished stone. He felt one come to rest against the tip of his shoe under the desk, and he delicately toed it back in her direction.

Yama crawled around on hands and knees retrieving the escaped records. He could hear what sounded distinctly like hot breathy sobs as she did so, but he still made no move to help her. How would she ever learn not to be weak if people fixed all her problems for her? No, he was doing her a favor, teaching her one small lesson today in what would be a lifetime of lessons she must learn if she intended to rise to anything beyond a common Corellian street girl.

It was the same lesson in humiliation he had learned from his classmates back in Bela Vistal, the same that all children learned. They either let it break them or used it to forge them into someone stronger, someone more worthy of power.

He waited until she was done before he spoke. "Of course, I'll have to add this to your permanent record, and appropriate disciplinary action will no doubt be taken. It's for your own good, really. You see that, don't you?"

The girl said nothing, and he didn't expect her to. She bent and finished gathering the boxes, this time more steadily having already learned her lesson, and walked to the door. Just as she passed through, Winshur's other employee, Monti Calay, entered. The two assistants briefly locked eyes, and Winshur thought he saw a flash of something unexpected in Monti's face. Was that disapproval? No, Monti had never given him trouble, had only admired Winshur. But for a moment he thought he saw something that looked like revulsion.

Well, that look must have been meant for Yama, not him. Yes, that made much more sense. After all, it was her behavior that was in question, not his. Winshur was blameless.

CHAPTER 5

MORNING DAWNED HOT AND wet over Myrra, Akiva's capital city. It had rained steadily through the night, and a thick mist still hung in the morning air. The yellow sun shone weak and waterlogged across the narrow alleys of the city proper and the verdant fields of the more generously landed outer settlements. Puddles gathered ankle-deep in the pockmarked dirt roads and gutters, filled to overflowing, dripping intermittently off the clay-tiled rooftops. Just outside the city among the settlements of family farms, Wedge Antilles dragged himself out of bed, put a pot of caf on to boil, and stepped outside into the relentlessly muggy morning.

"It's like sticking your head in a happabore's mouth," he observed to no one as he stretched his arms over his head and let loose a huge yawn. Something in his shoulder tweaked, causing a sharp pain in his lower back. He rubbed at the spot, mumbling a mild curse. That pain hadn't been there before. He must have aggravated something weeding the garden with Norra yesterday. Wedge had been tortured by Imperials years ago and still bore the results. His body just wasn't what it used to be. Of course, he reminded himself, old age was just as much of a culprit. Not as nefarious as the Empire had been, but even more relentless.

He stepped off the back porch and made his way across his yard. It was a modest yard, just as the house was a modest house, but it suited him and Norra just fine. Big enough for the two of them and the occasional guest. Two bedrooms, a study, a kitchen, and an outhouse. Out back was a water collection system with a purifier and septic tank and the standard parcel of one hectare to farm. Norra had insisted they plant three varieties of peppers and plenty of the stubby maize native to the region. There were also two rows of purple tubers and a koshar melon vine and, of course, the poultry house Snap had built for them last time he visited. When was that? Wedge had a hard time remembering. Must have been a while now, well before Snap and Karé Kun had gotten married.

It was early enough in the day that none of Wedge's near neighbors were out yet, and it felt like he had the whole world to himself, even if that world consisted of a misty water garden. The weather reminded Wedge of the stories Luke had told him about Dagobah. Now, there was a name he hadn't thought of in a long while, certainly not since Luke had gone off seeking . . . well, whatever he'd gone off seeking. Luke hadn't really explained much to Wedge, but then he didn't owe him an explanation. They had been kids together, really. Endor was

a long time ago, and Yavin was even longer. Wedge
didn't have to look at a calendar to know that. He
could feel it in his bones. In the ache of his joints in
this damn humidity, in the fact that his eyes didn't
work as well as they used to, and now in the throb
of pain in his lower back. Norra encouraged him to
go to the doctor and have his ailments checked out.
"They have medicine for those things, you know,"
she had teased him last time he had complained, but
he had earned his aches and pains, hadn't he? He
was one of the lucky ones. So many of his friends
hadn't survived the war. They didn't get to live long
enough to complain about the trials of old age. So
he brushed Norra's advice off and lived with the
pain another day, a warped badge of honor.

Wedge filled two bowls with clean water from the
purifier next to the house and carefully carried them
over to the keedee coop. He set them down on either end of the fenced-in enclosure and filled another bowl with feed. The tiny creatures inside were
awake and restless so he let them out to get their
exercise. They scampered out on two feet, fluffing
their multicolored tail plumage with a lot of chirp-
ing and flapping, leaving bursts of bright blue and
yellow feathers in their wake. He removed a wide
square cloth from his pocket and spread it out. He
could see there were almost a dozen eggs waiting for
collection in the now empty nests, and he got to
work retrieving the pale-green orbs. He remembered a game he used to play with his students at the
academy called stack-sticks. They all thought it was
a waste of time, but then his students had thought

that anything that didn't get them in the air and fly-ing was boring. Typical pilots. He'd tried to teach them that flying was more than just hotshot maneu-vers and force of will. You had to have finesse, too. Judgment. A willingness to take your time and make the correct choices so that when you were in the heat of battle you had learned to keep a cool head, and if your head failed you, then maybe your mus-cle memory would do the job instead. They didn't get it at the time, but he hoped they eventually did, and it would serve them well in the future.

The last of the eggs collected and wrapped safely in fabric, Wedge headed back to the house. He'd leave the keedees out for a couple of hours and come back before lunch to check on them. There weren't many predators that would bother them this close to town, and especially not on a soggy day like today, but he didn't like to take too many chances with the birds. They were a bit like part of the family now. He shook his head. When had he become so sentimental, and when had collecting eggs from docile fowl become the most dangerous part of the day? He was glad to be alive, that was for sure, but sometimes he wondered if his friends who had burned out fighting had the right of it. Re-tirement was no easy mission for an old soldier like himself.

Movement from above caught his eye, and he looked up through the hazy air. A flash of metal and the familiar roar of engines as two starfighters streaked through the lightening sky. His pulse sped up. For a moment his fingers flexed in shock, loosening around his makeshift egg basket, and he almost dropped his day's bounty. He braced the basket from underneath and tightened his grip.

He would recognize those starfighters anywhere. The telltale cruciform, the sound of the engines as the sleek ships broke through the atmosphere. Those were X-wings. Now, what were they doing on Akiva, and—more important—why were they coming back around to land . . . here?

"It's gotta be him," Wedge muttered as the first ship made its descent. He pressed back against the keedee coop and turned his face away from the sudden gale the ship stirred up. His bathrobe danced about him and the keedees squawked and screamed. At least they had the sense to go inside their coop, Wedge thought, instead of standing out here watching like bug-eyed worrts. But soon enough the starfighter was down and right on its heels, the second one.

Silence descended suddenly as the engines shut off. Surely his neighbors had noticed that he had some visitors by now, but he looked out over the open field and saw the shutters of the nearest house still tightly closed. Hiding, he thought, but not for long. It was possible his neighbors took the landing in stride, but unlikely. Curiosity would get the best of them after a while, and they'd come asking. Of course, Akiva had been one of the first planets to join the New Republic, so maybe they didn't mind seeing a couple of X-wings land in Wedge's yard. On the other hand, a lot of folks were looking for the First Order to come in and clean up the mess that the fall of the New Republic had caused. The irony being that the First Order had caused the mess to begin with, but people didn't think of it like that. All they saw was that the New Republic had made promises and failed to keep them. And now there was a new boss in town who would make things better. Wedge knew the lie in that, but he tried to keep the peace mostly, so he let it lie. Norra had gone toe-to-toe with some of their more opinionated neighbors back when they still got invitations to dinner parties and get-togethers, but those had stopped coming since the last time she'd threatened to knock someone out. After that, the neighborly friendliness had dried up. Most of the people around here knew he and Norra had a past with the Rebellion, though none had the will to make trouble for them. But something like the X-wings in his yard? Well, that was rubbing it in their faces, wasn't it?

Wedge laughed quietly. They could use a little face-rubbing, he decided. Things were too quiet around here, anyway.

The closest ship popped open its cockpit with a hiss, and a well-missed face greeted him. Karé Kun waved vigorously and he could see her big smile from here, her blond hair catching the light. She shouted something he couldn't quite hear as she unbuckled her restraints. Wedge grinned. If Karé Kun was in the first starfighter, then his suspicions were right. It had to be . . .

He turned eagerly to the second ship. The cockpit opened and all Wedge could see from this distance was a dark head and a familiar astromech droid.

Wedge dropped his egg basket, all but forgotten, and walked as fast as he could to the second X-wing. Before he knew it, he was running and shouting, arms outstretched.

Snap Wexley jumped lightly from the ship and landed on the green grass of Akiva. He opened his arms and caught Wedge in a hug.

"Snap!" Wedge said, tears threatening to break. He never cried, but this? This was worth a few tears of joy. "Your mother will be so happy to see you!"

"I'm glad to see you, too," Snap said, "but we're here with some news. Let's go inside."

They broke from the hug. "Yes, come say hi to your mother. I'll make an omelet. Oh." He looked back over his shoulder at the place where he'd dropped the eggs. "I'll make toast, then," he corrected himself, laughing.

"As long as you've got caf, we'll be fine."

"Of course. Come on in, Snap. Welcome home."

The older man led the younger one across the yard, and the blond woman joined them as they made their way to the house. As they reached the back door, the sun broke through the lingering clouds, chasing away the morning gloom. It was going to be a sunny day after all.

"Norra!" Wedge called as soon as they entered the house. "Come see who's here. Norra?"

The back door led directly into a small mudroom where Snap and Karé Kun paused. Wedge could see the two of them taking in the domesticity of it all. Garden tools hanging neatly from the walls, fertilizer and poultry feed arranged in marked bins, a bench where one could sit to remove muddy boots and overalls.

"We're not soldiers anymore," Wedge said with a shrug. But what did Snap and Karé expect? He and Norra had come back to Akiva to make a simpler life, to put aside the killing and fighting. It had been a good idea while the New Republic was in charge. But now, with the kids looking and judging, it felt selfish and indulgent, like he was ignoring the larger galaxy out there.

"I know you're not," Snap said with a reassuring nod. "This is all great. It looks like you and Mom are really happy."

"We are," Wedge said, and meant it.

He led them into the house proper. The room adjacent to the mudroom was the kitchen. It was dominated by a big wooden table surrounded by a low bench and an assortment of mismatched chairs. Back when they were still neighborly, the table could entertain a dozen people at once for meals. Now it was mostly just him and Norra and occasionally Snap's two elderly aunts. Behind the table was a cooking station with a nice-sized oven and cooktop and a spigot that ran to the water purifier outside. Open shelves of dried goods and the door to a root cellar half full of tubers huddled in the corner. Norra had insisted they build in a cellar despite the unfavorable climate. She had also insisted that there be a tunnel accessible from the cellar that led out to the edge of their property in case they needed a bolt-hole. To Norra's surprise, Wedge had agreed immediately. Norra had admitted she thought he would balk at the idea and think she was being paranoid. But both of them had been in enough close calls that neither would deny the value of an escape plan. So over a long two months in the dry season last year, they'd dug that tunnel. It would be a dirty unpleasant crawl if they ever had to use it, but knowing it was there seemed to appease Norra.

Above the door to the cellar were rows of plates, cups, and cooking utensils in a variety of colors and shapes. Wedge had gone on a kitchen improvement binge recently, which mostly consisted of tracking down various merchants in the local markets that sold culinary supplies and buying them out. It made for an eclectic mix, but he liked it. It reminded him of where he grew up on Corellia, or—more accurately—what he had never had while growing up on Corellia. His had been a drab house, functional, pragmatic. He owned some things now purely for the joy of owning them.

"It's colorful," Snap observed, eyes roaming the kitchen.

"And homey," Karé Kun added quickly, thumping her husband in the arm. "I love it."

"Have a seat," Wedge said, motioning the pair forward. "The caf should be ready. Norra?" he called into the house again. "Where are you?" She had to have heard him. Never mind him, she had to have heard those X-wings land. Which meant she wasn't coming out on purpose.

He caught Snap and Karé Kun exchanging a look.

"She's fine, son," Wedge protested. "She just gets in these moods sometimes. You know how she is."

"How could I forget."

Karé Kun stepped forward. "Why don't I pour the caf while you go check on her?" she said, moving toward the low-bubbling pot on the stove.

Wedge nodded, grateful. "Cups are up there. I'll just be a minute."

He paused as she laid a hand on his arm. "Take your time."

The hallway was dark and quiet, and Wedge felt a sense of foreboding growing in his chest as he made his way to the back part of the house. "Norra?" he called again as he dipped his head into the bedroom they shared. But it was empty, the bed made neatly, military corners and all. He checked the guest bedroom, just in case, but it was empty, too. Which left only one room—the place that, once he thought about it, he had expected her to be anyway.

Most of the rooms in their home were so clean and well kept that you could eat off the floor. The study was the only exception. Here chaos was allowed to reign, and reign it did. Shelves were packed to overflowing with various memorabilia from their trips around the galaxy. Here was a case of rare Carruthian brandy packed in next to the framed box where Wedge kept the various medals he had won as a hero of the Rebellion. There was his teaching certificate from the academy tucked in next to a box of Snap's old toys, which Norra's sisters had held on to and returned when she and Wedge moved in. They affectionately called it the Remembrance Room, because here they housed all their most precious memories. And there, in the sunlight streaming in through the window, stood Norra.

She was much as she had always been since he'd known her. Long and slim, silver hair cut short and practical, face a series of angles and sharp planes in profile. She had aged, wrinkles crowding her brown eyes, just as they did his, which only made her more formidable, as if she had acquired wisdom to temper her innate charisma.

She was looking out the window, likely right at the X-wings, and he couldn't see her clearly, but he could guess that her face was filled with conflicting emotions. He knew Norra well enough by now to understand that seeing those starfighters would have stirred up feelings and seeing Snap, whom she'd no doubt watched cross the yard with himself and Karé Kun, was never easy for her. Even after all these years, even after her son had forgiven his mother, Norra had never quite forgiven herself for leaving Snap behind as a child while she chased after her now deceased husband who had been arrested by the Empire as a spy. Which he was. And then, of course, it only got worse, because once she had found her husband, he had been ruined, brainwashed into an Imperial assassin. It was a mess, and one of the worst stories of Imperial cruelty that Wedge had ever heard, and he had heard a lot of them. And somehow Norra blamed herself for all of it. The problem was, she was a superior pilot, better than Wedge in a lot of ways—a fact he had no problem admitting. Good was good, and great was a whole other thing. Norra was great. But she was also . . . complicated. Haunted. Torn between her own needs and the demands of motherhood, her allegiance to the Rebellion and then the New Republic, and the people she loved. Day to day it was easier to set some of that aside, but with Snap here, and those X-wings? Well, no wonder she was in the Remembrance Room.

"How is he?" she asked as Wedge stepped inside. "Temmin. Is he okay?"

"He goes by Snap, Norra. You know that. And he's fine. More than fine. Karé, too. Why don't you come out and see for yourself?"

She had not turned away from the window, so Wedge approached her, wrapping a reassuring arm around her waist. She flinched slightly in surprise, and he tried not to take it personally.

"I thought . . ." She stopped and started again. "I thought, Why would they come without letting us know first if it was good news? To just show up and to land right here instead of in a proper port in town, well, it has to be bad news, doesn't it, Wedge?"

"Not necessarily," he said, his voice soothing. "Snap's never been one to follow rules, especially back here on his home planet. He probably feels like he's entitled to park wherever he wants." And landing out here let him avoid snooping authorities and people in town who might not remember Temmin Wexley all that fondly. He had been a small-time criminal before he joined his mom to hunt down Imperials. Nothing too terrible, as Wedge under-

stood it, and it seemed doubtful to Wedge that anyone would remember the troublemaker Temmin
had been as a kid, but maybe Snap thought better
safe than sorry.

She sighed, her shoulders relaxing slightly as she
finally turned to face him. "You're right. Of course
you're right." She shook her head as if ridding herself of bad thoughts. "I just saw those X-wings . . ."

"And all the old memories came back. Hey, I get
it. I was there, too, you know."

"And I love you for it," she said, finally favoring
him with a smile. She leaned in and kissed him. "Besides, I don't think anyone else could put up with
me."

"Well, there is that."

She punched him lightly in the shoulder. "Hey
pot, watch who you call a kettle. We've both got
our share of war memories." She glanced around
the room pointedly.

"Sure we do. But there's room for new memories,
isn't there, Norra? Quiet days on the farm, grandchildren running around, nights watching the stars
instead of flying between them."

She gave him a long look, her eyes narrowing, lips
puckered tight.

He winked. "Gotcha."

She exhaled, relieved. "I thought you were serious. I mean, of course I want the farm and grand-
kids, but . . ."

He nodded, a little sad. He had been serious even
though he played it off now for Norra's sake. She
was struggling as it was, trying to fit in with the

neighbors and forgive herself for her past mistakes, and he would do what he could to help. Besides, he knew what he had signed up for when they got married, and that was Norra, as complicated as she was. But he wouldn't trade her for all the credits in the galaxy.

"Yeah. Me, too." He gave her an encouraging smile. "Now let's go see why Snap and Karé are here and have some caf before it gets cold."

Snap and Karé were seated on the long kitchen table bench, heads together. They pulled apart, guilty as academy cadets caught canoodling after hours.

"Mom," Snap said, getting to his feet. "Wow, you look great."

"You do, too, son." She hugged Snap briefly and then Karé as she stood to be embraced. Norra motioned them to sit again, and she and Wedge joined them. Karé had brought the caf to the table along with four mugs. She had already poured herself and Snap a cup, and Wedge did the same for himself and Norra. Norra wrapped her hands around the mug and breathed in the fragrant steam. "It's great to see you, Temmin, and you and Karé are always welcome here, but Wedge said you had news?"

"I'll get to that," he said, sounding a bit evasive, "but first tell me how you've been."

"We've been the same as always," she said, a little sharply. "There's not much change out here in the Outer Rim."

"Did the news of Hosnian Prime not reach you?"

Norra blushed. "Of course it did. I'm sorry, is that what you meant?"

He nodded. "How has the local government responded?"

"An emergency election was called," Wedge said. "They voted out the governor and voted in some wealthy merchant known to be friendly with the First Order."

"A hedge against occupation," Norra said. "But no one's showed up demanding to take over the planet, yet. And day-to-day things have stayed the same. What's it like out there in the galaxy? We haven't gotten any news in ages."

"We came from Ikkrukk," Karé said. "Do you know it?"

"A Mid Rim world. The capital is Grail City. Made a few cargo runs there before."

"The First Order came knocking and demanded they surrender to immediate occupation. When they refused, the First Order opened fire."

Norra glanced at Wedge. "Just like what we expect to happen here."

"Luckily, we were in the vicinity," Snap said. "General Organa had sent Black Squadron there on a related mission. It was rough for a while but Poe showed up at the last minute to pull us out of the fire."

"Literally," Karé added.

"How is Poe?" Wedge asked. "He was one of my best students. Besides you, of course," he added hastily for Snap's sake.

"Now I know you're lying," Snap countered. "I was a terrible student."

"You were a terrible student," Wedge agreed.

The three of them laughed, but Norra frowned, mouth tight.

"What do you mean Poe Dameron showed up at the last minute? Isn't he Black Squadron's leader?"

"Snap was flying Black One on this mission," Karé said, a note of pride in her voice.

"That's great, son," Wedge said, beaming. "I knew you would lead your own squadron one day."

Snap lowered his head. "It was more out of necessity. Poe had another mission." He sipped from his mug and then straightened. "And here we come to some of the bad news."

Norra stiffened. "I knew it. Who's dead?"

"Norra," Wedge admonished her softly. "Snap didn't say—"

"We weren't there," Snap said, cutting him off, "but Poe filled us in on the important information. There was a battle at some backwater called Crait and . . ." He shook his head sadly.

"And who?" Norra said, voice taut.

"Everyone," Karé said gently.

"Not everyone," Snap corrected hastily at the look on his mother's face. "But the Resistance leadership is gone. Admiral Holdo, Ackbar, Statura. The entire fleet."

"Leia?" Norra asked, voice breaking.

"No, General Organa survived. Somehow. But she's still not entirely well, Poe said, and she can't run the Resistance by herself."

"I don't understand," Wedge said. He stood up and took a few steps away, as if he wanted to put space between himself and Snap's news. "Admiral Ackbar is gone?"

Snap nodded.

"But he survived Endor. And Jakku. I thought . . ." Wedge ran a shaky hand through his graying hair. "I thought he would live forever. How?"

"Does it matter?" Norra asked.

Wedge looked at her, but she shrugged and looked away.

"There's one more loss. Wedge, you better sit down."

Oh no. That was a sure sign Wedge preferred to stand. He leaned back against the edge of the kitchen counter and crossed his arms. "Tell me," he commanded, his voice hard.

"Luke Skywalker."

Wedge swayed. He reached back, gripping the counter. Not Luke! Could he even be killed? Didn't Jedi live forever or something?

"You okay?" He looked up and Karé was standing next to him, holding him by the elbow. He shook her off gently. "I'm fine. I'm not an old man, damn you."

Karé stepped back, eyes big. Her mouth turned down, clearly wounded. Wedge sighed, telling himself to get a grip.

"I'm sorry, Karé. I didn't mean to snap. It's just . . ." His hands really were shaking now. In fact his whole body seemed to be shaking.

"Everyone," Norra said, repeating Karé's earlier

word, her voice barely a whisper, but Wedge heard her. His eyes met hers, and all he saw there was defeat.

"Then it's over," he said. "The Resistance is over. The First Order has won."

CHAPTER 6

WINSHUR LOOKED UP FROM his datawork to find Monti Calay staring fixedly at him from the doorway to his office. It was not the first time he had caught Monti staring at him, as if he were studying Winshur. Well, he supposed he did cut a fine figure, and Monti probably wanted to know how he could rise in the ranks, too, like his boss. But really, the staring was starting to be too much. He suppressed a shiver of unease at the younger man's intensity and carefully sat back, folding his hands in his lap.

"What is it, Monti?" Winshur asked his assistant. "It's already been a trying morning, so please don't test my patience even more."

"A message from central command, sir. For you. It was marked urgent and confidential, so I thought I should bring it to your attention immediately."

Ah, something from command. And marked confidential! He motioned the cadet forward. Monti handed him a datapad. It was a slim, silver model that was the latest in First Order technology. Winshur kept his on his person most of the time, but he had left it with Monti last night to run the laborious backups the handheld device required. Unlike other communications devices, this particular datapad could not simply be remotely backed up but instead had to be physically plugged in to a port that accessed the larger network. Before he had been assigned Monti and Yama, Winshur had stayed the extra hours after work once a month to run the backup himself. But it was boring work and entirely uneventful, unless staring at a screen with a rotating planet to signify the passage of time was considered an event. So there was one thing he had managed to delegate after all.

Winshur stared at the screen a moment. The twirling planet was gone, replaced by the prompt for his password. He frowned.

"Did you try to access the data?" he asked Monti.

"No, sir."

"Then why is it prompting me for a password?"

Monti hesitated. "I-I thought to look before I disturbed you. I could hear you were busy."

"If the transmission is marked confidential, then it is meant only for me. I am the owner of this device." He held up the datapad in one hand as if to illustrate his ownership. "Don't do that again."

"Of course, sir. I was only trying to help."

Winshur appreciated the boy's enthusiasm, the direct opposite of Yama's lackadaisical attitude, but it was misplaced. Nevertheless, no harm was done. The datapad was secure. He typed his password identification into the keypad and then pressed his thumb against the pad that read his fingerprint. The screen cleared and he saw the visual that Monti had glimpsed as the transmission came in: The words URGENT and CONFIDENTIAL blinking at him in bold red letters. He skimmed over the long disclaimer about accessing data that was not meant for his eyes and clicked the agreement at the end that avowed he knew what he was doing. Finally he was presented with a hologram message option, which he accepted. A woman in a gray First Order uniform manifested just above the datapad in a show of lights. He recognized his superior officer, the same one who had interviewed him for the position he now held.

"This message is intended for Executive Records Officer Winshur Bratt of the Corellian Command Base. If you have accessed this in error, you continue under penalty from the First Order." Winshur was both annoyed and intrigued. What in the world had she sent him? He paused the transmission.

"You may leave, Monti." The young man had been standing silently. If Winshur didn't know better, he would have sworn Monti was trying to go unnoticed, perhaps hoping that Winshur would forget he was there altogether. A natural curiosity, but clearly this information was for his eyes and ears only.

"Of course, sir." Monti snapped his heels together in a gesture of farewell and turned crisply.

"And close the door on your way out. I'm not to be disturbed."

Monti released the doors, allowing them to close behind him. Now that he was alone, Winshur acti-

vated the transmission again. The hologram continued:

"I am now transferring you three highly sensitive
documents that the First Order has been compiling
for a while. The first is a list of subversives. High-
profile individuals whom we believe threaten the
peace and order of the galaxy and should be detained for questioning immediately. As you can
imagine, this is very sensitive information. If this list
were to leak, these individuals, once forewarned,
might go underground and be lost to First Order
justice forever.

"The second document is even more sensitive. It
is a list of Currently Detained Individuals that the
First Order has in custody. We know that some of
these individuals under our control no doubt have
connections and acquaintances in hostile governments and extrajurisdictional bodies that we believe
would like nothing better than to liberate their
friends. We cannot let that happen.

"The third document is a subset of the second list.
It includes the names of fifteen high-profile prisoners that have been deemed inappropriate to hold at
our standard security locations and are therefore
transferring to Corellia. In fact—" The woman
paused and seemed to smirk. "—you might recognize some of the names on the list. Your job, Executive Records Officer Winshur Bratt, is twofold.
First, you are to bury these documents in your archives where they may only be retrieved by myself
or another at high command, and second, you are
to equally bury these prisoners."

Winshur pressed a suddenly sweaty hand to his heart. It was unusual but not a problem to hide the records themselves. He could keep them isolated and off the larger network, difficult to find at the best of times and impossible if the searcher didn't know what they were looking for. But that last part. Had he heard her right? She was sending fifteen prisoners here?

He hit the REPLAY button and listened again. Yes, fifteen prisoners were being sent to Corellia and he was to receive them. And do what? He wasn't a prison warden. He let the transmission continue.

"They will be accompanied by their own First Order security under the guise that they are prison labor, which is in fact the truth. None of these prisoners are considered a high security threat, as we have taken precautions to neutralize any danger they might have once posed. In fact, you will find them quite weak, but not too weak to work." The hologram woman leaned in. "This is the opportunity you were waiting for, Officer Bratt. I need you to personally work with their accompanying officer from the Reform Office to oversee the placement of these prisoners into the shipyard labor pool. The dirtier the job, the better. But they are to be kept alive and above all, they are to work. Prisoner reform through labor is a vision the First Order embraces. Vocation, discipline. These are purifiers. Do you understand?" The woman straightened. "Do this, and do it well, and it will be no time at all before your leadership qualities are noticed and you are invited to leave Corellia and join us here at high command. And perhaps we'll see about that raise."

The woman disappeared. Winshur pressed a button on his datapad that brought up the last document. A scrolling list of fifteen names crossed before him. By each name was the prisoner's origin planet, species, crime, and sentence. Winshur pressed another button on his datapad. This time, the first document appeared. He perused the most-wanted list but recognized none of the names. Disappointed, he flipped back to the Corellian Fifteen—as he was starting to think of them—and looked at the names more closely.

He was glad he was sitting down.

These names. He thought he recognized a few from the newsnets, and others had designations like DIPLOMAT or ATTACHÉ; SENATOR was even listed next to one. Winshur's heart raced as he wiped a hand across his forehead. These weren't just criminals who needed hard labor to atone for their crimes; these were political prisoners, many of them former New Republic leaders who must have been offplanet when Hosnian Prime was eradicated. And now the First Order was clearly planning to hide them on Corellia, losing them in obscurity or breaking them in hard labor while in service to the glory of the First Order.

"Opportunity," he told himself quietly. "This is just an opportunity to prove my quality." Winshur had never been political. Since he had come of age after the Galactic Civil War, he hadn't really seen the alleged horrors of the Empire at its height, and the presence of Imperial troops in Bel Vistal had been limited. By the time he was old enough to notice, the stormtroopers that his mother had often complained about occupying the town had mostly gone. When the First Order came, people had grumbled. Some had protested and a few politicians had openly opposed the occupation, but they had quickly been voted out. People had been scared at first, but life had gone on. A few more checkpoints, a curfew, restrictions on public gatherings and some kinds of speech, but generally people had adjusted. Even when their most outspoken neighbors had been arrested and taken away. Even when their rights were slowly eroded. What could you do, after all? Politics was too big for average citizens to wrap their heads around.

"A chance to be someone important," he said, his eyes running across the list again. These people had been important before and look at them now, lower than Winshur Bratt. He smiled, his moment of conscience fleeting, lost in a rising tide of ambition. Yes, he could do this. Easily. Joyfully.

He checked the time. They were to arrive well after midnight when only the skeleton crew was present. Well, it would be a long day and a late night, but Winshur didn't mind. He would send Yama or Monti out to bring him takeout for a working dinner. He had plenty to catch up on, and he'd want to get a look at the job roster so he had a better idea of where to assign the prisoners. He'd have to retrieve that himself. In fact, he should do that now.

"Monti," he called before he remembered he had closed the door and it was unlikely the cadet would hear him.

The door opened immediately. Winshur looked up, surprised, to find Monti standing in the entrance. Had the boy been waiting for him to finish? Possibly. Likely, as that was his job.

"I need to step out for the morning to retrieve some records from the Employment Department. Can you manage the office while I'm out?"

"Of course," Monti demurred.

"And why don't you plan to stay late tonight. I'll have an errand for you to run before you leave for the day."

The boy nodded his assent without complaint. Oh, if only Yama could be taught to be so professional.

Winshur retrieved his hat and coat and slipped his hands, the same hands that had been sweating minutes before but were now cool and dry, into his gloves. And he left his office, daydreaming about greater things.

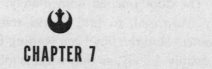

CHAPTER 7

WEDGE'S STATEMENT HUNG IN the air and for a moment, no one seemed to know what to say. Finally Snap met Wedge's eyes, his face a mask of determination.

"No, Wedge," he said. "The Resistance is not over. I'm here. Karé's here. Black Squadron is out there right now looking for allies who will join us. As long as General Organa is alive, there is hope."

"Even she can't live forever, Temmin," Norra said. "And why should she be expected to?"

"She doesn't have to." He turned to his mother. "Poe said as long as even one of us is alive and willing to fight, the Resistance lives on. We won't give in to tyranny."

"And that's why you're here," she said, cutting to the meat of the conversation. "To ask us to come back and fight."

Wedge raised his head. "Is that it, Snap?"

Snap nodded. "You are both heroes, leaders. You could do a lot of good right now."

"Or," Norra said, her voice dry, "we could just go back and die."

"Better dead than living under the First Order," her son countered.

"You could stay here," Wedge said, suddenly. "Both of you. It will take years for the First Order to notice Akiva. We have nothing of value, no export or industry they want. We're so far out on the Outer Rim, they would consider it a waste of time and resources to attack or occupy the planet."

Karé scratched at her cheek. "Didn't you just say your provincial governor was gearing up to hand the capital city over?"

"It's all bluster," Wedge said. "It won't happen."

Snap shook his head, dubious.

"I thought maybe you were here to tell us you were having children," Wedge blurted.

Snap stared for a minute, long enough for Wedge to look away, mildly embarrassed. Was that a strange thing for him to want? Another generation to carry on after him?

"I won't raise a child only to have them live under the First Order," Snap said firmly.

"It's never that cut and dried, Temmin," Norra said.

"My friends call me Snap," he said sharply.

Norra reared back as if struck. Their voices had been growing louder, more heated, and now there was silence. Wedge could hear that the rain had started again outside. Not a sunny day, after all.

Snap clasped his hands together and took a deep calming breath. "Mom. I'm sorry. I didn't mean it."

"It's fine," she said, but her voice sounded anything but fine.

"I think maybe everyone is a little wound up," Karé said, doing her best to soothe tensions. "Maybe we should all take a break. It's a lot to take in."

That's an understatement, Wedge thought. But Karé had the right idea.

"How about I make us some breakfast," he offered. "We've got eggs, those tubers you used to like, all the spices you probably haven't had since you left, Temmin . . . Snap. Let us feed you both and then we can talk some more. Brains work better on full stomachs, anyway."

"We don't really have time—" he started before his wife laid a hand on his knee. "Fine," he said, sighing. "Breakfast, and then we need to leave."

"Actually," Karé said, "my ship could use a few repairs. The weapons system is still not acting right after it got taken out at Grail City. I've got my astromech working on it now. I think I'll go check on him."

"And then Karé and I have an errand to run in town later, right, Karé?" Norra said.

"What errand?" Wedge asked.

"You know, that thing I told you about."

Wedge shook his head no.

"Well, anyway," Norra said, brushing his concern aside, "I'll do that thing I need to do and get a feel for if anyone's taken an interest in our guests. Oh, and pick up something for dinner, too. We should do something nice, don't you think?"

"We don't have time to stay for dinner," Snap protested.

"Let's play it by ear," Karé said. "Should we go,

Norra?" Before Wedge could protest further, Norra and Karé were up and heading out the door.

"They're coming back for breakfast, right?" Wedge asked no one in particular.

Snap shrugged. "Hard to say. Mom's up to something but Karé loves to eat. Could go either way."

"Norra's definitely up to something," Wedge agreed.

"And there's nothing you can do to stop it," Snap said. "She'll be fine or she won't, but you won't be able to stop her."

"You think I don't know that?" Wedge said airily. "I've lived with her for how many years now?" He said it lightly, but part of him worried. Well, Snap was right that there was no stopping her.

Snap tapped a knuckle against the table. "So, food?"

"I left my eggs outside," Wedge said absently. "Likely broken, but I'll see what I can salvage."

"I'll get them." Snap made to stand up.

"No," he said hastily. "I'll do it." Wedge pulled three big purple tubers from the pantry, dropped them on the table, and handed Snap a knife. Best to keep him in the house, since he didn't trust him not to disappear, too. "Want to cut these up?"

"Do I have a choice?"

Wedge chuckled. For a moment, Snap sounded just like the kid he had been when he met him. Impulsive, strong-willed, and so sure he was getting the raw end of the deal at all times.

"It's like practicing knife skills, right?"

"Who needs knife skills when you have a blaster?" Snap sounded genuinely baffled.

"Because . . . oh, never mind. Just cut the tubers and I'll get the eggs."

"Sure." Snap pulled the bulbous purple vegetables closer. "You want them cubed or sliced?"

"Cubed is good."

Snap nodded and cut into a vegetable. "Although I was serious about us not really having time for all this. I told Poe that—"

"Hush, now, Snap. One thing at a time. Surely the First Order won't destroy what's left of the Resistance before breakfast. Even war heroes have to eat."

Norra and Karé did in fact return for breakfast, and, after a quick and surprisingly tense meal, headed back out the door on their mysterious errand. The rain was falling again, but Norra assured them that a little water falling on Akiva never stopped anyone from getting things done. Karé told Wedge that repairs were going as quickly as possible and she thought they'd be done by the time she and Norra returned.

"They're doing this on purpose, you know," Wedge said once he and Snap were left alone in the house.

"I know," Snap said, a wry smile barely touching his lips. "Karé always knows how to settle things down." He sighed and leaned back, resting his big hands across his chest. "I'm the hotheaded one, coming in here and laying all this information on you and not even giving you time to process it. So"—he spread his hands—"she's giving you time."

"Your mother, too. She's the one that will need convincing."

Snap barked a laugh. "Norra? She's already half-way out the door."

"What do you mean?"

"I mean she lives with a foot halfway out the door. I'm surprised you've gotten her to settle down for as long as you have. Out here raising keedees and growing crops. I can't believe she hasn't run off on some life-threatening half-doomed mission yet."

Wedge looked at him incredulously.

"It's kind of her thing, Wedge."

The older man laughed. "I guess it is."

Snap leaned across the table. "But what about you? Will you be okay leaving all this behind?"

"I thought this was what I wanted," Wedge said, gesturing at this kitchen, "but seeing you and Karé again, knowing that so few people are left to fight, that so many have died. I can't stay here and let the Resistance die without doing my part." He sighed. "I'll miss my keedees. I was thinking of giving them names."

"Well, maybe you still can. When you get back."

Wedge stared out the window and let that well-meaning lie sit between them. He couldn't see much from where he was, just a slice of storm-gray sky that seemed to stretch endlessly.

———

"I want to sleep on it," Norra said, sitting on the edge of their bed rubbing lanolin into her roughened hands.

"What?" Wedge asked, surprised. He was wearing the loose pants he liked to sleep in and a worn collarless shirt.

"I said I don't know what I want to do yet, and I want to sleep on it." She finished moisturizing her hands and slipped into bed, pulling the covers up around her. "Karé and I had time to talk today, and she brought up some very good points. I know Temmin is all ready to have us die for the Resistance, which, frankly, is not something I ever expected to hear from my son, but his wife is a bit more level-headed."

"But I thought you already had one foot out the door!"

She paused in the act of reaching to turn off her bedside lamp. "I had what?"

"Temmin said—"

"Oh, what does Temmin know about me? Children always think they've got their parents figured out, but it's not true." She pushed herself up on one elbow. "I'm happy here, Wedge. With you, with our little piece of land. I know I gave you a hard time about grandchildren and domesticity earlier, but I was only half serious. If we go back to help rebuild the Resistance with Leia Organa, we're looking at certain death. I think we both know that. So maybe I chafe a bit at Akiva," she said, shrugging. "That doesn't mean I want to die."

"Are you saying the Resistance is a lost cause?"

"No, I'm saying I want to sleep on it. And you should, too. We go into this with our eyes wide open if we go at all." She reached over and turned off the lamp, leaving him standing in only the pale glow of the moon.

"You're right."

"I know. Now good night, Wedge. We'll decide in the morning."

Wedge stood for a while, watching Norra until he could hear her soft snoring. Then he went to the closet and pulled out his old flight knapsack. He stuffed a change of clothes, a warm jacket, and some basic toiletries in it. He pulled their emergency stash of credits from the top drawer of the dresser, not bothering to count it. The bag seemed a little lighter than he remembered, but maybe Norra had borrowed some and forgotten to mention it. He put the knapsack under the edge of the bed, next to his boots. Norra might need to sleep on it, but he had already made up his mind.

CHAPTER 8

LEIA CURLED UP ON her makeshift bed and tried to pretend it wasn't time to get up. But she kept dreaming of sausages and those big fluffy biscuits they had on Hosnian Prime back when she was in the New Republic Senate. She vividly remembered sharing one with Ransolm Casterfo, the young, charismatic senator from the Inner Rim planet Riosa. Ransolm had been her rival and then her co-conspirator and friend and her enemy again when he had revealed that Darth Vader was her birth father to the open Senate, and thus the entire galaxy. The timing and manner of the disclosure was devastating and essentially ended her legitimate political career. But she had been chafing at the reins of respectability anyway, the Senate being so contentious and at odds that it had become a useless partisan body. Nevertheless, Ransolm's betrayal had stung. Badly.

In the end he made amends for his betrayal of their friendship and faced his own trials—framed and falsely accused of terrorist activities and the assassination of Leia's good friend and senator, Tai-

Lin Garr. He was arrested and taken for trial to his homeworld, a planet that embraced the death penalty for such crimes. Ransolm's final fate remained unknown. Leia had tried to start an inquest to clear his name, but her political clout was in ruins and she worried that an association with her did more harm than good. Afraid lending her voice to his cause would only hurry his demise, Leia left it alone, but she never forgot him. In the end, he had been a friend. Just thinking about him made her melancholy. He was a good man who had not deserved his fate, a man who would have been an asset to the Resistance. Someone who could have made a difference. Exactly like the type of people they needed now. And he was quite dashing. She smiled, remembering how he had swooped into her meeting with the notorious crime lord Rinnrivin Di thinking he was saving her when, in fact, Leia had been leading Di into a trap.

"Rinnrivin Di!" she exclaimed, sitting up.

Work paused around her. Lieutenant Connix, Rose Tico, and Finn had been talking quietly at a nearby table. They looked up now, concern on their faces.

"Rinnrivin Di!" she said again, excitedly.

"Is that a place, ma'am?" Rose asked politely.

"No." She good-naturedly waved Rose's inquiry aside. "It's a person. Was a person. I first met him when I was in the Senate and we were investigating the existence of a crime syndicate interfering with Ryloth's shipping lanes. He had an underground operation on Bastatha."

Rose leaned forward, interested. Leia had noticed that the young woman had a hunger for war stories, or any stories, really, about the Resistance. *She's invested,* Leia observed silently, *and looking for connection.* They were good qualities, and she made a note to herself to encourage Rose's interest. Rose was still impulsive, as her unauthorized mission to Canto Bight evidenced, but she was competent and genuine and, most important, she cared. *She's someone who wears her heart on her sleeve,* Leia thought. *Young, emotionally vulnerable, but infinitely likable. And she reminds me a bit of Luke.*

Leia knew Lieutenant Connix well, although she was disappointed that she had supported Poe's actions on the *Raddus*. She should have known better, but Poe was convincing, and Leia understood Connix had meant well. She was an asset to their cause, and Leia was glad she was here, but she needed to make amends for her role in Poe's mutiny.

She didn't have as solid a reading on Finn, but Poe vouched for him and that mattered. She knew Finn was brave, and it was a bravery hard-won. He was one of the First Order's orphans, a participant in a horrific program meant to instill ultimate obedience into child soldiers. Finn had somehow retained his humanity despite the conditioning, and once he had seen the opportunity, he had fled the First Order. Along the way he had become part of the Resistance, but Leia wasn't sure where his heart lay. She guessed somewhere with his friends Poe, Rey, and Rose. And why not? If they weren't fighting for their friends, what were they fighting for?

"And is Rinnrivin Di here now?" Finn asked, dragging her back from her reverie, and obviously confused.

Leia laughed. She motioned Rose over. "Help me up," she said, sliding her legs off the bed and letting her feet touch the ground. She had fallen into bed fully clothed, exhausted after spending all night at the communications deck, and hadn't bothered to even take off her shoes. Now she was glad she didn't have to waste the time getting dressed.

Rose hurried over dutifully and helped Leia to her feet.

"Rinnrivin Di is dead," she said by way of explanation. "Which is a very good thing, because he was a very bad man. When I was in the Galactic Senate on Hosnian Prime, the Ryloth ambassador petitioned the Senate for help investigating Di. He was sure that Di's criminal operation was interfering with Ryloth's shipping lanes, possibly funneling funds into a terrorist organization."

"Was he?" Rose asked, sounding awed.

Leia blinked. "Yes." It occurred to Leia that the places she had been, the people she knew, must seem fantastical to Rose. She made a mental note to tell Rose about the memoirs she had recently recorded. They might be of interest, and besides, it would do no one any good for the young not to know the galaxy's history. That, no doubt, would doom them to repeat it.

"So if Rinnrivin is dead," Finn said, "why do we have to worry about him now?"

"Worry about him? Who's worried about him?"

"You are," Rose said, giving Leia a grin that bordered on the patronizing smile you gave your senile grandmother when you didn't want to offend her.

Leia huffed in irritation. "No. I don't care a thing about Rinnrivin Di. I was thinking of pastries and it reminded me of an old friend who then reminded me of Di."

"Ah," Rose said. "Got it."

"I don't think you do have it," Leia said. "Or else you'd be showing a bit more enthusiasm. Because I think I know where we can find help."

Rose, Connix, and Finn exchanged looks and then turned back to her, expectantly.

"Keep up, please," Leia said. "We're going to Ryloth."

"Of course," Finn said. "Makes perfect sense." But the look on his face said Leia was in fact not making sense.

"So is there an old rebel stronghold on Ryloth that we can revive, like on Crait?" Connix asked, excitedly, following along much better than the other two.

"Not an old stronghold," Leia corrected her, "but there is an old rebel, a friend. And he owes me a favor."

Leia hurried to the cockpit where she found Rey, Chewie, and Nien Nunb. They were arguing, voices low and urgent. Rey looked up when Leia came through the door.

"Did we wake you?" she asked, concerned. "We were trying to be quiet."

"I'd slept long enough. What's going on? Is there a problem?"

"We're low on fuel," Rey said. She was strapped into the pilot's seat. *It's where the girl belongs,* Leia thought. Han would have approved.

"We need to refuel but we've only got enough for one jump. If we choose wrong, we're grounded."

Leia frowned. "That bad?"

Rey nodded. "Nien Nunb thinks Tovash Tchii would be safe, and it's within range, but Chewie says he knows an old smuggler's way station where he and Han used to lay low sometimes. It's farther out, but he says we should try there."

"What do you think?" Leia asked.

Rey blinked, as if she hadn't expected Leia to ask her opinion. "They both have pros and cons . . ." she started.

Nien Nunb cut in, arguing his point. Leia held up a hand to quiet him.

"Rey?"

The girl continued. "If we go to Tovash Tchii we're more likely to find the fuel we need, but we're also more likely to draw the attention of the First Order. If we go to the place Chewie's talking about we'll get our privacy, but if the fuel isn't where he says it is then we're definitely stuck."

Chewie roared a complaint.

"I'm not saying that," Rey countered. "You said yourself that you weren't sure it was still there."

"I have a third idea," Leia said. "Ryloth." She quickly sketched out her plan to the trio.

Rey leaned over her console, hands working the

navicomputer. "It's within range," she said after a moment. "Not a bad option, but are we any more certain of what we'll find there?"

"No," Leia admitted. "But I'm willing to take the chance." She looked to Chewbacca and Nien Nunb.

Neither had an objection.

"Then Ryloth it is," Rey said. She nodded to Chewie, who accepted the coordinates and set their course. Within minutes they were burning the last of their fuel reserves and hurtling through hyperspace on the strength of Leia's wild idea.

Leia sat in the seat behind Rey, her pulse racing and her mind running through a dozen scenarios. She wrung her hands, anxiety getting the best of her. She knew it was a risk, but the Resistance would not be welcomed no matter where they chose to go. At least they had a potential ally on Ryloth. And if they didn't? If her gamble didn't pay off and they were stuck without friends and without fuel . . . no, she wouldn't let herself think that. It would work. She would make it work.

They were all silent as the *Millennium Falcon* hurtled them closer to their fate, the hours in hyperspace passing, the weight of their limited options sitting heavily in the cockpit.

"Are you well, General?" came a voice from behind her.

Leia startled as C-3PO entered the cockpit. She had been so lost in her own thoughts that she hadn't heard him approaching. She forced herself to take a deep breath, and then another, before she glanced over at the fussy protocol droid.

"I'm great," she said, brightly, heart still racing in her chest. "Why do you ask?"

"I can't help but notice that your cheeks are slightly flushed, and your heart rate is elevated. It would not surprise me to discover your blood pressure is higher than the recommended range, which current medical standards set between—"

"It's called nerves, Threepio," she said, cutting him off gently. "I'm just a bit anxious."

"I am familiar with the emotion, Your Highness— I mean General." he replied primly. "Nevertheless, it is my duty to inform you that the medical droids did advise you against becoming agitated so recently after your illness."

"Thank you. So noted."

"But Your Highness, I must insist—"

"We're coming out of lightspeed," Rey informed them.

Leia watched as the telltale blur of stars disappeared abruptly and the planet of Ryloth filled their view. It was beautiful, a blue-and-red ball with bands of green, the swirl of weather systems wrapping the planet in shades of white. She'd spent very little time on Ryloth and knew less than she would have liked about the planet's history and people. She wished this visit could be under better circumstances, but she didn't have that luxury.

"Something's coming up on the scanner," Rey said tersely from the pilot's seat. "Looks like ships approaching. Any chance that we're expected?"

"Not likely," Leia admitted. "Our luck with communications hasn't been the greatest, if you recall. So I thought we'd just . . . show up."

Chewie growled a response.

"They could be just patrolling their local space," Leia agreed, "but we haven't even entered orbit yet."

"And those are fighters," Rey said. "Two ships, *Can-Cell* class. Reading as Ryloth interceptors registered out of the capital city, Lessu. Official government call signs. Shields up?"

"Not yet," Leia said. She was more wary than worried at this point. "We come in peace. Let's not give them a reason to think we don't."

"How do you know they won't fire on us?"

"I don't."

Chewie made an urgent sound.

"He says they've powered up their weapons!" Rey exclaimed.

"I know," Leia said through gritted teeth. Now she was worried. She knew a hostile welcome was a possibility, but it still surprised her that the Ryloth government would be willing to shoot first and ask questions later of a simple cargo ship. Perhaps things were worse here than she realized.

She hurried to the corridor. "Finn," she called down the long hallway. Finn appeared at the entrance to the main corridor, Lieutenant Connix and Rose at his side. "We might have a problem. I need you and Rose on the turrets, just in case."

Finn nodded sharply, and he and Rose ran for the guns.

"Is there anything I can do?" Connix asked.

"Get on the communications console in the crew cabin. Run through our ally frequencies again. Anyone within shouting distance of Ryloth in case—"

"Leia!" Rey's voice was high and sharp. Leia gestured Connix away before she turned back to the cockpit.

The transmission light on Rey's console blinked green. Leia had been expecting the worst, but that light meant they wanted to talk. Relief flooded her body. They had a chance.

"Answer it," she said to Rey.

Rey looked back at her, eyes wide.

"Go on."

The green light blinked, more insistent.

"Oh my!" C-3PO exclaimed. "You must answer their hail. Protocol rule 12B6 states that when entering any c-class planet's sovereign orbital space, it is required to respond to a government—"

"What do I say?" Rey asked, voice panicked.

"You'll think of something," Leia assured her.

"I thought that was your job!"

"I'm too well known. I don't think we want to reveal who we are quite yet, just in case the First Order beat us here."

"Won't they know the *Millennium Falcon*?"

"Maybe. But they won't necessarily know I'm on the ship. And we won't know anything for sure until you answer that."

"I-I can't!"

"Of course you can," Leia said simply. "And now."

"I—"

Chewie roared, exasperated, and reached over to flip the green button on. The cockpit filled with the slightly threatening masculine voice. "YT-1300 freighter, identify yourself and your purpose in the Ryloth system or we will be forced to bring your ship down. You have thirty seconds."

"Ominous," Leia murmured. "I guess they don't get many visitors." She was being flippant, mostly for Rey's sake. Of course they didn't get many visitors. She imagined most of the galaxy was hunkered down and waiting, terrified that their skies would fill with a First Order occupying force at any moment. Or worse, a red pulse of light like the one that had decimated the Hosnian system. These were dark times and Ryloth had good reason to be wary, even of an old Corellian freighter. She was of two minds about it herself. On the one hand she had meant it when she said that it might not be wise to identify themselves to the Ryloth government. She didn't think they would be specifically hostile to the Resistance, but they had never joined the Republic and had certainly never taken sides when the Populists and Centrists had ripped the Senate apart, politically. She couldn't imagine they wanted to be openly seen supporting either side. She had hoped to slip onto the planet and track down her old friend without engaging with the government, but she should have known better.

"YT-1300 freighter," the voice repeated, "identify yourself and your purpose—"

Chewie groaned. C-3PO muttered something quietly worried. Leia waited, eyes on Rey.

"This is . . . Rey!" the girl said suddenly. "And we're out of the . . ." She paused and then, ". . . Han system! We're carrying medical supplies to the southern region." She grinned excitedly, clearly extemporizing. "We're expected!"

It wasn't bad. It would at least buy them some time.

"Pilot Rey of the Han system, transmit your clearance code now."

Rey looked at Leia, eyes big. *What do I say?* she mouthed.

Think of something, Leia mouthed back, letting her know she was to solve this problem on her own.

"I . . . we lost our code. Terrible incident on Teedo Minor. Do you know it? But I assure you we—"

"I'll take it from here, Lessu command," a female voice cut in, saving Rey from whatever she was going to say next.

The voice was authoritative and sounded like it expected to be obeyed. Rey frowned, and then whispered, "Another ship on the scanner. *Rycrit*-class. Stealth model." She let out a low, impressed whistle. "That's a nice ship."

"Identification?" Leia asked.

"Transponder's not broadcasting one."

Leia frowned. Friend or foe? "Get those shields ready just in case, Rey. We don't know if this new ship is on our side or we're about to jump from the skillet into the scalder."

"Copy that."

"—not your jurisdiction," the first ship, the Ryloth government party, was saying to the new ship. "We can handle this."

"Sorry, but I'll be pulling rank on you, Lessu," the female voice from the second ship said crisply. "You are to disengage this freighter under the authority of the RDA. We will take it from here."

Silence on the *Millennium Falcon* as they waited. Rey kept her finger ready to bring up the shields on Leia's order. Chewbacca muttered into his mike, a command for Finn and Rose to hold steady. The whole ship seemed to hold its breath.

"Copy," the male voice said, finally. "RDA One, we have received your authorization code and are disengaging. With our apologies."

"Copy, Lessu."

Again, silence as the *Millennium Falcon* waited and then, "Corellian YT-1300 freighter, I am switching communications to a secured channel at the following frequency. Please engage in three, two . . ."

Rey let out a gasp of surprise. "It's the Resistance channel." She quickly punched in the new frequency. Leia leaned over Rey's shoulder and pressed the TRANSMIT button. "Who is this?"

"*Millennium Falcon,* you are required to follow me."

"This is General Leia Organa of the Resista—"

"We know who you are, General. Please follow us. We'll explain once we get on the ground. You're attracting too much attention up here."

Leia raised an eyebrow at no one in particular. They weren't exactly being rude, but they were being obtuse. Well, perhaps that's what happened when one showed up unannounced. And they did have a point.

"Do as she says," Leia said, dropping back into her seat. "Let's see where this goes."

Chewie growled an acknowledgment, and the *Millennium Falcon* fell into formation behind the ship.

"They're leading us away from the capital city," Rey reported.

Not surprising. "Which way?"

"Toward the southern hemisphere. There're forests near the equator, but after that, it looks like open desert." She made a small distressed sound. "Looks like Jakku," she said, so quietly that Leia almost didn't hear her.

Leia waited, but when Rey didn't elaborate, she said, "Well, you did say the *Millennium Falcon* was headed for the southern hemisphere, so maybe they're covering for us."

"Why would they do that?"

"Maybe they want our cover story to stand up, too." Well, as far as it could. They weren't actually carrying any medical supplies, of course, but maybe way out here no one would look too closely if they were parked at the right place and left when expected. Or maybe it would be easy to make them disappear out here. No one would remember the Corellian freighter on such a routine run.

Soon they had crossed the equatorial forests and were flying over vast expanses of red-rock desert, cresting dunes and scattered striated mesas. Small settlements dotted the landscape but nothing that looked like a city.

A wide flat-topped mesa came into view. The lead ship, RDA One, flew in close, dipping into a canyon that blended effortlessly into the landscape. The *Millennium Falcon* followed.

"I don't like this," Rey said quietly. "Not a lot of room to maneuver down here."

"Stay the course," Leia reassured her. The cockpit thrummed with tension, all of them waiting to see if her gamble paid off. Only Chewie looked calm, as if following strange and potentially hostile ships into unknown territory was all in a day's work.

The opening narrowed. Despite her earlier protests, Rey handled the challenging landscape easily. RDA One dipped abruptly, and Leia saw it was leading them into a cave of some kind, a natural opening in the mountainside.

"Do we follow?" Rey asked, voice taut.

"We've come this far," Leia replied.

"It could be a trap."

"I don't think so. If it was a trap, why bother bringing us all the way out here?"

"To hide the evidence?"

Leia glanced at Rey to see if the girl was joking, but her face looked serious. "I don't think so," she said.

"Excuse me, General," C-3PO interrupted. "I don't mean to counter your years of military experience and expertise—"

"Then don't," she murmured.

"—but the statistics are alarmingly high that a trap is likely considering—"

"Thank you, Threepio," she said, as politely as she could manage.

"They're landing," Rey said, sharply, and Leia turned her attention back to the scene in front of her.

They had entered a hangar of some kind. The cave expanded exponentially, the ceiling lost far above them in the darkness. The floor below was buffed to a gleaming obsidian, traced over with glowing lines that delineated acceleration lanes and landing pads. They were in a cave, deep inside the side of a desert mountain, but in a fully functioning landing base.

"What is this?" Rey asked quietly.

"The RDA, apparently," Leia said. She laughed quietly. "I think we've stumbled into exactly what we need."

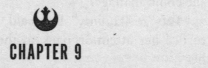

CHAPTER 9

"SHOULD I LAND?" REY asked.

Leia could see that a rectangular pad was pulsing brightly a few hundred meters in front of them, an obvious invitation to set the ship down.

"Yes," Leia said. "Let's go see what, and who, we've found."

Rey brought the ship in smoothly, putting it down between the green glowing lines. The *Millennium Falcon* settled gently, the first time it had touched solid ground in what seemed like weeks.

Leia exhaled and pushed herself up from her chair. She realized she hadn't had a chance to clean up and had slept in her clothes. Well, whoever was waiting for them below would have to excuse her breach in civility.

"Shall we?" she asked, unnecessarily. They were all on their feet, awaiting her command. She led the way and Rey, Chewie, Nien Nunb, and C-3PO followed her out of the cockpit, the droid keeping up a steady stream of disapproval, citing terrible statistics and probabilities. Leia ignored him, focused on the task at hand. So much was riding on finding someone friendly on the other side of that door.

Finn, Rose, and Connix joined them at the outer doors. She gave them each a tight smile. Strength in numbers, she told herself. Even if the combined age of her entourage, not including Chewie, was nearly equal to her own. Well, maybe it wasn't quite that bad—she wasn't *that* old—but looking at their faces, knowing that their futures were not guaranteed, she certainly felt so today.

Chewie made a questioning sound.

"Open the door," Leia said. And to the others, "Weapons close but not drawn. I'm still hoping this is a friend."

Chewie punched the button. The boarding ramp of the *Millennium Falcon* lowered. Leia prayed that she wasn't about to get anyone killed. She straightened her back, rising to her full height and lifting her chin. She was tired and hurting and it took effort. She reminded herself that she was still a princess so she damn well better look like one, even now. Especially now.

The view opened onto the bay they had seen from the cockpit view. Approaching them were two Twi'leks. A female with orange skin and eyes, dressed in a fitted sand-colored jumpsuit that had a definite utilitarian cast. Everything about the way she held herself said fighter, including the blaster in her hand. The other Twi'lek was male, pale purple with dark eyes, his lekku wrapped in black leather. He wore a version of the same jumpsuit. Leia noticed an unfamiliar insignia on the chest: two arms raised to fists, the chain connecting them broken down the center. She didn't recognize the symbol, but she made note of it. Both Twi'leks looked competent and professional. Whatever they had stumbled into was, as she had deduced on the ship, an organized fighting force. She dug through her admittedly feeble knowledge of Ryloth history, trying to recall if there was any sort of guerrilla army on the planet anymore. The most notorious guerrilla leader had been Cham Syndulla, who had liberated Ryloth from the Separatists during the Clone Wars. But that was more than fifty years ago. These days Ryloth had a government and no need of an underground army. At least that had been her presumption.

"Welcome, Leia Organa," the woman said, and Leia recognized her voice from the earlier transmissions. She also noticed that the woman had not used any of Leia's numerous titles to address her— princess, senator, general. Interesting. Oversight? Insult? Or some sort of Twi'lek emphasis on egalitarianism? She would find out soon enough.

"Our mysterious escort," she said, acknowledging the woman with a nod.

"Hahnee Brethen," the woman introduced herself. "Pilot for the Ryloth Defense Authority."

"Ah." And there was Leia's answer. "You'll pardon my ignorance, but I'm not familiar with the defense authority."

"And why would you be unless you've recently spent time on our planet?" the male Twi'lek asked, stepping forward and giving Leia a small bow.

"Charth Brethen. Ambassador of the Ryloth Defense Authority."

"Oh dear," Threepio said from somewhere behind Leia's shoulder. "I'm scanning my data banks and I find no record of the Ryloth Defense Authority."

The woman looked slightly startled but the man, Charth, responded easily. "That's because we aren't officially part of any record you would have access to, droid. If we were, we wouldn't be doing a very good job of staying off the scope."

"And whose scope do you wish to stay off?" Leia asked pointedly.

Hahnee barked a laugh. "Who do you think?"

"You'll have to excuse my sister," Charth said, cutting in smoothly. "We're a bit on edge after what happened to the Hosnian system, and not everyone thought it was a wise decision to allow you to land here."

"I understand," Leia said.

"I don't know that you do," Charth said. "We're taking a risk, having you here. Should the First Order find out that we've given you aid, we become targets ourselves. You could drag us into war . . . or worse."

Leia nodded. Despite Charth's accusation, she was all too aware of the danger that trailed the Resistance. "We are grateful," she said simply.

His eyes locked on hers, considering. Leia held his gaze until, finally, he broke it, with a small shrug. "It wasn't our call," he admitted, gesturing to encompass himself and his sister. "It was his. So an exception was made."

His. Leia smiled. She had gambled correctly. "I'd like to see him now, if I could. We don't have much time."

Charth nodded. "Then by all means, let us not keep him waiting any longer."

Despite Charth's assurances of expediency, Leia found herself waiting while he offered them all a chance to eat and refresh themselves first. Leia remembered that the Twi'leks took hospitality seriously and was loath to decline, but time felt precious. She had spent enough of it already without any measurable progress. Soon enough Black Squadron would be heading back and she needed a place for them to call home, at least temporarily. She already knew she was going to have to talk fast to convince the RDA that this mysterious place in the desert was it.

A door on the right side of the cave slid open and two Twi'leks, purple-skinned like Charth and no more than school-aged, rolled out a cart laden with platters of food and pitchers of fresh water.

"For those of you who are staying," Charth explained. "I know you don't want to go far from your ship, so we will bring Ryloth hospitality to you."

They all watched as the two set up a table and chairs right in front of the *Falcon*'s landing ramp. One of the youths caught Leia's eye, a familiar look of awe on her face. She quickly looked away when

Leia noticed. Leia heard the girl whisper "princess" to her companion who stole a glance, too, before Charth pointedly cleared his throat. The two quieted immediately, focusing on their work.

"You're a bit of a legend," Charth said, leaning slightly toward Leia. His tone was wry but not without its own touch of awe. "You'll have to excuse their curiosity."

"Are they relatives?" Leia asked, her keen gaze picking out similarities in the facial features between the ambassador and the two children.

Charth blinked, surprised. His lekku twitched and he hesitated a moment before saying, "Yes. These are my offspring."

And you are having them serve us, Leia thought. She recognized it for what it was—a gesture of trust.

"You must be very proud," Leia said earnestly, hoping he saw that she understood what he was doing. Charth watched his children for a moment, face expressionless.

"Yes," he finally said, giving Leia the briefest of acknowledgments. "I am."

The two children were done with their setup and Charth clapped his palms together briskly. "Please, help yourselves."

The crew of the *Millennium Falcon* did not hesitate.

"Sure beats rations," Finn muttered as he stuffed a leaf-wrapped tube of dried fruit in his mouth.

"Don't forget to chew," Rose scolded him lightly.

He ducked his head, chastised, and slid into a waiting seat. Rose gave him a smile. "We represent the Resistance now," she told him. "We have to act like it."

Chewbacca roared in agreement and then dipped his big hairy paw into the vat of clear noodles in the center of the table. They all laughed, including Chewie, and for a brief moment some of the tension faded over the prospects of a meal shared with friends and potential allies. After the laughter faded and most of the crew had committed to eating, Leia pulled Chewbacca aside.

"I want you and the others to stay with the ship," she said. "Keep an eye on things. Connix can handle any communications that come in, and Finn and Rose can stand guard."

Chewie growled in concern.

"I'll be fine. I'll take Rey and Threepio."

Chewie protested, a low sound in his throat.

"If they wanted us dead, we'd be dead," Leia countered. "But just in case . . ." She turned her palm over, revealing a comm. "If there's a problem, try to reach me. If you can't, then follow my signal."

Chewie gave an affirmative growl.

Leia turned back to her hosts. "Shall we?" she asked.

Rey fell into step beside her as Charth and Hahnee led them away. Rey had readily agreed to accompany Leia, but she had insisted on bringing her staff and a blaster. To Leia's mild surprise, their escorts didn't object. C-3PO trailed them, happily commenting on Leia's wise decision to bring him along since, as a protocol droid, he was most qualified to assist her.

They crossed the length of the cave that remained relatively bright and airy. The rock ceiling stretched so far above their heads that Leia didn't feel claustrophobic in the enclosed space as she thought she might. She watched Rey to see if the girl minded, but she seemed calm and observant, in her element. Leia was pleased to see it. C-3PO, however, insisted on rattling off half the known history of Ryloth as they made their way deeper into the caverns, which appeared to annoy Hahnee and amuse Charth. Leia found it mildly educational and appreciated C-3PO's efforts.

The droid said, "Did you know that early in the Clone Wars, your ancestor Anakin Skywalker helped fight for Ryloth against the droid armies? The Ryloth forces were led by Cham Syndulla, a terrorist—"

"Freedom fighter," Hahnee growled, getting in C-3PO's face.

"I beg your pardon?"

"He's a hero here, Threepio," Leia corrected him. "While Imperial records may have labeled him a terrorist, here among his own people he's considered a freedom fighter."

"Oh, of course. I meant no offense. My historical records are often, well, historical. I will make the notation immediately."

"Great," Leia said brightly. "Continue." They'd entered another passage, this one seemingly lit from within.

The droid continued. "Freedom fighter Cham Syndulla. In addition, his daughter Hera Syndulla served as a general in the Rebellion and New Republic. Her contribution to the record is quite remarkable. Now, I may be incorrect, but from my *historical* records I can extrapolate that the Ryloth Defense Authority is a direct descendant of Cham Syndulla's Free Ryloth movement."

"Not a direct descendant," Charth corrected him amicably. "But certainly a philosophical one. After our history of oppression and slavery, certain factions have vowed to never have it happen again. There are those of us who have dedicated our lives to the continued liberty of our world, for ourselves and our children. Against any comers, First Order or otherwise." He gave Leia a pointed look, his black eyes bright in the shadowy cave light.

"So you are part of the government," Leia said.

"We operate with the full knowledge and support of the Rylothian government, yes," Charth assured her. "But we are also somewhat . . . autonomous."

"A secret police force?" she asked.

"A supplemental militia," Charth corrected. "Recent events have made it clear that Ryloth needs a backup system, shall we say, should something incapacitate the capital. We are that backup system. We operate independently but with their full blessing."

"Not for this," Hahnee reminded them.

Leia pursed her lips, thinking. The last thing she wanted was for the RDA to see them as a threat to Ryloth's freedom. "It is what drives the Resistance as well," she said, picking her words carefully. "It is what we have in common."

"We heard the Resistance is all dead," Hahnee spit bluntly.

"Bloodied in the fight," Leia admitted freely. "Hurting, but not all dead."

"That is good," Charth said. "We admire this fighting spirit. Better dead than a boot on one's neck." He paused. "And we are here."

They had reached a wide, round stone door. The door was a deep garnet-colored stone. Burned into the door was the same symbol Charth wore on his chest, the symbol Leia had come to think of as "chainbreaker." Charth pressed his hand against the door until it lit from within, bathing them briefly in a blood-red light, and then he pressed the door open. Hahnee went through first, stepping over the low threshold and ducking slightly to pass underneath the lintel. Charth gestured Leia in next, and she followed, Rey on her heels. He came through last, pulling the door shut behind him.

At first glance, Leia thought they had entered a throne room. The space stretched before them over a hundred meters, stone under their feet, the same garnet as the door behind them. The walls were equally distant, a pale-pink stone heavily veined with silver and white, and Leia could see they were lined with . . . were those books? Scrolls, maps, bound books, and various forms of what looked like paper records filled shelves that looked like they had been carved out of the stone walls. Directly in front of Leia, the cave opened onto a massive balcony that overlooked the entire desert valley. She could see the hint of a sunset blossoming outside past the energy shield that held the blowing sand out and kept the chill in. In fact, this room was noticeably colder than the rest of the cave system had been, enough that she shivered and rubbed her hands along her arms. And there, between her and the balcony, where she expected a throne to be, sat a desk. Regal in its own way, its size three times that of a normal table and carved from a single piece of what looked like petrified wood. It was also practical, piled with holocards and a communications transmission module. And sitting behind it, the man she had come to Ryloth to see.

He stood now to approach them. He wore a heavy robe, black with blue and silver embroidery, draped over his broad shoulders. His face was lost in the hood, but as he came closer, he lifted blue-skinned hands and pushed the hood from his face. It was a Twi'lek face, more handsome than Leia had remembered him. Age had been kind to him, had chiseled away some of his previous boyish appearance and left him looking distinguished. His lekku were patterned in a molten swirl of sky and ocean, and he wore them tied back with a sort of golden headpiece that reminded Leia a bit of a crown. But the man she had always known had no interest in power, and certainly this room he surrounded himself with didn't speak to power as much as it spoke to a reverence of knowledge, despite its grandiosity.

"Have you become a scholar in your old age?" she asked by way of greeting.

"I have dedicated what is left of my life to preserving my people's history," the man admitted. "I don't know if that makes me a scholar, a collector, or a fool."

"A bit of all three?" she ventured.

He laughed, which was the response she was hoping for. So he wasn't so much changed, despite appearances. They met in the middle of the room and he paused, deferentially, as if waiting. She took the initiative and leaned in to embrace him briefly. He returned the welcome.

"Princess Leia," he said, his voice resonating with respect.

"It's general now," she joked, warmly.

"Princess, senator, general. Is there nothing you cannot do?" he observed.

"It doesn't look like you're doing too poorly yourself."

"This isn't mine," he said. "This was once the Ryloth Historical Society's library. When they decided to found the RDA, they wanted us out of the capital, far enough away from Lessu that if it was lost, there would be a place to regroup. This"—he gestured to take in the room, the cave, the entire facility—"was available."

"They moved you out of the city and into the desert."

"And I let them," he acknowledged, voice wry.

"Ah," she said, archly, "there's where the 'fool' comes in."

He grinned, obviously charmed. "Indeed."

She took in his rich robe, the coronet that held back his lekku, and then let her gaze travel around the room. "And what should I call you these days?

Certainly not fool. So scholar, historian, librarian?"
She paused. "General?"

"No, Your Highness. You call me what you've
always called me. My name."

She smiled, fully confident that she could still call
this man a friend. A friend that she was about to ask
to risk his life, his home, and his very people. But
she had no choice.

"Hello, Yendor," she said.

He acknowledged her with a solemn nod. The
previous lightness of their banter had all but evaporated, replaced with the tension of expectation and
need.

"You need my help."

"Desperately."

He gestured toward the terrace behind him.

"Come. Let's talk."

They took their tea on the vast balcony overlooking
the red mesas of Ryloth. Yendor himself served
them before taking a seat at the table with Leia,
Rey, and Charth. Hahnee preferred to slink around
the perimeter, in constant contact with someone on
the other end of her comm.

The tea was served in a clear vessel within which
Leia could see a bouquet of dried purple-and-black
flower heads unfolding under the influence of the
heated water. They blossomed anew, releasing a rich
fragrance into the desert night. The tea was accompanied by a plate of the same leaf-wrapped dried
fruits Leia had seen Finn eat before they left the
crew back at the *Millennium Falcon*. She took one

out of civility and set it on her fired-clay plate. She hadn't eaten all day, but the very idea of food made her stomach roil. She wouldn't relax until she had secured some kind of assurances of Yendor's aid. The way their conversation was going, however, she wasn't sure if that was going to happen.

"Ryloth doesn't get involved," Yendor was saying, his long fingers steepled under his chin.

"I'm not asking you to get involved," Leia said. She reached over and took the liberty of pouring herself more tea. "I'm asking you to let me and my friends impose on your hospitality for a while."

"You and your friends?" Yendor repeated, incredulously. "Is that what we're calling the Resistance these days?"

C-3PO, who had been hovering a few meters away, turned to the conversation. "Technically, General Organa is correct—"

Leia held up a hand, and C-3PO stopped talking.

"Yendor, you were a rebel once. And the Ryloth Defense Authority? What is that if not a tool to fight the First Order? We're on the same side."

"I still am a rebel in here," Yendor said, tapping a fist to his chest. "But it's not just me. I have to think of my people, too." His eyes cut to Charth.

Charth sat up straighter and cleared his throat. "Not just the RDA, but all of Ryloth. Our neutrality has been hard-won, and we will not fall under the influence of any foreign government." He glanced at Leia. "Even yours."

Leia shook her head, amused. "What government? We're barely a ship. If you think we're in any shape to be a threat to your independence . . ."

"I did hear the rumors," Yendor said, thoughtfully. "Reports of a destroyed fleet, rumors of Luke Skywalker seen again and then gone . . . is it true?"

"It's true," Leia said, and the admission only hurt a little.

"Ahh . . ." Yendor shifted in his seat. He reached over and poured himself more tea, even though his cup was barely touched, eyes focused down. "And how was Luke? Will he be joining . . . is he part of this?"

"Luke is gone," Leia said quietly, and that one hurt a lot, after all.

Yendor glanced up. "You mean . . . ?"

"Yes."

The Twi'lek leaned back in his chair. "So there are no more Jedi."

"I wouldn't go that far," Leia said. She gave Rey a reassuring smile, but the young woman only looked at her like a frightened skittermouse. Yendor watched the exchange curiously.

"I'm afraid I've forgotten your name," he said to Rey.

"I'm Rey," she said quickly. "I'm just a junker from Jakku."

"I doubt that if you're with Princess Leia."

"Or I was. Now I'm . . . a pilot."

Yendor gestured expansively. "A pilot is someone," he said, and gave Leia a conspiratorial wink. "I was once a pilot, and a damn good one, until they made me wear these robes and take meetings. What kind of ship do you fly?"

"All of them?" Rey winced. "I mean, any of them. Right now . . . the *Millennium Falcon*."

Yendor whistled in appreciation.

"She was also Luke's apprentice," Leia said, laying a hand on Rey's arm.

Yendor looked even more impressed. "Well, that's someone, Rey of Jakku. That's someone, indeed."

Rey flushed scarlet and took a gulp of her tea. She choked briefly and quickly set the cup down. She pressed a hand to her mouth, coughing hard.

"Are you all right?" Charth asked, leaning forward.

"Fine," she said, coughing again.

"Shall I hit you in the back?" C-3PO offered.

She shook her head no in alarm. "I'm fine!"

"Perhaps you'd like to refresh yourself?" Charth said.

Rey pushed herself to her feet with a nod, and Charth waved Hahnee over. The woman led Rey away until Leia could no longer hear her cough echo through the oversized room.

The three of them sat quietly for a moment, soaking in the growing darkness of the evening, the warmth of good tea in the belly, all at odds with the tension that crowded the room.

Finally, Leia pressed her hands on the table and leaned toward Yendor, bringing all the weight of authority she had left to bear. All those years in the Rebellion, in the Senate, in every role she'd played came down to this. "Let me be blunt, Yendor. I'm calling in a favor."

When he spoke, it was with reluctance, but he said, "After what you did to rid Ryloth of Rinnrivin Di and his crime syndicate, you have that right."

Leia nodded. It wasn't what she'd call enthusiastic, but it wasn't a no.

She spoke briskly. "We need a place to lay low, and Ryloth needs to be it. We need shelter, food, and communications equipment, a place to park some ships and do repairs . . ." Yendor's eyes had gotten a bit wide, so she slowed down. "It's not so much, if you think about it."

Yendor's laugh was bitter. "Maybe not so much, but it's politically dangerous."

"Not if no one knows we're here, and I certainly don't want anyone to know until we can regroup, find some allies."

"It can't be done," Charth cut in.

Leia stared, and he tipped his chin in apology.

"I don't mean to be rude, General," Charth said, "but logistically, it just can't be done. We don't have the facilities to house hundreds of Resistance fighters—"

"One ship."

"What?"

"The *Millennium Falcon* is all we have left." Her voice didn't waver when she said it. Her eyes moved back and forth between the two men before she shrugged. "Give or take. Once Black Squadron and my other pilots come in with help, I'm hoping to double, maybe triple that. But not hundreds, not even a hundred. And for now? Just the *Falcon*."

Silence descended. This one thick with grief unspoken.

"I-I'm sorry to hear it," Yendor said after a few moments, his voice quiet with loss.

"Me, too," Leia said, less quiet, and moving toward angry. She didn't like rehashing all she had lost to convince Yendor and Charth that they should do the right thing, the thing Yendor had admitted he owed her. She just needed a safe place to rest, and the time to do it.

The older Twi'lek man ran a long finger around the edge of his cup. "I'll have to talk to Lessu. Chancellor Drelomon won't like it, and General Ishel even less so." He leaned forward, intent. "You know what you're asking, Leia. If the First Order finds you here, they will crush us. Oh, we'll put up a fight, but Ryloth is under no illusions as to how we would fare against the First Order and the military might they have amassed. No one wants to risk being the next Hosnian system."

Leia wanted to reassure him that Starkiller Base was destroyed, that he need not fear the demise of his planet simply for rendering the Resistance aid, but she knew she could make no such guarantees. She might well be talking Yendor into signing his planet's death warrant. Part of her wanted to leave, right then and there. Find somewhere else, somewhere remote like Hoth or abandoned like Crait where she would not be putting friends in harm's way. But deep down, she knew there was no safe place. Not for Yendor and Ryloth, and certainly not for her. Even if she had never brought the Resistance to his door, the First Order would come eventually. And they would ask of Ryloth what it could not give, and when it refused, they would bring war, and they would destroy Ryloth. It was their way.

"Father," Charth said, alarmed. "You can't be seriously contemplating this."

Leia let out a small noise of surprise. Son? Charth was Yendor's son? Oh stars, somehow that made it all the worse.

"I dedicated my life to fighting for what's right, Charth," Yendor said, voice firm. "I didn't do that to turn my back on people fighting for the same cause when they need help the most. Ryloth will maintain its neutrality, but helping refugees is not taking a political stand. It's simply doing the right thing for fellow people."

Charth stood to pace, legs moving him back and forth along the polished red floors. "I understand, Father, and I'm sympathetic. But we're calling the Resistance refugees now? No one will buy it."

Yendor shrugged. "I don't think I care."

His son barked an incredulous laugh. "I thought your freedom-fighting days were over."

"So did I, but apparently not."

Rey returned, and Yendor gave her a kind smile. "Who knows, maybe I'll get to pilot an X-wing again?"

"What's going on?" Hahnee said, trailing Rey as she walked over.

"Dad's made up his mind," Charth murmured, and despite his earlier protests, Leia was sure she heard a hint of approval in the younger man's voice. Charth turned to his sister. "It looks like we've joined the Resistance."

CHAPTER 10

"**WEDGE, WAKE UP! THERE'S** someone in the yard."

Wedge woke immediately, fully on alert. He looked to his side, but Norra wasn't next to him in bed. He sat up. There she was, at the window, standing to the side where no one could see her but giving her a clear view of the yard. Early dawn filtered through the glass, casting her face in shadow. Only her silver hair gleamed white in the burgeoning sunlight. The morning must be just shy of full sunrise.

"Who is it?" he asked, his voice a low whisper. "Nosy neighbors?"

"Too far to see faces from here, but they look official. No armor, but I see a few that look like enforcers of some kind."

His mouth felt dry. He reached for the bottle of water by the bedside and gulped it down. "Could it be the local government from Myrra come to investigate the X-wings?"

"Could be. Probably. But there's something about the way they carry themselves . . ."

"First Order," he said, grimly. He'd said earlier that he didn't think the First Order had established a presence on Akiva yet, but maybe that had been naïve.

Norra didn't answer him, which was sign enough that she agreed. He pushed himself out of bed and padded silently over on bare feet to join her at the window. She moved to make room, and he looked out on the yard for himself. He counted six figures moving brazenly around his yard. Norra was right. No stormtroopers but . . .

"Third on the right," Wedge said. "That looks like a blaster rifle. Can you guess the model?"

Norra looked. "Could be standard-issue F-11D, but since when have stormtroopers served out of uniform?"

Wedge shrugged. "I don't know, but do you want to take a chance?"

"No."

Wedge hesitated. "Norra . . ."

She looked at him, eyes bright. He had expected to see conflict there, a wariness of things to come. Perhaps even reluctance after her words last night. Instead all he saw was determination. Calm.

"Looks like the fight has come to us," she said.

"Does that mean . . . ?"

She hurried to her side of the bed and pulled a bag from underneath. Wedge recognized a flight knapsack. "I packed a few things," Norra said, sounding sheepish. "I know we said we'd sleep on it, and I meant it . . . but I thought . . . just in case."

Wedge laughed and pulled his own packed bag from his side of the bed, grinning.

Norra laughed. "I thought I was giving you time."

"I thought I was giving *you* time."

"You were. And I thought about it. But I didn't have to think long."

"So we're in this," Wedge asked. "We're going back to war, back to being rebels. Even if it means . . ."

"It's always meant that, hasn't it?" she said quietly, eyes intent. "And we've lived long lives . . ."

"Longer than many of our friends," Wedge agreed.

"And Leia needs us. The galaxy needs us." She exhaled. "Our children need us."

Wedge couldn't argue with that. And something inside him brightened, feeling some of the same determination that beamed from Norra's smile.

"Well," Wedge said, "now that's decided, why don't we wake the kids?"

They woke Snap and Karé, filling them in on their suspicions about the people in the yard.

"We can take four of them, no problem," Karé said, sounding confident. "Probably even from here."

"Well, before we go shooting up the Akiva countryside, maybe we can think of another plan," Snap suggested. The others looked at him. "Or not."

"Snap's right," Norra agreed. "We should at least consider a less violent option."

Norra and Snap were the voices of reason? Wedge found that hard to believe. "It's like opposite day in here," he murmured, but nobody heard him.

"Do they have restraints for the X-wings?" Karé asked. "Anything that would keep us grounded?"

Norra shook her head. "I didn't see any, but maybe they just came to investigate."

"Likely a neighbor called it in as a nuisance," Wedge agreed. "They send out a few troopers to scope it out, see if it's the real deal or just an overactive neighborhood watch."

"We don't take any chances," Snap said, decisively. "We need those X wings. They can't have them."

"Okay," Wedge said. "But maybe we can get them out without killing everyone."

"Do you have a plan?" Norra asked.

Wedge nodded. He'd been thinking about it as they talked. "As a matter of fact, I do."

Snap and Karé left first, slithering through the tunnel that led from the kitchen to the edge of their property, Norra's bolt-hole coming in handy after all. The couple took their own gear as well as Wedge's and Norra's, leaving the older couple to dress quickly. Norra layered her housecoat over her old flight suit, and Wedge did the same with his robe. Wedge's flight suit had been a tight fit, but there was no shame in the bounty he had found in middle age. It just meant the garment was a little snugger than he'd liked. No doubt Resistance rations would change that.

"You look great," Norra said, and kissed him fiercely, a grin on her face.

He decided that was good enough.

Wedge rechecked his pocket for the stash of credits, and then they each tucked a blaster in their pocket and headed for the back door. Wedge paused a moment, taking in the old house. The place had grown on him. This life had grown on him. He would miss it. But greater things called to him now, and he had never been afraid to answer such calls.

Norra reached over to muss his hair. He looked at her questioningly.

"So you look like you just got out of bed," she explained. "Although I always did like your hair a little long."

"Now you tell me," he said. "Right before I join up again."

"The Resistance will let you keep your hair. Have you seen Poe Dameron?"

"He does have nice hair," Wedge agreed.

"Yours is nicer," his wife said, winking. "Now let's go get into trouble."

They had barely made it a dozen meters out of the house when they were confronted by three of the security guards Wedge suspected of being First Order goons.

"Drop your weapons," one of them shouted, raising a rifle.

"What weapons?" Norra asked, her voice shaking with feigned fear. "We don't have any weapons. We're just farmers."

The guard with the raised rifle hesitated but the

second guard, a light-skinned man with eyes that paled to a frost-crusted green in the dim morning light, sneered. "Farmers? Who just happen to have two X-wings in their field?"

"They're not ours," Wedge offered hastily. "The people who were flying them, the pilots, they paid us some credits to park them here. The growing season hasn't been too kind, and we could use the extra, so we took it." Wedge dug into his pocket, the one not holding the blaster, and pulled out a handful of credits. He held them out toward the man. "See?"

The green-eyed man stepped back, frowned. His face creased in thought.

"Where are these pilots now?" the man asked sharply.

"We didn't ask," Norra said, her mild Myrra accent exaggerated. "We were scared to say no."

"And they were paying." Wedge thrust the credits forward again.

"Don't believe a word they say," came a voice from the other side of the house. They turned as a female Abednedo approached. The Abednedo's skin was cream-colored, spotted with dull gray; the sparse hairs on her head were white, and her black eyes protruded from her long rectangular head. Norra stiffened. Wedge had pinned her as another guard but it was their neighbor, the one Norra had almost come to blows with over political differences at a community dinner party.

"Tukalda . . ." Wedge began, trying to cut her off

before she said anything damaging, but Tukalda was already drawing herself up, shoulders set.

"That one," Tukalda said, pointing a long digit at Norra, "is a former rebel. Wouldn't surprise me if she was a Resistance sympathizer, too. She's trouble."

"I'm going to give you some trouble," Norra growled, taking a step toward the Abednedo.

Wedge touched his wife's arm briefly, a warning to stay focused. "You have us wrong, Tukalda. We don't get involved in politics. We mind our own business."

The guard, the green-eyed one who was clearly in charge, glared at them both. "I'm going to need to see some ID," he said. Over his shoulder, Wedge caught movement. He could see shadows near the poultry house. Snap and Karé had made it out of the tunnel and were working their way stealthily toward their starfighters. But there were guards at the ships, too, and they'd have to incapacitate them. They needed more time.

"Now, look here," Wedge started.

"I don't have ID," Norra protested at the same time, throwing her hands up in indignation, her voice raised.

"Then you'll have to come with me." The guard gestured his companion forward. "Arrest her."

Wedge stepped between them. "Wait! Maybe we can come to an agreement." He proffered the credits again, this time straight to the man's face. He slipped his free hand into his pocket.

Annoyed, the man slapped Wedge's hand to the

side. The credits flew into the air. Behind them, near the ships, someone screamed and was abruptly cut off. The green-eyed man turned his head back toward the X-wings in alarm.

Sound, too loud and too close to Wedge's ear.

He ducked on instinct and looked up in time to see the green-eyed man stiffen and fall, the side of his face destroyed by blasterfire.

Wedge looked back at Norra. She stood there, momentarily still, her blaster raised and smoking.

Tukalda screeched and Norra's fist hit the pulpy side of her face with a squelch. The Abednedo went down like a log. That left only the guard with the rifle. Wedge whirled just in time to see the man's finger close on the trigger. He shot his own blaster, already raised, hitting the man in the shoulder. The rifle jerked skyward, his aim skewed, and Norra lunged to the side, the lethal shot going wide. Wedge pulled the trigger again, and this time the remaining guard collapsed, a hole in his chest.

Silence descended, and Wedge stood for a moment, staring. He'd killed a man. He'd done it before. Many times. It was what soldiers did, and it had been a war. Was still a war. But he'd never killed here, in his idyllic garden among the keedees and the pepper stalks. His throat felt dry and he tried to swallow past the thing, the emotion, stuck there, threatening to choke him.

"Let's go," Norra said, breaking him from his reverie. He looked up at her. Her eyes were bright but wary, as if she understood what was going on in his head all too well.

"Is Tukalda . . . ?"

"No, she'll have a headache and a story to tell about her crazy neighbors, but she's fine."

Wedge tried again to swallow, and this time he succeeded.

Norra had discarded her housecoat, and Wedge quickly emulated her, dropping his beloved old robe in the grass. Behind them, they heard the X-wings rumble to life. Snap and Karé had made it to their ships and were firing up, ready to leave.

"What do we do now?" Wedge asked. For some reason, his brain wasn't cooperating, wasn't letting him think through action and consequence and next step.

Norra was patting down the dead guards, looking for something. "When Karé and I went into town yesterday, I thought we might end up having to make a run for it eventually, so I rented us a shuttle. It's not fancy. One of those leisure shuttles that people use to vacation offplanet, but it will get us to wherever the Resistance is hiding. I re-upped my guild pilot's license, so it looks like I'm flying some locals to Cardo Minor for some sightseeing, but once we're out of Akivan space I'll disable the trackers and the ship is ours. I hate to steal, but I don't see any other way."

Wedge nodded along numbly. What was wrong with him?

Norra had pocketed a comm device from one of the guards and had moved on to search the other. "You and I will have to get to Myrra undetected," she said, not looking up, "but that shouldn't be too hard at this time of the morning."

"What about the bodies?"

Now she looked up at Wedge, surprised. "What?"

"We should do something with them." He gestured to the dead guards.

"Leave them, Wedge," Norra said, her voice quiet. "With Tukalda as a witness, what we've done won't be a secret for long. We'll tie her up and leave her in the tunnel, the bodies, too, but eventually . . ." Norra paused. "Unless you think . . ."

She raised her blaster and gestured toward their unconscious neighbor.

It made sense and would buy them some extra time. Plus, they could just leave all the bodies in the field, a mystery for the neighborhood and law enforcement to solve. But, no. Everyone had seen the X-wings. And many knew Wedge and Norra's history. And . . . it was wrong. Tukalda was an annoyance, but she didn't deserve to die.

Wedge shook himself, getting rid of the fog in his brain. "You tie her up and gag her," he said, making a decision. "I'll start moving the bodies back behind the house. The tunnel is overkill. The west side of the house under the trees should be enough."

A house they could never come back to. A place that would no longer welcome them. Wedge knew it was the way of things, but it still stung. He had tried to make a home here. But the truth was, his home was out there in space. It always had been. And now he was heading back, once and for all.

Norra nodded and holstered the blaster without

further argument, and they got to work. Fifteen minutes later, while the sun rose in full over their farm, the field was pristine, as long as no one looked too closely at the spatter in the pepper beds. And Wedge and Norra were on their way to the capital city.

CHAPTER 11

POE PEERED OUT OF the cockpit of his borrowed starfighter. Behind him, and shrinking quickly, Ephemera swirled pink, blue, and green, a beautiful, tranquil marble that he was more than happy to leave behind. Disappointment sat heavy in his chest, and when BB-8 asked him what was wrong, Poe answered truthfully.

"I guess I expected more," he told the droid.

BB-8 beeped a question.

"More empathy for one," Poe answered. "More passion for the Resistance, more information. Just . . . more. More everything."

BB-8 whirled in sympathy.

"Maybe my expectations *were* too high," Poe admitted. Or maybe the problem was the messenger more than the message. Maybe Maz didn't trust him, didn't respect him. These days, he barely trusted himself. The mission to Grail City with Black Squadron had been a reprieve, a moment of reassurance among the people who loved and trusted him most in the world. But now the doubts were closing in again, making him question how he was going to overcome the mistakes above D'Qar and the mess he had made on the *Raddus*. Black Squadron had at least understood, and Leia seemed to understand, even if he still suspected she was disappointed in him. He could only imagine how the rest of the galaxy, the people who weren't his squadron or his friends, would react. Would every new person he met know about the errors in judgment he had committed and the huge cost in lives it had exacted? And if they didn't know now, wouldn't they eventually? It was a shame he would have to live with for the rest of his life, and the only thing he could think to do to make up for it was to give his all, everything he had—body and blood and soul—to rebuilding the Resistance.

But here, his first mission out to secure the Resistance major support and he had failed miserably. Well, he supposed he had also failed to obtain any direct aid from the Grail City prime minister. He laughed to himself, low and bitter. So far things were going great, just great.

BB-8 beeped, letting him know a call was incoming. He checked the frequency. It was the *Millennium Falcon*. For a moment his stomach dropped, his hand hesitating over the reply switch. What if the news was bad? What if something had happened to Leia and Finn and the others and he had failed them, too? He squeezed his eyes shut, forced himself to take a deep breath. BB-8 asked him again if he wanted to accept. Quickly, not allowing himself to overthink it any further, he asked BB-8 to put the call through.

"This is Poe Dameron," he said quickly. "Everything all right?"

"Poe!" came an enthusiastic voice on the other end. "Good to hear your voice. You find Maz Kanata?"

"Rose," Poe said, recognizing the young maintenance worker's voice. "Everything okay on the *Falcon*?"

"*Falcon*'s on land," Rose said. "We're hoping you and Maz will join us."

"Maz isn't coming," Poe said, regret and annoyance coloring his voice. "I'm afraid she's decided to sit this fight out."

"What? Why?"

"She didn't say," Poe said, which wasn't exactly true. But he wasn't going to explain that Maz had her own priorities and they didn't include the Resistance to a woman who had lost her sister in the evacuation of D'Qar. Poe hadn't known Paige Tico well, but her sacrifice was etched into his memory. He was responsible for her death, too. It had been his command that had sent Paige's bomber over the dreadnought *Fulminatrix,* a decision that had taken out the First Order's monster ship—but at the expense of Paige's life, among others. So many others. Blood on his hands, and he wouldn't forget it. He wouldn't regret it; unlike his mutiny, he still felt taking out the *Fulminatrix* was the right call. But he would not forget it.

Rose was talking, and Poe pulled himself back to the conversation. "—shelter on Ryloth."

"The Ryloth system?" Poe asked, picking up the end of her sentence. "Did I hear that correctly?"

"You did, Commander. Leia has secured us temporary shelter on Ryloth."

Poe laughed. Leave it to Leia to make his failure with Maz irrelevant. "How did Leia pull that one off? I thought Ryloth didn't pick sides."

"She's Leia," Rose said simply.

"She is, indeed," he agreed.

"I'm sending Beebee-Ate the coordinates now," Rose said. Poe watched them come in and render on his display. He frowned. "This says head for the outermost moon. Is that correct?"

"Ambassador Yendor has asked our starfighters to meet there. Once everyone's collected, he'll bring you in under cover."

"Ah," Poe said. "So we're not officially on Ryloth."

"It's a bit of a stealth mission," she admitted. "The government knows we're here but they can't acknowledge us. We're working directly with the Ryloth Defense Authority."

"The Ryloth Defense Authority? I don't know what that is, but it sounds promising."

"Leia can explain once you're here. Any word from the rest of your squadron?" Rose asked.

"Negative, but I'm just clearing planet orbital

space. I'll follow up with Black Teams One and Two shortly and give them the coordinates."

"Affirmative," Rose said. "Leia also wants you to follow up with Inferno Squadron and give them the coordinates, too."

"Can do."

"Great. See you soon, Commander."

"Out," Poe said, and ended the transmission. "Beebee-Ate, open a secure channel to Black Team One."

Seconds later, Snap Wexley's voice came alive in his ear.

"Is that you, Poe? Everything okay?"

"All good, here, Snap. Checking in on the status of your mission and to give you coordinates to a meeting place."

Mild cursing filled Poe's ear and a shouted "Yes!" before Snap's voice came back clearly. "Copy that, Poe. And your timing is excellent. Karé and I have left Akiva with Norra and Wedge in hand."

"Any trouble?"

"Nothing we couldn't handle. Some local opposition and some less-than-effective surface-to-air cannons. We took care of it."

"Good to hear," Poe said. "And everything's good with Wedge and . . ." Poe paused. He didn't mean to pry, and asking Snap directly about his mother felt like prying. On the other hand, he was Snap's commanding officer, and if one of his pilots was feeling mentally unfit or compromised for personal reasons, it was his business to know and take remedial action.

". . . and your mom?" Poe asked, keeping his voice neutral.

"Oh, she's crazy as ever," Snap said with a low laugh. "But aren't we all these days? It's her life, right? I'm going to let her live it."

"Good to hear," Poe said enthusiastically, but he made a note to follow up once they were all on Ryloth. "Sending coordinates to you now," he added.

A moment passed before Snap said, "Received. I'll get them to the team. Listen, we're going to make a couple of detours to see if we can find any of Phantom Squadron still kicking around."

"Phantom Squadron?" Poe asked, surprised. "They haven't flown together since my mom was still an active pilot." He remembered that Wedge had built Phantom Squadron back in the days of the New Republic, a squadron of castaways and burnouts, pilots who wouldn't balk if their missions were less than sanctioned. They'd seen action in the liberation of Kashyyyk and again at Jakku, but that was about all that Poe knew about them.

"We need people, right?" Snap asked.

Not just people. Leia wanted leaders. But who knew who Snap might track down? "I'm listening."

"Won't take long. We'll see you on Ryloth before you know it."

"Watch your back out there, Snap," Poe said.

"Always do."

Poe ended the communication. "Beebee-Ate, can you—"

But he didn't even have to finish his request before BB-8 had connected him to Black Team Two.

"Poe!" Suralinda's voice screamed in his ear. "I can only talk for a sec. Real busy here!"

"What's going on?" he asked, concerned. "Are you and Jess under fire?"

"Uhh . . . you could say that." Suralinda screamed. The communication went dead.

"Beebee-Ate, what happened?"

The droid beeped, just as distressed as Poe was.

"Well, can you reconnect?" he asked.

BB-8 answered.

"Well, keep trying," he said, the soft pulse of the unanswered transmission in his ear. He knew Suralinda and Jess were on Rattatak, a place notorious for its warlords and gladiatorial societies. The chances of them running up against the First Order there were minimal, but an encounter with the warlords of Rattatak was inevitable. He could delay his rendezvous on Ryloth to go to Rattatak, but even if he left now, where would he start his search for Black Team Two? It was a big planet, and he had nothing to go on but Suralinda's vague assurances that there was an ex-Imperial there who was sympathetic to the Resistance, or at least hostile to the First Order. He assumed that wasn't something one advertised openly, even in a place like Rattatak. He exhaled some of the jumpy energy eating at his nerves. No, running to Rattatak to try to save the day would just be more reckless behavior. He had to trust Suralinda and Jess to handle themselves, even if he didn't like it.

He was about to ask BB-8 to end the communication attempt, when Jess's voice popped into his ear.

"Poe?" she asked loudly. "Is that you?"

"Jess," he breathed, relieved. "We got cut off. Everything all right?"

"Oh yeah. I just tagged Suralinda into the ring, so she had to go." He realized now Jess was panting like she had been running, deep heaving breaths. A roar went up somewhere in the background like the sound of a crowd.

"Where are you?"

"Barterus. Gladiatorial ring. The ex-Imperial Suralinda was looking for? Teza Nasz? She wouldn't see us unless we bested her greatest warriors in hand-to-hand combat, so Suralinda thought—"

Poe swore. "Suralinda thought she'd throw two very much needed Resistance pilots into the death pits of Rattatak for the sake of simply talking to an ex-Imperial who may or may not be of help to us?"

A moment of silence and then another crowd roar. Jess's voice came back, chagrined. "Well, when you put it that way."

"Get out of there, Jess," Poe said, decisively. "It's not worth losing either one of you. We need you flying for Black Squadron more than we need this Teza Nasz."

"Yeah, I'm afraid it's a little too late for that, Poe. The Rattataki don't take kindly to quitters. It's sort of a win-or-die situation. But don't worry. We got this in hand. Oh!"

Something crashed in the distance, and then the

distinct sound of a vibro-ax sparking to life roared through the comm.

"I'm up! Gotta go, Poe. Don't worry."

Don't worry. Easy for her to say. "Beebee-Ate will send rendezvous coordinates to your onboard. Just get there as soon as you can. Don't mess around. And don't die! That's an order."

"Order received," Jess shouted, and then she was gone, the transmission dead.

"Insanity," Poe said, irritated, but part of him had to laugh. He was the commander of Black Squadron for a reason, and it was becoming more apparent every day that the reason was they were a bunch of hotheads who deserved one another. There was little he could do now but get back to Leia and company and hope that Jess and Suralinda hadn't bit off more than they could chew.

Poe asked BB-8 to make one last call.

"Shriv here."

"Shriv, it's Poe. How's your mission going?"

"Oh, you know. Lots of flying around and getting doors slammed in our faces. But we did find a couple of old friends of the Rebellion. I think Leia will be pleased."

"We're headed for Ryloth. You think Inferno Squad can join us?"

"Absolutely."

"Great. We're sending the coordinates now."

Shriv confirmed. "Received. We're on our way."

"See you there."

He ended the call. "Are we ready to jump, Beebee-Ate?"

BB-8 answered, and Poe laughed. "Well, sorry to keep you waiting. Ready when you are."

Poe took one last look at Ephemera, now no more than a pink speck far behind him. Then he and BB-8 were leaving the planet behind in a blur of stars.

CHAPTER 12

"LEIA, ARE YOU THERE?" Yendor's voice came through the speaker at her ear. "We've got a problem."

Leia had been sitting back at the communications console on the *Millennium Falcon*, doing nothing. That wasn't quite fair. She was worrying. And trying not to think about why she still hadn't heard from Resistance allies and contemplating what they would need to mount any kind of useful strike against the First Order and how many things could go wrong along the way. So that was something, just the wrong kind of something.

Yendor had offered her a room and a bed in the expansive national-museum-turned-defense-authority-headquarters. In fact, he had offered her his room. But she had declined, not only because it felt wrong to dislodge him from his chambers, but because she preferred the *Falcon*. Yendor had not pursued the issue, and she had not explained further. If she had been pressed, she would have said that she wanted to stay close to the communications deck and hoped everyone was polite enough to overlook the *Falcon*'s missing dish and the RDA's perfectly functional communications console and accept her obvious lie. The real reason was that the ship had become a consolation, a familiar place that reminded her of Han and happier times and fueled her sense of hope. She could sit in the hard-backed chair in front of the deck and almost hear Han's voice shouting some outrageous maneuver at Chewie or complaining that, once again, the hyperdrive wouldn't engage. She found herself more than once laughing quietly to herself over a memory of flying off on some wild adventure or ill-conceived scheme that had been hatched right here where she sat. She could almost see Han's cocky smile, his insouciant slouch as he talked her into yet another debacle. Perhaps it was foolish to dwell on such nostalgia, but it gave her solace, and she clung to it. The *Falcon* felt like home.

"What is it, Yendor?" she asked, leaving her small comforts behind and focusing on the moment before her.

"We need to talk."

"I'll come down," she said.

"No," he countered. "I'll come to you. Are you on the *Falcon*?"

"Yes. Chewie can let you in."

She had not been the only one more comfortable on the ship than in Ryloth's caves. Chewie and Rey had stayed, too. Rose had volunteered to stay, but Leia had encouraged her, Connix, and Finn to stay in the accommodations offered and work with Charth to prepare for the imminent arrival of Black

Squadron and the others. Poe had confirmed that they were coming, and that they were bringing almost a dozen others including former members of Phantom Squadron, two former rebel commanders that Zay and Shriv had found after all, and an ex-Imperial that Black Squadron had tracked down. It was a motley bunch to say the least, but Leia was eager to see them all.

The distant sound of a door opening was followed by the steady fall of footsteps as someone approached. Leia stood as Yendor entered. He was wearing a long navy-blue robe belted at the waist. He still wore the golden headpiece around the base of his lekku, but the rest of his clothing seemed toned down, almost somber.

"What is it?" she asked.

He gestured for her to sit and she did. He joined her at the table, leaning in as he folded his hands in front of him. "We've gotten word of the First Order in Lessu."

"What?" Leia felt suddenly dizzy, her blood pressure rocketing. "We were careful," she said, mind racing. "They couldn't have followed us."

"I don't think they did," Yendor said, offering a steadying hand that he folded briefly over hers. "It seems their presence here is a coincidence. A terribly timed one, but . . ." He spread his hands. ". . . not your fault."

She took a deep breath, forced her body to calm itself. "So they don't know we're here?"

"All signs point to no. I sent Hahnee to the city to look around, find out what she can. I was waiting for her to report back before I brought the issue to you."

"And so you've heard back?"

He nodded affirmatively. Hesitated before he spoke. "It seems the First Order is here on a diplomatic mission." He bit off those last words as if they pained him, the sarcasm in his voice thick. "It seems they've lost some very expensive ships recently and need to levy some taxes to raise revenue. They've given us five days for the Ryloth shipping guild to voluntarily tithe to them before they blockade the shipping lanes in and out of the system and start leveraging tariffs."

Leia didn't mean to laugh. She was relieved when Yendor joined her. After a moment she gathered herself and asked, "Will they do it? Form a blockade?"

Yendor shrugged. "Already the business council is considering its options. Chancellor Drelomon thinks they are bluffing but who wants to take a chance? What I don't understand is why they would choose to blockade Ryloth, way out here on the edge of the galaxy. It doesn't make a lot of logistical sense."

"Pride," Leia murmured, and then louder, "Pride. They think a victory here will be a show of strength. To turn notoriously neutral Ryloth would be a feather in someone's cap."

Yendor leaned back, thinking. He templed his fingers, touching the pads together. It was a habit Leia had noticed. "It's possible," he finally admitted. "Or maybe we're not seeing a piece of the bigger picture here. Nevertheless, the fact remains that your window for staging any kind of mission out of Ryloth has just shrunk considerably."

"Five standard days," Leia acknowledged. "To get everyone here and figure out what comes next."

"Less than five days. Drelomon's already making noise about what drew the First Order's attention to us. Most think it was bad luck, but if he decides it was the Resistance, I worry he'll betray you." Yendor's lekku twitched with some emotion. "I would never let that happen," he said, voice earnest.

"I would never ask you to fight your own government, your own people on my behalf."

"Then let us hope it doesn't come to that."

They sat together in silence, each of them thinking their own thoughts, until Yendor said, "What do you wish to do, Leia?"

"We stick to the original plan." What else could she do? The Resistance ships were expected to arrive tomorrow. Poe had assured her that they would all be on the far side of the largest moon by then, awaiting her signal.

"All right," Yendor said, sounding resigned. "Who knows? Perhaps the spirits of our ancestors will smile on you."

Yendor had explained that tomorrow was the Longest Night, a Twi'lek holiday where all three of Ryloth's moons were at their lowest phase and darkness was most complete in the most populated hemisphere. The holiday kept most people indoors to spend a quiet evening with their families. A good night to avoid prying eyes. It was even possible,

Yendor told her, that people this far out in the remote southern desert had never heard a starfighter engine and would attribute any sounds to the restless ghosts of the dead who were known to roam on Longest Night. Leia found that doubtful, but Yendor didn't seem concerned, so she wouldn't be, either. Although Poe and the others making planetfall under the cover of the restless dead seemed a bit too fitting.

"We can hope the First Order isn't looking our way," he continued, "but there're no guarantees. You should apprise your commanders of the situation and tell them to be prepared to fight."

"Of course," Leia said, but inside her heart felt heavy with disappointment. She had wanted a reprieve, a moment of peace away from the war, if even for a few days. She still bore the injuries from the *Raddus,* still carried the bone-deep weariness that had settled around her after Crait. Fight. Flee. Fight again. She closed her eyes briefly, letting the sorrow she felt follow its course. When she opened them again, Yendor was watching her.

"We'll be ready to fight," she assured him. "Even if it kills us."

"Which it will, eventually," he said, a sad smile stretching across his mouth. "But perhaps not yet."

She wanted to argue the point, but she saw the truth in his words and let it lie.

Leia watched Poe, Black Squadron, and the rest of the hope for the Resistance come in over the open desert. They practically skimmed the ground, running low with minimum lights despite the dark of night. If she hadn't known they were there, and what they were, she might have thought them some sort of natural phenomenon, a swarm of light-emitting migrating insects or some strange desert illusion. As the ships grew closer, she heard the telltale howl of X-wing engines. Well, there was no disguising that. But you had to be close to hear it, and Yendor had assured her that the locals, what few there were out here, were loyal Rylothians.

The last of the ships, this one not a starfighter but a small transport that looked more yacht than anything else, crossed over the desert and disappeared into the mountain below her. She sighed. That was it, then. She'd counted ten X-wings, an A-wing, Poe's loaner from the Hutt, two smaller civilian transports, and that yacht. Not a lot with which to fight your enemy but more than they'd had yesterday. And so it would go. Every day more than yesterday until they had a fighting force. Or at least that was the idea. She tried not to think about the losses they would take along the way.

Leia left the library to go and greet the arriving fleet. As she made her way down the tunnels to the incoming ships, she was joined by R2-D2. She hadn't seen the little droid in days. She guessed he was mourning Luke in his own way so she had let him have his space. But she was glad to see him now, and he rattled off a happy greeting.

"Aren't you supposed to be helping Rey with repairs to the *Falcon*?" she asked.

R2-D2 replied.

"That's good news," Leia agreed. "I'm glad it's done. Now we see what Poe and his Black Squadron have brought us."

Another round of beeps, and Leia nodded.

"Inferno Squad, too," she amended. "All good pilots. Good people. But we need leadership, Artoo, not just soldiers. I need thinkers, strategists, battle experience."

R2-D2 beeped.

She laughed. "You do have a lot of experience. You would make a good leader."

They left the side tunnel and entered the main hangar. It hummed with noise and activity and the smell of ships that had recently been flying among the stars. Leia embraced it all. It was expectation. It was hope. It was what would keep them alive.

The ships groaned as they settled into the Ryloth gravity and dry desert air. Excited voices called to one another in greeting, and astromechs whirled and beeped requests for fuel and repairs.

"Leia!" a voice called, and she looked up to find Poe Dameron heading her way at a steady clip.

R2 beeped a question and Leia pressed a hand briefly to his head. "Yes, go say hello to Beebee-Ate," she said, and the droid spun merrily away.

"Commander," she greeted Poe as he approached. He flushed brightly. He ran a hand through his thick dark curls and dipped his chin, chagrined.

"General," he amended his greeting with a nod. "Sorry for the informality. Just glad to see you."

"I'm glad to see you, too, Poe." She hadn't really meant to correct him, just remind him that they were here in front of potential new leadership and that they should set an example. "Walk with me and tell me what we have."

He walked her through the hangar, pointing as they went. "The two pilots there you know from Black Squadron, Jessica Pava and Suralinda Javos. The woman with them is ex-Imperial-officer Teza Nasz. They found her on Rattatak after fighting in the death pits."

He pointed to the eastern quadrant where Jess and Suralinda had parked their ships. Jess was bent over, talking to her astromech. Her dark hair was matted on the side with what looked like blood. Leia made a note to make sure the pilot got medical attention immediately. To her left, Suralinda was greeting a woman who had made her way over from the civilian transport ship. The woman was imposing, unusually tall and rippling with what seemed to be hard-won muscle. She wore a one-shouldered jumpsuit that looked like it had been stitched together from a mixture of animal hides and discarded armor. Her exposed arm displayed an elaborate stretch of short slashing lines that had been cut into her dark skin from shoulder to elbow, and below the elbow she wore a leather bracer. Her thick hair was dyed blood red and she held it back in dreadlocks that trailed down her back.

Leia stifled an incredulous laugh. "That warlord is ex-Imperial?"

"So they say," Poe said. "She was an officer in the Imperial Navy. Some sort of genius strategist involved in the Battle of Jakku, but when that went sideways for the Empire, she was assumed dead on the *Ravager*. Turns out she just went to ground and only popped back up on Suralinda's scope because of a story about Rattatak fielding a shockball team in some major tournament. Suralinda recognized her from a background picture. They used to know each other."

Leia pressed her lips together, thinking. "Well, she looks like a warrior, not a strategist, but perhaps I shouldn't judge by looks alone. If she dropped off New Republic scopes that thoroughly and was able to rise to power on Rattatak, she's probably both. What's her name, again?"

"Teza Nasz."

As if hearing her name, Nasz turned her head toward them. Her face was painted in streaks of ocher and coal lines vertically crossing her cheeks, and she narrowed dark watchful eyes at Leia. Leia returned her gaze until the woman turned away. Oh, she would be interesting.

"Who else?"

"Princess Leia?" an excited feminine voice cut in. Both Leia and Poe turned.

Zay Versio beamed at them and stepped forward to shake Leia's hand. The young pilot's short dark hair was tousled, and her eyes looked tired under the thick black eyebrows that dominated her delicate face. But she smiled gamely, and her handshake was strong.

"It's good to finally meet you in person, Zay," Leia said, greeting the young pilot. "Where's Shriv?"

"Over here," a blue-skinned Duros said, joining

them. He looked tired, too. His skin looked sallow under the cave lights, and lines ran like rivers under his large red eyes. He swiped a hand over his nose-less face and grinned through thin, almost nonexistent lips. "Good to see you again, General."

"How was your mission?" Leia inquired.

"Well, we survived," Shriv said laconically. "But I did get a rash in an unmentionable place that still hasn't cleared. Don't suppose you have some kind of cream for that?"

Leia gave him a grave look. "I'm sure someone in medical can fix you up."

"And I could use a nap. And some food. I hear they've got fruit here. And meat. Is it true, or did we arrive too late for all the good stuff?"

"The Twi'leks have been very generous. There's plenty to go around."

"Sweet!" Shriv rubbed at his face and stifled a yawn that threatened to crack his jaw. "Then I'll excuse myself. I really got to fix up this rash."

"Did you find anyone, Zay?" Leia asked once Shriv had wandered off.

The young girl nodded. "Over at the civilian transport. I think you'll be pleased."

They made their way over, Zay filling in with small talk about her and Shriv's mission. "We looked everywhere," she said, sounding exasperated. "Most of the leads were dead ends and some of the people we were trying to find were . . . well, they were dead. More dead people on our list than alive." Zay's face clouded over. "And a handful that have just disappeared. One day they're going about their own business and the next they don't show up for work. Their families have no idea where they are, the authorities won't take it seriously and say they must have run off, but it doesn't make sense."

"Disappeared," Poe chimed in, expression concerned. "Maz told me something similar."

"What does it mean?" Zay asked.

"The First Order, most likely. If we know about these potential allies, so do they. They're just getting to them first."

They had reached the edge of the ramp to the transport shuttle. A motley group of people were gathered there. Leia spotted Charth's two children moving among the crowd, offering hot towels and pouring pitchers of water into clay cups so the newcomers could refresh themselves. There was a low hum of chatter among the group that broke off as Leia approached.

A man separated from the small crowd, and Leia's brows raised in disbelief.

"This is—" Zay began.

"I know who this is," Leia murmured. "General Rieekan."

The Alderaanian man grinned through a nest of thick wrinkles, his blue eyes still as bright and intelligent as Leia remembered. He stepped forward and embraced her. After a moment he stepped away, holding her at arm's length. She could see tears gathered in the corners of his eyes. "How long has it been, Leia? Thirty years?"

"Feels more like forty," she said with a rueful shake of her head. Leia felt a surge of relief. A familiar face, and one she had looked up to long ago. Emotion threatened to overwhelm her, and she felt her own tears looming. The burden she had been carrying since Crait lifted, if only a little.

"I'm glad you've come," she said, her voice warm with feeling.

"I couldn't not come. When Zay and Shriv showed up at my door, the answer was obvious. And Ryloth beats Hoth as a command post, even if we are in the middle of nowhere."

"To die by ice or fire," Shriv quipped morosely as he joined them, the silver corner of a packet of medicated cream peeking out of the breast pocket of his jacket. "Our options are underwhelming."

"Who says we're going to die?" came another voice.

Rieekan stepped aside to usher the new speaker into their circle. "I brought a friend," he explained.

"Princess Leia." The Dressellian male who had spoken greeted her with a bow. His fur-lined cream-colored cape flared out around his short frame. The fabric was a shade lighter than his orange-tinted skin, and his hairless head was a map of brain folds. He wore a jaunty black patch over one eye; the other gleamed dark as night.

"Welcome," Leia said politely. The Dressellian looked familiar but she couldn't quite place him.

"This is Orrimaarko," Rieekan said, saving her from having to ask.

"Of course," Leia said brightly, remembering immediately. "The Battle of Endor. You were there."

"Ah, not in the thick of the ground fight like

yourself," Orrimaarko demurred. "But I did my part."

"You helped plan the attack," she recalled. A battle strategist. Wonderful!

He nodded. "A decisive victory it was, thanks to you."

"I had help."

Shouting erupted somewhere behind her, and Leia turned, searching for the source of the argument. A commotion, back near the quadrant where she had seen Jess Pava and Suralinda and that formidable ex-Imperial. Voices rose in what were distinct fighting words, and then that telltale sound of knuckles against the flesh of someone's cheek.

"A fight!" Zay shouted, sounding excited.

Poe and Shriv took off running toward the growing melee, and Leia let out a long heavy sigh. Who was it? Yendor's people? Black Squadron? That ex-Imperial who looked like a walking invitation to rumble?

Well, she thought as she and the rest of the crowd headed toward the fight, she'd find out soon enough.

CHAPTER 13

WINSHUR WATCHED WITH NAKED fascination as the prisoners arrived. Stormtroopers escorted them in, legs chained in ankle shackles as they shuffled single-file from the transport vessel to stand in line for inspection. Winshur had pressed his jacket and shined his boots well past the point of necessity for the occasion. Part of him had known his preparation was excessive, but now that he was here to greet the ship, he was glad he had done it.

He had meant to stay in his office and observe from his window, perhaps send Monti Calay down to dole out the work assignments and the rest. Sending Monti would have been a stroke of genius, a well-barbed insult. How it would have offended them to have someone of such a low rank be the only person there to greet them, a clear message letting the prisoners know they weren't important, not important at all. But in the end Winshur had decided that he personally should oversee the transfers. He trusted Monti to do such a simple job, but if anything went wrong . . . well, he couldn't have that happen. And besides, he couldn't resist seeing the prisoners' faces up close. He wanted to know what it was like to fall from such a height. If it marked a person in some noticeable way, some impenetrable stain on the soul that showed through.

But he was disappointed.

These former senators, former diplomats, and once powerful people of the New Republic were irritatingly bland, basic even. They looked like any other downtrodden creatures who had spent time in chains and darkness and labor and were destined for more of the same until their deaths. Nothing . . . nothing . . . they were nothing special at all.

He snapped his fingers and Monti Calay stepped up beside him, ready to serve.

"My datapad," Winshur commanded, holding out a hand.

Monti hesitated.

"Is there a problem?" Winshur asked.

"No, sir. It's just . . ."

Winshur waited.

"What did they do wrong?" his assistant asked.

"Their crimes against the First Order are numerous."

"Are they going to kill them?"

"Is that what you think the First Order is, Monti?"

"No. Well, I'm not—"

"It's not that they don't deserve to die," Winshur continued, "if justice demanded it. But the First Order is merciful and believes in giving people, even undeserving criminals, a chance at reform through hard labor."

"Is that what this is?"

Winshur frowned. "What else would it be? Now, enough questions." He motioned for the datapad.

Monti placed the device in his open palm. Winshur entered his password and pressed his thumb to the pad. Immediately the screen revealed the list. Winshur read it carefully, trying to match names with faces. He paused over a familiar name and scanned the prisoners. There she was. An auburn-haired woman in a dull-gray jumpsuit. She looked hollowed out, empty, her brown skin pale from lack of sunlight and her eyes cast toward the ground. He was sure the woman was Hevasi Joy, that singer who had openly opposed the First Order on the entertainment newsfeeds, condemning them for the destruction of Hosnian Prime and calling for people to join the Resistance. Well, it was a pity to see her come to this, but Winshur had always preferred the singer Gaya to Hevasi, anyway. He tapped the screen, bringing up a list of job assignments he had entered earlier. He matched Hevasi Joy with sanitation and moved to the next prisoner.

This one was a hairless male from some species he didn't recognize, but the list said he was a former attaché who had been offplanet when Hosnian Prime was destroyed and had tried to hide from the First Order. Apparently unsuccessfully. He went to sanitation, too.

The next was a tall muscular woman who strained at the binders that held her. Obviously a new capture, and physically dangerous. Winshur felt his insides shrink just looking at her. He assigned her to sea animal control. The last person who'd held the job was recently deceased, bitten in half by a pulsar skate. It had been the talk among the cadets for days, most afraid that they would be assigned to the opening. Winshur could only hope a similar fate befell the physically imposing woman.

And, ah, what was this? Another name he recognized, and his pulse couldn't help but quicken at the idea of seeing someone so famous. This prisoner was special, notorious even. A former senator fallen from grace, indicted, tried, and found guilty of plotting the assassination of a fellow senator. How delicious. Although Winshur had thought the man was long dead. If he recalled correctly from the newsfeeds, the man had been put to death for his crimes. But here he was, standing in front of him.

"Ransolm Casterfo?" he said and realized he had whispered it for some reason. He cleared his throat and spoke again, this time with authority. "Ransolm Casterfo?"

"Prisoner 876549C," a voice cut in smoothly.

Winshur turned to see a First Order officer, his uniform an impeccable teal, standing on his other side, opposite Monti Calay. Ah, this must be the reform officer that he was told would oversee the employment placements. The officer didn't look at Winshur, instead keeping his gaze on the prisoner, but Winshur could feel the censure rolling off his body. He cringed, and then straightened. It wouldn't do to look weak.

"Of course," Winshur said. "I was . . . only curious."

"It's not your job to be curious," the officer said, and now he cut his eyes to Winshur. They were the ice blue of a polar cap and just as cold and distant. The man's mouth turned down. "I assume you have an appropriate assignment for Prisoner 876549C?"

Winshur did indeed.

"Sewage pipe fitter in the shipyard, sir," Winshur offered. "Filthy work. With a high accident rate. Pipes have been known to slip and allow those crawl spaces to fill with lethal gas. According to employment records, we've lost a dozen people that way since the yards were recommissioned by the First Order."

The officer, who still hadn't told Winshur his name, narrowed his eyes. "Is that right?" he murmured.

"I did check the records."

The man turned back to Ransolm. No, it was Prisoner 876549C, Winshur corrected himself.

"Very well," the officer said. He pressed a gloved hand briefly against Winshur's shoulder. Heat radiated down Winshur's arm, like the lick of an open flame. "See that the rest of them are so aptly assigned. I have business elsewhere but I'll come back to ensure you've completed your task to satisfaction." His eyes bore into the records officer. "The First Order is counting on you."

Something roiled nervously in Winshur's gut, and he felt sweat gathering on the back of his neck.

The officer must have seen him sweating because

he made a noise, somewhere between amusement and disgust, then turned on his heel and was gone. Winshur waited until the sound of his boots against the cold floor had faded to exhale. When he did, he looked up briefly.

Prisoner 876549C was staring directly at him.

"Is there something wrong?" Yama asked.

Winshur looked up blurry-eyed from behind his desk. Yesterday, he hadn't left his office until 0400, intent on making sure that the prisoners were all assigned and accounted for. He had made the trudge home just as the sun was rising and only had time to shower, change into a fresh uniform, and down a nutrition drink before turning around and making the trudge back. He was tired but determined to be ready when that mysterious blue-eyed reform officer paid him a visit today. The man would find Winshur's report impeccable, his handling of the matter unassailable, and if Winshur himself looked a bit fatigued, well, that just went to prove how hard he worked and how seriously he took the matter. Although he wasn't sure he appreciated his insolent assistant pointing it out.

"What makes you say that?"

"You just seem . . . upset."

"I seem—?" He ground his teeth, working his jaw in frustration. No, it wouldn't do to show such weakness, especially to the likes of Yama. He must command the respect due him, and looking weak or, as Yama accused, upset would undermine that. "I'm perfectly fine, Yama. Why don't you worry about whether you've completed the indexing tasks I assigned to you yesterday? Perhaps I need to assign you something more difficult, since you clearly don't have enough work if you're worried that I'm *upset*." He said that last word with a contemptuous sneer.

Yama's eyes widened. "No way," she protested.

" 'No way'?" he asked, mimicking her voice. "Is that the vocabulary of a First Order cadet?"

"No w—" She cut herself off. "I mean, no, sir. And you look great. Sir."

Winshur sniffed, only slightly placated. The truth was he was very upset, but he was sure he had done everything within his power to correct any perceived mismanagement on his part. He would just have to do something else to impress. He wasn't sure what that was, but he'd figure it out, and before that First Order officer came around to check on him. He was so deep in thought that it took him a moment to realize Yama was still talking to him.

"What is it?" he snapped, irritated.

"Your appointment, sir. With Hasadar Shu."

In the excitement of the clandestine prisoner assignment, Winshur had forgotten all about Hasadar Shu. Meeting the man had been a bit of a fluke, really. He had sat next to the local politician and businessman at an informational session on a new park being built in the government district, and they'd struck up an awkward but ultimately useful conversation. The man was the owner of a metal parts business that had been trying to make inroads with the First Order in the hope of landing one of the lucrative First Order contracts in the shipyards.

Winshur might have mentioned that he worked for the Corellian Engineering Corporation and had sway with the First Order. He might have exaggerated. He had meant only to impress the man and never have to see him again, but somehow the man had gotten on his calendar.

"Who made that appointment?"

"I did," Yama confessed. "He said he knew you," she explained, sounding apologetic. "That you were old friends from Bela Vistal and that you had asked him to contact you."

Well, that last part was true enough, but he had never expected the man to take him up on it. Winshur pulled up short. "He knew my hometown?"

"And your mother's name. Should I have not taken the appointment?"

"He knew my mother?" What were the chances? And now Winshur wondered if the transmission he had received from his mother yesterday was simply a coincidence, or something more. A warning? He snorted. No, that was paranoia talking, an aftereffect of his meeting with that First Order officer. It was much more likely the man had realized they were distantly related and was trying to use that to curry favor with him. But Winshur was sure he hadn't mentioned where he was from, and certainly he would never have told the man who his mother was. It was strange.

Winshur shook his head. He didn't have time for this. That First Order officer could be arriving at any minute.

"Tell him I'll have to cancel. Something's come up."

"But he's here, sir."

Winshur frowned. "Here?"

Yama stepped aside so Winshur had a clear view of the open foyer outside his office. Sure enough, there was a man there in the typical dress of a wealthy Corellian. He wore white pants and a matching knee-length overcoat, both in what looked to be expensive linen. His shoulder-length black hair was slicked back from a wide handsome face with prominent brows and cheekbones. His skin was a few shades darker than Winshur's, and he crinkled dark eyes as he talked to the yellow-haired man standing next to him in a teal First Order uniform. Winshur gasped. The glacial-eyed reform officer from yesterday.

His mouth went dry and he swallowed noisily, trying not to panic. He jumped to his feet, almost knocking his datapad from the desk. He righted it and wiped a hand down the front of his trousers to straighten any rogue wrinkles. He hurried over to the hook where he had hung his jacket and slipped it on, trying to keep his skyrocketing anxiety at bay. He thought about putting his hat on but decided against it. They were indoors and it might seem like he was trying too hard. He walked quickly over to the two men, passing Monti Calay who was seated at his small assistant's desk to the left of the door.

"Gentlemen," Winshur said, and winced as his voice cracked, his volume a little too loud for the small space. The First Order officer looked over, his face slightly annoyed. Winshur realized immediately he should have greeted a superior officer by his title, but of course, the man had never told Winshur his title, making it impossible. All Winshur knew was that he wore the teal uniform of a superior. The businessman's sharp eyes glanced between the two, and Winshur knew Hasadar Shu had picked up on the tension immediately. That's why he hated businessmen like Shu. Too shrewd for their own good.

"Bratt," the officer said. "You didn't tell me that you knew Hasadar Shu."

"Well, uh, yes. We are acquainted."

"Old friends, wouldn't you say?" Hasadar mused, a strange grin on his face.

Winshur felt overwarm. He knew he was missing something here, some crucial bit of information about Shu that he should have known. But he was afraid to ask, worried that no matter what he said it would be wrong and he would look stupid in front of his superior officer. How had he stumbled into this situation when he was usually so good at controlling the people and places around him? He glanced about, frantic, and caught Yama's expression as she turned away. She was smirking.

He gaped and then quickly snapped his mouth shut. Was she laughing at his misfortune, or had she engineered this debacle somehow? She had admitted that she'd put Hasadar Shu on his calendar. Had she somehow convinced the blue-eyed officer to show up, too? He pushed down the flash of rage. Paranoia, again. She was a silly girl, barely capable of serving in an office. She couldn't have . . .

"Bratt? Are you all right?" Hasadar asked. Winshur turned back to the conversation. Both men were looking at him, concerned.

"Of course. Just . . ." He shook his head, made himself focus.

"Shall we go to lunch, gentlemen?" the businessman continued. "And while we're there, perhaps I can tell you about the latest innovations Shu Industries has made in microwelding. It's very exciting."

Winshur was sure it was the opposite of exciting, but there was no graceful way to bow out of the luncheon now. The two men seemed to close in around him, and Winshur was swept out of his office without a chance at a backward glance.

CHAPTER 14

MONTI CALAY SAT AT the bar at the Dead Aeronaut, his favorite cantina in Coronet City, profusely sweating. The lunch crowd was sparse, a few regulars bellied up to the bar sipping on watered-down gadje. Monti had ordered an ale, but he was much too nervous to drink it. Or maybe he should drink it to calm his nerves. He didn't know. He felt like there were a lot of things he didn't know. Like, had he done the right thing? His hands flexed involuntarily around the leather satchel he held against his chest. He could almost feel the datapad he had stuffed in the front pocket before he had rushed out of Winshur Bratt's office. Almost feel Yama's shrewd eyes on him as he made excuses about going out to lunch. But he trusted she wouldn't care enough about his weird behavior to look into it any further. More than trust, he was betting his life on it.

Something large and heavy crashed loudly behind the bar, and Monti almost jumped out of his skin. He looked around frantically, expecting stormtroopers to be surging through the door, ready to arrest him, but all he saw was Smokey, the old bartender, stooping to pick up a bucket that had held the blue ice that he'd emptied into the drinks display moments before.

"Breathe, Monti," he whispered to himself, and decided to take that drink of ale after all. He swallowed the deep-golden beverage, alcoholic calm radiating through his body, and he immediately felt better. When he sat the ale down, he'd drained half the glass.

"How is it?" a voice to his right asked.

He startled, almost dropping the leather satchel. He clutched it closer to compensate. "Beg your pardon?"

"The ale. Is it good?" The human asking was of medium height and build, their head shaved to skin on the side facing Monti, revealing a tattoo of a white circle on their scalp that looked vaguely serpentine. Their brown hair was long and full on the opposite side, and trailed down to their shoulder. Their features were somewhat sharp, almost vulpine, set in freckled light-brown skin, and they wore thick white liner around their green eyes. Monti recognized the makeup as a way to avoid the cams the First Order employed. He noticed a white scarf coiled around their neck, big enough to pull up over mouth and nose, another facial recognition blocker. Gray pants tucked into boots, a gray jacket, and white gloves completed the ensemble. Monti frowned. This person looked like a criminal.

But then he remembered why he was here and

hoped to the all-knowing that at least they were a competent criminal.

"The ale is good," he said beneath a cough. "How's the weather in Doaba Guerfel?" It was the pass phrase they had agreed on, but it felt weird and contrived coming from his mouth.

"Ah," the stranger said, sliding onto the stool next to him, "fair and fairer, I hear. Clouds are clearing and a disinfecting light is expected to spread."

Monti pressed his lips together. It wasn't the exact phrase his contact had suggested—a bit too flowery—but it was close enough.

"What brings you to the Dead Aeronaut today?" Monti asked cautiously.

The stranger smiled. Their teeth were very white. "Lunch."

Monti wasn't sure how to react. He'd never done anything like this before and felt out of his depth. Should he continue the subterfuge, or should he get right to the point? He decided spycraft was not his strength.

"I have something for you," he said, thrusting the satchel forward.

The stranger didn't take it. Instead they lifted a disapproving eyebrow and kept it raised until Monti, flushed with embarrassment, pulled the bag back against his chest.

"Have lunch, my friend," the stranger said. "It's a noticeable thing for a First Order man to be at the bar at lunchtime, is it not? And then for him not to order lunch?"

And to be talking to someone that looks like you, Monti thought. The stranger was right. He was terribly conspicuous.

"What will you order?" they asked.

"I-I . . ."

The stranger motioned toward the menu, a flimsy data sheet that scrolled the daily specials. Monti read it and picked a meal at random.

"Salted squid," the stranger said. "A delicious choice. I'll have the same." They gestured to Smokey, who hobbled over to take their order. Once he was gone, Monti leaned close to whisper.

"I don't have much time," he explained. "I'll need to be back before my boss."

"You'll have time," they assured him. "Hasadar will make certain of it."

Monti blinked. The politician in Winshur's office. "Is he . . . ? I mean, does he know?"

"Not exactly," they said. "His wife is a good friend to the Collective, a benefactor if you will. He knows to delay the First Order men as long as possible without arousing suspicion."

The Collective. Monti knew them. Well, he didn't *know*, know them, but he'd heard of them. They were an underground organization of engineers, technicians, and scientists bent on stopping the spread of authoritarianism in all its forms via the use of technology. Some people said they worked hand in hand with the Resistance. Others said they were completely independent and hated the Resistance as much as they did the First Order and wanted only to spread chaos throughout the galaxy.

Either way, they were known to be dangerous and untrustworthy, tricksters and thieves, a public menace.

"I thought I was dealing with a solo operator," Monti said, feeling more than a little scared. He took another look at that tattoo on the person's head. He recognized it now as the white-horned serpent. A water species known to symbolize a capricious or mercurial nature, and the symbol of the Collective. What had he stumbled into?

"No, Monti Calay," the stranger said, voice low with threat. They gestured with their chin to his satchel. "With something this valuable, it takes a team."

Their meal came, but Monti couldn't eat. He could barely look at his plate. Why had he ordered squid? He felt his stomach turn.

The stranger, on the other hand, dug in, eating as if it had been days since their last meal. Monti watched for a while, strangely fascinated, until he finally blurted, "I don't know how to get the list off the datapad. I do know it's encrypted, but I don't have the key."

The stranger slurped down a long pinkish tentacle before answering. "We've got the key. And I'll do the downloading, don't you worry. Cracking First Order security is my job." The stranger softened for a moment, eyes growing distant. "A Doaba Guerfel woman died for that encryption key," they said quietly. "She was a friend."

"I'm sorry," Monti said. It seemed like the right thing to say.

The stranger smirked, as if sensing Monti's lack of genuine empathy. "And who did you lose? What made you join the Collective?" they asked.

"What?" His voice was too loud, and a few patrons looked his way. He hunched, trying to hide, and the stranger winced.

"I haven't joined the Resistance or the Collective or any of it," Monti said, much more quietly. "I-I don't . . . I didn't lose anybody." He shook his head for emphasis. "I'm just doing the right thing." At least he thought he was. When he'd seen the prisoners last night, all shackled and broken, something inside him had shifted. And the way Winshur lorded over them, his glee at seeing their suffering. His platitudes about reform through hard labor when anyone with half a brain knew those prisoners had been tortured just by looking at them. Most of them could barely stand.

Monti hadn't liked it. No, more than that. He had felt it was wrong, morally wrong. The intensity of the emotion had surprised him. He hadn't been part of the First Order for very long, and for the most part he had no complaints. Winshur Bratt was perhaps not the best boss, but he was no worse than the handful of others that Monti Calay had worked under in his life. A bit more petty, more ridiculous, if he thought about it. And a snob, to be sure. But he had never thought of him as evil, of what the First Order did as evil. Oh, he knew about Starkiller Base and the destruction of the Hosnian system like everyone else, and yes, that was evil. But that was high command's doing. It had nothing to do with what he saw of the First Order on Corellia. Here the First Order brought order and jobs and pride in one's accomplishments. What happened to the Hosnian system felt distant, unreal. After all, Monti hadn't known anyone personally who had died there, and there had been no newsfeeds showing actual people suffering. The evil, if that's what it was, was decidedly divorced from his everyday reality.

Until last night.

Monti was no saint. He passed people in the street every day as they begged for food or work, and while he occasionally gave the truly wretched a few credits or a leftover meal, he mostly remained morally unbothered, willing to look the other way if it meant he could maintain his comfort. But something about last night had gotten under his skin. Maybe it was the intimacy of it, the up-close mundanity of men and women in chains for the smallest of crimes ferried to Corellia in secret and clearly meant to die laboring in anonymity. It had driven it all home in a way the other things he knew about the First Order had not. It had felt intimate. Real. Like something that could easily happen to him if he stepped out of line.

"Perhaps you should give me that bag, now, friend," the stranger said.

Wordlessly, Monti handed it over.

"Six minutes," they said, sliding off the stool. Monti watched them head to the bathroom. Six minutes wasn't long, but now he had nothing to do but wait. He drank another mouthful of ale and picked at his squid.

A commotion at the entrance drew his attention. Two CorSec guards swaggered through the doors. Monti felt his heart rate climb through the roof, sweat immediately gathering at his neck. The guards scanned the room, clearly looking for someone, and Monti snapped around to face front. He drained his ale and, instinct kicking in, stabbed at his squid, thrusting a forkful into his mouth. It tasted like ash and seawater. He ate more.

Out of the corner of his eye, he watched the guards make their way around the room, checking IDs and asking questions. There were only a handful of patrons in the place, and at least three of them were so drunk they practically fell out of their seats when prodded for identification. They were getting closer. Monti forced himself to breathe normally.

The squeak of a bathroom door and Monti turned, heart pounding. He caught the stranger—he had never learned their name—walking out. He widened his eyes, trying to tell them to go back or to run or to do anything but come over to him. The stranger must have caught the mood in the room because they froze, catching a glimpse of the guards, and then eased their way back into the bathroom, letting the door close silently.

"ID?" asked a voice to his left.

He swiveled around to face the guard. A woman, light hair pulled back in a severe bun, dark eyes serious.

"Of course," Monti said. He sounded flustered. The guard narrowed her eyes skeptically. It wouldn't do. He needed to sound like a righteous man in a

First Order uniform, not a boozy Corellian caught in an act of treason. He straightened, pulling his identification card from his pocket, and thought of his boss.

"What is this about?" he said, channeling Winshur Bratt at his most haughty. "If there's something amiss, I should inform the First Order. I doubt CorSec has the resources to handle it." He let his voice drip with contempt.

The woman took his ID and fed it into her handheld datapad. He could see his information come up on the screen. Name, residence, job details. Some things he didn't know they tracked, like known acquaintances. He blushed when he saw his ex's name. Monti hadn't thought about him for ages and preferred not to be reminded.

"Nothing we can't handle, sir," the woman said. "Reports of Collective activity in the area."

"The Collective?"

"White face paint, white headscarves. Known criminal element."

"Can't say I've seen anyone like that, and it seems outrageous to be harassing innocent citizens over a criminal you can't be bothered to . . ." He drifted off as the security guard's eyes took in his lunch.

"Two orders of salted squid?" she asked skeptically.

A moment of panic, but then Monti thought again of Winshur and raised his chin, looking down his nose at her. "Is there a law against a man liking salted squid?"

She glared at him, mouth pursed. When it came

down to it, Monti doubted CorSec would actually cross him. He was First Order, after all, and they were just locals. Locals who clearly didn't appreciate his presence, but surely wouldn't want to cause an incident over it. If he kept his cool, he would be fine. He hoped.

The other officer joined them. "No one's seen the slicer," the partner said. "Place is clear."

"Check the bathrooms."

"Why? If no one's seen them . . . ?"

"Just do it."

Monti thought to protest, to cause a distraction, but what? Surely the stranger could fight their way out of the situation. Isn't that what criminals did? Monti briefly closed his eyes. It was in fate's hands now.

The partner slouched over to the bathrooms looking annoyed, and Monti braced himself for what was to come. The guard drew her weapon, a long electrified baton, and kicked the door open, weapon raised. She entered, and the door swung closed behind her. Monti held his breath.

After a moment the door opened, and the guard came out alone. "Empty," she said. "Just like I told you."

Her partner grunted and handed Monti's ID back. "Sorry to bother you, sir," she said, not sounding particularly sorry. She motioned to her partner and they both turned away. Monti watched them wend their way back among the tables past the indifferent patrons and through the front doors. Only when they were out of sight did he dare breathe again.

He exhaled, coughing furiously. His hands were shaking, and he clamped them around his ale glass until they stopped. After a few moments, he stood on wobbly legs and made his way to the bathroom. He opened the door, tentative, and peered in. He saw only a toilet, a sink, and pale walls. Completely vacant. He spied a window. It was small but big enough for a small and clever person to squeeze through in an emergency.

A hysterical giggle escaped his lips, and only intensified when he realized that his satchel and the datapad it held were nowhere in sight. The stranger may have gotten away, and likely copied the data, but Monti was without a datapad to return to Winshur's desk unmissed. He stopped laughing, swallowing to hold back terrified tears instead. He would be arrested for this. Beaten. Tortured for information and then likely convicted of treason and put to death. Or maybe he would join those poor pathetic prisoners, shunted off somewhere to work until he was dead. He stumbled dizzily into the wall. Sobs threatened to rack his body, but he held them back by sheer force of will. Surprisingly, he had no regrets. He was glad he'd done it. Glad the information on the list was out in the world now. It was, he believed, worth it.

I'll run, he thought. Simply run. Disappear into the city, maybe join this secretive Collective. Or even go offplanet. Somewhere in the Outer Rim, where the First Order would never find him.

Heartened by that bit of dreaming, he pushed himself upright. He took three deep breaths until he almost felt normal, and then, back straight and feeling resolute, he walked out of the bathroom of the Dead Aeronaut. He paused at his seat to leave enough credits to cover both his and the stranger's bills, and then he made himself walk toward the front door. At first his steps dragged, heavy and impossible, but as he realized that losing the datapad meant he had gained a kind of freedom, they lightened. He might be wanted, hunted for the rest of his life, but he would be reborn, somewhere and someone new.

The only problem was, he liked being Monti Calay.

By the time he reached the exit, he was dragging again, tears threatening to drown him.

"Calay," Smokey said from the corner of the bar. His voice was a wavering creak, and the reason the patrons all called him Smokey.

Monti stopped.

"Your friend left this for you." The old man lifted up a leather satchel and handed it over the bar. He took it with unsteady hands, unbuckled the clasp, and looked into the front pocket. The datapad was there.

Monti collapsed against the bar in relief. He felt his stomach heave, and he gagged back the anxiety threatening to manifest itself as half-digested lunch and sour ale. After a moment he felt an old gnarled hand patting his hair.

"Now, now," Smokey said. "The salted squid ain't that bad, is it?"

CHAPTER 15

POE ARRIVED AT THE fight just as one of the pilots Wedge had brought in from Phantom Squadron went sliding across the floor, his feet skidding out from under him in a streak of blood.

"What in the hell?" Poe murmured, taking in the scene. To his left was the ex-Imperial, Teza Nasz. She was breathing hard, her chest rising and falling rapidly. She had a cut above one of her eyes that bled freely, streaking the ocher on her cheeks and dripping on the floor like rubies against the black stone. The woman surged forward, a pillar of muscle, but Jess hurried to stop her. She wrapped a hand around the woman's arm, pulling her back, pleading in words that Poe couldn't hear this far away.

To his right, Wedge and another man were helping the Phantom Squadron pilot Poe didn't know up from the floor over his protests that he was fine and didn't need their help.

The gathered assembly had created a loose circle around the two combatants, clearly ready to cheer on the fight. Poe looked at their faces. They were a fair mix of rebel veterans—graybeards left over from the war with the Empire—and fresh faces that looked like they couldn't be long out of flight school, if they ever attended flight school at all. The absurdity of it all flashed through his mind. The old and the young, both caught up in this war, both fighting for the same things, yet somehow fighting each other. *Might as well punch yourself in the face,* he thought. That last thought stopped him in his tracks. Is that what Maz had been trying to tell him? That he was fighting himself?

"Poe Dameron," a familiar voice called. Poe shook the unsettling thought from his mind and looked over to see his old flight instructor, Wedge Antilles.

"Antilles," he said, voice threaded with anger. "What in the hell is going on?"

"Agoyo swung first," Norra Wexley offered. She was standing beside Wedge, clearly evaluating the ex-Imperial with something that looked like appreciation.

"I'm not sure I care," Poe said, somewhere between disgusted and tired. "We're all on the same side here. What is this about?" He waved his hand in the general direction of the circle of bystanders.

"You should care!" shouted the young pilot Norra had named as Agoyo. He was back on his feet, but the uniform he wore was streaked with blood that wasn't his. That uniform wasn't his, either. Or at least it had belonged to someone else before Agoyo claimed it. For one, it was at least a size too big, but the giveaway was the Phantom

Squadron patch. This kid was way too young to have been part of Phantom Squadron.

Poe raised an eyebrow. "Identify yourself, pilot." He hated to call the young man out, but he also knew that he needed to put an end to whatever this was right now, before grudges were formed and things got even more complicated.

Agoyo tossed his black hair out of his eyes defiantly. He crossed thin arms over a square chest, and his expressive mouth twisted now in something close to contempt. Poe shook his head. Agoyo was this close to insubordination.

"Name, pilot," he repeated crisply.

"Pacer," the kid practically spit. "Pacer Agoyo."

"Pacer." Poe gave him a nod of acknowledgment. "You know who I am?"

Pacer nodded. "Poe Dameron."

"No. I'm your commanding officer," Poe corrected him. "And frankly, right now I'm not impressed with what I see. I understand you've come a long way to join us . . ." He left the statement open until Pacer offered: "Nuja. My dad flew with Phantom Squadron at Kashyyyk but he's dead. So I came instead."

That explained the uniform. "I appreciate your father's service, and your willingness to join the Resistance, but unfortunately, it looks like you're not a good fit for this mission. You're free to leave." Poe very purposefully turned his back on the pilot. Small gasps of shock echoed around him, and then silence. He caught Leia's eye. She was standing back at the edge of the crowd, watching.

Poe heard Pacer shifting in his boots. He cocked his head slightly to indicate he was waiting.

Finally Pacer spoke. "Poe . . . I mean, Commander Dameron. I-I want to stay, sir. Please. It's just . . ."

Poe could almost feel the emotion flowing off the young pilot like a living thing. The kid was deep into it, whatever it was. Not embarrassment, not regret . . . righteousness. Righteousness and rage.

He turned. "It's just what, Agoyo?"

Pacer wasn't looking at him. He was focused on Teza Nasz. And his gaze burned hot, all that rage bubbling to the surface.

"Do you know each other?" Poe asked, a suspicion forming in his mind.

"She murdered my brother!" Pacer growled. He took a step forward, fists rising.

"Agoyo!" Poe barked sharply, drawing the young man's attention to himself.

Pacer froze.

"Eyes on me," he said, and now their eyes met. "You will stop menacing Teza Nasz, or I will have you thrown in the brig until you can cool down. Is that understood?" Poe wondered if they even had a brig, but certainly they could improvise, if necessary. He hoped it wouldn't be necessary.

Pacer Agoyo paled. Wedge, who had been standing near the young man and watching, placed a hand on Pacer's arm and leaned in to whisper in his ear. At first Poe thought Agoyo would shake him off, but instead some of the bubbling anger seemed to dissipate, and he let Wedge pull him back.

Poe breathed a silent sigh of relief and made a note to speak to Wedge later. But first, he had to bring Teza Nasz on board, too.

"Well?" Poe asked, turning to the ex-Imperial. He knew next to nothing about the woman, but he would have to figure her out quickly. He needed everyone's buy-in, or this wouldn't work. Simmering resentments, distrust, and personal grudges would kill this new Resistance just as quickly as an attack by the First Order.

Teza turned a painted, blood-streaked face toward Poe. "It's possible I killed his brother," she admitted coolly, "but I don't remember." She straightened to her full height, easily just shy of two meters, her eyes roaming over the gathered crowd. "It's possible that I killed all of your brothers. And cousins. And mothers and fathers and former lovers." Her voice was flat and unforgiving. "It was my job."

"Then why are you here?" Poe asked, voice calm, curious but not accusing.

Teza focused back on Poe, looking mildly surprised. "Because it was wrong," she said simply. "But I didn't know it at the time."

"You were young and ambitious," Poe said, taking a guess, "so you joined the Empire."

His conjecture was rewarded with a startled nod. "Mostly hungry," she murmured, "but yes."

"You joined the Empire," Poe said, eyes roving the room before resting on Wedge, "just like you."

The older man blinked but didn't hesitate. "It's no secret I attended Skystrike Academy," he said, spreading his hands. "But I left once I realized what the Empire was doing."

Poe gave him a knowing nod and turned to Zay. "And your mother," he said.

"My mother was an Imperial officer," Zay said quietly. "But she defected. She and my father. They died for the Resistance. Ask Leia. She knows."

"Suralinda?" Poe called, raising his voice slightly. Suralinda was sitting on a bench watching the scene before her with glittering eyes, no doubt taking mental notes for another story. "I didn't give a care about either side much," she admitted breezily. "I was ready to sell Resistance secrets if it would get me what I wanted. Oh wait, I did." She laughed at the stunned faces around her. "Relax," she said. "I came around."

Poe smiled tightly and tried not to think about yelling at her to choose her words with a bit more care, but she had made his point.

"And you?" Poe asked, turning lastly to Finn, who had been idling in the background next to Rey.

Finn stepped forward immediately. "Used to be a stormtrooper, but now I'm rebel scum," he said, pressing a fist over his heart. "Until the end."

"My point," Poe said, turning back to Agoyo, "is that many of us have dubious beginnings, but it is how we end that counts."

"My father was Darth Vader," Leia said, pitching her voice so that it rang out clearly through the room. "Is there anyone who wants to question my loyalty to the Resistance?"

The room was wisely silent. Poe nodded his thanks, and she returned it before stepping back.

"Now, is there anyone else with a grudge that needs airing? Something that's bothering them? Someone in this room that they can't wait to knife once their back is turned?" He got a few laughs at that, as he had meant to, and the tension lessened a bit. He waited a moment longer until it looked like no one was going to speak, started to pass the floor to Leia when a new voice called out from the crowd.

"I got a question."

Poe bit his lip to keep himself from cursing. It was one of the old rebel pilots, someone Wedge had found from the original Phantom Squadron. He resembled a human, but his skin was a dusty gray and his pate was hairless, either by genetics or by design. Poe didn't know him, but he knew his type immediately. The way he stood, legs planted wide, shoulders squared from carrying that chip around. He was going to be a pain in the ass, but he also looked like someone the other pilots would follow. Poe had a feeling he needed him on their side, troublemaker or not.

"Go on," he prompted.

The veteran pointed a finger at Poe. "What about you?"

"What about me?"

"I heard the stories," the man said. "About what happened on the *Raddus*. To Holdo." The man thumped his chest. "I fought with Holdo. She was a good leader."

Poe felt queasy. Panic fluttered in his chest, and

his hands felt clammy. Some small voice inside screamed that he was caught, that his worst nightmare was coming true. Part of him wanted to hide, to shrink back and let someone else handle it before he royally screwed it all up again, but Maz's admonition rang in his head. Was he a leader or not? Was all his talk about giving his blood, sweat, and tears to the survival of the Resistance just that? Or did he mean it?

He made himself breathe deeply and then exhale. He met the man's accusing gaze head-on.

"I agree," Poe said simply.

"You *agree*?" the veteran sneered. He propped massive hands on his hips. "That's not what I heard, Poe Dameron. That's not what any of us heard."

He gestured to the pilots around him. Wedge and Norra, too, but Poe couldn't tell if they concurred or were caught in the crossfire. Snap, who was just to Wedge's right, looked flushed and ready to defend his squad leader. It occurred to Poe that Snap must have told Wedge what happened, and Wedge must have told Phantom Squadron. Not out of animosity, but because those were the facts and people deserved to know the facts before trusting their lives to him.

"You're the one who should be in the brig," the veteran said, emboldened. "Or better yet, tossed out of an air lock."

Grunts and murmurs of approval, and Poe's heart sank. They were right, to a degree, but they also hadn't been there. Hadn't seen their forces decimated, hadn't felt the desperation, the fear. Poe was a man of action and he had been grounded, made helpless, and he had almost burned it all to the ground because he couldn't take it.

"You're right," Poe said, loud enough to carry over the crowd. "You're absolutely right. I disobeyed a direct order, I got people killed, I undermined my commander, and led a mutiny. And if you don't think that eats me up, that it haunts me every day, every minute, then you don't know a damn thing."

Restless movement, some of the pilots muttering, but they were listening.

"And yeah, you could lock me up, throw me into space, but you tell me how that helps the Resistance? How that brings down the First Order? Because, trust me, if I thought my death would bring them down, I'd sacrifice myself in a heartbeat." He snapped his fingers.

"Poe," Finn said, shaking his head.

Poe started to warn Finn off, but Jess stepped forward. "Poe's my squad leader and I trust him with my life. There's no one else I want leading Black Squadron."

"He saved our butts over Grail City, just a few days ago." That was Karé.

"And he saved mine on Jakku," Finn said.

"And mine on Crait," someone else said.

"And mine," came another voice.

The testimonials rose to a crescendo, a dozen men and women bearing witness.

Poe bowed his head, overwhelmed. It was more

than he could have asked for, more than he deserved.

Finally, the declarations died down, and a calm settled over the crowd. He looked up, scanning the faces, stopping for a moment to smile at Finn and nod to Wedge, willing their support to buoy his voice. There was one more thing to say.

"We've all made choices," Poe said. "Choices that caused harm, led to destruction, even at times death. We are all responsible for our deeds. The great and the terrible. But if we define ourselves only by what we've done, only by our failures, then this Resistance, this spark? It dies here and now."

He waited a moment, but no one interrupted. *Keep going,* he told himself.

"We're all here because we have a chance to change things. A chance to change the galaxy. A chance to change ourselves. But we have to make that commitment. That choice. A choice . . ." Poe hesitated. It sounded good when he'd started, but now he was fumbling. He looked around as if trying to summon the words from the air around him.

"A choice to be better." A voice pierced the silence, and the girl Zay stepped forward. She was young, easily the youngest among them, but her voice was clear and strong and her eyes shone with conviction.

Poe pressed a fist over his heart, grateful. There it was.

"A choice to be better," he repeated.

Murmurs crept over the crowd with nods and smiles of assent. Someone clapped, but the noise quickly died down as no one else joined in. Poe appreciated it all the same.

Wedge said something Poe couldn't quite hear to make everyone around him laugh, and the tension evaporated like it never was. The crowd began to break up, pilots going back to care for their ships, hungry men and women inquiring about food or fresh clothes or other mundane needs, the fight and what caused it forgiven among patriots to the cause.

Zay idled, eyes roving the room, hands thrust nervously in her pockets. She looked like the teenager she was.

"Thanks for the assist," Poe said, approaching her.

She nodded, a blush spotting her cheeks. "I didn't mean to interrupt. It just felt right, what you said."

"No, I appreciate it." He grinned and ran a hand through his hair. "I was losing my way out there."

She shrugged. "You were doing okay."

"Your parents were pilots?" he asked.

"Yeah. My dad was more of an engineer, but Mom . . . Mom loved to fly."

He grinned. "Mine too."

"Cool."

Leia's voice drew his attention. "Commander."

"Gotta go," he said to Zay, and hurried over to where Leia was standing with a smaller contingent.

Leia had already gathered her new leadership around her. Most were people whom Poe expected to see—most of the crew from the *Falcon,* Orrimaarko, Rieekan, Antilles, the Wexleys, and Shriv

Suurgav—but others—Nasz and the veteran who had challenged him—were a surprise.

"I would like you all to join Ambassador Yendor and me for tea," Leia said. "There's much we need to discuss, and little time to do it."

CHAPTER 16

POE WHISTLED LOW IN appreciation as he stepped past the deep-red stone door and into what Leia had called Yendor's library. It may have been a library at some point, but now it was a full-on war room. A large round table had been placed in the center of the polished garnet-colored floor, and above it rose the shadowy outline of a holo readout. Poe could see what looked like alarmingly short inventory lists—people, ships, rations, and a number of other logistical shortfalls. He knew the Resistance didn't have much, but to see it laid out so starkly was sobering. The group Leia had brought with her had been quietly talking, some of the excitement of the evening keeping the conversation lively, but as they all gathered around the table, a deep solemnity descended.

Leia stood among them, a small figure that radiated power. *But at what cost?* Poe wondered. She couldn't be well, not after what she had been through. She must be running on fumes. *And it's my job to help her through this,* he reminded himself.

I'm supposed to be her right hand, her go-to commander, and, more important, her friend. He felt buoyed by the scene in the hangar moments ago but he knew he needed to check in with Leia, too. Make sure she was doing okay.

A heavy hand came down on his shoulder, and he looked up to find the veteran who had challenged him smiling down at him. He towered over them all, even over the tall ex-Imperial. The man squeezed his fingers, and Poe swore he could feel something pop in his shoulder.

"I am called Sanrec Stronghammer," he introduced himself, "and I want you to know that I forgive you, Poe Dameron." Stronghammer's voice was a deep rumble. "Just do not think to challenge me when I am in command." His grin spread wider, showing a mouthful of broken teeth. "Or I will kill you."

Poe felt tiny beads of sweat breaking out on his forehead. "What did you say you'd been doing since the Battle of Jakku?"

Stronghammer scratched at the scruff of a silvery beard that was a shade whiter than his gray skin and shrugged. "I was security."

"For who?"

Stronghammer shrugged. "Whoever paid." He shrugged. "I am not proud of it. But I had to eat."

"No flying?"

The big man looked into the distance, ash-colored eyes misty. "I had not been behind the controls of a bird in almost twenty years when Antilles called me up. I honestly did not expect to get another chance. They do not make X-wings in my size."

Poe could believe that. "What do you like to fly?"

"Ah, give me a U-wing and I will show you how a real pilot operates, Dameron."

That was a big bird all right. No way it could outrun Poe in an X-wing. But then, Poe didn't have an X-wing anymore.

"It's not a competition," Poe said, thinking he could smoke this guy, X-wing or not.

"Are you afraid to try?"

"I'm not afraid of anything," Poe scoffed, and it was almost true. He wasn't scared of anyone, and certainly not Stronghammer. But he was acutely aware that he did not want to fail Leia and the Resistance again; that, he feared.

"Is it a bet then?" Stronghammer asked under the sly lift of an eyebrow.

"You really think you could outrace me?"

The big man leaned in close. "I know it."

The two men laughed, and Poe relaxed. This was good, the banter. The implied camaraderie. He couldn't help but feel that he had passed a test. But he'd meant what he'd said before in the hangar. He was determined to honor the Resistance, to make up for his mistakes, and to do Holdo and the others who had lost their lives proud.

"You're on," Poe said, "as soon as we get you a U-wing." The two men shook on it, Stronghammer's meaty palm engulfing his own. Poe started to pull his hand back, but Stronghammer held tight.

"I win and you cut your hair like mine, eh?" Stronghammer whispered with a wink.

"What?"

"So I know you mean it. So I know you will really try."

There was no way to save face now, and, besides, he would win. He had to. He loved his hair.

"It's a deal."

The bigger man nodded and patted Poe on the back so hard he stumbled forward a step. Well, at least they weren't wrestling. Stronghammer would crush him on the ground, but no one beat him in space.

"I'm glad you're all here." Leia's voice cut through all the side conversations, quiet but forceful. Poe and the others turned their attention to her. "I know many of you came at great personal cost with small hope of success. I can't promise that we will survive this. That we will all still be alive tomorrow, or the day after. But I can promise you one thing. I will fight beside you until the end."

A beat of silence as everyone absorbed the truth in her words. Poe felt them, too. Deep in his bones. Hope was there, but this was a last stand.

"If I may," Norra Wexley said. Leia motioned for her to continue. Norra lifted her chin, eyes shining in the light cast from the holo. "Everyone in this room knows what they signed up for, General. This isn't our first battle, although it might be our last. We're done with 'homes.' We've made our choice. This"—she gestured around the table—"this is our home now. The Resistance is our family. And just like you, we're ready to die for it."

Leia lowered her eyes, but not before Poe caught the gleam of tears. "And the rest of you? Is that how you all feel?"

"Yes," said Poe, immediately.

"Yes," from Orrimaarko.

"Yes," and another "Yes," and a "Hell, yes!" from Stronghammer.

When Leia looked up, her eyes were dry. "Then we have work to do. Yendor?" She stepped back, ceding the floor.

Yendor came forward. He was a handsome Twi'lek, distinguished in both his long robes and his commanding manner. "Welcome to Ryloth," he said simply. "Like Leia, I thank each of you for all that you have sacrificed. We are all here for the same purpose: to stand against the tyranny of the First Order." His face clouded momentarily, as if lost in memory. "Those of us from Ryloth know a thing or two about standing against tyranny."

A few nods to that, but Poe was unfamiliar with Ryloth history. He made a note to ask C-3PO about it later.

"I and my children and those who are part of the Ryloth Defense Authority offer you all we have, but as you can see, we are few."

"You called the Resistance's allies from Crait, did you not?" Rieekan said, turning to Leia. "Others will come."

Leia grimaced, lines forming around her mouth. "So far the only allies we have been able to reach are the ones you see in front of you. We suspect that the First Order has been rounding up and imprisoning those sympathetic to the Resistance, and we think that they've figured out how to block our frequencies, but we aren't sure. We can't rely on reinforcements. Not at this point."

Rieekan frowned. "Do we know if the roundup rumors are true? That's a bold step for a movement with no official government."

"They destroyed Hosnian Prime," Wedge said, anger edging his voice. "I think bold isn't a problem for them."

"I only meant they don't have the infrastructure to house prisoners, do they?" Rieekan said solicitously.

"Of course they do," Norra countered. "I think you underestimate how massive they've become."

"Besides, what do they need?" Wedge asked, not ceding the point. "A few local governments to look the other way, a few dark holes to lose people in. It's not hard."

Another Twi'lek whom Poe had been only briefly introduced to leaned in across the common table. "Speaking of local governments," Charth said, "you should all understand that while Ryloth welcomes you in your time of need, there has been a complication."

"A complication?" Norra asked.

"The First Order has come to Ryloth," Leia explained. "Not because of us," she said quickly, cutting off the worried voices already beginning to ask questions. "As far as we know, they aren't aware of our presence here."

"Then what do they want?" Stronghammer asked.

"The usual," Charth said. "Money. Power. They want to tithe our shipping lanes to raise money to rebuild the vessels they lost fighting the Resistance." Charth's charge was without accusation, but there was a moment of strained silence. He quickly moved on. "We will refuse, of course, but it does put us all, Ryloth and the Resistance, in a precarious situation."

"I suggest we act quickly," Leia said. "Given our time and our limitations, I am most concerned with rebuilding our forces, giving us another week, another month. A foundation. I had hoped for time to find more leadership, but . . ." She looked around the table, making eye contact. "I want ideas."

"Ships," Poe said. He reached over the table, hand passing through the holo that had been hovering above the round table. He paused, his finger highlighted the ship inventory. "Is this up-to-date?" he asked the room.

"Yes," Rey said from her perch in the corner. She was so quiet Poe hadn't noticed her there until she spoke. "I saw Rose account for the arriving ships before we met here."

Poe nodded his thanks. "I see a handful of starfighters, a few transports, a yacht. It's not a fleet, and we can't fight much less expect to win any kind of battle against the First Order with equipment like this. We need ships."

"I agree. How do you suggest we get these ships?" Leia asked.

"We could steal them," Norra offered. "The First Order's actively building fighters. You"—she pointed to Charth—"just said so."

Charth nodded. "The rumor is the Corellian shipyards are running continuously to meet the quotas."

Poe slapped his hands together. "Then we go to Corellia."

"Too high-profile," Wedge countered. "And we don't have enough people to stage a raid."

"Send me in with a handful of pilots and I'll get your ships for you," Poe said.

Leia raised a hand. "Wedge is right. We can't risk the few pilots we have to liberate a handful of ships. We need a more strategic plan."

Poe thought to argue but stopped himself. Hadn't he just sworn to be better? Leia looked at him expectantly, like she knew he hated holding his tongue, but he didn't rise to the bait. She smiled approvingly. Well, that was something, he supposed.

"Bracca." That was Shriv. Eyes turned to him and he shrugged. "It's just a thought."

"Bracca is a junker planet," Agoyo said. "I know it. I have a sister who moved there for the work and joined the Scrapper Guild. I didn't go with her because I wanted to fly, but . . ." He lifted a shoulder in a shrug. ". . . it pays good."

"We don't need junk," Poe said. "We need good ships. Usable ships."

"Bracca has become the place that the First Order sends any and all claimed New Republic ships to be decommissioned and junked," Finn told the room. "It's bound to be a treasure trove of the kind of ships we want. Parts, too. We could fix up those X-wings out there. Besides, beggars can't be choosers, and let's face it. We're beggars."

A sound, and they all turned. It was Connix, and she stood breathless at the door, like she had run there.

Poe's pulse sped up. Surely the enemy was not already at their door.

"A message came in on the *Millennium Falcon*," Connix said, eyes on Leia. "From Maz Kanata. She said you'd want to see it immediately, or I wouldn't have interrupted."

"Can you patch it through?" Leia asked.

Connix looked to Yendor, and he nodded. Charth stepped to Connix's side as she lifted the datapad in her hand. They conferred and then Connix entered the proper commands. The inventory lists faded and in their place rose an almost life-sized projection of the diminutive space pirate.

"Greetings, Leia." Maz's voice echoed in the oversized room. She looked around. "I see you're doing well collecting your allies to you."

Leia's smile was small and tight. "We would be better if you had joined us."

"Ah, of course, of course. But the ways of the Force are mysterious, and it was not my time."

Leia seemed to bristle momentarily, but her voice was calm and amicable when she spoke. "I hear you have news for us, Maz."

"Yes! Did Dameron tell you of the list?"

"A rumored list of First Order political prisoners and dissidents," she confirmed.

"It's not just a rumor anymore. I've seen it. Well, parts of it."

Murmurs around the room until Leia lifted a hand to silence them. "How?"

"A rule I live my life by: If you have anything worth stealing, someone will eventually steal it."

Leia's voice lifted, amused. "Someone stole the list?"

"Fortunately, the thief who has acquired it is an old acquaintance of mine."

"Will they give it to us?"

"Hard to tell. Nifera can be mercurial. She likes games."

"We have to play a game for it?"

"Not exactly, but then again . . ." Maz shrugged. "She's holding an auction at her birthday party. Invitation-only to the party, and the auction will happen sometime during the event. List goes to the highest bidder. You know how thieves are."

"When and where?"

"The party will be held on Corellia, in Coronet City. As for when, you'll just have to be ready to move quickly when the information comes in. I should know soon."

A soft murmur of surprise drifted around the room, but Poe grinned. The auction gave them another reason to go to Corellia. "As long as we're in Coronet City, might as well pick up some ships," he said.

"The Force does work in mysterious ways," Leia

murmured. Louder, she said, "Maz, you said it's invitation-only? Can we—"

"I've already taken care of it. Two invitations secured. One for a handsome but unscrupulous profiteer from Canto Bight and his junior business partner, and one for the ambassador of Ryloth and guest. It's the best I could do under the circumstances. You'll have to improvise."

"Who's the profiteer from Canto Bight?" Poe asked, confused. "There's no one like that with the Resistance."

"Well, of course not, Dameron. I made him up. Pick someone, whoever you like. But," she added, leaning forward with a wicked smile, "I was thinking of you when I said he was handsome." She winked.

Poe frowned. Stronghammer, who was still standing beside him, laughed, slapping a hand against his back. "The little woman has you there," he said. "You are a handsome man."

Poe wasn't sure what to say to that, so he said nothing.

"Thank you, Maz. We accept the invitations," Leia said, saving Poe from further embarrassment.

"Leia," Rieekan said. "How do we know this list is even real?"

"Who said that?" Maz asked, leaning forward and adjusting her spectacles. "Hmm . . . it's real because I just confirmed it's real. Didn't you hear me? I've seen it."

"You said you saw a partial list. So even if we concede it's real, how do we know it's useful?"

"It doesn't have to be useful," Poe cut in. "Those are people being unjustly held. People who were willing to speak out for what's right. It's our duty to free them."

"They could be friends and family," Norra added. "Poe's right. We should help them."

"And we will," Leia said. "But Rieekan has a point. Our funds are limited. Before we commit to spending them at some thief's auction, we should know more."

"We could just steal it," Shriv said. "I mean, the list is stolen. We could just steal it again."

"Is that really the best idea?" Poe asked, unconvinced.

"We're talking about stealing ships, aren't we?" Shriv said with a shrug. "What's the difference?"

"Lifting a few First Order fighters is payback," Norra agreed.

"I'd rather not turn the Resistance into a den of thieves," Leia said with a sigh. "But we'll do what we have to do."

"You'll have to pay the reserve to be allowed into the auction," Maz said. "After that, it's up to you. But if you get caught with your hand in the biscuit bin, there won't be a nice trial and punishment, you know. These people will kill you."

"Your friend sounds charming," Leia said.

"Meh," Maz said. "Rich, yes. Charm? Charm was never her strong point."

"I still think we should see who and what is on this list before we commit to any action," Rieekan said. "Maz, can you share what you have?"

"It will come over encrypted." Noise sounded in the background, and Maz turned. "Have to go," she said when she came back. "Hope I see you in Coronet City. Especially you, Dameron. And wear something nice. This Canto Bight fellow is quite dapper. I hear." She pressed a palm to her mouth and then threw a kiss in his direction. "Tah!" she said, and then she was gone.

"Did we get the partial list?" Leia asked.

"She just sent the invitations," Connix said, fingers moving deftly across the datapad. "No list yet."

Leia nodded. "Thoughts, while we're waiting?" she asked the room.

"Even if we do get to Coronet City and Poe and Charth and whoever are able to lift a few First Order ships, it's not enough," Shriv said. "We'll still need more."

"I agree," Leia said. "That's why I want you to go to Bracca. Put a team together. Take whoever you need and go get as many starfighters as you can."

Shriv laughed. "You want to give me command of a squadron?"

"I do."

"We really are desperate," he quipped.

Leia tilted her head. "What was your first clue?"

"Okay, okay." He lifted long-fingered hands in surrender. "That's what I get for opening my big mouth, I guess. All right." He turned to Pacer Agoyo. "You, kid. What are you doing?"

"What?"

"That's what I thought. You're on the team. And

Zay, too." He scratched at his nonexistent nose. "Who else? Hey Stronghammer, want to go get some junk?"

"Leia," Wedge said, moving around Shriv, who continued to list off possible team members. "I know Maz thinks Poe should go after the list, but I think I should lead the team to Corellia."

Leia glanced at Poe, and he stepped close so that he could hear.

"I'm listening," she said.

Wedge gave Poe a tight smile. "No offense, Dameron, but I was born there. I know Coronet City. I can get that list for you."

Poe shrugged. He wasn't sold either way. He'd prefer a battle out in the open, something he could take on face-to-face. Sneaking around in a disguise wasn't his preferred style, really, but he'd do what Leia wanted him to do.

Leia held up a hand. "Slow down, Wedge. I'm not convinced this is the best use of our resources, yet. Let's see the list before we start making plans to—"

"It's here," Connix said. "Transmitting now . . ."

They all turned back to the holo and waited. Anticipation thrummed through the air. Poe suspected that many people in the room had friends and family members lost to the First Order. To think that some could be alive, could be found. It was a lot to ask.

Finally the holo cleared and a graphic of the First Order appeared across the screen, the sixteen-rayed sun with the hexagon in the center, a symbol Poe had come to hate. After a moment, the insignia scrolled up. The header SUBVERSIVES appeared, followed by a list of scrambled names and last known locations. Poe squinted, reading through the list.

"Hey Poe," Finn said. "You're finally on someone's most-wanted."

Poe frowned, looking for what Finn had seen. There was someone with a first name *P* and last name *D* followed by a mix of numbers, letters, and symbols. It could be him, but it could easily be any number of individuals with his initials. How many could that be in the galaxy? Billions? But then the last known location was clearly listed as Crait. That narrowed the likelihood by a couple of factors.

He quickly skimmed the list for other names with Crait beside them. There were half a dozen more. Well, it shouldn't come as a surprise that the First Order knew who they were.

"This is an assassination list." Norra was staring at the hologram, face ghostly in the reflected light. "This is why we can't find our allies. They're hunting them down, one by one."

"Well, they're not going to get us," Finn said firmly.

Norra's eyes cut briefly in his direction, face doubtful. Poe had to agree. Confidence was great, but there was something chilling about realizing the First Order knew you by name and was actively trying to find you.

The list broke off after several encrypted names with the last location listed as Castilon and another list appeared, this one headed CURRENTLY DETAINED. The list, much like the first, included encrypted names of individuals identified only by their initials, but instead of LAST KNOWN LOCATION there was a CURRENT LOCATION listed for them. In addition was a column headed CONVICTION. There, titles were listed—senator, diplomat, local union leader, business owner, celebrity, athlete—followed by the "crime" the person had been detained for. Poe whistled low and distraught. The crimes read like a joke, except they were all too serious—speaking ill of the Supreme Leader, loitering in a restricted area, questioning an official directive, failure to comply with a direct order.

"So this friend of Maz's, the thief, she can decode these names?"

"That's my understanding," Leia murmured, gaze focused on the list.

"It's smart," Wedge said. "The auction list, I mean. Offer enough information to make people think that someone they know is on the list but with no guarantees."

"People will pay their last credits for even the possibility of finding their missing loved ones," Norra agreed.

"When it could all be a false hope," Snap said. "Foolish people and foolish dreams."

"Nothing foolish about hope," Rey said quietly, but Poe heard her.

"These titles . . ." Nasz said. "These are people from all walks of life, not just those directly associated with the New Republic. Did they arrest anyone who has ever spoken against the First Order?" She sounded impressed.

"Looks like it," Snap said. "Hey, C. H., athlete. Could that be Cutar Har? The grav-ball champion?"

"I thought he was dead," Norra said. "Didn't he die in the Turclom Riots?"

"Apparently not," Wedge said. He lifted a hand as if to touch a finger to the hologram.

"We've got to help these people," Finn said.

"Agreed," said Poe. "And look at some of those other titles. Senator, diplomat. These could be the leadership we're looking for. What do you think, General?" He turned to Leia and sucked in a surprised breath.

Leia stood with her hands braced against the table. She looked like she had aged years in only a few moments. Her head was bowed, and instinctually, Poe reached to steady her. She was frail under his hands, her shoulders trembling. When she looked up, her eyes were filled with tears, but her lips curved in an incredulous smile.

"What is it?" Poe asked, confused by her reaction. "Are you okay?" Maybe this had all been too much. She should be resting; it was his job to lead now. "Do you need to take a break?"

"It's the list," she said, and there was disbelief in her voice. Disbelief and pure joy. "I-I never knew. I thought he was gone."

"Who?" he asked. He looked back at the list, but none of the initials were familiar.

"An old friend," Leia said. She patted Poe's hands, still resting on her shoulders, his arm holding her up. She straightened and he let his hands drop.

"And if I'm reading it right, he's being held on Coronet City."

"Leia?" That was Rieekan.

"I could be wrong," she admitted. "But look." She pointed to a line halfway down the CURRENTLY DETAINED list. The initials were R. C., the conviction read "Senator—Crimes against the state, conspiracy, murder," and, sure enough, the location was Coronet City.

"Another coincidence?" Rieekan asked.

"It doesn't feel like a coincidence," Leia murmured.

"Rieekan's right. It could be a trap," Norra said. "Bait to get us to Coronet City."

"No," Poe said. "The First Order doesn't know we want ships from their shipyards and they likely don't know this list is even stolen yet, much less being auctioned off in Coronet City."

"Who is R. C., Leia?" Rieekan asked.

"Someone I thought long dead."

"False hope," Snap said, gently.

Leia straightened. "You're right, of course. I'm not unaware that the chances of this being my old friend are . . . unlikely. But it fits. And we're going to be there anyway. And I just . . ." She shook her head, as if to clear it.

"So we're going after the list?" Poe asked.

Leia looked around the room, taking in the nods of affirmation. "Yes. And the ships. And, if you can, Senator Casterfo."

"Leia," Yendor breathed, sounding surprised. "Do you think it could be?"

She pressed her lips together and nodded once.

"And if we can't?" Poe asked. "If he's not there, or it's not him?"

Leia exhaled, and the light that had brightened her face moments ago faded. "Then I'm a fool. But it doesn't change our mission. We rescue those prisoners, anyway."

Poe nodded. It was smart. They needed a win, and rescuing those prisoners would certainly be a win. If some of them turned out to be leaders, well, that was just the bonus. The real prize was the Subversives list. That list could be the future of the Resistance. And if they meant to find that future, which was no doubt scattered across the galaxy, they would need ships to do it. And that's where Bracca came in.

Three missions. Three teams. Poe turned to Shriv.

"Do you have your team together?"

"At your service," the Duros pilot said. "Ready to go get us some starfighters."

"Good." Poe pointed to himself. "I'll lead the team to retrieve the list of subversives and galaxy-wide prisoners."

"I'll join you," Charth said. The Twi'lek man smiled, showing pointed teeth. "That second invitation was for Ryloth's ambassador. That would be me."

"Or me," Yendor said, lightly.

"Of course, Father. I didn't mean . . ."

Yendor waved him off. "I'll stay here with Leia and oversee operations. I leave the sneaking around to younger men."

"We need a third team to go after those prisoners; it looks like they are being held in Coronet City," Poe said.

"I'll do it." That was Wedge. "I know Coronet City."

"I'm with you," Norra said immediately.

"Good," Poe said. "Get the rest of your team together and be ready to leave on my word."

Everyone broke apart at Poe's unspoken dismissal, dividing into their teams to hammer out logistics. Leia drifted to Poe, looking bemused.

"Thank you, Commander," she said, a small smile playing on her lips.

"For what?"

"It seems you have everything in hand."

Poe flushed, abashed. "I didn't mean to overstep—"

"No, no. You misunderstand." Her smile spread. "I'm grateful."

"Oh." Now it was Poe's turn to grin. "I'm just doing my job."

She arched an eyebrow. "So you are, Commander Dameron. So you are."

She turned to leave, but he stopped her. "Leia."

She looked up.

"What you said, about the First Order being on Ryloth. Do you think it's safe for you and Rieekan and the others to stay?"

She shook her head wryly. "No. But there is no 'somewhere safe' for us anymore. We'll stay as long as we can, monitor the missions and give tactical support."

"And if the First Order finds you?"

She patted his arm. "Then we do what we always do," she said. "Fight." And then she was walking away.

He let her leave, but something nagged at him, left him unsettled. He didn't know what he would do if he lost Leia, what any of them would do. But he had his mission, and the best he could do for her was complete it. Still . . .

He shook off the disquieting feeling and went to find Charth. They had work to do before they could crash a birthday party in Coronet City.

CHAPTER 17

"**WHAT ARE YOU DOING** in there?"

Monti froze, heart thudding in his chest. He forced himself to stay calm and purposefully pressed the button that closed Officer Bratt's interior office door as if he was meant to be there.

"I asked you a question," Yama said. "Don't make me repeat myself."

The door whispered shut under Monti's direction, and only then did he turn to face his co-worker. "Winshur asked me to tidy up for him while he was gone." He was having a hard time keeping his voice from shaking.

Yama was standing in the center of the foyer, her hands full of packing material. He recognized the shipping supplies that the Records Department kept in the storage room. She must have been down in the basement retrieving it when he had returned from his cantina meeting to find Winshur's office empty, the man himself still at lunch as the stranger had assured him he would be and, in a stroke of luck, Yama absent, too. But now she was back, an accusing look on her face. He brushed past her to sit at his desk. He made himself move deliberately, settling himself in his chair as if his mouth wasn't dry and he didn't feel faint.

"Why are you sweating?" she asked.

He wiped his palm across his brow. Great suns, he was sweating. He clutched at the cloth he kept in his pocket, the one for shining his boots, and dabbed his forehead. "I'm sick, if you must know," he said, thinking quickly. "I think I ate some bad squid at lunch." He folded the cloth and tucked it back in his pocket. He folded his hands on his desk. "But why are you asking me all these questions? You're not my boss."

Yama's eyes cut to Winshur's closed door. She clearly suspected something.

"You expect me to believe Officer Bratt's office needed tidying? I was in there before he left. It was spotless."

Monti blanched. He could try to bluff some more, channel some outrage and perhaps cow the girl into leaving him alone. Or he could try to allay her suspicions through friendliness. After all, he and Yama had always been friendly. He had been sympathetic when Winshur had yelled at her, treated her like an incompetent child. He'd never spoken up for her or anything. That would be a bit too much. But he had felt sorry for her. He had certainly considered helping her when Winshur gave her some of the more tedious assignments. He never had. But he'd thought about it.

But Yama never gave him the choice. "I know what you did."

"W-what?"

"You stole his datapad."

Monti considered vomiting. "T-that's ridiculous," he stuttered. "Why would I do that?"

Her eyes narrowed. She was still holding her packing supplies, and Monti thought she looked a bit absurd standing there like that. Except, of course, for that look on her face.

"I don't know why you stole it," she said, "but I'm going to report you."

"Yama!" He bolted to his feet. She dropped the supplies to reveal that she had a box knife in her hand, the blade out.

"Whoa!" he said, raising his hands. "Calm down. I didn't steal anything." He jerked his chin toward the closed door. "Go look for yourself. The datapad's right where Winshur left it on his desk."

"Officer Bratt," she corrected him. "You should call him Officer Bratt." She moved toward the door, blade still in her hand and eyes never leaving him. He kept his hands raised, taking her threat seriously. Monti had never been a fighter. In fact, he abhorred violence. It was one of the things that had convinced him to give the list to the Collective to begin with. He was not so foolish that he didn't see the irony in a man who proclaimed his aversion to violence joining the First Order, but he hadn't joined the stormtroopers now, had he? He worked in an office. He processed records and contracts and archives. He was a *datapusher*.

Yama had opened the door and peered inside, no doubt seeing the datapad right where Monti had placed it moments ago. She pulled the door shut.

"It wasn't there when I looked before," she said. "Before I went to the supply basement. I checked to see if Officer Bratt needed his desk material replenished and the datapad wasn't there."

"You must have overlooked it," Monti said, trying to sound sympathetic. "It was definitely there."

She seemed to consider his words. He let himself relax a bit, lowering his hands. Yes, he would just convince her that she was mistaken.

"Do you think I'm an idiot?" she growled.

He blinked.

"You think I don't know what I saw?"

"I . . . uh . . . Yama." Her name came out as a plea. He thought to tell her everything. Convince her that he'd done the right thing, that Winshur was rotten, that perhaps the whole First Order was rotten, and she didn't need to protect Winshur or it.

"Why are you defending him?" he blurted.

Yama drew in a breath, her hand tightening around the box cutter.

"He hates you," Monti hissed. "He thinks you're nothing. Trash. Worse than trash. He would throw you out with the garbage if he could."

She flinched, and he knew he'd hit a nerve.

He came around the desk now, hands raised again, eyes focused on her. He had been scared before, bumbling in his shock, but now he knew how to fix the problem. The truth that neither of them could deny.

"He won't believe you."

Her mouth opened, as if she meant to protest, but then she snapped it shut.

He dropped his hands to his sides. "So go on. Report what you think you saw. Tell Winshur whatever you want. I'll deny it . . . and then you'll have nothing."

Yama's lips pressed down in a thin line, her brow wrinkling. She didn't say anything, just stared daggers at him, because what could she say? He was right, and they both knew it.

A chime went off down at the end of the far corridor, drawing their attention. Footsteps could be heard, coming up the hallway. They both stared, waiting, like shaaks in line at the slaughter. Yama still held her blade in a death grip. Monti pulled himself up, back straight and chest out. He could feel the sweat gathering at the back of his neck, but he ignored it.

Winshur Bratt entered the outer office. He had his hands in his pockets, and his head was down. He was muttering quietly to himself, clearly preoccupied. He didn't notice them until he was a handful of meters away, and then he jerked his head up suddenly, a small gasp of surprise escaping his lips.

"What are you two doing?" he shouted, breathlessly. His eyes went to Yama with a laser focus, and when he spoke, his voice practically dripped with contempt. "Yama." He said her name as if it pained him. "Why are these supplies on the floor in the middle of the room?"

The girl just stared, unable to answer.

"And what are you holding? Is that a knife?"

Yama lifted the blade up helplessly.

"A box cutter," Winshur said, a touch of relief in his voice. "Well, whatever you were doing, get it done. And pick these things up. They're blocking my path."

"Officer Bratt . . ." Yama's voice was barely a whisper.

Monti watched her, motionless.

"And then get me those reports I asked for before lunch. Honestly, Yama, if you can't—"

"Officer Bratt," she said again, louder, cutting him off.

A visible chill rippled across Bratt's shoulders. "What?" he said, voice slick with annoyance.

The girl looked over at him, eyes huge. Seconds ticked by, and still she didn't speak.

Winshur grunted, sounding exasperated. He looked away from Yama, and for the first time his eyes seemed to catch on Monti.

"Why are you standing there?" he asked. "And . . . are you sweating?"

"Not feeling well, sir," Monti said, and this time it was true enough.

"An illness?" Winshur immediately held a hand over his mouth and took a step back. Then he seemed to reconsider and hurried forward, giving Monti a wide berth.

"Go home," he called over his shoulder. "I don't want you getting me sick." He opened his door, quickly disappearing behind the safety of the barrier. And just as quickly as he had come, he was gone.

His two employees still stood where he had found them.

"Go on, then," Monti said cruelly. "Go tell him. If you can even get the words out."

When she didn't move, he shrugged. Went around to his desk and collected his things, including his leather satchel. Monti pulled the strap over his head and adjusted it across his chest. Gave her a small bow before he walked resolutely out of the office, knowing that whether she reported him or not, he was never coming back.

CHAPTER 18

SHRIV AND HIS TEAM were the first to leave Ryloth. They had reconfigured into a mix of squadrons, and he had now affectionately started to refer to his own as Dross Squadron. Pacer Agoyo had bristled at the name, but the rest of the team had taken to it easily enough.

Stronghammer had laughed. "Might as well call us garbage," he said.

"Garbage sounds so uncouth," Shriv said as he settled into the captain's chair in the transport ship they were taking. "If there's anything I am, it's couth."

"What does that even mean?" Zay asked as she took the seat next to him.

"I don't know, but I'm committed now."

Zay rolled her eyes. She'd been doing a lot of that lately and Shriv wasn't impressed. Was this human puberty? He'd asked her that once and she'd punched him in the arm, hard. Totally unnecessary, but he didn't ask again.

There would be six of them on the team. Pacer

had been an obvious choice since his sister was part of the Scrapper Guild, and Shriv had hopes that she would help them get onto the planet and wherever they needed to go. Zay came along because they were Inferno Squad. Plus, Shriv was her uncle, wasn't he? And he had a responsibility. Stronghammer because Pacer had said the guild recruited big men like him to be Cutters, and if they were going to sell themselves as a work crew, they needed light-footed Riggers like Pacer and Zay as well as big men. Shriv fit somewhere in between, Pacer told him, as did the other two team members, a wife-and-wife longhaul cargo team from Mygeeto. One of the women, Wesson Dove, was small and compact, pale skin and deep blue eyes, indigo hair cut short. She was a former member of Phantom Squadron, and that would have been good enough for Shriv, even if her business partner and wife, Raidah Doon, wasn't a former athlete and champion stormsailer. Raidah was long and lean, skin light brown and a thick dark braid of hair trailing down her back, a physical contrast to her partner. But Pacer thought that Shriv and the two women were in the physical range required and could pass as Hazmats.

"Hazmats?" Shriv asked dubiously. "What's a Hazmat? That doesn't sound good."

"We only need to pass long enough to get into the facility and take a few ships," Zay had piped up. "We can totally handle whatever it is for that long."

Shriv supposed he could, but he wasn't thrilled. However, his comfort was low on the priority list. The plan was that with six pilots, they could fly six ships back, the transport included, and tow a few more if they needed.

The team had said their farewells quickly and left Ryloth behind, passing out of the atmosphere and into space. Once the view out of the cockpit was a solid mass of black, pinpricks of distant stars notwithstanding, Shriv turned to Zay, who was seated next to him.

"You got coordinates on this Bracca?" he asked her.

"Locked and loaded," she answered.

"Locked and loaded," he snorted. "Where'd you hear that?"

"Wesson," she said, throwing a nod back toward the cargo hauler.

Someone shifted in a seat behind him, huffing noisily. "I'm the only one who's been to Bracca." It was Pacer, sounding less than happy. "Shouldn't I sit in the navigator's seat?"

Shriv considered ignoring the kid, but decided some rules needed to be understood if he was going to make Dross Squadron work. First rule, he was the boss. "If I wanted you in the seat, I would've asked," he said.

"Just seems like you're playing favorites," Pacer muttered, loud enough for everyone to hear.

Zay, who had been ready to send them into lightspeed, opened her mouth as if to speak. "Belay that thought," Shriv said, cutting her off. "And hold us steady."

He swiveled in his seat until he was facing Pacer and the rest of Dross Squadron. "What are we doing here? Hmmm? Are you having a pissing contest, Agoyo? Because I drank a liter of that damn Rylothian green juice they had back there and I guarantee you that if there's a pissing contest about to go down, I'm going to win."

Pacer's face clouded over with indignation; Wesson, sitting directly behind Pacer, frowned in disgust.

"I was just saying—" the boy started.

"Chain of command, Pacer," Shriv said, tapping the back of his right hand against his open palm for emphasis. "You learn about it back at the academy?"

The kid crossed his arms.

Shriv narrowed his eyes. "Then practice it. I'm in charge. I make the decisions. You follow orders. Easy enough?"

"He's right, pilot," Stronghammer said to the younger man.

"You heard the man," Shriv said, gesturing with a toss of his head toward Stronghammer. "I'm right. So have a seat." He gestured to the third row, the back row of the shuttle. Actually, he could have been gesturing toward the cargo area just behind the passenger seating and that would have worked for him, too.

Pacer made a show of moving back a row and trading seats with Wesson, who moved up to take his old seat.

"What's his problem?" Zay asked quietly, her dark eyebrows bunched in distress.

"Who cares?" Shriv said lightly, turning back to

the front of the ship. "You know how space babies are. Always trying to prove themselves."

Zay's frown deepened. "What's a 'space baby'?"

"Kids born offplanet, in space stations or on board ships. No foundation, nothing to keep their feet and minds on the ground. Makes them spacey." He tapped a blue finger to his skull. "So, you know, space babies."

"How do you know he's a space baby?"

"I got a hunch."

Zay's voice was quiet when she said, "I'm a space baby."

His voice was flat with amusement. "You don't say."

"I was born aboard the *Corvus*."

Shriv chewed the inside of his cheek and kept his eyes forward. He could feel Zay watching him, possibly gearing up for another eye roll.

"Well?" she finally asked.

"I'm not saying it explains a lot of things about you, but . . ."

And there it was. The eye roll.

"It's a joke," Shriv said.

"I'm not laughing."

Shriv shrugged. He liked to tease Zay, and at least she didn't get her undergarments in a knot like that new kid back there.

"Are we ready to go to Bracca?" she asked, still sounding annoyed. "Time's wasting and you're in a mood today."

"Yeah, yeah." He scratched at his jaw. "Punch it, kid. Let's go liberate some New Republic ships."

Zay did as she was told, and the pinpricked darkness outside their window blurred to the rushing haze of lightspeed. After a moment Shriv leaned over. "Hey, Zay?"

"Hmm?"

"For the record, your parents would be proud, space baby or not."

"Hmm," she said, sounding unconvinced.

"Especially your mom, especially Iden."

The girl was quiet for a while. "I know."

"No, you don't. Not really."

She was silent again and Shriv hoped it was enough of an apology, enough truth to show he meant it.

"I miss her . . . and Dad," she said finally.

"Me, too."

And then they both ran out of words and instead focused on hurtling through space on their way to a world made of castaways and salvaged parts.

They came out of lightspeed on the far side of Bracca. The planet spun below them, a murky ball streaked in shades of blues and grays, the edges of its distant sun glazing the northern pole.

"It's kind of pretty from up here," Zay commented.

Shriv snorted. "Sure, if you like depressing industrial space junk."

Stronghammer spoke up from behind them. "I hear there is a great being that they keep captive on the planet, and they feed it metal night and day and harvest the excrement for credits."

"Sounds lovely," Shriv quipped. "Who suggested we come here, again?"

"You did," Zay said.

"That's right." He sighed dramatically. Waved a hand over his shoulder without turning. "Okay, Pacer, you're up. Riggers, Hazmats, all that. Run everyone through it again."

The young pilot hadn't spoken since their earlier disagreement, but he didn't seem to be radiating frustration like he had earlier. Shriv guessed that Pacer was the kind of kid who walked around looking for a fight, a chance to prove he was just as big and bad as the larger people around him. Shriv knew the type, may have been the type himself once upon a time. He figured the trick was to give Pacer enough room to prove himself and maybe the kid would settle down. In their flight through hyperspace, he'd already been thinking about how that would all go down, but he wanted to see what the boy had to offer them first.

Pacer leaned in between Shriv and Zay.

"Bracca is run by the Scrapper Guild," Pacer explained. "My big sister joined up a year or so back. She told me all about it last time she was home. The guild is divided into Riggers, Hazmats, and Cutters. Different jobs for different kinds of people. She also told me about the Ibdis Maw and the decommissioned New Republic ships it eats."

"She tell you how we can steal a few ships?"

"No, but she said the work is hard, though the pay is good."

"Great, maybe we'll all join up if we survive this."
Shriv was only halfway joking.

"My sister is a Rigger," Pacer continued like he
didn't hear him. "She said they're always looking
for new recruits."

"So what exactly is a Rigger?" Zay asked.

"Demolition and salvage in hard-to-reach locations. Climbers, mostly. Daredevil work."

"Cool."

"Will she help us?" Wesson asked.

Pacer nodded confidently. "She hates the First
Order as much as I do."

"Good enough for me," Shriv said.

He spoke over his shoulder, pitching his voice to
address the rest of the team. "Remember, we don't
need martyrs on this mission. We need live bodies to
fly these ships home. So if we're caught, our cover is
that we're an unsavory lot of junk traders looking
to score a few New Republic ships. We are not the
sad remnants of the Resistance known as Dross
Squadron."

Silence. Finally Stronghammer spoke. "You're a
strange man, Shriv Suurgav."

"Strange doesn't cover it," Raidah murmured.

Shriv touched a finger to his temple in a salute. "I
aim to please."

"We're being hailed," Zay said. "By the guild."

Shriv turned his full attention back to the front of
the ship. "Okay, Dross Squadron, buckle up. Here
we go."

CHAPTER 19

"SO WHAT'S THE STORY on Leia's friend, Senator Casterfo?" Norra asked as they loaded their bags into the shuttle craft. It was an old Imperial model that belonged to Teza Nasz and had carried her to Ryloth from Rattatak.

"Leia said that he had been framed by some paramilitary terrorist group, the seeds of the First Order, a few years ago."

"That seems strange. Is she sure this is the same guy?"

Wedge shrugged. He motioned for Norra to hand him the crate of supplies closest to her and she did. He took it, tucking it under the seats in the back of the cargo hold. "She admitted it's a wild guess. But he has the same initials, and the list called him a senator. How many senators can there be with the same name?"

"Depends," Snap said as he sauntered up the ramp. "Is it a popular name on . . . what did she say was his home planet?"

"Riosa," Karé filled in.

"Right." Snap gave his wife a smile. "Just seems unlikely that he's been in prison all this time, hidden away. Especially with a list of crimes like that."

"Not that strange," Teza chimed in. She was stretched out on a long bench in the cargo area, eyes closed. "You kill people, you run the risk of making them martyrs. But you imprison them for life, let them grow old and feeble, drive them insane with your well-concealed tortures, and then trot them out for public consumption every so often." She folded her hands over her stomach, eyes still shut. "It's much more effective. No one follows a martyr out of pity."

They all paused for a moment, staring. The ex-Imperial cracked one eye open. "What?"

"Are you sure she has to come?" Snap asked.

"It's her ship," Wedge said.

"And you'll need me to get through First Order security."

"I can get us through," Norra countered.

Teza rolled over onto her side and met Norra's gaze. "You'll need me if you want to sneak in and avoid bloodshed. If my idea doesn't work, then by all means we'll shoot our way through."

Norra raised her hands briefly in surrender before continuing to pack.

"And they called me a barbarian warlord," Teza murmured.

Wedge sighed. He wasn't thrilled about bringing Teza along, but she did have a point about both the ship and her knowledge of the security systems they could expect once they hit Coronet City. He knew they needed a shuttle that could carry Casterfo and any other prisoners they found, and leaving it to chance to steal one was too risky. But he sure did wish they had Snap and Karé in their starfighters backing them up. If he was honest, he wouldn't mind flying something a little faster and a little sleeker himself.

"We got everything?" he asked.

Affirmative answers from the two Wexleys and a silence from Teza that he took as a yes. He dropped the jumpseat down and strapped in. He was mission leader, but he'd given the captain's chair to Snap. Teza pushed herself to her feet and slouched toward the cockpit. She leaned down to talk to Snap. Wedge couldn't follow the details of their conversation, but as long as she was on their side, he would let Snap handle it. Norra dropped into the seat next to him, buckling her own restraints. Her eyes were bright, and she grinned.

"It feels good, doesn't it?" she asked. "To be doing something again."

He nodded tightly. His stomach was in knots. Not because of the danger of sneaking through First Order lines; he'd done much the same a hundred times as part of the Rebellion. And not because Leia was counting on him to rescue her friend and return him safely to her. But because he was headed home.

Wedge hadn't been back to Coronet City since he was a teenager. After a string of odd jobs, he'd gotten a gig flying cargo ships out of the busy port. That lasted until the Empire recruited him to Skystrike Academy. It had been a dream come true. But dreams have a way of turning into nightmares, and his was no different. When Sabine Wren had showed up to help him defect to the Rebellion, he had been more than ready to go.

The ensuing decades seemed to have gone too quickly. So many friends lost, so much ground gained and then lost to his enemies, and through all of it he had never gone home, back to Coronet City. Well, he was going now. He only hoped his first trip home in all these years wouldn't also be his last.

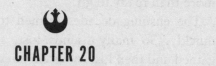

CHAPTER 20

POE FOUND FINN SITTING on his bunk in the *Millennium Falcon* deep in conversation with Rey. Their heads centimeters from each other, knees touching side by side. Rey was speaking in a hurried whisper, shoulders tense, her whole demeanor focused. Poe was torn between not wanting to interrupt and being tempted to listen in. Not that he wanted to eavesdrop. He just felt at a disadvantage around Rey. He still didn't know her well and she clearly meant a lot to Finn, and Finn meant a lot to him, so Rey mattered. But she was private, cagey almost, and so far she had not been willing to open up to him. Spying seemed like a logical solution. How else was he going to get to know her? Even so, he wasn't that much of a jerk.

He cleared his throat loudly. "Sorry to interrupt."

The two jumped apart. Rey's ever-present staff had been resting against the bed, and her sudden movement sent it careening toward the metal floor. She reached for it before it could hit, reflexes lightning-fast. Poe whistled low in appreciation. She flushed, embarrassed.

"I should go," she said as she stood, staff in hand.

"Rey . . ." Finn started, but she was already pressing past Poe, who moved out of her way with a murmured apology. She was gone before Finn could finish his plea.

"Sorry," Poe said. "I wouldn't have interrupted if it wasn't important."

Finn leaned forward, resting his arms across his knees. He looked distracted, worried. Whatever they had been talking about, it had been serious.

"If you need to go find her, finish the conversation . . ."

"No." Finn gave a little shake of his head, as if clearing it. "It's fine. Rey will work it out on her own. She's smart like that."

"I have no doubts." Poe hesitated before he asked, "So the two of you aren't . . ."

Finn looked puzzled at first, but then his expression shifted to amusement. "No, nothing like that. Just friends."

"And Rose?"

"Oh." Finn shook his head no. "We talked about it, and Crait was . . . a moment. But that's it. Friends there, too."

Poe laughed. "I can't keep up with your 'just friends,' man."

Finn flushed, rubbing self-consciously at his neck. "I know. It's been a lot. But never mind all that. I know you didn't come to talk about my love life, or lack of one. So what is it that couldn't wait?"

"You heard that Leia wants me to go get that political prisoners list?"

"The auction in Coronet City," Finn confirmed. "Going undercover to sneak into some mysterious thief's private party."

Poe grinned. "That's right. I have room for one more on the invitation."

Finn tilted his head. "Oh yeah?"

"I want that to be you."

"Wait, wait, wait." Finn held up a hand, eyes narrowed. "You want me to go with you to an occupied city and pretend to be some crime lord at an underworld auction so we can steal a list of the First Order's top-secret most wanted? A list the First Order and a number of unsavory sketchy types would happily kill us for if they knew we had it?"

Poe hesitated. He had been sure that Finn would be up for it. "What? That doesn't sound like fun to you?"

"Hell, yes, that sounds like fun. I'll do it!" Finn said, clapping his hands together and laughing. "Anything to get me off this planet for a while. I mean, I am dedicated to the Resistance." He pressed an open palm over his heart. "Dedicated! But I'm crawling out of my skin with counting supplies and tallying rations and fuel and . . ." He shuddered dramatically. "I thought sanitation work on Starkiller Base was dull. This making lists and counting stuff edges out mopping up after muddy combat units by a kilometer."

Poe grinned. "Glad to hear you're in." He offered

his hand and Finn shook it with enthusiasm. "We'll leave in an hour, once Charth has the ship ready."

"Who's he bringing?"

"Not sure yet, but we should go find out."

Finn rummaged around under his bunk and pulled out a bag. "I don't need an hour. I'm ready to go."

Poe shook his head, amused. "Do you stay packed like that?"

Finn paused before he answered. "Force of habit, I guess," he said, voice somber. "Never had a home before, and it wasn't unusual to get reassigned. You always had to be ready to leave a place. To leave your friends."

Poe pressed a sympathetic hand against Finn's arm. "Sorry," he said quietly. "I know it must have been rough."

Finn shrugged. "I didn't know any different then." His eyes rested on Poe's, and the commander held his gaze, unblinking. Finn's voice was quiet, barely above a whisper. "I didn't even have a name."

Poe squeezed the younger man's shoulder.

"But you've got both now," he said. "A name, and friends. And maybe a place to unpack before long."

Finn stood up. He embraced Poe briefly. Emotion passed between them that neither needed to articulate. Finn returned the slap on the shoulder, and the two headed out of the *Millennium Falcon*.

"Hey," Poe said, as they made their way across the hangar to Charth's ship. "I know you said Rey had it under control, but is everything okay? With Rey? That conversation looked serious."

Finn's brow furrowed in thought. "She's gone to talk to Leia about it. She didn't want to burden her, but I told her Leia needed to know."

"Whoa," Poe said, hand grasping Finn's arm and bringing him to a stop. "Is there something I should know, too? If Leia's in danger . . ."

"Rey will handle it," Finn said. He sounded confident, assured. Poe wasn't convinced. But what choice did he have? Leia had always managed to take care of herself. She didn't need Poe to be her bodyguard. And Rey was formidable. She wouldn't let anything happen to Leia.

Finn started walking again, and Poe double-stepped to catch up.

"What's the plan?" Finn asked.

Poe could feel the anticipation building. He wasn't much for undercover work, but he was glad to be doing something. And part of him wanted to see Coronet City and the famed shipyards of what had once been Corellian Engineering Corporation. He knew now the legendary shipbuilders were under the First Order's thumb, but occupation or not, Corellia still built some of the greatest ships in the galaxy. And if he and his team happened to liberate one or two for the return trip? Well, hadn't they just determined that the Resistance needed ships?

"The plan is that we find Charth and his teammate and then we get our asses down to Coronet City."

———

"Suralinda?" Poe asked, again.

Charth nodded. He was dressed in a deep shade of blue, the fabric rich and expensive looking. He wore a cape over a matching shirt and pants, with a black-and-gold coronet around the base of his lekku that was similar to the one Yendor always wore. Poe wasn't sure what it meant, but it must signify rank of some kind. The RDA insignia had been replaced by the official Ryloth emblem.

"Is that a problem?" the ambassador asked. "I thought you would appreciate me bringing another member of Black Squadron. I considered my sister, but if something were to happen to us, I wouldn't want my father to lose both his children." He said it matter-of-factly, but Poe could read the tension in the set of his jaw, the way his lekku seemed unnaturally still, like he was trying very hard not to give any emotion away.

"Of course," Poe said, reassuringly. "She's a great choice. It was just a surprise. I didn't know you were acquainted."

Poe had never seen Charth smile before but he did now. "She's quite something. Fierce. A warrior. She could almost be a Twi'lek."

"High praise," Poe said. "I'm sure she would appreciate it."

"Appreciate what?"

They both turned to see Suralinda approaching. She had changed out of her pilot's uniform and wore, of all things, a dress. The dress was formfitting until it hit the ground, where it cascaded across the floor in a puddle of bright-purple silk, only a shade off from Charth's skin.

"Where did you get that?" Poe asked before he could stop himself.

"Yendor gave it to me. There's a whole wing of historical clothing here. Do I look like an ambassador's girlfriend?" She struck a pose, hand on her hip. In her other hand she carried more clothing. Suits on a hanger, wrapped in translucent sheeting.

"I was thinking you would be my attaché," Charth demurred. Poe wasn't sure that Twi'leks blushed, but if they did, Charth was definitely blushing.

"Oh." Suralinda shrugged, unconcerned. "Whatever works, as long as I get to wear the dress." She dragged the hangers with the clothes over her shoulder. Slapped them against Poe's chest. He instinctively clutched them to his body.

"Got something for you and Finn, too," she said with a mischievous grin.

"What are you talking about? And how did you know Finn was coming? I *just* invited him."

"Lucky guess," she said, the grin on her face growing wider. "Anyway, the clothes from the historical clothing collection are here. Maz said you needed to look dapper, so I brought you dapper."

Poe sniffed at the garments suspiciously before holding them out at arm's length for inspection.

"The clothes are not going to hurt you, Poe." She rolled her eyes toward the stars.

"I know that," he said, defensively. "It's just—"

"We're all set!" Finn said, walking briskly toward them. "Connix transmitted the confirmations and the money for our buy-ins. We have cover stories, too. You," Finn continued, looking at Poe, "are Lorell Shda, notorious weapons dealer who wants that list to free some old brothers-in-arms who were caught up in the First Order sweeps of your home planet. I am your business partner, Kade Genti, who—"

Poe laughed. "Really? That's your name?"

"You don't like it?"

"It's a bit . . ."

"A bit what?"

"Kade Genti, Master of Section Nine!" Suralinda exclaimed.

"Who?" Charth asked.

"A program on the entertainment feeds when we were kids. Well, when I was a kid, at least. That is where you got it, right?"

Finn looked sheepish. "Connix asked, and I had to think fast. I remembered the comics from when I was a kid. FN-1971 would sneak them in. They weren't regulation, and they would have sent us to reprogramming if they'd known, but man, were they great." He frowned. "Do you think anyone will notice?"

"That your name is the same as a dashing cartoon character from Coruscant?" Suralinda shrugged. "Who cares? Half the people there will be using aliases. Might as well pick a great one."

Relief flashed across his face, but he looked to Poe for confirmation.

"Sure, why not?" Poe said. "I'm Lorell . . . what was the other name?"

"Shda. He's a notorious—"

"Yeah, I got that part. Okay then." He checked the chrono he wore on his wrist, the same one everyone else on the team had been issued for the mission. "We don't have much time before the auction starts. I suggest we head for Coronet City."

"Aren't you going to change your clothes first?" Suralinda asked.

"What's this?" Finn held a hand to his ear theatrically. "We have disguises?" He rubbed his hands together gleefully. "This mission just gets better and better."

"Historical clothing," she corrected. "I guessed your sizes, so they might not fit perfectly. But I think we can make it work." She took the bags that Poe had been patiently holding and held them up individually. "This one is for you," she said, handing Finn a silver jacket and pants. Even through the plastic, Finn's outfit flashed and sparkled in the light.

"And this one's for Poe. I mean, Lorell Shda."

Poe took the suit she proffered and sliced open the plastic with his thumbnail. The suit was a solid gleaming black and consisted of a velvet-lapelled jacket, a vest, and a pair of slim-fitted pants. A white button-up shirt and a black ascot embroidered with fine red threads finished the outfit.

"No shoes?" he asked, jokingly.

"Oh, I got both of you shoes. A few to choose

from in the back, but you really didn't want me guessing your shoe size," she said, winking.

"We should go," Charth said. "Time is passing quickly."

Poe nodded, sliding his tuxedo into the bag. Finn looked disappointed. "Don't worry," Poe assured him. "We can dress on the way to Corellia."

"It's not that. It's just, I got arrested at the last fancy party I was at."

"Really?" Suralinda sounded impressed.

Finn shrugged.

"Well, this may be fun after all!" Suralinda quipped.

Finn grinned, his face lighting up. "Oh, we'll have fun, if it's the last thing we do."

"There's the spirit!" she said, delighted. "This might get us killed, but at least we go out in a blaze of glory!"

Usually Poe liked the bravado, the inevitable big talk before a mission. It was part of the process, psyching yourself up before putting your life in danger. But now it bugged him. "How about we don't go out at all," he said, his voice a bit sharp.

"Live free, die young," Suralinda said, unconcerned. "Like heroes in a story."

But this isn't one of your stories, Poe wanted to protest. *If we die then the good guys lose, the Resistance has no future, and evil is that much closer to overtaking the galaxy. There's nothing heroic about that.*

He held back his dark thoughts, knowing it would

do no good for anyone to hear them. He said simply, "Let's just try to stay alive."

"Sometimes death comes for you," Charth said quietly, black eyes on Poe, as if he could read his mind. "No matter how hard you try."

CHAPTER 21

THE BRACCA GUILD OF Scrappers, Union Local 476, commanded Dross Squadron to land their transport shuttle on a long narrow platform that jutted out into a murky sky like a leaf on a dead metal tree stripped bare by winter. Around them were other platforms, just as long and narrow and open to the elements, all spiraling down the central trunk of the landing structure. Shriv could see a few more ships here and there, arriving or possibly awaiting clearance to leave, but overall it cut a desolate picture.

It was eerie up here in the thick fog, and while Shriv had the feeling that there was a hive of activity somewhere below them, lost to sight, it felt like they were all alone. He didn't like it. Alone meant singled out. It meant not blending in. Their whole plan was riding on blending in.

"Well," he said to no one in particular. "No use delaying. Let's go see the salvage capital of the galaxy."

They all began to unbuckle their restraints and move toward the exit at the back of the ship.

"Except for you," he told Zay, holding out a hand to stop her.

She paused awkwardly, already in the act of standing up. "What?"

"I want you to stay with the ship."

She looked back at the others, who had stopped in the corridor to listen. "I'm not a child," she growled, low enough for only his ears. "And you heard Pacer. You'll need someone like me to look like a team, to look like a Rigger."

"I know, but Pacer can be our daredevil climber. I need you here more."

"If you're trying to protect me after all we've been through . . ."

He shook his head sharply. "That ain't it, kid. You're our safety switch, our last line of defense. I'm leaving you behind because I trust you. If things go sideways down there because some junker gets an attitude and decides to try and kill us, I need you to find us and get us out of here—or if it's worse than that, get back to the Resistance and keep fighting."

Zay flushed, looking somewhere between flattered and frustrated. "Shriv . . ."

"I know you're touched," he said, waving a hand, "but save the pretty words for my funeral. And make sure I get one, okay? Something nice. Oh, and make Leia go, and all the rest of those bigwigs. Make them say nice things, like he was a giant among mere mortals, or he was strikingly handsome despite that persistent rash he acquired on Inya Prime."

Zay held back a smile. She nodded.

"Okay, then," he said after a moment. He clapped a hand against her shoulder. "Take care, space baby."

He marched out of the ship, the others letting him pass first. All but Zay, who dropped back into her chair. He couldn't shake the feeling that he should have said more. Said something about how she meant the world to him and maybe he was protecting her but he was allowed to do that, right? He was allowed to protect his kid. He hesitated, but then he went anyway, and he didn't look back.

The transport train rattled and hummed as it wound its way through the soupy atmosphere on the planet's surface. The train was a monorail that swayed and rolled in parallel to the curve and swoop of the geography around them. Geography that Shriv couldn't see out of the narrow gap of a smog-blackened window. But he certainly felt it as the train leaned left, and then right, and then farther right, and he braced his feet against the filthy floor and held tight to the ceiling strap. Someone bumped against him, forcing him to step back and reset his stance. Shriv waited for a muttered apology but none came. He looked around at the bowed heads and resigned set of the many hard and unfriendly shoulders that were crowded into the train with himself and Dross Squadron. The train rolled to the side again, and everyone shifted accordingly, but still no one looked up. Maybe it was better this way, he thought. He'd been worried about standing out when they landed up there on that bare platform, and now they were lost in anonymity, just like he wanted. So why was he so anxious?

On the next turn, he let himself bump gently against the person to his right, Wesson. She bumped back, and he felt the hard metal of a blaster concealed beneath her nondescript Scrapper's jumpsuit. Pacer's sister had left them each a jumpsuit and work belt concealed under a pile of trash in a maintenance corridor a few blocks from the train station. Six sets of guild uniforms, of which they only needed five, in various sizes and configurations that fit them mostly, if not well. Pacer's was the best. Raidah's was too short at the ankles but too loose through the waist. Wesson's was too long altogether, and she'd had to roll it up at both the feet and hands. Shriv's kept riding up in the back, which honestly felt like what he deserved. Stronghammer's . . . well, Stronghammer's hadn't fit at all, but he'd managed to combine the girth of two tool belts, including the one Zay would have used had she come, to rig something that looked appropriate for the job. Or at least Shriv hoped so. He had surreptitiously inspected the other Scrappers on the train. Dross Squadron all seemed to fit in well enough. Pacer's sister had left a note to head for platform thirty-three, where she would meet them. She had bribed a handful of her team members to call in sick so Dross could pass as fill-in scrubs. Pacer seemed confident that it would work, and it was better than the other plan Shriv had, which involved more shooting and running.

They pulled into a station and the train slowed, finally coming to a halt. The mechanical doors slid open with a hiss of steam and Shriv, afforded a momentary view, peeked out to the world beyond the train. He wished he hadn't. Both Stronghammer and Pacer had mentioned a giant creature of some kind that consumed metal like a living trash compactor, but Shriv wasn't prepared for the glimpse of the massive mouth he had seen in the distance, all those teeth. And was that grayish-pink thing a tongue? He shuddered as the doors mercifully closed.

He was so distracted by the mouth that he didn't immediately notice the new passengers that the train had picked up, and by the time he did, it was too late. Stormtroopers. Four of them, with rifles held close to their chests. He straightened, hand sliding toward his own concealed blaster, but then he dropped his hand into the pocket of his jumpsuit and allowed his shoulders to slump in feigned indifference. The stormtroopers weren't doing anything. Just riding the train like everyone else. He knew the First Order had a presence here, and he'd hoped, perhaps foolishly, that with a party as small as Dross Squadron they might get in and out undetected. And they still might, if they kept their cool.

A solid thump against his shoulder, and this time he didn't even bother to expect an apology. But then Pacer was passing him, and he caught a glimpse of the young man's expression. Shriv groaned quietly. Pacer's face was a mask of rage: mouth set in a grim line, jaw clenched, eyes narrowed on his target. A target that was clearly the stormtroopers.

"Kid," he whispered, grasping for Pacer's arm. But the pilot shrugged him off, intent on his mark.

Shriv cursed under his breath. Reason was telling him to let the boy go, allow him to get in whatever mess he wanted to. Let him fight, get arrested, or worse. They had a higher mission, and Pacer Agoyo could be sacrificed. But his instinct was screaming at him to stop the pilot. Tackle him to the ground if he had to, anything it took to stop him from reaching those stormtroopers and starting whatever personal war he meant to start with them.

Shriv realized he had never asked Pacer exactly what he had against the First Order. Nobody in the Resistance had any love for the First Order, of course, and pretty much all of them had lost friends, family, and sometimes homes and entire planets to their atrocities. But Shriv was the leader of Dross Squadron and he had allowed Pacer to join them—encouraged it because they needed his contact on Bracca—and Shriv hadn't even asked him why he hated the grimy planet-killing bastards. He hadn't gotten to know Pacer at all. Just humiliated him in front of the rest of the squad.

"Not smart," he muttered under his breath, and he swore to apologize if they made it out of here in one piece.

Which, frankly, was looking less and less likely.

"What are you going to do?" came a voice in his ear.

It was Wesson, leaning in close enough that her

breath licked hot at his skin, making him shudder involuntarily.

"He's going to start a fight," Raidah said, leaning in to cite the obvious.

"And get us all killed," Stronghammer added.

"I can see that," Shriv spit, annoyed.

"Well, are you going to stop him?" Wesson asked.

"How do you suggest I do that?" He said that a little too loudly, and a few heads turned toward them, curious. Shriv made himself take a deep breath. Pacer was almost at the stormtroopers now. They hadn't noticed his approach yet, but it was a matter of seconds.

The train pulled into the next station. Shriv scanned the scrolling feed of information above the door. Platform thirty-two. One more stop and they were there. But this wouldn't wait.

"Damn space babies," he muttered and started to move.

The doors opened, disgorging a handful of guild workers and letting on six more stormtroopers. Shriv moaned quietly. Ten against five in close quarters on a moving train. He didn't like the odds. And, surprise enough to stop his heart, maybe Pacer didn't, either. He pulled up short, no more than four or five meters away from confronting the stormtroopers, and he allowed the Scrappers who flowed through the open doors to push him away, back toward Shriv and Wesson and Stronghammer and Raidah at the far end of the train.

He sighed with relief as the younger pilot stopped at his shoulder.

"What did you think you were doing?" Shriv asked, his voice considerably calmer than it had any right to be.

"Troopers raided my hometown," he said, every word sharp with bitterness. "Hurt my sister. Burned our house to ash."

"That's bad," Shriv said, the words themselves inadequate perhaps, but the emotion behind them, the empathy . . . he made sure Pacer heard that.

The young man looked up, brown eyes wide with grief. "Yeah."

"And we'll make the bastards pay," Shriv assured him. "But we don't make them pay by punching a few grunts on a train. We make them pay by winning a war."

Pacer stared at him, unconvinced.

"Listen." Shriv hesitated. Looked around the train as they leaned into another curve. "We need you," he said, his voice a harsh whisper. "This mission . . . we can't do it without you. You understand?"

The young pilot narrowed his eyes. "Is this your apology for what you said to me on the ship?"

"Geez, kid, what can I say? I got a mouth, and leadership . . . eh. Not really my thing. But I'm glad you're here. And yeah, I'm sorry."

His words seem to mollify the young man. "We're gonna win this war?" he asked.

"Definitely." It was a lie, but he sure said it with conviction.

Pacer shot one last glare at the stormtroopers before grabbing an overhead strap and letting himself sag forward. "Yeah. Okay."

Shriv exhaled, relieved. One disaster dodged.

The train slowed as it came into the next station. The info scroll informed them that this was platform thirty-three.

They had done it. Made it after all.

He motioned Pacer forward, and he and the rest of Dross Squadron filed off the train. Stronghammer had just crossed the threshold, bringing up the rear, when Shriv heard the voice.

"Hey, you, all of you! Stop right there, by command of the First Order."

"Keep walking," he murmured to his team, and they all picked up the pace.

"I said, Stop!" The sound of rifles being raised into position behind them and the distinct click of some kind of vibro-weapon engaging brought them up short.

"Hands up!"

Shriv lifted his hands as he turned, hoping his team had the sense to follow his lead. He put on what he felt was a friendly smile. But considering he wasn't the friendly-smile type, really, and Duros didn't have much in the way of lips, he knew his smile wasn't very convincing.

"Something wrong?" he asked, his voice sounding like someone befuddled but wanting no trouble.

"Her," the stormtrooper in the lead said, motioning toward Raidah. "She's coming up wanted on my ID recognition. A known criminal on Gheia Six."

Shriv stared at Raidah incredulously.

She tossed her dark bangs out of her eyes and shrugged, hands still raised. "I maybe liberated some First Order funds for redistribution a while back. I seriously didn't think it would come up."

Shriv closed his eyes, forcing himself to calm. *Get to know your crew,* he repeated to himself, *so you can weed out the personal vendettas . . . and the wanted criminals. Otherwise, Shriv Suurgav, it's your own damn fault.*

"We don't know her," Wesson said, stepping forward. She had her hands up by her ears, tight to her shoulders. Shriv could see the glint of the hilt of a blade at her neck, halfway hidden by her indigo hair. "She joined our crew at platform twenty, and we just let her tag along." She stepped a little closer. She gestured with a raised hand. "Take her."

Stronghammer started to protest—Shriv could see it in the set of his chin as he opened his big mouth—but Pacer ground his heel into Stronghammer's foot, and the big man was stopped short before he could get a word out.

The stormtrooper in the lead paused, eyes moving over them all, as if deciding what to do. His posture loosened a bit, and he pointed toward Raidah. "You! Come quietly, and we'll let the rest of you go."

"I don't think so," came a new voice from behind the stormtroopers. It was dry and brimming with disdain, and Shriv felt his belly drop. The white-armored guards parted smartly to let the owner of the new voice through. A man, dressed in a gray uniform, bearing the insignia of a First Order officer. "Colluding with a known criminal is an offense," he said, eyes roving over Dross Squadron. "We take them all in for questioning."

"Now, listen here," Shriv said, ready to try to bluff his way through, but it was too late. Wesson's fingers closed around the hilt of the knife hidden at the back of her neck, Pacer and Raidah drew their blasters through the holes in their jumpsuit pockets, and Stronghammer let out a roar loud enough to shake the ceiling above them.

The stormtroopers froze, stunned, for a crucial second. It gave Wesson enough time to throw her knife. It landed true, right in the First Order officer's throat. He clutched at the blade, eyes bulging, before he slumped to the ground, dead.

And then all hell broke loose.

CHAPTER 22

POE CHECKED HIS REFLECTION in the mirror and, quite frankly, liked what he saw. He had been dubious of Suralinda's sartorial choices, expecting that she had picked him out something loud and flashy to wear to this auction, despite Maz's proclamation that he, or rather Lorell Shda, was a refined and dapper criminal. But he should have trusted her. The Black Squadron pilot had picked him out a fine suit, indeed. A black tuxedo cut to fit with matching vest and pants and a white shirt made of the finest fabric, textured and solid under his fingers. The suit didn't require a tie, but rather an ascot. He arranged it around his neck now, the silk soft against the roughness of his chin. He should have shaved, but a razor, Suralinda had forgotten. No matter. The day-old beard suited the look.

Suralinda had given him a small bottle of oil meant for his hair. He poured some in the cup of one hand and ran it through his curls. It made them shine. He inhaled the scent. It, and now he, smelled expensive.

He grinned. Lorell Shda was a handsome bastard. And he was about to rob a few Corellian thieves blind. Maybe being undercover wasn't so bad.

Someone rapped sharply on the bathroom door.

"Enter," he said.

Suralinda's head appeared from around the corner. "We're approaching Coronet City. Are you ready?"

He turned to give her the full view, hands spread. "How do I look?"

She narrowed her dark eyes, evaluating. "You'll do," she said, her voice purposefully bland.

"Hey!"

She laughed. "Hard to believe you're part of the rag-tag Resistance in those threads."

"Isn't that the idea?"

"Absolutely. You have the chip card I put in the garment bag?"

Poe patted his pockets, found the card, and withdrew it for her inspection.

"Just remember your cover story. You're a business associate of Hasadar Shu's. He does ships, you do weapons systems for ships."

"Hasadar Shu?"

Suralinda crossed her arms, irritated. "I told you this. He's the businessman and aspiring Corellian politician whose wife's birthday party we're attending."

"The wife is Maz's friend, right? The one who stole the list."

"Even criminals have birthday parties."

"Did we get her a present?"

"Do I look like an amateur? Don't answer that. Of course we got her a present. Well, Charth and I did, and you and Kade did. We shared a ride, but we're not together, remember?"

It took Poe a moment to remember that Kade was Finn's cover name. "Nice. What did we get her?"

"Charth and I got her a lovely necklace of Rylothian jade."

"Classic. I suppose I got her something similar. Jewelry, something rare and unique."

Suralinda's eyes sparkled with mischief. "Your gift is a surprise."

Poe frowned. He did not like the sound of that. "Suralinda—" he started.

"Just remember to play the part of the wealthy immoral businessman," she said airily, cutting him off. "And go find Finn. We're landing soon."

And she was gone before he could clarify what exactly he had brought the wife of Hasadar Shu for her birthday. Well, it didn't matter. It was all a ruse to get him in the door, and hopefully it wouldn't be one he would have to play for long.

He spared one last glance in the mirror and then he went in search of Finn. It didn't take him long to find him. All he had to do was follow the sound of ranting.

Poe couldn't remember ever hearing Finn curse, but a string of unflattering adjectives flowed at high volume from behind the closed door of the sleeping chamber on the ship. Poe paused to listen. He wasn't even sure Finn was speaking Basic.

He knocked, and the ranting cut off abruptly. "Finn?" he called. "Everything okay in there?"

His answer was a growl of frustration and the distinct sound of something breaking against the wall. That didn't sound good.

"Finn?" he called again. "Open up, man."

"I'm fine," Finn said, his voice the low flat sound of defeat.

"Let me in. Maybe I can help."

"I said I was fine."

"You don't sound fine."

No answer, and Poe tried another tactic. "We're entering Corellian orbital space. Setting down any minute now. You're going to have to come out sooner than later, so . . ."

Another moment of silence. Just when Poe was contemplating forcing his way in, the door slid open. Finn stood in the doorway with one hand braced against the side jamb. He had the silver suit on, which ended up being a bit closer to white than it had looked in the plastic garment bag. It fit him well, smooth across his shoulders, and the pants tapering tight to the ankles.

"You look great," Poe said.

Finn made a face.

"What?"

He waved Poe in. He entered hesitantly, unsure what he'd find. Besides an overturned table, all looked to be in order.

"Here," Finn said, thrusting something toward Poe. Poe took it. It was a long strip of silver silk fabric. It had a subtle sheen, expensive and understated.

"Your tie?" Poe asked.

Finn nodded, widening his eyes in exasperation, and Poe understood the problem.

He motioned the younger man over and took the tie from his hands. He looped the silver silk around Finn's neck under the collar, letting the long tapering ends trail down either side of the line of cloth-covered buttons.

"There are different ways," Poe explained as he crossed the thicker side over the thinner one and brought it up and through at the collar. "But this is the one my dad taught me. It's my favorite." He let the thick side fall forward then brought it around the other side, and back through at the collar. Once more over and through and then he tucked the end through the knot he had made at the base of Finn's throat. He pulled the end tight and adjusted it until the two tails were almost even, leaving the thin side a bit shorter.

Finn held up a silver pin he had retrieved from his pocket.

Poe took it, turning it over in his palm. It was an Alliance starbird, the symbol of the Rebellion and, now, the Resistance.

"Where did you get this?" Poe asked.

"I found it. On Crait. I . . . I didn't tell anyone because it didn't seem right to keep it, and maybe I didn't deserve it. But I'd like to wear it. Tonight."

"We'll likely be mixing with the First Order. Do you really think that's wise?"

Finn looked up, fire in his eyes. "I don't think I care if it's wise. It means something to me. Besides," he said, lifting his chin, "Kade Genti's not afraid of a few stormtroopers."

Poe grimaced. It wasn't just unwise, it was foolish. It might draw the wrong attention. But he understood. He fastened the pin over the tie, holding the fabric in place. He smoothed the tie one last time before turning Finn around so he could see himself in the mirror. The younger man's eyes were wary at first, but soon went soft with wonder.

"They don't teach you how to tie a tie in stormtrooper training," Finn said quietly.

Poe didn't say anything, just pressed a reassuring hand against Finn's shoulder until the younger man gave him a half smile.

They met Suralinda and Charth at the doors to the craft.

"If you two are here," Finn asked, "who's flying this thing?"

"We're on a tractor beam now," Charth explained. "We're being brought in to a secured location adjacent to the home of Hasadar Shu. I expect we'll encounter First Order security forces of some kind."

Suralinda leaned forward to meet Finn's gaze. "No turning back now," she said, eyes sparkling.

"Not a consideration," he said, his hand moving to the starbird pin in his tie.

The ship rumbled under their feet as they made contact with the ground, forcing them to sway slightly. Suralinda braced a hand against Poe's arm. He steadied her, and she gave him a small smile.

"Careful out there, Black Leader," she said. Her voice was sad, almost melancholy, and it was so out of character for her that it gave him pause. But before Poe had time to ask her what was wrong, the doors to the craft opened and they stepped out, walking down the ramp to catch their first glimpse of Coronet City.

They were high up, that much Poe could tell, likely on the rooftop of a skytower. Around them rose other skytowers—long fluted office buildings, glass-domed chapels, and antenna-topped landmarks. And beyond them, a vast ocean. The air was redolent with salt and the smell of seawater but around them was a verdant and precisely manicured park. Central areas of green grass, well-shaped trees, and tall buildings encircled them, stretching into the dark of the sky beyond. Pathways curled around pools of crystal-clear water lit from below in shades of blue. A moving bridge at least fifty meters wide stretched skyward to end in an arching doorway. People streamed up the walkway to the doors, laughing and talking, the flow of the wealthy and fashionable glittering like jewel-toned confetti strewn around glass.

Movement behind him and Poe turned in time to see their ship moving away on a conveyor belt, making room for the next partygoers to land. He frowned. That was going to be a problem. How were they going to get back to their ship in a hurry?

Someone, Finn, cleared his throat loudly, and Poe hurried down the ramp to join his companions.

"Invitations, please."

A row of stormtroopers, six on each side, lined the white stone pathway where the landing area met the gardens. The voice had come from one of the stormtroopers, who now held out an expectant hand. Charth was nearest, and he stepped forward, offering the stormtrooper a chip card similar to the one Suralinda had given him.

He watched the stormtrooper slide the card into a datapad. Poe held his breath. The datapad took a moment, but then it emitted a chime, and the stormtrooper waved Charth and Suralinda through to the next trooper, who patted them down for weapons.

Poe stepped up next, handing his card over. The stormtrooper inserted it, and Poe watched Lorell Shda's information scroll across the display. The stormtrooper studied it and cocked his head.

Poe tensed. "Something wrong?"

"Lorell Shda."

"That is my name."

"And you're from Coruscant."

"Canto Bight more recently, but yes, I was born on Coruscant. A lot of people are from Coruscant," he said lightly.

"Of course, it's just . . ."

Poe looked pointedly at the chrono on his wrist. "We're holding up the line," he said. "If there's not a problem . . . ?"

The second stormtrooper came over. "Does the invitation check out?"

"Yes, sir. But this man looked familiar. I swear he looks familiar."

"Perhaps you've seen me on the newsfeeds," Poe said smoothly.

"There was that one deal," Finn said, snapping his fingers. "With the . . . uh . . . at the fathier track. That race you won." He spread his arms. "Huge money. So much money." He grinned and leaned in conspiratorially to the stormtroopers. "We couldn't get away from the reporters. Constant coverage. I swear he had a fan club for months."

Poe smiled big, showing pearly white teeth and willing Finn not to lay it on too thick.

The second stormtrooper sounded bored when he said, "See? He's famous." He gestured toward Poe as he spoke. "There're a lot of celebrities here. That's why you recognize him."

"I don't think that's it," the first stormtrooper said.

"You're overthinking it," he said, shaking his head. "This is supposed to be a cushy babysitting detail. As long as he's got an invitation and he's not armed . . ." He shrugged.

The first stormtrooper hesitated.

"What's the holdup?" shouted someone behind them in line.

The second stormtrooper waved a hand. "Move him through." He turned to Poe. "Move through."

Poe moved, Finn trailing behind him.

They were checked for weapons and pressed through the line. Once free of the security checkpoint, they caught up with Charth and Suralinda.

"What was the holdup?" Charth asked quietly.

"Nothing," Poe said. "I looked familiar."

Suralinda tapped her fingers against her chin, thoughtful. "You are known to the First Order. We probably should have gotten you a prosthetic of some kind. A fake nose or something."

"A wig?" Finn suggested.

Poe held a hand to his hair. "You wouldn't dare."

They moved up the crystal stairs toward the doors in the sky. Just another group of partygoers at a lavish gathering. Charth drew them to a stop at the entrance to the Shu mansion.

"Here's where we part ways," Charth said. "Suralinda and I will make our thanks to our hosts first, so hold back a bit until you see we're gone. We don't want them to think we are more than simple acquaintances sharing a shuttle down to the planet's surface. Lorell Shda is a friend of the Rylothian government, so it is not so remarkable for him to accompany the ambassador's son. But the eyes that watch us need not know more than that."

"Okay, and after that?"

"It is my understanding that invited guests must present a gift to Nifera Shu. If she approves of your gift, she will present you with a gift in return. This gift is the next step in reaching the auction."

"Do you know what she's supposed to give us?"

"I assume a map of some kind, but I'm not sure."

"Poe, your gift." Suralinda reached into a dress pocket, pulled out a small square box, and presented it to him with a flourish. "Careful. It's fragile, so don't shake it." She giggled. "And don't open it until you're in front of Hasadar and Nifera." She grinned, wistful. "I wish I could be there to see it."

"I don't like the sound of this," Poe said. "At all."

"The rumor is that Nifera does like the unusual, and you need to make an impression. We couldn't risk you not getting into the auction, so I made sure you would make an impression."

"You got her a necklace!"

Suralinda sniffed. "We're dignitaries. You are a rogue of sorts. I picked gifts that fit." She took Charth's outstretched arm in her own and leaned in to give Poe a kiss on the cheek. "Good luck!"

Charth nodded his farewell. And then they were melting into the crowd.

Poe held up the box, listening. He heard scratching and wrenched his head away. Was there something alive in there?

"Don't shake it," Finn reminded him.

"I'm not."

"What do you think it is?"

"No idea, but knowing Suralinda, it will be interesting. Now let's go find the Shus and get this over with so we can get that list."

The box jerked in his hand, and he held it a little tighter, wondering what the hell Suralinda had given him.

CHAPTER 23

LUNCH WITH HASADAR SHU and the blue-eyed officer, whom Winshur finally learned was named Colonel Genial (surely a joke of a name!), was a disaster. Not only had it been horribly awkward, Winshur seeming to trip over every other word, but every topic of conversation had felt like a trap waiting to be sprung. When the first course had come, a white paste spread over lumpy bread, Winshur had made a remark about the snows of Bela Vistal, hoping to lighten the mood and perhaps get Hasadar to say more about how he knew Winshur's hometown. Instead, Genial had made a snide remark about simple men and provincial palates that could not appreciate urban delicacies. Winshur had turned a shade of burgundy and choked on his bread until Hasadar, looking concerned, had offered him a glass of water.

The luncheon had dragged on for almost three hours, an impossibly unreasonable time to spend away from work. When he'd finally returned to the office, it was almost time for his staff to go home for the day. Monti Calay was practically already out the door, saying something about feeling an illness coming on and, honestly, sweating abnormally. Winshur sent him home immediately, not wanting to catch whatever germs the young man was incubating. Yama was acting a bit strange, too. He'd made a note of it in her file and told her to stay late to cover for Monti in case he needed assistance. Because there was simply no way Winshur could leave. He had too much work to do. Work he had put off to handle the prisoner assignments. He would just have to stay all night again.

The day was already fading when he sat down at his desk, opened his datapad, and got started. By the time he looked up again, the light that filtered in through his small window from the ship hangar was the harsh yellow glow of artificial electricity. He yawned, rubbing at his eyes, and checked his screen for the time. Well past time to go home.

He wavered. It had been almost two days since he'd truly slept but the thought of Colonel Genial catching him with work uncompleted was enough to drive any thoughts of rest from his mind. He would stay, he decided. Just another hour. But first he'd get Yama to make him some caf. Surely he deserved that.

"Yama?" he called through the open doors. No answer from the girl, so he called again. Still nothing and, his temper shortened by exhaustion, his irritation at the girl became anger. Had she left after he specifically told her to stay?

"Yama!" he yelled a third time. Still nothing, so

he dragged himself out of his chair, back aching and feet swollen, and lumbered stiffly to the door.

The girl was there, head down and sleeping at her desk. Her cheek rested on crossed arms, and she was snoring softly, a line of drool tracing her open mouth. That mouth. She had smirked at him earlier, he was sure of it now. Laughed at his awkwardness with Shu and Genial. And for weeks now, she had shown him nothing but disrespect. In the way she dressed, in the way she spoke, in her very presence. And here it was. The final straw. She didn't even have the professionalism, the *courtesy,* to stay awake while he worked. Or, heaven forbid, bring him caf while he labored.

He took two long steps toward Yama, hitched his foot under the edge of her chair, and pulled. She went sprawling across the floor.

An irrational rage boiled up from inside him and the humiliations and injustices of the day, of his life, the final irritation of Yama's insolence, exploded all at once. Winshur felt a pounding in his ears, and his vision went black.

The next thing he knew, Winshur was staggering from his office, blindly groping at the walls until he found the restroom. He vomited into the nearest sink, all the fancy overpriced food he had eaten at that ridiculous luncheon coming up in bile and bits. There wasn't much left and soon he was dry heaving, tears streaming down his face. What had he done? *What had he done?*

Yama had deserved it, he told himself. Deserved

the kicks to her head and stomach, the violence that he had done her. But even as he thought it, it felt like a lie.

Finally he calmed. Washed his face while doing his best to avoid his own reflection in the mirror. He didn't want to see what he looked like.

A sound behind him, someone clearing their throat, and he whirled around so quickly he almost lost his balance. He gripped the edge of the sink to keep from sliding on the cool white tiles. In front of him stood his nightmare.

"Colonel Genial?"

"Bratt," the blue-eyed man said, drawing out the *t*'s in his name and then cutting them off with a sharp note of disdain. Winshur's throat was tight, his pulse racing. How long had the colonel been standing there. What had he seen? Did he know what he had done?

"We have a problem," Genial said.

"I-I can explain . . ."

The colonel raised a thin yellow eyebrow.

"About the girl . . ." Winshur started.

"Interesting you should bring up the girl," Genial said, voice silky with some emotion that made Winshur feel dizzy. "She paid me a visit earlier this evening."

Bratt had been ready to confess his weakness, his irrational loss of his temper. To protest that he wasn't the kind of man who would beat a child. But it all froze in his throat.

Genial pointed a bony finger at Winshur. "You have an employee problem."

"The girl. I know. I—"

"Not the girl, you fool. I just told you the girl is exemplary."

"I . . . then who?"

"Your other employee, Monti Calay. Yama tells me he disappeared this afternoon with your datapad."

Winshur gaped, unable to process what Genial was saying. "That can't be right . . ." he started.

"Oh?"

"Monti Calay has never been a problem. Yama Dex on the other hand. Her file is thick with disciplinary infractions." He shook his head. "She's lying."

"And why would she do that?"

"She . . ." Winshur racked his brain, trying to think of a reason why Yama would say such a thing about her co-worker. "I don't know. But I wouldn't trust her. That girl—"

"Deserves a good beating?" Genial cut in smoothly, cocking his head to the side, eyes boring into Winshur.

Winshur had never felt quite so small.

Genial tsked, a thick ugly sound in the quiet of the restroom. "You really are a terrible judge of character, Winshur Bratt. But now I suppose it doesn't matter. I can only say that I am glad I was here to stop this disaster before it went any farther. You are lucky Yama Dex had the judgment to come to me."

"I am?" Winshur asked, feeling stupid.

"It seems that your datapad was in fact breached,

and the prisoner list that high command entrusted to you was stolen." The colonel paused, obviously waiting to see how his declaration affected Winshur. Winshur could only stare.

"You understand that Monti Calay committed this crime while he was under your supervision. Therefore the ultimate blame rests on you, Bratt. You—" He pointed a finger at Winshur. "—will have to answer to high command for it." An unsettling grin spread across Genial's face. "You may envy the girl her beating on that day. Hers only lasted a matter of seconds. I don't think it will go so well for you, my friend."

Winshur felt faint. Only his grip on the sink kept him on his feet.

"I've already sent the full contingent of stormtroopers stationed here ahead to disrupt Calay's little plan," Genial said primly. "They should be rounding up the guests to start the interrogations imminently."

"Plan? Guests?" He was lost.

"I'll be honest with you, Bratt, Yama Dex only implicated Calay, but I find that hard to believe. A young man, promising by all accounts. Why would he do such a thing? Unless he was instructed to do it."

Winshur still hadn't caught up fully with Genial's accusations, and he was even more confused now.

"No," the colonel said, resting fingers against his chin, as if thinking. "While Yama Dex's loyalty to the First Order is without question, she is young. Well meaning. I'm afraid her best intentions may have led her to not be quite as forthcoming as she should have been. Yes, I think she was protecting someone."

"Who?" Winshur blurted.

"After I realized the list had been leaked," he said, continuing as if Winshur hadn't spoken, "I asked Intelligence to monitor their networks, listening for increased chatter. It didn't take long before they had something. Seems that Hasadar Shu's wife is holding an auction tonight and it's attracting quite the attention of Coronet City's more unsavory citizens."

"Hasadar Shu? The politician from lunch?"

"The very same. Now, I suppose you expect me to think that a coincidence. A man you just happen to know."

"I don't know him!" Winshur protested. "I mean, I barely know him. I just met him."

"You were scheduled to meet with him today, had been carrying on with him for a while, as I understand it, after some rendezvous at a clandestine assembly for environmental activists."

"It was a public land-use meeting!"

"Ecoterrorists." Genial leaned closer. "You see. It's very bad for you right now. Very bad, indeed."

"But it's not true. None of it is true." He held a trembling hand to his mouth. "I've been set up!"

Genial shook his head. "Here's what I think happened. You meant to have lunch with Shu and turn the list over to him. But then I showed up unexpectedly and accompanied you, so you couldn't carry out your treachery. Thwarted, you then somehow alerted Calay to deliver the list instead."

"But you were with me the whole time. How would I have done that?"

"I'm not sure yet," Genial said, "but it would be easy enough. A predetermined signal, a secret hand gesture, a quick transmission when my attention was turned."

It was so ridiculous, so outrageous, so *untrue,* that Winshur laughed.

The blow to his head, entirely unexpected, sent him stumbling. Genial loomed over him, hand raised as if to strike him again.

"Laugh now, Bratt," Genial said, voice low and quiet. "You won't be laughing when high command is done with you."

Winshur was done for. He knew it deep down. Genial hated him, had hated him from the beginning. The man had already decided Winshur's guilt, already had his story, and nothing, no amount of protests on his part, would change that. His bowels felt loose and all he wanted to do was be alone to weep in terror.

"But . . ." Genial held up a hand. "All is not lost. We know Shu has the list. If you help me retrieve it before the auction we might be able to remedy this disaster. In that case, I might, *might,* put in a word for you. Ask that they show you mercy."

"Mercy?" Winshur latched on to that word. "What must I do?"

"Clean yourself up and meet me downstairs. I'll explain on the way."

Winshur cleaned up as best he could. He dared not go back to his office to fetch a clean shirt. He was afraid of what he might find there. Yama still curled in a ball on the floor, or, worse, Yama dead. Or—and perhaps this was what he feared most— Yama bruised and beaten by his own hand, staring accusingly at him, smirking at his weakness, and now under the protection of Colonel Genial.

CHAPTER 24

HASADAR AND NIFERA SHU'S home had been transformed into an underwater kingdom for the occasion of Nifera's fiftieth birthday. Blue sea shimmered around them in eerily realistic holoprojections, and strange fish in brilliant colors swam through the crowd of guests who exclaimed in appreciation at the subterranean display. The food was ocean-themed, and Poe and Finn found tables heaped with all manner of edible sea creatures, including twen-chok battered and fried in perfect tubular bits, colo clawfish coated in pink salt, huge prawns with eyes and antennae intact piled on mountains of smoking ice, and half a dozen species of fish displayed on beds of multicolored seaweed that Poe had no name for. Even the drinks that the waitstaff passed around referenced the oceans on Corellia in shades of green, blue, and storm gray. They bubbled merrily in long fluted glasses, and Poe was sure he heard the distant sound of waves crashing on the shore when he held one to his mouth to take a sip.

"This place is wild!" Finn exclaimed, already in

possession of a plate heaped with the saltwater delicacies. "Have you ever seen food like this?"

"Once," Poe said. He shuddered involuntarily.
"Not a great memory."

"Right." Finn stuffed an entire yobcrab leg in his
mouth, bit down, and winced in pain.

"You have to take the shell off first," Poe said,
amused.

Finn looked indignant. "Well, why didn't they say
so?"

Poe clapped a hand against the younger man's
arm. "Did I ever tell you how much I appreciate
you?"

Finn grinned. "Not as much as you should."

Poe drained the glass he had been holding in his
free hand. The drink, a bright-green libation, had
tasted like sunlight streaming through kelp forests,
or at least what Poe thought that might taste like.

"You ready to go present our gift to the Shus?"

"Let me just . . ." Finn stuffed a piece of dark
fleshy fish in his mouth. He rolled his eyes in pleasure. Dusted his hands off. "Okay, now I'm ready."

They wound their way through the crowd of hu-
mans, Twi'leks, Sullustans, Barbadelans, and a
dozen other denizens of the galaxy. It was a diverse
crowd, multicultural, multilingual, but all having
one thing in common. They looked very, very rich.

"Hey, Lorell," Finn said, mouth close to Poe's
ear. "Did you notice something alarming about this
crowd?"

Poe looked a little closer, past the glittering wealth

and seascape, and immediately understood what Finn was getting at.

"Did you know half the attendees at the shindig would be First Order?" Finn asked.

"It's more like a quarter," Poe said without turning, "but no. I think we underestimated the First Order presence in Coronet City, and that they'd all be here tonight."

"You think?" Finn said, as another officer walked by, dipping his head in a nod of acknowledgment.

"You still want to wear that pin?" Poe asked.

"Are you kidding me? Now more than ever." Finn hesitated. "You'll have my back in a fight, though, right?"

Poe laughed. "Inevitably."

It was strange to see so many First Order officers here, but perhaps that was the nature of the occupation. The local merchants and politicians courted the favor of the First Order elite, and high command mostly left them to their business—as long as their business was supplying the First Order with ships and cheap labor and anything else they needed. It was ugly, but it wasn't the first time Poe had seen it happen to a planet. And it never lasted. Sooner or later, the First Order would want more than Corellia could give, and the fist would tighten. And squeeze. And Corellia would either fight back or be left a used-up husk.

They'd reached the receiving line and joined the guests waiting for a moment of the Shus' attention.

"Still got the gift?" Finn asked.

He held the box up in response. It let out a strange hissing sound. Not encouraging.

They didn't have to wait long before they were face-to-face with Hasadar and Nifera. Hasadar was a handsome man. He wore a sea-green robe, tied at the waist with a belt of shark teeth. He smiled broadly in greeting. His wife was a head taller than him with ebony skin that glowed in the strange translucence of the artificial underwater world. Her hair coiled regally atop her head, and she wore long earrings that curved around her lobes and draped across her broad shoulders. Her dress was fashioned from hundreds of tiny white shells and flared out at her hips only to pinch in at her knees and finally scrape the floor like a tail. She wore a living albino eel around her neck as if it were a necklace. Poe shook his head, amused. Suralinda and Charth's gift was impressive, but it was no eel.

"Lorell Shda," Nifera Shu greeted him. "A pleasure to finally meet you. Our mutual acquaintances speak quite highly of you."

Poe took Nifera's outstretched hand and brushed a kiss across her knuckles. Her dark eyes glittered in delight. "The pleasure is mine."

"This is my husband," she said with a gesture toward Hasadar. "He is not familiar with your previous work but is surely a supporter."

Poe nodded to the man, who nodded back in acknowledgment. Nifera hadn't come out and said she knew that he was part of the Resistance, but her words were opaque enough to suggest it.

"My associate, Kade Genti," he said, moving aside to allow Finn to present himself.

"A queen of the sea," Finn said, kissing Nifera's hand, "on her second twenty-fifth birthday."

The Corellian woman laughed loudly. "Oh, you are charming. And what a name." She arched an eyebrow at Finn. "An admirer of the firebird, I see."

Finn touched his pin briefly. "And yourself?" he asked, recklessly.

Her eyes met his, bright with mischief. But wary, too. "Brave," she murmured. "Or very impetuous."

"I like to think I'm a bit of both," Finn countered.

She turned back to Poe. "Do you have a gift for me, gentlemen? Besides your charm and flattery?"

Poe presented her with the gift. It fit neatly in Nifera's palm, the gold-flocked wrapping flimsi catching the light.

Her face brightened as she unwrapped the box with eager fingers. Now it hissed and chittered in her hands. Her eyes widened as the flimsi tore away to reveal a tiny metal cage and inside that cage, a tiny living insect.

"Oh!" she cried.

"Oh!" Finn shouted, surprised.

"Oh," Poe moaned quietly.

There was a scroll attached to the top of the cage and Nifera peeled it free, handing the cage back to Poe. He took it, peering in at the creature. It had six legs, ridged in a hard shell of armor, not unlike the yobcrab leg Finn had tried to eat earlier. Spiked mandibles snapped at him, and tentacles waved through the bars of its cage, as if to reach out and grab him.

"It's a miniature lylek!" Nifera exclaimed, sounding delighted as she read from the scroll. "A native of the Ryloth equatorial rain forests, they usually grow to immense size, big enough to eat a full-grown man. But this one has been specially bred to stay small, as long as you don't feed it flesh." She widened her eyes in mock horror at Poe, but he could tell she was not afraid in the least. If anything, she was fascinated. "And," she continued, "this one is a queen."

She rolled the scroll back up and handed it to her horrified husband. Poe held the cage out, the strange beast still chittering and waving its tentacles menacingly.

"I love it!" Nifera Shu said, clearly pleased. "I do believe this is the best gift I have received, Lorell Shda." She leaned in conspiratorially. "I don't know how you knew that I trained to be an entomologist as a young woman, but I am impressed."

Poe blinked. Had Suralinda known? Surely not.

"I am glad you appreciate this small token of my appreciation of your . . . birth."

"I do, indeed. And now I have a gift for you." She handed the lylek to her husband, who immediately handed it off to a servant waiting nearby. Nifera dipped her hand into a pocket and drew forth a tiny black clam-shaped packet. She took Poe's hand and pressed the packet into his palm, temporarily holding his hand in both of hers. Her skin was warm to the touch.

"Best of luck," she whispered, loud enough only for his ears, "and may the Force guide you in your endeavors. The games will begin five minutes past the hour."

And then he and Finn were being moved down the receiving line and the next guests were presenting their gifts to the couple.

They wandered the undersea room a little longer, careful to avoid any First Order guests. Finn made another run at the banquet table, and Poe searched the room for Charth and Suralinda. He finally found them by a rushing waterfall filled with brightly striped fish. She was facing outward to the room and he reached past her to fill a nearby cup with whatever strange libation was pouring from the falls.

"Nice gift," he said drily by way of greeting. "Did you know she was an entomologist?"

Suralinda's jaw drop was enough of an answer.

He drank from the cup. It tasted like the tropics—like the vacation he had spent on Spira. He sat the cup down and gave her a smirk.

She narrowed her eyes. "I assume that means you got the packet."

He patted his breast pocket. She handed him a comlink. "Stay in touch." And then she was gone, back into the party.

He went looking for Finn by the buffet.

"Hey, try this," Finn said, handing Poe a slice of gelatinous yellow cake on a small plate. He had one for himself and took an oversized bite.

"What is it?"

"Who cares? It's delicious."

Poe looked closer at the layer of icing. "Are those . . . sea worms?"

Finn stuffed what was left of his cake in his mouth. "De-lic-ious."

A bell chimed somewhere, marking the hour.

"Come on," Poe said. "Let's find somewhere private and see what Nifera has given us."

In the far back corner of the massive room they found a balcony that looked out over Coronet City. Poe handed Finn the comlink Suralinda had given him and motioned for him to stay and keep watch at the balcony door as he himself stepped through into the humid sea air.

He opened the clamshell packet and poured out the contents. Inside was an imagecaster with a single individual earbud. He slipped the bud into his right ear and pressed the button on the caster. A holo projected itself in front of his eyes. It was an adjudication droid holding a gavel. The droid greeted him as Lorell Shda and displayed the credit account that Connix had created for him. He whistled low in appreciation. That was a lot of money, probably the majority of the credits that the Resistance had. The gravity of the situation hit him all at once, and he swallowed nervously. The holo of the droid prompted him to choose an avatar that would represent him in the anonymous bidding. In keeping with the party's theme, each avatar was a sea creature of some kind. Randomly, Poe chose a red crotty from the list. The holo in front of him blinked a

confirmation that the red crotty was now associated
with his account and asked him to please wait. He
had no choice but to do as he was told.

"How's it going?"

Poe jumped at Finn's voice in his free ear.

"I'm waiting for the auction to begin."

"Great! All clear out here." Finn gave him a
thumbs-up.

The hologram started to change, and Poe turned
his attention back to the screen. Something was
happening. He watched curiously as the adjudication droid dissolved and in its place a horned serpent appeared. It slithered across his visual, thick
and white, its scales shining, until it looped itself
into an O shape, head rising above the juncture
where the body and the tail met. It turned its horned
head toward Poe and opened its mouth. Holographic words seemed to flow from its mouth. Not
in Basic, but in a language Poe didn't know. But he
didn't need to read the words to know what it said:
All Knowledge Must Be Free.

He knew that slogan. It was used by the Collective.

Poe was surprised. He knew the Collective and
had had occasion to deal with the criminal organization in his past. They were mostly encryption
breakers, network slicers, and data pirates. Criminals with a cause, but criminals certainly. Of course,
the Resistance wasn't exactly on the right side of the
law these days.

The horned serpent unwound itself and slithered
off the screen, replaced by the familiar adjudication

droid and Poe's avatar and the Resistance's credit account amount. Poe watched as his credits were cut in half.

"What the hell?" he said, alarmed.

"Thank you for your generous donation to the Collective," the droid said. "This donation is nonrefundable. The bidding will begin in approximately three minutes. Please stand by."

"They've already taken half our credits!"

Finn poked his head around the corner. "Did you say something?"

"The auction. They've already claimed half our credits as a 'donation.'"

"Criminals," Finn said, shaking his head in disgust. "Can't trust them."

"That's not the point," he said. "Well, not entirely. The point is that if this auction gets pricey, we won't be able to compete."

Finn grabbed his arm, face intent. "We've got to get that list, Poe. That's why we're here. The future of the Resistance is that list!"

"I know, I know." He scratched at his chin. "I'll think of something."

The droid said, "Bidding to commence in five . . . four . . . three . . . two . . ." A bell chimed in his ear, and the same document that he had seen back in Yendor's library appeared on his screen—a list of encrypted names and locations under the heading SUBVERSIVES and another under CURRENTLY DETAINED. This was it.

"Opening bid at ten thousand credits," said the droid. "Do I hear twenty?"

Poe grimaced, but he was determined to win.

"Twenty," he said into the mike. "You have twenty."

After that, the bidding came fast and furious. Poe had a hard time keeping up, especially with Finn asking him how it was going every few seconds. Back and forth, back and forth, and Poe tried to determine just how many parties were bidding, but everything was happening too quickly to keep track. If the bidding kept going at this rate, they simply couldn't keep up. He covered the device in his ear for a moment, sheltering the mike and causing the holo to flicker off.

"Fi—I mean, Kade," he whispered harshly. "Go look around for other bidders. See if you can identify anyone that looks like they're spending a lot of credits."

Finn looked at him quizzically.

"Just try," he said, motioning Finn forward with his hands. "Go. Tell me what you see."

Finn shook his head doubtfully but stepped back into the main area of the room, leaving Poe alone. Poe lifted his hand and fell back into the thick of the auction. In the few seconds he was away, the price had shot up another hundred thousand credits. He slumped. The exponential jumps were almost too big for him to comprehend. Another few minutes at this rate, and he would have blown through the Resistance's maximum.

Finn came back.

"Anything?"

He shrugged. "They all look rich to me."

"Anyone with an earpiece?" he asked, exasperated.

"Not that I can tell, Poe. But I saw Suralinda and Charth. They'll keep an eye out, too."

Poe nodded. It was the best they could do. Because he was certain now that he was not going to win this auction. Sure enough, the bidding climbed by exponents again, blowing past the Resistance's funds. His avatar went dim and the droid said. "You have exceeded your reserve. Please add more funds at this time. If you fail to add more funds, this device will self-destruct in sixty seconds. One, two . . ."

Poe ripped the device out of his ear with a muttered, "Dammit!"

"What is it?" Finn asked over his shoulder.

"We're out."

"What?"

"Too rich for us."

"What do you mean? Already?"

Poe nodded grimly.

"So this whole mission is a bust?" Finn asked, outraged. "A waste of time?"

"No." Poe scanned the room. He knew the list had to be here. Suralinda had said that the winners had to be physically present to claim it, as it could only be transferred to a personal device and would not be open to the larger network or be broadcast or transmitted anywhere. So maybe entering this auction at all was going about it the wrong way.

A shout of alarm drew his attention to the grand entrance. Stormtroopers were pouring in across the bridge and through the front doors. The room that had been crawling with First Order officers earlier now seemed to have a distinct lack of them, as if they had been forewarned to clear out and within minutes had simply disappeared.

"Something's up," he murmured to Finn.

Bright party conversation faded to the silence of shock. The only sound in the room was the strange underwater music that continued to play from hidden speakers and the continued pounding of stormtrooper boots on the floor as they spread through the party, eerie white figures moving through the artificial deep.

Behind them came a First Order officer, cold and spectral, stretched skeletal thin in his black uniform.

"This is an illegal gathering," he declared loudly. "Under the joint authority of CorSec and the First Order, all guests will be detained and questioned. If you are innocent you have nothing to fear. However, if you resist, you will be shot."

Hasadar Shu stepped forward in his regal robe and belt of shark teeth, putting himself between the soldiers and the party guests. He held out a hand.

"Stop!" His voice carried over the party. "This is a private residence! What is the meaning of this?"

The stormtrooper in the lead lifted his rifle and pointed it at the man. He didn't hesitate. He simply pulled the trigger.

Hasadar Shu pitched back, neck snapping violently. He went down, a blaster hole in his forehead.

A loud crash as someone or something outside of Poe's direct vision knocked one of the towering banquet tables over. He caught the edge of a massive silver tower, full of ice and seafood, thundering as it hit the floor. The deafening boom reverberated through the room, loud and unexpected as a bomb. One of the stormtroopers, no doubt rattled by the noise, fired wildly into the crowd.

And that's when the screaming started.

CHAPTER 25

"WHERE IS EVERYONE?" WEDGE asked as they brought their craft in to dock. Nasz's codes had worked like a charm, the woman at the other end of the transmission passing them through security with barely a second glace.

Snap answered first. "As I understand it, Coronet City is under First Order occupation, but the local government's still technically in charge."

"Technically," Karé said, laughing softly. "We know how that goes."

"They've repurposed much of the shipbuilding, but CorSec still decides who comes and goes."

"Really?" Norra sounded skeptical.

Her son shrugged. "They didn't seem interested in us."

Snap was right. If they really were holding high-value prisoners here and building secret starfighters, destroyers, and ground attack ships, shouldn't there be a little more security?

"Maybe there's some other priority tonight," Karé suggested.

"Or," Nasz said, "maybe the populace has risen up in rebellion and the Resistance has vanquished the enemy on Corellia without having to lift a finger."

Silence, until Snap said, "You don't have a lot of friends, do you?"

"I don't have any friends." Nasz smiled. "And that's the way I like it."

"Any thoughts about where they all went, Wedge?" Karé asked, bringing them back on topic. "You know this place best. Is it a high holiday or something? Evacuation of some kind?"

The ship landed smoothly. Snap really had become an exceptional pilot. Not that flying a cargo ship was the height of the art, but to fly an X-wing and a bulky toad like this with equal skill? Well, it showed talent. Patience.

"No idea," Wedge said. "I haven't been home for a very long time."

"Well," said Nasz, standing. "Let's go see for ourselves."

"We're still going in armed," Norra said.

"Of course. We're not stupid."

The exterior door opened and the ramp lowered. Wedge unbuckled his restraints and pushed himself to his feet. He took the blaster Norra handed him and put it in the holster strapped to his waist. Checked over his disguise, which wasn't much of a disguise at all: brown pants and a jacket over a lighter shade of brown shirt. Something to make him blend in as a worker or a mechanic on his day off. The rest wore similarly nondescript clothes. All except for Nasz, who still wore her animal skin and armor one-shouldered jumpsuit, but at least had thrown a canvas jacket over it to tone it down to the casual viewer and hide the marks on her arm.

Karé elected to stay with the ship, certain that a quick getaway would be needed, and Nasz insisted on coming, so the four of them—Wedge, Norra, Snap, and Teza Nasz—disembarked and made their way across the massive hangar.

It was strange that no one was here. Sure, it was late, but this was a big intergalactic city. And Charth had said the First Order was building ships around the clock. Something was definitely going on. They'd made it all the way to the main doors that led into the heart of the building before anyone stopped them.

"Halt, trespassers!" came a voice from behind them.

"Easy," Wedge murmured when he saw Nasz reach for the blaster in her waistband. "We talk our way out first."

Her fingers lingered at her holster for a moment before she raised her hands with the others and turned to face their accuser. It was a young man, dressed in First Order black and bearing no insignia to denote his rank. Wedge guessed he couldn't be more than seventeen. He gave Nasz a look and she shrugged.

"Hey," Wedge said brightly. "We're a little lost."

The boy glared. "You shouldn't be here at all. This is a restricted area." His eyes narrowed. "Show me your work badges."

"Work badges?"

"You are mechanics, aren't you?"

"I'm not," Nasz said.

Snap snorted and Wedge sighed loudly. The boy's eyes darted between the two of them. The understanding that he was in danger seemed to dawn on him, and he took two steps backward, eyes wide. He fumbled for the comlink attached to his belt, but Nasz was on him before he could pull it free. She landed a right hook directly to the cadet's cheek and he went down immediately, his comlink skittering across the floor.

"Really?" Wedge said. "You couldn't just say you were a mechanic?"

"Oh come on, Grandpa," she said. "It was taking too long. At least I didn't shoot him."

"You would make a terrible spy," Snap said, quietly. Wedge wasn't sure if he was talking to him or Nasz, but he chose to believe the comment was meant for the ex-Imperial.

Norra shook her head and motioned Snap over. Together they lifted the unconscious young officer by his arms and legs and carried him to a corner. They dumped him there in the shadows and hurried back to Wedge and Nasz.

"We should have asked him where everyone is," Snap observed.

"Yes," Wedge said drily, "and I would have. If someone wasn't so quick to solve every problem with their fists."

"I said I was sorry," Nasz said.

"No, you didn't."

"Well, I thought it."

"I doubt that, too."

"Hey," Norra cut in. "Are you sure you two aren't the married couple? Let's go."

They passed into the main building without any other interference. Everyone really was gone. The building looked much like any other building, except that its long hallways were lined with framed blueprints of various ship makes and models. Interspersed between the framed pictures were dozens of award plaques and glass display cases presenting parts of old ships for interested eyes.

"It's like a museum," Snap observed, his voice hushed.

"Look at this," Norra said, excitedly. "This is the original blueprint for a *Baleen*-class heavy freighter. Those things are monsters."

Wedge and Snap stopped to look, but Nasz kept walking. "This isn't a tour," she threw over her shoulder.

They made their way down another hallway, this one lined with windows that looked out on the hangar from which they had just come. They were building ships here, all right. And not just massive freighters. Wedge spied a familiar TIE model and a couple more that looked like innovations on the fighters but were entirely unfamiliar. And one that made him sigh in appreciation: a Corellian CR90 corvette.

"Look at that thing," he said to no one in particular.

"An old blockade runner," Norra answered at his shoulder. "Now wouldn't one of those be handy."

"We'll see what we can do on the way out," Snap said.

"I do wish we had more time here," he said, voice wistful. "Did I ever tell you that I had an aunt who worked for Corellian Engineering?"

Norra smiled. "Maybe we'll really come back for a vacation sometime when the place isn't occupied by the First Order."

The hallway ended at a lift, and beside it, a screen that when Nasz pressed her hand to it displayed a directory.

"Where to?" Snap asked.

"Records," Nasz said confidently. "If the First Order is anything like the Empire, they'll be meticulous record keepers."

"Can't we access the records we need from anywhere?" Norra asked.

"Maybe. Maybe not. But I say best to start at the heart of the operation if you can." She ran a finger down the display until she found what she was looking for. "Not so far. Seven floors up."

Norra pressed the button to call the lift and they waited, weapons drawn. The floor numbers ticked down from four, three, two . . . as the lift descended. Wedge held his breath, expecting trouble. The lift stopped, emitting a soft chime to signal it had reached the hangar level.

"Get ready," he said, shifting the grip on his blaster.

The doors opened. To an empty car.

He exhaled, relieved. Snap went first, checking the lift, even poking at the mesh roof to confirm no one was hiding above.

"Clear," he said.

The air in the lift felt stale, heavy, nearly claustrophobic as they crowded in.

"I'd almost rather we encounter some fighting," Snap said, shaking out his arm. "This lack of engagement is making me nervous."

Norra nodded. "It's like the enemy is hiding, waiting to pounce."

"Be glad we haven't seen trouble, yet," Nasz said. "Plenty of things could still go wrong."

"Absolutely no friends, huh?" Snap's comment wasn't a question as much as a statement of fact.

They'd reached the seventh floor, and Wedge motioned them to silence. He knew it was idle chatter to get rid of some of the adrenaline, but he was trying to focus and for some reason the babble was bothering him today.

The doors opened and they entered the hallway before them. Wedge signaled for Norra and Nasz to lead. He and Snap took the rear. They moved slowly from cover to cover, checking corners and doors, methodical and careful. They had almost reached the executive records office when they heard noise to their right. Norra motioned them back and they took cover just as a First Order officer exited from what looked to be a bathroom. His hair was disheveled, and he tugged at his uniform as if trying to straighten the crumpled fabric. He looked exhausted, eyes heavy with bags and skin sallow. His expression was haunted, his cheeks hollow, and a red welt was rising on his cheek. He made his way on weak legs to the lift, and they let him pass unmolested.

They listened for the ding of the lift doors opening, and when they were sure he was gone, they continued down the hall. Norra went through the executive office doors first, blaster raised. Silence as they waited for her all-clear. Seconds ticked by, and then a full minute.

Snap motioned worriedly to Wedge. Wedge jerked his chin toward Nasz, and just as she was about to go, Norra came out, a strange look on her face.

"There's a girl," Norra said, her voice cold. Wedge recognized that tone. Norra ran hot at all times, a blaze of a woman, except when things were really bad. Ice in her voice meant she was trying to hold back some emotion, usually a murderous one. But she'd holstered her blaster and her arms hung by her side, so the danger had passed, whatever it was, leaving only her icy fury. "She said she'll help us."

"What is it?" he asked warily.

"Come in. See for yourself."

Wedge and Snap exchanged a look. He knew that coldness, too. Whatever it was, it wasn't good.

"Come on," Norra said. She turned and left them no choice but to follow.

The office doors opened to a foyer with two desks, one on each side of the main path through the office that led to another set of doors. These doors were flung open and through them Wedge could see an-

other desk, this one bigger than the two in the greeting area. Beyond that desk was a rectangular
window at eye level that looked out to what Wedge
guessed was the hangar seven stories below them.

But it was the girl that drew his attention. She sat
at one of the desks, her head bowed. Her orange
hair was matted with blood and she held a rag to
her nose. It was soaked red.

"What's going on?" Wedge asked.

"This is Yama Dex," Norra said quietly. "How
old did you say you were, Yama?"

"Fifteen," she said morosely.

"Fifteen," Norra confirmed, eyes cutting to
Wedge. "And who did this to you?"

The girl sighed heavily. She said something that
Wedge couldn't hear, but Nasz did and whistled
low. The woman took a few steps away, laughing
quietly, shaking her head in disbelief.

Wedge wasn't sure what her reaction meant, but
he could guess. As an ex-Imperial, she'd experienced
the brutatily of the Empire up close and personal.
The viciousness of the First Order probably felt all
too familiar, and against one of their own, at that.
There were probably a lot of stories Nasz could tell
about her time as an Imperial that had turned her
into the woman she was, but he wasn't sure he had
the stomach to hear them.

"Who did this?" Wedge asked, echoing Norra.

The girl looked up. Wedge flinched. She had been
beaten badly. Her nose looked broken and the area
around her eye was quickly swelling, the blood vessels smashed into tiny tributaries. He'd seen dozens

of beatings in his time, taken his fair share and doled out more, but he wasn't sure he'd ever seen something so stark as this girl sitting calmly behind her desk in the records office, her face a mess of blood and bruises.

"Executive Records Officer Bratt." Her voice was a low wail of grief. Whoever Bratt was, he had been important to her, and he had broken not just her body but something deeper.

"The man leaving the bathroom?" Wedge asked Norra.

"That's my guess."

The girl sniffed, and then winced at the pain. She looked at Wedge through bloodshot eyes. "She said you were looking for one of the prisoners."

"That's right," Wedge said.

Nasz had paced back to them. "Do you know where they're being held?"

"I was there when Officer Bratt assigned them to their duties. I can find them."

Wedge blinked. Too much of a coincidence? A trap? Or ridiculous luck?

"If we give you a prisoner's name, do you think you can look him up in your records?" he asked.

"Officer Bratt kept the list on his personal datapad, and it's locked."

"We can break the lock," Nasz said confidently. "Where is it?"

The girl's gaze flashed briefly toward the big desk in the adjoining room.

"On it," Snap said. A moment later he was back with a handheld datapad. He handed it over to

Nasz. She pushed the box of tapes off the top of the empty desk across the room and climbed up, sitting cross-legged on the top. She removed a drive from a pocket at her hip. "This has every encryption key the Empire ever used, at least up until Jakku. It's possible the First Order has their own, but we'll try these first. If they don't work, I have some other ideas."

"How long will it take?" Wedge asked.

The ex-Imperial shrugged. "Could be a few minutes, could be an hour. Could not work at all."

Wedge turned back to the girl. "Do you know where your boss went? And if he's coming back?"

She shrugged and shook her head no.

"Surely there're only so many places in this building they could keep prisoners," Norra said. She turned to Yama. "Is there a place that workers live? The ones they keep on-site? A camp or a dormitory or—"

"—a detention center," Nasz murmured.

"They'll probably want them to blend in."

"Not too much. Else they start making allies, talking about where they're from, what they used to do for a living, family, pets, the good old days. They can't have that. They'll be isolated together, close enough not to draw outsider suspicions but able to be placed on lockdown if necessary."

Snap had pulled a chair from the office behind them and positioned himself as a lookout, weapon resting but ready in his lap. "How do you know these things?"

"Part of the old job."

"There're dormitories," Yama offered.

Wedge and Norra exchanged a look. "Ransolm could be there," he said.

"Ransolm . . ." Yama murmured. They all looked at her. She looked back with big eyes, and then flushed.

"Do you recognize the name?" Wedge said, breath bated.

"Prisoner 876549C."

"Are you sure?" Norra asked.

"I have an eidetic memory. That's why they put me in Records. Officer Bratt never asked why they would assign him a fifteen-year-old cadet, so I never told him. But I remember everything. Always have."

"And you are saying that Prisoner 876549C is Ransolm Casterfo? He's definitely here?" Part of Wedge had doubted they'd find the man, despite what Leia believed. She had been guessing, after all. Following a hunch based on a few letters and half-guesses. But he should have known a hunch from Leia was always more than a hunch, and here was the confirmation.

"I saw him," the girl confirmed. "He was assigned to sewage pipe fitting in the shipyard."

"Do you know where that is?" Norra asked.

She shook her head no.

"But I do," Nasz said. She held the datapad up. "That part's not encrypted." It took her a few moments to find what she was looking for, but she found it. "Hmm . . ."

Wedge walked over to look at the screen. "What did you find?"

"No Ransolm, obviously, and no Prisoner 876549C. But there's a new hire that was added to the detail this morning, and is being housed in . . ." She punched a few more buttons. "Dormitory F."

"Dormitory F is closed for renovations," the girl said, sounding puzzled. "I walk by it on my way to the office. No one's housed there right now."

Nasz looked up, grinning, and Wedge returned the smile.

"We got him."

CHAPTER 26

ONCE AGAIN, LEIA FOUND herself gazing out of the windows of Yendor's library that she had turned into a war room. It had become a favorite spot rather quickly. There was something peaceful about the view, the expanse of desert that stretched out for kilometers before her, seemingly empty but no doubt teeming with life, great and small. Desert rodents, birds, and the myriad insects that lived in the sparse landscape. Secret flowers that bloomed only at night, succulents bursting with moisture, roots that ran deep below the dry ground seeking out the underground waters. All of it hidden, but very much alive.

The metaphor was not lost on her. Roots for the Resistance were exactly what she was hoping to plant herself. Here, or somewhere else. With these companions, old and new, or perhaps others. She didn't know. But she knew in the end it wouldn't be her choice. Life had not given her many choices beyond the edict to survive. So she did. Knowing that it was her purpose to survive what came next, and what came after that, and after that. And as long as she woke up the next day and did something to feed and water and nurture those roots, then it was a good day.

"Leia."

She turned from the view to find Yendor waiting patiently for her attention, hands clasped behind his back.

"Sorry," she said. "My mind was somewhere else. How long have you been standing there?"

"Not long," he demurred. "And I've always loved this view. It's one of the reasons I took this post."

"It is lovely," she agreed. "And peaceful. At least until I showed up." She gestured to the center of the room where the table and holo were. Even now a handful of people milled about, datapads in hand or studying star maps and logistics and whatever else Rieekan, Orrimaarko, and the others had set up.

Yendor shrugged. "It was getting boring out here in the desert. Besides, we've been over this."

"I know," she said, raising a hand. "I'm just aware of how much we've imposed."

Yendor smiled. "I thought that's what royalty did. Impose."

"Generals, too," she said, teasing.

"Of course, but I wouldn't have it any other way." He gestured to the door. "Someone else has been waiting to talk to you, too."

Leia peered in the direction he had pointed. "Rey?"

Despite the distance, the girl heard her and perked up. She waved.

Leia shook her head, amused. She was still surprised that Rey had asked to stay behind on Ryloth. She thought for sure that she would have wanted to accompany Finn and Poe on their mission, or at the very least join Wedge's rescue team. After all, she was a formidable asset. But Rey had come to her, hot off a conversation with Finn, saying she had a feeling that she would be needed here, with Leia. Leia had taken one long look in her eyes and agreed. She didn't know what Rey felt, but she knew to respect it, just as she had learned to respect her own premonitions. Nevertheless, Rey had to be anxious; all the waiting wasn't pleasant for any of them.

"Excuse me," she said to Yendor before walking toward the door. Rey met her halfway. They stopped in front of the holo table.

"General Organa," she said.

Leia thought to correct her, to remind her once again to call her Leia, but she had corrected her half a dozen times already. General it would be. "Is there something wrong, Rey?"

She chewed at her lip.

"Spit it out," Leia said.

"How are the missions going?" she asked hurriedly. "Finn and Poe, the Bracca retrieval, the prisoner rescue? Everything all right?"

Leia narrowed her eyes. "As far as I know. Why do you ask? Are you . . . ?"

Rey nodded. She took a deep breath before pressing on. "I have that feeling again. I thought it would go away, but it hasn't and . . ." She looked lost.

"Rey," Leia said gently, a notion of understand-

ing leading her words. "You and I, we have something special. Something that means feelings aren't
just feelings. Do you understand?"

Rey nodded. "The Force," she said, voice barely
a whisper.

"So you better tell me."

"That's just it," she said, frustration bubbling
over. "I can't! Because I'm not sure what it means.
It's just . . . a feeling."

Leia studied her face. The girl was close, so close
to something big. Bigger than Leia, maybe even
Luke, if that was possible. But Leia knew that she
wasn't the one to ultimately get her there; that
would be someone else. Nevertheless, she would do
what she could for Rey while she could.

"Let's check in on the missions, then, shall we?
See if there's any news."

Rey sagged, relieved.

They made their way over to the communications
console where Rose and Connix sat. Each had their
headphones draped around their respective necks,
eyes busily studying the boards in front of them.
R2-D2 was there, too, and he beeped a greeting that
Leia returned with a nod. She leaned in over Rose's
shoulder.

"Any news?"

Rose startled. "General Organa!" she said in a
rush. She sat up straighter, pulling the headphones
away and setting them on the console. "I didn't see
you," she confessed. She gave a small smile to Rey.
"Hi!"

"Hi," Rey said with a nod.

"Any word from Bracca or Corellia?" Leia asked.

"Zay checked in at oh nine hundred hours. She said they had made planetfall and Dross Squadron was headed to their rendezvous point with their contact from the guild."

"Dross Squadron?" Leia asked, amused. "One guess who came up with that name. Did she report any problems?"

"No. I mean, negative. All seemed to be going smoothly. But she said their away team would be out of comlink contact for a while. Something about interference on the planet's surface."

"Good." She turned to Connix. "What about the Corellian teams?"

"Team One has landed and is at the auction," she said. "They're out of comlink contact, as well, but for safety reasons. Seems there's a substantial First Order presence where they are. But I'm monitoring that here." She pointed to four small blinking red lights on the screen.

"So do we know if the auction's started?"

"We do," Rose said. "We had a communication from Maz Kanata."

"Did she report any problems?"

"None so far."

"And the other Corellian team?"

"No word from Corellian Team Two, either," Connix said. "But the minute I hear something, I'll let you know."

"Thank you," Leia said. She turned to Rey. "Does that help?"

"Yes," Rey said. "But I still feel something. I can't

explain it." She paused, mouth open as if searching for the right words, but finally shook her head, giving up. "I can't explain it," she repeated.

"That's okay," Leia said gently. "When you do know, come find me and we'll—"

Rey jerked her head up. Her voice was soft with terror. "They're here!"

A proximity alarm blared through the room. Massive metal doors thundered down over the glass windows, quickly obscuring the desert view.

"All hands!" Yendor shouted from across the room. "Sound the alarm. The First Order is here. We're under attack!"

CHAPTER 27

"SCATTER!" SHRIV SHOUTED, BUT for Wesson, it was too late. He watched the indigo-haired pilot drop with a blaster shot to her ribs. Raidah screamed. Shriv cursed and dived to his left, his own blaster firing as his shoulder slammed into a thick metal post. He winced at the pain, ducking down behind the limited cover. The others on his team did the same, taking shelter behind the wide steel columns that lined the corridor. It was weak refuge, and they were still too exposed, but so were the stormtroopers. Both sides were taking fire at close quarters, but the stormtroopers were more exposed on the open platform. Dross Squadron had better cover, as meager as it was. A small advantage, but Shriv was grateful for small things.

He shot, taking out a trooper. He looked around frantically for some kind of exit. Their only hope was to move farther down the hallway into the unknown. He shuddered, remembering the metal-eating creature's mouth and wondering which he would prefer—dying by blasterfire or being a monster's lunch. He was pretty sure it was blasterfire, but then Stronghammer cried out, and Shriv's attention shifted across the hall to where the remaining members of Dross Squadron were pinned. The big pilot had taken a hit to his leg and was down on one knee, clearly in pain. Pacer was trying to pull him back out of direct fire, but there was nowhere safe. They were stuck, and it was only a matter of time before the First Order picked them off, one by one.

"Fall back!" he shouted, although what good it would do them, he wasn't sure. He caught Pacer's gaze and yelled it again, but the young pilot shook his head and motioned frantically toward the troopers. Shriv turned just in time to watch a stormtrooper pitch forward, helmet shot through with a heavy arrow.

"What in the depths of Mustafar . . . ?" Shriv murmured as another trooper went down with an arrow through the head. And then the entire platoon seemed to realize they were being attacked from the rear and turned to face the new threat. Which allowed Shriv and the others to do the picking off, and just like that the tide turned from impossible to winning. Between Dross Squadron and their mysterious bow-wielding allies, they made quick work of the First Order forces.

Pacer was the first to venture forward, well before Shriv could counsel him to caution. A handful of guild Scrappers materialized through the smoke, weaving between the bodies of dead stormtroopers. Four of them were holding modified bowcasters that looked like they were meant for setting anchors for zipline cables, not shooting people, and Shriv put the puzzle pieces together.

The woman greeting Pacer was short like him and wore her thick black hair in a straight bowl cut that circled her brown face like a cowl. Her expression was set in grim lines, and Shriv surmised that this must be the sister—and that Pacer's intensity must be a family trait.

"My sister, Puwanini," Pacer said by way of introduction as they strode toward Shriv.

"Call me Puwan," she said quickly.

"Call me Shriv," he said. "A thousand thankyous for the assist. Now how do we get out of here?"

She holstered the bowcaster in a contraption on her back. "Well, the First Order knows you're here now. I expect reinforcements to show up any minute. Probably on the next train."

"Which gives us how much time?"

She glanced skyward as she did the math in her head. "They run every fifteen minutes, and one just pulled out, so I'm guessing you've got more like twelve or thirteen minutes, tops."

That was more than he had expected. "We can work with that. Just show us which way to those ships."

Puwan's thick black eyebrows rose. "You still want to try to lift some New Republic scrap?" She looked pointedly behind Shriv.

Shriv glanced back over his shoulder where Wesson lay sprawled and panting on the ground a few meters away, Raidah hunched over her, hands pressed to her injured side. Wesson was silent, but tears leaked down her cheeks and through Raidah's fingers, he could see burned flesh. Hell, he could smell it. Wesson noticed Shriv watching her and she lifted her chin.

"We complete the mission," she said through gritted teeth.

Shriv sighed. He hated this, truly. Soldiers got injured. Sometimes, lots of times, they died. That's just how it went. Especially when the soldiers in question were fighting for the side he was on. So he said the only thing he could say.

"We complete the mission."

Puwan braced her gloved hands on her hips. "Okay, but no use trying to sneak them out now. Best way is to cross at the nearest entrance. You can power over to the open scrap platform. I tried to pick one out that I thought a bunch of Resistance pilots would appreciate, but I wasn't sure."

That was thoughtful of her and he said so.

She shrugged. "Anything for my little brother."

"What about Wesson?" Stronghammer asked as he joined them. He was limping badly. Shriv held back a wince. The big man's leg was a mangled mess below the knee. That he was standing at all was a miracle.

"Don't you worry about her," Raidah said. "I've got her."

"If we get those ships, it's all worth it," Pacer said. "Wesson's sacrifice will be worth it."

"She's not dead, you ass," Raidah growled.

Shriv whacked Pacer on the back, pointing him down the hall. "Go!"

Pacer shrugged and joined his sister, who was scouting their path down the hallway. "Kids," Shriv said to Raidah, trying to make light of it as he helped her pull Wesson to her feet. As of now, Dross Squadron was down to two fighters, two injured, and a hotheaded kid. Not the way he would have wanted it, but he would find a way.

Their progress was slow. Too slow. Shriv had offered to relieve Raidah and carry Wesson's weight, but the woman had waved him off. "It's my fault we got caught," she said, voice shattered. "It's my fault Wesson and Stronghammer are shot up. So I'll do it."

Shriv didn't argue. He knew how those things went, what they meant to a soldier. What it must mean to Raidah. But it was slowing them down, and Shriv was sure that blasterfire would break out from behind them at any moment. Blessedly, they reached the end of the corridor faster than expected. It dead-ended into the open air. Puwan made a beeline for a row of lockers tucked in an alcove to the right and Shriv, against his better judgment, toed to the edge of the platform to look out. He immediately wished he hadn't.

Below him spread the giant jaws of the Ibdis Maw. This mouth was even bigger than the one he'd spied earlier, and it occurred to him that either there were multiple creatures or multiple mouths on a single continent-sized creature—and neither option was comforting.

He watched in horrible fascination as, far in the distance, probably eight hundred meters across the expanse, a great ship tumbled into the creature's jaws. There was a groaning shriek and then a crunch and the whole platform rumbled beneath their feet. He hurriedly backed up, feeling much too close to the edge.

"How do we get across?" he asked, hastily joining the others at the lockers. They were strapping on what looked suspiciously like jetpacks. Shriv's stomach dropped to his feet. "Don't tell me we're going to fly across."

"Not exactly," Puwan said. She had drawn her bowcaster again and tapped a hand against the barrel. "I'll shoot you a line, and you can attach your rigging to the cable. The thrusters are just for momentum and direction. They'll probably slow your fall, but I wouldn't recommend trying it. And if you come off the cable . . ." She shrugged. "You saw what the drop does to you."

Lands you in the mouth of a monster, thought Shriv. "Great!" he said brightly. "So glad I thought of this plan."

Pacer snorted, and Shriv almost grinned. The boy had a sense of humor after all.

Puwan clapped a hand to her ear, and Shriv noticed for the first time she was wearing a communications device. "Time to go," she said grimly. "Stormtroopers are on their way."

Shriv shrugged into the heavy reinforced vest the Scrapper handed him and watched as she attached thrusters to the belt at his hips. She showed him how to control them through the gloves that he slipped onto his hands, and then did the same for Raidah. Raidah attached the belt and thrusters to Wesson, who bit down in pain on her lip so hard that it welled with blood. Pacer was already geared up. But when she got to Stronghammer, she paused. The big man was having none of it.

"Go without me!" he shouted through teeth gritted in pain. "I'm not going out on that wire, and those tiny thrusters won't hold a man as powerful as me. I'd rather die here on solid ground, fighting, than in the mouth of a monster."

"Didn't you hear me say the stormtroopers are on their way?" Puwan said.

"Let them come!" he roared. "Give me a weapon and I'll make them pay before I go."

Puwan threw up her hands and stepped away. "He's your problem," she grumbled. "You talk to him. I'm going to set the cables." Shriv watched her stomp over to the edge of the platform, take aim out across the stretch of what he had fondly begun to think of as the Chomping Abyss of Death, and line up a shot.

Raidah was bent down, whispering furiously with Stronghammer, and he left her to it for the moment, hurrying over to Puwan.

"Where are you aiming?" he asked.

"Platform thirty-three G. That's the one I thought you'd appreciate."

He scanned the dozen or so platforms visible from their spot. Thirty-three G was by far the farthest from them. He could just make out the telltale

cruciform wing shape of two of the ships there, patiently waiting consumption by the Ibdis Maw, and
another that he was pretty sure was an A-wing.

"Can you get us there?"

"It's far," she admitted, "but I've got the wire.
Not enough to double it up, so you'll be solo out
there with no redundancy, but no risk, no reward,
right?"

"That's a terrible saying," he muttered.

She grinned and then turned back to her target.
She aimed her crossbow and with an exhale let the
arrow fly. They watched the cable trail like a ribbon
on the end of a kite. It sailed across the Chomping
Abyss of Death and finally, after what felt like a
lifetime to Shriv, the arrow struck true.

Puwan grinned and let out a whoop. "See!" she
said. "Knew I could do it."

"Fine, you stubborn ass!" came Raidah's frustrated voice behind him. "Stay here and die."

Shriv turned back to his other problem. "What's
going on, Stronghammer?" he asked, but he didn't
need to. He'd already guessed that there was no way
the man was going to make it across the Ibdis Maw
attached to that wire, ruined leg or not.

"A man should get to choose how he dies," he
said, and Shriv could see sweat coating his pate like
a spring rain. "This is how I choose to die."

"No martyrs," Wesson said, anguished. "Isn't
that what you said on the ship, Shriv? No martyrs
on this mission."

Shriv nodded. He had said that.

Stronghammer dragged himself to his feet, a tremendous effort. Shriv could see there was a hole clean through the meat of his calf. He swallowed. "Does it hurt?"

"Like the fires of my homeworld are trying to consume me," Stronghammer said. "But I am not afraid."

"Sanrec . . ." he started, but the time for words was over. "I'm sorry."

Stronghammer laughed, his joy cutting off with a sharp inhale. "You are not a great leader, Shriv Suurgav," the big man said with a grimace. "Only mediocre. But maybe in time you will be great." He shrugged.

Shriv couldn't argue with that. "I told you not to expect a lot when this started."

"Commander Dameron said a person must make choices to do better. I do not regret my choice to follow you." He tempered the words with a half smile, but it didn't make Shriv feel any less like a failure. He should have never let them put him in this position. Two of Dross Squadron down, and nothing but empty hands to show for it so far.

In the distance they could hear shouting, the sound of dozens of feet coming their way.

"We're out of time," Puwan said. "Now or never if we all want to get across."

"Go," Shriv said. "You and Pacer first. Then Wesson and Raidah. I'll bring up the rear."

The Scrapper didn't argue. Just attached the carabiner on her harness to the wire she had laid out earlier and leapt off the edge of the platform. Pacer moved to follow her. Raidah attached Wesson and

pressed the buttons on her gloves to send her partner into open air; then, with one last look back at
Stronghammer, Raidah did the same.

"I wanted to fly one last time," the big man said
to Shriv, his voice heavy. "But I guess it wasn't
meant to be. Take those ships back to the Resistance," Stronghammer added. "And when you fly
that big bird through the atmosphere and reach
space, you look back down here and you think of
me, eh?"

"I can do that."

"There!" came a shout from the corridor, and
then Stronghammer was bellowing and firing the
rifle he had claimed from a dead stormtrooper, and
Shriv was running for the wire. He hooked himself
in, hands feeling clumsy in his navigational gloves,
and launched himself off the edge. Blasterfire echoed
through the hall he left behind.

He flexed his fingers in his gloves and activated
the thrusters attached to his rig, accelerating out
over the abyss. He kept his eyes focused on his destination, the platform with the X-wings almost a
kilometer ahead. He did not look down at the ocean
of teeth below him. And he did not wet himself, as
he so desperately wanted to do.

But when the cable above him suddenly went
slack, sagging as if it had broken loose from its
mooring, and Shriv started the slide backward and
down, quickly accelerating into a free fall, he did
scream.

CHAPTER 28

WHEN SHRIV WAS A child, he got into a nest of bluebarb wasps. He was stung so badly that his face swelled up, big as a Cardekkia cheese wheel. The medic had dosed him with so much antivenin that he had felt like he was melting, flesh dripping off bone to puddle like wax at his feet. Not exactly that bone-crushing feeling of stepping onto a high-gravity planet for the first time unsuspecting, but the drag and the pull and the pain . . . that was the same.

That's how he felt now, as his free fall into the Ibdis Maw was abruptly cut short when someone or something slammed against him, hurtling him into the solid beams of the metal tower just below the edge of the platform that had been his target. His head struck first, a solid hit to his temple, and he grunted at the impact. His body quickly followed, and only the reinforced ribbing in the vest Puwan had made him wear kept his insides from being crushed. His breath rushed out in an agonized grunt.

"I've got you," a distant voice shouted. He felt the vibration of the sound, the kiss of spittle and breath against his ear, but the voice seemed so far away. *Concussion,* he thought to himself. *Head injury. And I can't hear so well.*

The voice was shouting other things, things that sounded like "cut cable" and "close call" and "monster's meal," but he couldn't be sure. Rough hands shook him, and he finally pried his eyes open.

Pacer Agoyo was close to his face, looking concerned.

"You okay?" the boy asked.

Shriv wasn't sure, but he knew he wasn't dead because the pain in his head was worse than any afterlife could have dreamed up, even in his warped imagination.

"I think something's broken," he finally managed.

Pacer touched his head, surprisingly gentle, turning it this way and that. "Naw, you're fine. But you got your bell rung but good!"

"I can't hear." Which wasn't entirely true. It just sounded like everything was down at the opposite end of a deep well.

A sudden breeze scraped across the top of Shriv's head, making him shiver. Another cable like the one they had used to zipline dropped from an open panel above him. He looked up, and through the trapdoor in the platform floor he saw Raidah and Puwan. Puwan waved.

"We'll get you up there, boss," Pacer said, already attaching the new line to Shriv's carabiner. And within seconds he was being hauled unceremoniously up and through the hole. Hands pulled him the final few meters, and he found himself lying flat on his back against the warm metal platform.

"You okay?" Puwan asked, grinning wildly. "Because that was something else. Troopers back on the train station cut your cord and I thought for sure you were a goner. But Pacer launched himself over the edge and caught you. Never seen anything like it." She was beaming. "My brother is a natural Rigger."

"That's great," Shriv said. His head was still pounding and he still couldn't hear, but at least he was alive. And he owed it all to the kid. "Great," he repeated.

"They're up to something over there," Raidah said, hand over her eyes as she squinted back at where they'd come from. "Looks like they might be setting up some kind of weapon. A repeater cannon or something."

Pacer's head popped out of the hole next to Shriv. He pulled the rest of his body through, grinning. Puwan hugged her brother, talking breathlessly about his daredevil save.

"You got that sighter, Puwan?" Raidah asked, voice tense.

She handed Raidah what looked like a monoccular. The pilot held it to one eye. She sucked in a harsh breath. "Cannon," she confirmed. "If we're going, we'd better go."

The woman held out a hand and hauled Shriv to his feet. He looked around. The payload on the platform was even more spectacular than he could have hoped for. A whole freaking platform of X-wings.

Four T-70s just like he used to fly himself, an older model, T-65B, and one T-85 looking way too new to scrap for parts.

"Sweet buttered biscuits," Shriv murmured. "Dross Squadron's got starfighters."

"But only two of them will fly," Raidah said. "The T-70s are all missing an alluvial damper. I did get the T-85 to power up, though." She strode purposefully toward the ship in question, talking to Shriv over her shoulder. "It would have been easier with an astromech, but I think we can at least get them in the air. Not sure about weapons systems or hyperdrives, but they haven't been completely stripped for scrap."

"Can we tow them?"

"How?"

"Salvage all that cable, and we'll link them up. We'll fly the ones that we can get airborne and tow the rest."

Puwan, who had been listening, scratched thoughtfully at her chin. "Cable's strong," she acknowledged, "but I don't know if it's that strong."

"Only one way to find out."

Shriv's eyes wandered back to the T-70s. He headed over to the one that looked to be in the best shape. "You try to start this one?" he asked over his shoulder.

"It looks like it's missing its alluvial damper, just like the others. I didn't bother."

Shriv ran a hand across the metal hull, thinking. He'd hotwired his own ship enough times in the past to know how to bypass an alluvial damper. Of

STAR WARS: RESISTANCE REBORN   335

course, back then he'd had tools and an astromech to help, but it shouldn't be impossible.

"Start rigging up the tows," he commanded. "I'm going to see if I can power this baby up." He gazed across the abyss. "How's that First Order cannon coming along?"

Raidah raised Puwan's eyepiece again. "Still setting it up," she said, after a minute. "I think we're too far away or something. Looks like they're trying to rig something to compensate for distance."

"Well, let's do what we can before they figure it out."

They did, hauling up cable and fashioning hitches. They were almost done when the world below their feet started to slide sideways.

At first Shriv thought it was his head injury acting up, but as the others cried out and they all leaned forward, he realized what it was. He'd seen the way the platform with the big ships had tilted almost vertical to dump its load into the Ibdis Maw.

"Took them longer than I thought it would to find the tilt command," Puwan said, knees bent and arms wrapped around the landing gear of one of the X-wings. "But it was inevitable."

Shriv wanted to ask her why she hadn't bothered to mention it to him if it was inevitable, but he supposed it didn't matter now. "That's our signal to fly," he said through gritted teeth. "Lock and load."

Wesson, who had been sitting under the shade of an X-wing sweating and looking green around the edges, gave him a grin. She had blood between her teeth.

Shriv returned the smile.

"How're you feeling?" he asked as he approached. She held out a hand, and he got her to her feet.

"Might be a little hard to fly one of these ships, but I'll make it."

"I'll put her in a tow ship," Raidah said as she joined him. "That way all she has to do is hold on."

"You think you can handle it?"

Wesson's eyes were flint. "Absolutely, Dross Leader."

"Okay." He gestured for Raidah to get on with it.

Raider helped load Wesson into the cockpit of one of the T-70s in tow, attached to the T-85, where she took the reins. Pacer was already waiting in the T-65B. With a shake of his head Shriv hopped in the T-70 he'd been working on. The platform continued its slow tilt, and Shriv gave the command for the others to go. Pacer and Raidah lifted vertically off the platform with no trouble. Their tows were attached at the nose and the rear, so that once the primary ship had enough lift, the secondary ship would follow like they were stacked one on top of the other. Shriv watched nervously as the cables reached their maximum stretch and pulled tight. Puwan wasn't sure they would hold, but they did. Slowly, slowly they lifted off the platform.

With the other two clear, Shriv readied for liftoff.

The space in front of Shriv's fighter exploded. Platform debris pattered down against the transparisteel of his cockpit and he involuntarily ducked. The canopy held.

"Where did that come from?" he shouted into his comm.

"Cannon fire," Pacer's voice answered. "Looks like they figured it out."

"Want me to take them out . . . wait . . ." Cursing and what sounded like a fist against metal filtered through Shriv's earpiece. "Weapons system down."

"It's fine," Shriv said. "Your job is to get those ships out of here. Besides, you're hauling a second ship and your maneuverability will be compromised. I'll be fine. You and Raidah get those X-wings back and complete the mission."

Silence on the other end, and Shriv felt a spark of frustration ignite. "Follow an order, Agoyo!" he shouted. "Get out of here."

After a moment, Pacer answered. "Copy that. Dross Two and Dross Three away."

Shriv grinned. "Dross Leader, copy."

Another explosion, this one practically beneath him, and he realized the tilting platform must be moving him closer to the First Order cannon. The view outside his cockpit was also slanting increasingly toward rows of metal-grinding teeth, and the weight of the extra ship in tow at his back left him unsure if the T-70 would respond in time to get him clear. He'd waited too long, and now he was stuck. The only way out would be attempting a tricky sweeping maneuver down into the Ibdis Maw to avoid the cannon; if he tried a vertical takeoff, he'd do it directly into the line of fire. Slathering pit beast or First Order cannon? This scenario was feeling a little too familiar, but just like before, Shriv promptly decided he'd rather take his chances with the cannon. He flipped on the forward deflector shields, engaged the X-wing's thrusters, and said a prayer to whoever or whatever might be listening.

As he rose, the world around him exploded. The ship rattled violently. His already injured head slammed against the transparisteel, and for a moment he saw stars. The shield indicator light blinked and then dimmed, and the engine whined under the stress of the slow lift. He gave it more power, but the ship didn't respond. He needed an astromech to fix the shields, to boost the thrusters, but it was only him. He was all out of options, and he'd made a terrible mistake. The shield light went dark. Shields dead. "Shoulda went with the pit beast," he muttered. He braced for the impact of cannon fire.

More explosions, but these were in the distance. A shadow fell over the cockpit and he looked up. The transport vessel they'd taken to Bracca hovered above him, blanketing the train station populated with First Order troops with fire. He laughed. The transport didn't have much of a weapons system. It was only meant for limited defense against pirates and the like, but it was enough to decimate the train platform and the stormtrooper cannon.

"Zay!" he shouted into the comm. "Where did you come from?"

"You're all over the newsfeeds. Rogue guilders stealing ships. Guild's denying that you're one of them, but the First Order swears! You've started a galactic incident!"

"Great!"

The transport pulled away, and Shriv cleared the platform. "Where are the others?"

"They're away. I came back to check on you. Good thing I did."

"Sure is," he said, giddy with relief.

They passed through the thick atmosphere and above it, and Shriv had never been so happy to see the black of space. He spared a thought for Sanrec Stronghammer, like he said he would.

"Back to Ryloth?" Zay asked.

"You said it, space baby."

And this time, she laughed.

CHAPTER 29

CHAOS SWIRLED AROUND POE, a surreal overload of the senses as party guests panicked and ran for their lives. The crash of crystal cups and the shatter of fine furniture filled the air. Despite the edict against weapons, someone—several someones by the sound of it—must have sneaked a blaster in because soon the air was filled with laserfire, overturned tables, and chairs turned into makeshift shelters, as the people fought back.

The invading First Order had left open the grand doors and a wind straight off the sea swept through the building, slicking the white stone floors and leaving the salt and sea so thick in the air Poe could almost taste it under the acrid burn of smoke. All of it accompanied by the continuous sound of blasterfire and the strange illlusions of swimming fish and sea creatures. The scene was a nightmare mix of the surreal and the all-too-real, as people died on both sides.

Over it all, the skeletal First Order officer yelled for calm, but the damage had been done. No one was listening.

Poe took the opportunity to move through the room, keeping low, Finn at his side.

"We need to find Suralinda and Charth," he said over his shoulder.

"We need to find a couple of blasters," Finn countered.

"Both," Poe said. "Both would be good."

"Look!"

Poe followed Finn's directive and there, behind the artificial rocks of a waterfall, was Suralinda, returning fire with a fallen stormtrooper's rifle. They wound their way over to her, ducking behind columns and avoiding the frightened crowd.

"Where's Charth?" Poe asked as he reached her side, breathing hard.

Suralinda glanced his way, and they all ducked as another blaster shot shattered the rocks just above her head.

"He went for the ship. What happened?"

"They must have found out about the auction." He gestured toward her blaster with his chin. "Don't suppose you have another one of those?"

She smiled, showing fangs. "Go get your own. I did."

"A little help, then?"

She leaned out, taking her time to aim despite incoming fire, and took down the stormtrooper closest to her. Finn darted forward to retrieve his weapon, Suralinda giving cover fire. He grabbed the blaster and ran to a large column a dozen meters away.

"Good?" she asked.

"We can't leave yet," Poe said. "We've got to get that list."

Suralinda frowned. "The list is lost," she said. "We've got to get out of here alive."

Suddenly the lights went out, plunging the room into darkness.

"What now?" Poe muttered. Small floor illuminators blinked on around the room, offering just enough light to avoid tripping over his own feet, but not enough to see who was coming for them.

"At least that damn ocean holo is off," Suralinda said.

She was right. For the first time since they'd arrived, the oversized room was devoid of its strange artificial underwaterscape.

Something caught his eye, a glimpse of glowing white hurrying up a flight of stairs behind Finn. It was Nifera Shu, still alive and likely running for her life. Her white shell dress glowed even in the darkness. And something else glowed, too. The serpent around her neck.

Of course.

"You and Finn find Charth and get to the ship," Poe said, an idea forming in his mind.

"What? Where will you be?"

"I'm going to get that list."

He caught up to Nifera Shu on the edge of a second-story balcony, frantically trying to reach someone with the comlink in her hand.

"Nifera!" he shouted.

She spun to face him, panic widening her eyes. The albino eel slithered around her neck, looking as distressed as its mistress. Poe eyed it warily.

"They killed my husband," she whispered breathlessly. "They murdered Hasadar in front of me. In front of everyone."

"I know," Poe said. He'd spread his arms wide to show he wasn't armed, that he meant her no harm. "Because of the list." He glanced at the eel. He could see now that the creature had the stubs of tiny antlerlike horns protruding from its head. It was so similar to the creature that he had seen open the auction holo that it couldn't be a coincidence. "Because of the Collective."

Something in her face crumbled. "Because of me," she said, her voice a low wail.

"And they're coming for you," he said. As if to reinforce his words, something below them in the main room collapsed, powerful enough to shake the balcony they stood on. Poe crashed shoulder-first into the wall. Nifera gripped the railing to keep herself from falling.

"I've got to get out of here," she said. She lifted her comlink again, pressing the buttons. Nothing happened.

"They've blocked your signal," Poe said, taking an educated guess.

"No," she said, shaking her head. "I dropped it when they shot . . ." Her whole body heaved. "I-I think it's broken."

"And the list?" he asked, heart pounding.

She touched her hand to the head of the horned

serpent. "Here." She lifted the creature's head and pressed gently on either side of its jaws. It obediently opened its mouth. Poe could see a tiny datachip resting on its tongue.

"I can get you out of here," he said. "We've got a ship."

"The Resistance?" she asked knowingly. "That is who you're with, Lorell?"

He nodded. No reason to hide it now.

"And what will it cost me?"

He thrust his chin in the direction of the serpent. She seemed to hesitate.

Footsteps sounded on the steps behind them, and Nifera's face paled at whatever she saw behind his shoulder.

"Now or never," Poe said urgently, eyes focused on Nifera, back itching from not looking behind him. "Give that list to the Resistance or take your chances with the First Order. Do we have a deal?"

She nodded sharply. "Deal."

"Great." Poe reached out and grabbed her hand, pulling her to the edge of the balcony. Twenty meters below them was a dark pool of water, one of those that graced the ornamental gardens they had passed through on their way to the party.

"How deep is that water?" he asked.

"I-I have no idea."

He climbed over the railing, and helped her follow, awkward in her shell dress. "Let's find out," he said.

And they jumped.

———

They hit the water together.

The cold enveloped him immediately, water rushing in to soak his limbs through his clothes and surge over his head. He felt Nifera's hand start to slip from his, the weight of her dress dragging her down, and he tightened his grip, pulling her closer. He fought to keep his mouth closed, to hold his breath until he could get his bearings. He looked around frantically, his world an undulation of dark salty waters punctuated by blue beams of light.

It was the light that helped him orient. The lamps were at the bottom of the pool, which meant down. Which meant swimming away from them was up.

So he kicked up, dragging Nifera with him.

Finally, his head broke the surface and he gasped, gulping in air as fast as he could.

Rough hands reached into the icy water, dragging him to dry land by the back of his jacket. He looked up, half expecting to see First Order troops, but it was Finn, a wide grin of relief on his face. "I can't believe you jumped," he said, laughing.

Next to Poe, Suralinda pulled Nifera to the sloping green shore.

"Your necklace!" Poe said, alarmed. She'd lost the eel creature somewhere in the water.

Calmly, the woman dipped a hand in the water and seconds later the serpent was slithering up her arm, all the way to its safe place around her neck.

"Cute trick," Suralinda observed.

"A better trick would be to tell me we have a way

out of here," Poe said as Finn pulled him to his feet. "Where's Charth?"

"Headed back to us," Suralinda answered. "No luck on the ship. It's locked down tight, the whole landing dock surrounded by stormtroopers."

"I thought you were going to get me out of here, Lorell," Nifera complained.

"I am. We are. We just . . . need to think of another plan."

"Well, I suggest we do it quick," Suralinda said. "I figure we only have a few minutes before we've got our own contingent of troopers to deal with."

She was right. They were too exposed here. There were shadows in the garden, trees with arching canopies and shrubbery two meters high that would help hide them, but once the chaos inside was controlled, the First Order would be sweeping the grounds. Sooner if they realized that Nifera had escaped.

"What about Wedge?" Finn said.

Poe turned. "Go on."

"He's here, right? And he's got a ship. We get to him, we got a ship, too."

"Brilliant," Poe said, meaning it. "Now all we need to know is where he is."

"I'll hail Connix back on Ryloth," Suralinda offered. "Maybe she can pinpoint Wedge's position."

She turned away, comlink in hand, and Poe could hear her talking, relaying their situation.

"What's going on?" Nifera asked, warily. She narrowed eyes at them. "Who is Wedge? And who are you . . . really?"

Finn stepped up. "We're with the Resistance, ma'am. And we're here to help."

The woman frowned, a hand going to her pet at her throat. "Lorell said as much on the balcony, and you with your starbird pin. But if you think I'm one of you, you're mistaken. The Collective doesn't support any government."

"We're not a government," Poe countered. "We're more like . . ." his gaze traveled to Suralinda who was still engrossed in her conversation, ". . . a ragtag group of heroes."

Nifera pursed dubious lips. "Heroes? I suppose that remains to be seen."

"Okay," Suralinda said, cutting the transmission as she turned back to face them. "I've got coordinates on Wedge's team, but we need to hurry. They're on the move."

"And Charth?" Poe asked.

"He'll meet us on the way."

"Where are we heading?"

"Corellian Engineering Corporation."

"You know the direction?"

"I do," Nifera offered.

"Then let's go."

They all followed Nifera across the garden, staying close to the shadowy greenery. Suralinda lingered behind, touching Poe on the arm to get his attention.

"Something wrong?" he asked.

"I didn't want to say more in front of Nifera, but there's trouble on Ryloth," she said, voice low.

"What kind of trouble?" he asked, concerned. "Is Leia okay?"

"Connix didn't go into detail," she said, "but she said they are evacuating."

"We've got to get back."

"And we will. We're trying. We need a ship for that. So we stick to the plan, get off this planet, and go rescue our people."

There wasn't much else they could do. A surge of helplessness rattled through him. He should be there to protect Leia, to help his friends on Ryloth. But he couldn't be everywhere. Right now he was here, and he had to complete this mission. Ryloth or no Ryloth, Leia needed that list.

Poe quickened his pace, scared that failure even now dogged his steps. But he wouldn't let Leia down again. He would not fail. He would get this right, even if it killed him.

CHAPTER 30

WINSHUR DRAGGED AS FAR behind Colonel Genial as he dared. They had climbed considerably, up far enough that if he looked back the way they had come, he could see the government and business districts shrinking behind them. Why hadn't they taken a transport to come this far? Maybe Genial thought the walk would be good for them. Maybe he hated public transportation, or maybe there were no transports available at this time of the night. Maybe walking simply gave him more time to berate Winshur.

The man had kept up a constant censure as they made their way through the streets of Coronet City to the wealthy district where Hasadar Shu lived. At first, Winshur had flinched every time Genial spit another insult at him. His words had cut bitter lines of shame across Winshur's conscience as if they had been physical blows, and Winshur was back in religious school all over again, degraded and deserving of his degradation.

Winshur felt spent. Undone. And here he was

marching willingly to his inevitable end on the weak promise of a merciful death from a man he did not trust to have any mercy in him.

But after the fifteenth biting remark about Winshur's traitorous ways, something snapped. He began to see the lie in it. He was not a traitor to the First Order. He could not be. He loved everything it stood for. He had given everything of himself to the cause, upheld its values and beliefs.

His gaze went to his surroundings. The bridge they were crossing was an arc that stretched over a wide expanse of water; an inland channel of the sea that Coronet City bordered ran far below them, waters cold as the sea itself. Usually the channel was filled with boats hauling goods or small pleasure craft escaping the city. But at this time of night, the water was empty. In fact, the streets around them were empty. Quiet. Except for Genial's grating insults.

Ahead of them, just over the cresting hill, Winshur could see the brightly lit home of Hasadar Shu. It had to be it. Even from this far away, he could hear the high hum of music and voices raised to be heard over the music. They were almost there, and then what?

For the moment they still stood in the generous gloom. Shadows pooled around them, creating a darkness that Winshur had never cared for before but now felt a profound kinship with.

He felt himself floating, high above the bridge, the colonel, too. Himself. As if he could look down from a great height and see the two tiny men on the tiny bridge with the vast ocean below and around them. At first, he didn't like what he saw. The one man tall and authoritative, the other small and beaten. But when he looked closer, he could see the smaller man was growing. Burgeoning. Spreading like the sea.

"Who is Winshur Bratt now?" he asked himself. "And who will he be?"

Colonel Genial turned sharply. "Did you say something?"

His voice was a challenge that a more timid Winshur, a Winshur of even ten minutes ago, would have ducked and evaded. But this strange floating Winshur, this other him, the growing him, the one who felt the possibilities of violence for the first time, simply smiled.

Genial's eyes narrowed. "Is this a joke to you?"

Winshur shook his head no.

"Then pick up your pace. We want to be there when the criminal is detained." Genial's mouth turned down cruelly. "And you are faced with your failure."

Screams punctured the air, small but distinct and growing. On their heels, blasterfire. All coming from the house on the hill.

"Dammit, we're late!" Genial growled. "Hurry up, Bratt."

Winshur made his feet move. They were like concrete at first, heavy and impossible. But as his resolve solidified, his feet became lighter, just like his consciousness, and soon he was running. Light as a feather. Light as moonlight.

Winshur didn't slow as he approached the colonel. He went faster, faster still, and tackled Genial below the waist. Genial slammed against the railing with a grunt, bending backward into the open air. Winshur heaved, lifted the taller man up, tipping him over the bridge railing. He did it quickly, before he could think. Before he could change his mind.

Genial's eyes widened in confusion, and then shock. His arms windmilled for balance, but it was too late. He was falling.

He tumbled through the Coronet City night, away from Winshur, away from the bridge. He struck the chill waters below without ever uttering a sound.

Winshur leaned against the rail, panting. Watching with terrible vision to see if the blue-eyed man would resurface.

He waited minutes.

Nothing.

He waited a little longer.

Still nothing and he found himself laughing. Louder, gasping for air, hysterical and wild.

He knew that if someone heard him now, they would think him insane. But he was the sanest he had ever been.

Was it that easy to vanquish your nightmares? Why hadn't he known? Why hadn't anyone told him?

He scanned the streets around him but saw no one.

Easy to explain, he thought to himself. Genial had slipped and fallen. Or the real traitors had gotten him, and Winshur had tried his best to fight them off. Look at the blow to his face that he had taken in the colonel's defense. Or perhaps he had never even seen Genial this night.

Yes, that was it. He would just pretend this never happened.

No. That was the old Winshur talking. The new Winshur could do better. He could find Monti Calay and drag the traitor to First Order justice himself. Then what would high command say? They would have to absolve him, maybe even give him that promotion, make him a hero. All he needed was Monti Calay's personnel file and home address in the records back at his office.

A smile leaked across his face, bright as shadow.

He was done with being afraid, done with cowering.

Darkness fell like a blanket around him, and at first, he thought it was his doing somehow. He looked around himself, amazed. Somehow, the lights in the big house on the hill had all gone out.

He gaped for a moment, exhilarated.

And then he was running as fast as he could, back to his office.

CHAPTER 31

WEDGE AND THE REST of the team followed Yama Dex through the sprawling campus of the Corellian Engineering Corporation. It consisted of three identical skytowers and all the adjoining gardens and water features that connected the buildings in a sort of industrial park. Wedge remembered that Coronet City, and Corellia itself, had always been a unique mix of the environmentally conscious and the unabashedly industrial. The city combined flora and fabrication with a kind of hubris that Wedge had always admired. He'd never seen another planet do it so well. Of course, maybe he was biased. He had grown up here.

They reached the dormitory building, which looked like all the other buildings surrounding it. Despite the lush grounds, there was something decidedly unfriendly in the design of these particular structures, something that screamed utility but lacked warmth. He said as much to Norra and she shrugged.

"Built by engineers," she offered. "Maybe they were more worried about function."

It made him miss his farm with its eclectic kitchen and colorful dishes. He was sure all the dishes here were a uniform colorless gray.

Yama pulled up short, looking back over her shoulder.

Nasz peered around the corner. "Guards at the entrance," she whispered. "We need to take them out."

Wedge said, "Let's try to keep the noise to a minimum."

"I can do that. Give me five minutes." Nasz shouldered her rifle and slunk off into the shadows.

They counted the five minutes down, tense as tauntauns.

Nasz came back promptly on the five. She motioned them forward, and they all followed. They stepped over the bodies of the guards. One had the side of his head bashed in, and the other had been garroted. Wedge tried not to wince, but Nasz caught him looking and grinned, showing her blue teeth.

"One day I'll ask you about Rattatak," he said.

"Please do."

"Dormitory F is up six levels," Yama said. "Do we take the lift?"

"Stairs," Wedge said. They'd avoid lifts from here out if they could. Too easy to be ambushed while stuffed in a tiny metal box.

Floor F was a soulless industrial wasteland that made the grounds outside that Wedge had thought

cold look downright welcoming. Rows of feature-
less doors greeted them, tiny barred windows at eye
level their only feature.

"A prison," Nasz said as she reached out to try a
handle. "What did I tell you?"

"How do we know where Ransolm is?"

"Prisoner 876549C?" Snap asked. "I guess we go
door-to-door."

"No, there's an office somewhere," Nasz said.
"And in that office, there's a list. I'm telling you, it's
the Imperial way, which means it's the First Order
way, too. Authoritarians thrive on paperwork.
Somewhere, there's a list."

Wedge wasn't convinced, but she had figured out
where to look in the records to get them this far, so
he didn't argue. "Go search for the list," he said.
"We'll start knocking on doors."

They split up, Snap taking one side and Norra the
other. Wedge and Yama started on opposite ends.
Most knocks yielded no responses. Either the rooms
were empty or the occupants were sleeping. One
knock produced a bloodcurdling scream that made
them all shiver, and then more responses came after
that. Some weeping, others begging. But no answers
came to the name Ransolm, which they had each
whispered as they moved methodically down the
halls.

"We can't leave them," Norra said, once they met
in the center. "This is awful. And these people are
our allies. We can't leave them."

Wedge felt the same. "So we get them all out."

"Can we fit them all on the shuttle?" Snap asked.

"Not in the shuttle we came on, but there's a whole bay full of ships back there. We'll figure out something."

"What if they don't want to come?" Yama asked.

"Why wouldn't they want to come?" Snap asked, face puzzled. "You think they want to stay in a First Order prison?"

"No, but not everyone wants to join the Resistance."

"They won't have to join," Wedge told her. "That's not how it works."

"We get them out," Norra said, "and we let them decide. They can come with us and try to get off-planet in a hurry, or they can go their own way. Either way is better than these cages." She shuddered.

"Agreed," Wedge said. "Now how do we get the doors open?"

An alarm shattered the night, three sharp bursts of a warning, and then the doors all opened at once. They stood, staring.

Nasz came around the corner at a run. "Found the office," she said. "There was a big button marked for emergencies, so I pushed it." She put her hands on her hips. "Look at that."

Slowly, people were emerging from their cells. Most looked confused, wary.

"Did you find Prisoner 876549C?"

"Cell eight."

Cell 8 was some distance down the hall. Wedge

made his way over, unsure what he would find. Behind him he could hear Norra and Snap explaining to the prisoners that they were free.

A man was emerging from cell 8. He was tall and gaunt like the others, but he had a presence, even now. His sandy hair had gone to gray. He had been washed and shaved recently, although not kindly by the look of the cuts on his face. He looked up at Wedge with intelligent but wary blue eyes.

"Ransolm?" Wedge asked. "Ransolm Casterfo?"

The man didn't acknowledge the name, but his eyes stayed fixed on Wedge.

"Are you Ransolm Casterfo?" Wedge tried again, trying to keep his voice gentle, the way he might for a scared cadet back at the academy.

"I was once," the man finally said, his voice a dry and painful whisper. "But no one has called me by that name in a very long time."

Wedge's shoulders dropped in relief. They had found him. "A friend sent me to free you."

Ransolm frowned, deep lines forming at his mouth. "I have no friends. My name is a curse, a bad omen. I am forsaken."

Wedge shook his head. "No, Senator."

Ransolm flinched at the title, and Wedge wished he could take it back.

He tried a different approach. "We've been sent by Leia Organa to find you."

"Leia . . ." He breathed the name like a prayer. And then, "They told me she was dead."

"She's very much alive," Wedge said reassuringly. "And she wants you to come with us. And I don't mean to pressure you, but I expect the First Order to show up any minute, so maybe we can discuss the details on the way."

Ransolm blinked. "Yes," he said quietly. "Best not to keep royalty waiting."

"Wedge." It was Snap. "I just received a communication from Karé back at the shuttle. She said a message came in via Ryloth. Poe's team has lost their ship."

"Lost?"

"There was some sort of commotion in the background, Karé said. She couldn't catch the details. Bottom line, they're stuck."

"Tell them to rendezvous here. We'll get them off the planet."

"How?" His eyes roved across the prisoners standing in the hall. "We're going to have trouble with the people we have now."

Wedge thought of that blockade runner that he'd spied when they first arrived. "We'll think of something. How many are coming with us?"

"Eleven. The other four prefer to be on their own."

"And the Subversives list? Did Dameron get the list?"

"Unclear."

Wedge rubbed at his cheek, worried.

Footsteps, and Wedge turned to see Norra running down the hall. "Someone's coming," she said, breathless, blaster in hand.

Wedge nodded. "Tell Karé to get Poe's team over here to our coordinates now. We'll hold as long as we can, but we've got to get these prisoners off the planet. They're in no shape to fight."

"And if he doesn't make it?"

"Tell Dameron that's not an option. He comes here. Now."

CHAPTER 32

WINSHUR ALMOST DIDN'T SEE the traitors.

He was so intent on getting back to his office and getting hold of Monti Calay's personnel file that his mind was somewhere else entirely. He caught a flash of orange hair and stopped in his tracks.

Yama. She was alive. Right here in front of him. And this was all her fault.

If she hadn't gone to Genial. If she hadn't provoked him.

Why did she constantly labor to vex him?

A film of rage darkened his vision. He should have killed her, crushed her head in when he had the chance. It was not too late.

The breadth of his audacity astounded him, and for a moment a sliver of doubt crept back in, the barest suggestion that he was a murderer contemplating yet another murder and that it was wrong.

And then he looked back at her, sneaking through the grounds, obviously doing something she was not supposed to be doing, and doubt fled. She had been put back in his path for a reason.

He watched her move stealthily through the night. Her pace was hesitant, and she paused at corners and in puddles of shadow to scout her way. Every so often she'd look back to whatever was behind her and then move forward again.

She headed down an underground passage that he knew ran beneath the main campus and to the far entrance to the shipyard. Why would she be going to the shipyard at this time of night? The reason didn't matter to him, but it felt all the more fortuitous. There were many ways one could come to harm in a shipyard.

He slipped from his own shadows and followed her.

Down they went into the long narrow walkway. The lights here buzzed low and disparate overhead, blinking uncertainly to illuminate the cold concrete underfoot in sporadic bursts. Winshur squinted through the poor light looking for her, but she had disappeared.

Impossible.

He hurried his pace, moving in and out of the darkness, looking frantically for a head of unruly orange curls. But he saw nothing. Just a long stretch of empty tunnel before him.

He was about to turn around and chalk the episode up to some kind of strange delusion brought on by the revelations of the night when she stepped from a maintenance alcove he had somehow missed before. She held a long stretch of metal pipe in her hand and her face, a face bruised by his boot, was set in determined lines.

He grinned. This was better than he could have expected. Killing an innocent was one thing, but a fight, an actual fight—well, no one could fault him for defending himself.

He walked forward, hands spread. "You must be angry with me," he said, hoping to lure her closer. "But do you remember what I told you, Yama, about power coming from discipline? I was disciplining you." It was a lie, of course. He had only meant to hurt her, to make her suffer, as he always had. But it sounded good coming from his lips, and he clung to it.

Her grip tightened on the pipe. A memory of her standing the same way, a box cutter in her hand, flashed through his mind. Understanding dawned. She must have confronted Monti in his office, must have been threatening him with that blade when Winshur interrupted them. She had tried to tell him something, he remembered, but he assumed it was more excuses for why she wasn't working. Perhaps if he'd listened, things would be very different right now. Or perhaps she would have told him lies.

"You told me discipline meant controlling your baser instincts," she said.

He hesitated. "I did . . ."

"But you didn't!"

Her voice was a wail, a plea for understanding. *She still admires me,* he thought. *She still wants me to guide her.* Something shifted inside him, something shameful that he thought he had suppressed. Nausea rose like a wave in his gut.

"You beat me," she continued, "for no other reason than because you were angry, at yourself, your own weakness, and you took it out on me!"

"I . . ." Winshur blinked, feeling unmoored. Where was the darkness that had sustained him moments ago? The boldness?

"No," he said, finding his footing again. "I did it for your own good." But he remembered the horror he had felt, the loathing. "For your own good," he repeated, as if to convince himself.

He was close enough now to see that he had broken her nose and blacked her eye. Her bottom lip was split, too. He swallowed nervously at the sight of his own handiwork.

"Don't come any closer," she warned. She shifted her grip on the pipe, her hands sweating.

He took a step forward. "Yama," he whispered, her name echoing in the tunnel. He wasn't sure what he meant to do when he reached her. Hit her? Snatch the pipe from her hands and beat her with it? Or fall to his knees and ask for forgiveness.

She swung.

He sidestepped her attempt, but she reversed, bringing the pipe up for a downward strike, and he wasn't fast enough to avoid it. He took the blow across the shoulder. Pain radiated from the contact, and his rage bubbled up to the surface again. He grabbed at the pipe, catching it mid-swing. He wrenched it from her hands. Yama, pulled forward by the momentum, fell to her knees.

He stood over her, panting. The crude weapon was his now, and while he told himself he took no pleasure in defeating a child, a strange delight suffused his body. It warred with his other emotions, the shame, the confusion.

She was crying. He could hear her soft sobs. She looked up at him, face raw with feeling.

"I did everything you told me to," she said. "But I could never please you."

"Please me?" he asked, bewildered. "You tried to destroy me."

She blinked.

"The meeting with Shu, the smirks behind my back, the sabotage of my work. You went to Genial!"

"When you wouldn't listen. I-I did it for your own good!"

The words came out of her mouth, an echo of Winshur's own, and they both froze in horror.

"No," he whispered as he reared back to swing the pipe at her head.

"Wouldn't do that" came a voice from behind him.

He lurched to a halt. Still holding the pipe, he turned, incredulous, to see who had interrupted him.

A woman, tall and muscular and wearing a canvas jacket and jumpsuit made of fur and metal. She had a blaster on one hip, still holstered, and a rifle slung over one shoulder. She looked him up and down, as if judging. She shook her head in disappointment.

"So you're the piece of crap that beat up a defenseless fifteen-year-old girl?"

Winshur paled. He tightened his grip on the pipe.

The woman noticed and raised an ocher-stained eyebrow.

"Really?" she asked.

"Go away, barbarian," Winshur cried, frustration leaking into his voice. "You don't understand. This is none of your business."

"The name's Teza Nasz, former officer in the Galactic Empire, and that's warlord to you, Bratt."

Winshur swayed. She knew his name, and she was a former Imperial. He felt weak.

"Now this could go one of two ways," she said, voice casual. "You could hand that nice bit of metal in your hand back to my friend Yama, and she can beat you until your face approximately matches her own. Give or take."

He stared, not speaking.

"Or," she said, taking that rifle down off her shoulder, "I could just shoot you."

Winshur's lips twisted in a sneer. This foolish woman knew nothing, even if she did claim to be an Imperial. How dare she threaten him. He found some of his old bravado and scoffed, "I would never deign to allow this foolish girl to—"

He was cut off by the sound of blasterfire thundering in his ears and heat in his belly like he'd never felt before. He collapsed, his head striking the cold concrete. His mouth gaped open in shock.

"Good," Nasz said cheerfully. "We're kind of in a hurry, so thanks for making that easy."

Winshur lay there stunned, a hole in his stomach.

Footsteps approached at a run, but Winshur could only lie there and listen. His body wasn't working anymore, and his mind was fast following into oblivion.

"Everything okay?" a voice asked. Winshur saw that an older man with gray hair and wearing a brown jacket had spoken. Was he talking to Winshur? That couldn't be right.

"Everything's fine," said the woman who'd shot him. "A small problem. We took care of it." The woman walked past Winshur like he was already dead and held out a hand to the girl, pulling Yama to her feet.

"Why don't you and Snap take lead?" the woman said. "Yama's going to stay close to me until we get out of here."

"No problem." The man barely glanced at him before he was gone.

Time seemed to stretch and shrink in no particular order or reason. Winshur was sure there were other people walking past him. The sound of feet was loud in his head. His sight was dimming, the world around him fading to echoes and vibrations. He closed his eyes.

Something nudged him. A foot. He ignored it.

Another nudge and he reluctantly peeled one eyelid open. He recognized the face staring down at him. Prisoner 876549C.

Winshur thought to laugh. He was dying, bleeding out on cold pavement, and fate thought to deal him one last humiliation? But what could this man do to him that had not already been done?

The prisoner reached out a hand.

Shame flooded him. Winshur caught a sob in his throat. He closed his eyes.

Another nudge, but Winshur refused to look. He forced himself to roll over, a slow agony that was sticky and wet with blood, until he faced the wall and could no longer see the man or the glimpse of pity, of forgiveness, that he'd seen in his eyes.

The man was foolish. Winshur was dying. There was no saving him now.

"Leave me," he mumbled, but it came out garbled, unintelligible even to his own ears.

He waited for another nudge, but it didn't come, and he let loose the sob that had been stuck, a defeated mournful sound, more animal than anything else.

The footsteps passed and he was alone again.

He hurt, inside and out, but the pain was fading. Betrayal. That's all he could feel now. Not by Monti, or even Yama. It was violence that had lied to him. It had made him promises of power, but in the end, it had not saved him. It had damned him.

CHAPTER 33

LEIA SAW HAHNEE FALL.

When the attack had started, Yendor's daughter had been the first through the library door, yelling a warning about betrayal in the capital city. Now she was the first to fall, a blaster shot to her chest.

Yendor was holding the south end of the hangar so he didn't know when it happened. He and a handful of RDA fighters were keeping the First Order forces at bay so that Leia, Orrimaarko, Rieekan, the droids, and the rest of the command base could make their escape. But when Hahnee went down, a piece of Leia's heart went with the Twi'lek warrior. Then the general did the thing that came most naturally to her: She picked up Hahnee's rifle and took her position.

She pressed the trigger on the big gun and it bucked, sending fire into the enemy's advance. They cowered back, taking shelter. But the rifle was hot in her hands, already running close to empty, and Leia knew the folly of her position immediately. There was no way one person with limited firepower could hold for long. Still, she only had to hold long enough for everyone to make it to their respective ships.

"Rey!" Leia shouted over her shoulder, hoping the girl could hear her over the din of the firefight. And then Rey was there with a blaster in hand, no questions asked. They fought side by side as if they had done it a hundred times before. Gradually the assault on their position faded.

"They're retreating!" Rey shouted.

Leia nodded grimly. For now, at least. Or more likely, finding an easier advance. Or just doing the smart thing and waiting to pick them off as they exited the cave. That's what she would have done.

Chewbacca was roaring an all-clear, which also meant "Get your ass on the *Millennium Falcon* right now," and with Rey covering her back, Leia hustled across the bay and up the ramp.

Rose was there to greet her, eyes wide with worry.

"Status," Leia said, voice clipped with exhaustion.

"All personnel accounted for and on board their respective vessels. We're ready to get the heck out of here, as soon as we get word that it's clear out there."

"Clear out there," Leia echoed. "What does that mean?"

"That they're not waiting to pick us off as soon as we leave the cave, ma'am."

Leia laughed, and it was a bitter sound. "Yes, I know. And I think that's not going to happen. We'll have to take our chances. It's either that or stay here and let them regroup so they come at us again."

The rage she had been holding back surfaced momentarily. She could believe that someone in Lessu had betrayed the Resistance. After all, there was no love for them here on Ryloth, and Yendor's contacts had made it clear that the clock was ticking on their tolerance of the Resistance's presence. They had overstayed their welcome and were now suffering the price. But to betray Yendor? After his years of service, his pride in his people? That made Leia see red.

And now Hahnee. Leia would have to be the one to tell him. It was her fault, after all.

As if on cue, Leia's comm beeped furiously.

She flipped it open. "Go on."

"Leia!" Yendor's voice was a hoarse shout, and she could hear the ongoing firefight in the background. "What's your position?"

"We're all in place and accounted for," she told him. "Except . . ." She paused, trying to find the right words to tell her friend that his daughter was dead. But before she could find what she wanted to say, Yendor was talking again, but this time not to her.

". . . take two men and head for the cannon."

"Cannon?" Leia asked, surprised.

She thought she heard Yendor laugh. "Surface-to-air cover. A little surprise from the RDA that the dirtbags back in Lessu don't know about, and the First Order won't see coming. It's not much but it should give you some cover."

"You are full of surprises," she said, feeling a little awed. She took a deep breath, exhaled. There was no easy way to say what had to be said. She had hoped there was, but she knew from experience that there wasn't.

"Hahnee . . . She didn't make it. She's dead, Yendor."

Silence on the other end, and Leia thought perhaps he hadn't heard her. But she could still hear the sound of blasters through the comlink, so she tried again.

"Yendor . . . ? Did you hear me?"

"Copy, General," he said, and his voice was steady. But underneath, Leia could tell that the man was not.

"I'm sorry. She died defending us. It was a good death."

Another beat of silence before he said, "There are no good deaths, my old friend. Only death."

And with that she didn't argue.

"The children?" he asked quietly. "Charth's children?" Leia looked around the room for an answer. Rose Tico gave her a thumbs-up.

"The children are safe and accounted for."

A heavy intake of breath and then, "Okay, then. Get them to their father."

She hesitated, because she thought she knew the answer to the question before she asked it, but ask it she did. "And what about their grandfather?"

"Tell them he died directing the cannon. Tell them he died defending a free Ryloth, same as their aunt."

Leia recognized that it was the grief talking. Grief at the loss of his daughter, grief at the loss of his planet, the betrayal from Lessu. Yendor's worst nightmare was playing out around them, all the things he had warned Leia might happen, all the things she had agreed were possibilities. The Resistance was the kiss of death, to friends and allies alike.

"Yendor . . ."

"Excuse me, General Organa." It was C-3PO.

"What is it?" she asked, distracted.

"Chewbacca asked me to tell you that they are short an X-wing pilot. It seems that one of the Phantom Squadron pilots did not survive the initial First Order attack."

Leia grimaced. They could ill afford to lose a pilot, or a ship. She considered telling the droid to handle it on his own, but then a thought came to mind.

"Yendor," she said. "How do you feel about flying again?"

"What?"

"We've lost a pilot but his ship is prepped and waiting. If you can get there, we could use you."

Silence, and for a moment, Leia thought he would say no. That he would give in to his grief. But then: "I'm on my way."

"Thank you," she said, relief rushing over her.

"No, Leia. Thank you."

The communication ended and Leia turned to Rose.

"Tell Connix and Nien Nunb to get to the turrets. We're going to need the firepower. And I want to be in communication with Rieekan and Orrimaarko's ship at all times. Can you handle that?"

"On it," she said.

Leia dismissed her with a nod and made her way to the cockpit. She strapped into her old chair as Rey and the Wookiee engaged the thrusters. The *Falcon* slowly rose.

"We make a run for it, like Yendor said," Rey explained over her shoulder. "The X-wings will lead, and the others will follow."

Follow us where? Leia thought. Back into running, searching for a home, losing friends and family? But all she said was "Okay."

"Leia."

She looked up. Rey was staring at her, expression intense.

"We have to fight," she said simply. "I know it's hard, but what's the alternative? Let the First Order win? They wouldn't spare our friends and family. At least we fight for what we love this way. As long as we fight," Rey continued, "there's hope."

Hope. A small word, but so precious. So difficult to maintain and easy to lose. But Leia wouldn't let herself lose it. She could do that much. For Han and Luke, for Hahnee and the Phantom Squadron pilot whose name she didn't know. For the living, too. All of them. For Rey and Rose and Poe and Finn and for the future of the Resistance that she hadn't even met yet.

"There's always hope," Leia agreed. "Drops of water, right?"

Rey's nod was solemn. "Which we will build to an ocean."

And then they were airborne, shields engaged and dodging cannon fire. Leaving Ryloth behind.

CHAPTER 34

ALARMS SHRIEKED ALL AROUND them, eardrum-poppingly loud. Wedge tried to ignore the awful sound, but it was overwhelming. It kept him on edge, as it was no doubt meant to, and he expected the team to turn a corner and find themselves face-to-face with a battalion of stormtroopers at any minute.

A vicious curse ahead of him drew his attention to the front. It was Nasz. She had paused to take aim at a speaker up in the rafters of the nearest building, obviously fed up with the noise, too.

"It's not going to—" Wedge started, but he didn't have a chance to finish before she'd pulled the trigger. Silence. Merciful silence, and their menagerie of prisoners and pilots paused in appreciation.

But the relief was short-lived as another alarm kicked in, this one even louder, he was sure, as if indignant about the fate of its predecessor.

He met Teza's eyes. She shrugged. *I tried,* she mouthed.

Snap approached, crouched at a low run.

"We're getting close," he said. "I've seen a couple

of patrols now. Whatever drew the stormtroopers away earlier must be over. Everyone's headed back this way."

Wedge frowned, worried.

"Any word from Poe?"

"Karé gave him our coordinates. We should expect him and his team soon. Otherwise . . ." He spread his hands.

"Everyone's okay, right? Finn, the others? No reports of injuries?"

"Looks like it. But they did pick up an extra passenger."

"He say who?"

Snap shook his head. "Suralinda said they'd explain when they got here."

"Okay," Wedge said. He chewed at his lip, thinking. Their window of escape was closing, he could feel it, but they couldn't leave without Poe and his team.

"Thoughts?" Snap said, sounding tense. He knew they were running out of time, too.

Stay? Go?

"Wedge?"

"We stay," he said. "We don't leave without Poe."

"Then we might not leave at all." That was Nasz.

Wedge turned. "What do you mean?"

"Over there."

A small group of people in First Order uniforms were running their way, blasters clearly visible in their hands.

"I count five," Snap said grimly. "Easy enough."

"I take the two on the right, you take the left," Nasz said, unshouldering her rifle. "Wedge, you take the middle."

"Wait!" That was Norra, shuffling up behind them. "They aren't First Order. Look closer."

Wedge peered across the grounds through the darkness. The figures resolved, two in white, three in what looked like black, or colors close enough to be black in the dark of the night. But two wore dresses and one wore a robe. And one was a Twi'lek.

"It's Poe," he breathed, relieved. He stood from his crouch and waved. The group noticed him and swerved their course to intercept. Moments later Poe was there, Wedge embracing him in a welcoming hug.

"We sure are glad to see you," Poe said. "Thought we'd lost our ride for a while there."

"What happened?" Wedge asked.

"First Order caught wind of the auction and raided the party. Shut down the port and weren't letting anyone out. We lost Charth's ship."

"It's a small thing," Charth said. "We got what we came for."

"The list?" Norra asked.

Poe motioned to a woman who had been hanging back, as if taking in the scene. She wore a dress of white shells that hung heavy and waterlogged on her frame and a serpent of some kind curled close around her throat. "This is Nifera Shu. She has the list. We get her off the planet, she gives us the list."

She nodded an acknowledgment.

"Do you know there's a water serpent on your neck?" Nasz asked, eyebrow raised.

Nifera smiled. "Yes."

"Okay." The ex-Imperial lifted her hands in innocence. "Just checking."

"Everyone accounted for," Norra said. "Time to get the hell off this planet."

"Ideas on how to do that?" Poe asked.

"Stormtroopers ahead," Snap told them.

"How many?"

"Sixty. Maybe more. They're guarding the entrance to the shipyard."

Poe grimaced. "As if we were expected?"

"Our luck was bound to run out," Wedge said. "Yama," he called over his shoulder. Yama came forward. She stopped at Nasz's side, sticking close to the larger woman. "Is there another way around?" Wedge asked the girl.

"We can go through the building," she said, pointing a thumb back toward the skytower they had passed. "But the halls are narrow and there's a lift and a checkpoint."

"So our best bet is entering here," he said to Poe, filling in the blanks, "only we need a way to get past the troopers?"

"Create a distraction," Norra offered. "Wedge and I can lead them off while the rest of you get through."

"No guarantee they follow you," Snap said, already looking worriedly at his mother.

"We'll make it worth their while," Norra said. "We'll go in the way Yama said. We'll make a lot of noise, make them think we're bringing in the prisoners that way."

"Mom . . ."

"We only need to split them. If we can get even half of them to follow us—"

"That's still two against thirty," Snap countered.

"Snap," Poe said, voice quiet. "It's not a bad idea."

"Then I'll go," he said.

"Son." Wedge hadn't spoken yet, letting the debate play out. But now he did, picking his words with care. "We can do this, Norra and I. You get the prisoners out of here. Find us a transport big enough for everyone."

Snap's face brightened. "Maybe that blockade runner?"

"A man after my own mind. You think you can fly it?"

"Oh yeah." And then his face fell, as if remembering the plan. "But what about you and Mom?"

"We'll be okay," Wedge assured him.

Snap stared at Wedge, emotions cycling over his face as quickly as the weather changed on Akiva. Wedge knew he wanted to protest but he didn't. He pressed his lips together until they were thinned to white and nodded once before turning away.

Norra sighed, gaze lingering on her son.

"Okay," Poe said, breaking the tension. "Go. We'll make our move when we see the troopers split." He thumped Wedge on the shoulder. "See you on the other side."

———

The plan worked almost too well. Wedge was sure that all but a few of the sixty stormtroopers that Snap had spotted guarding the shipyard entrance were now firing at them. They had the slightly higher ground, and from their vantage at the top of a winding ramp, he could see the entire hangar spread out before them. And there, in the far corner, their shuttle.

A laser blast flew past him, too close for comfort, and he ducked back down behind the heavy metal desks he and Norra had piled up to serve as cover.

"How long do you think we can hold?" he asked. His blaster was overheating in his hand, and while he had a backup strapped to his belt, after that one was done, they were done.

"Long as we need to," Norra said between gritted teeth. She leaned out to take a few more shots.

"And then what?" he asked.

She looked back at him.

He laughed. "Guess this is what I get for wanting to be a hero."

"Since when have you wanted to be a hero?" she scoffed.

She was right. All he had ever wanted to do was be a pilot. Being a hero was secondary, and other people were better suited for the spotlight. Wedge had only ever wanted to do his best, recognition be damned.

"There!" Norra said.

Wedge peered over the edge of their makeshift

shelter to see Snap and the rest of his team leading the prisoners at a run through the hangar. The group broke into two, Nasz and Charth leading the weak and injured to the Imperial shuttle where Karé ushered them inside, and the rest of the team, including Finn, Nifera, and Snap, headed for the big blockade runner. Everyone was accounted for except . . .

"Where's Poe?" he asked. "And Suralinda?"

"They can take care of themselves," Norra said. "Keep shooting. We're almost out but we're not there yet."

Wedge took aim at a stormtrooper who had pressed forward again. He pulled the trigger, but the blaster didn't respond. It was spent.

He muttered a curse and dropped it, reaching for his backup. But it was too late. Blasterfire, and his arm lit up in pain like it was on fire. He cried out and fell back, instinctively reaching for the place where he took the hit.

"Wedge!" Norra screamed. She crawled over to him, careful to stay low. She looked out only long enough to take down the trooper who had shot him. Then she was at his side.

"Are you okay?"

He shook his head, tears coming unbidden to his eyes. "Hurts like a bastard."

"I bet." She probed gently at the burned material and charred flesh. A grimace slipped over her face but was gone just as quickly.

"That bad?"

He didn't have to ask. He could smell it. See a glimpse of white bone through his shirt.

"And it's my shooting arm," he said lightly.

"Well, it's about time you get ambidextrous, husband," Norra said, slipping his backup blaster from its holder and slapping it into his good hand. She turned him, careful not to jar his arm, until he was propped up, leaning just slightly over the edge of the desks. He squeezed the trigger, tentative, and then with more confidence. His aim was terrible, but it was better than nothing.

Norra gave him a tight smile and crawled back to her position.

The next time he managed to look out over the hangar floor it was all clear, which meant everyone had made it to their respective ships. As if in confirmation, the cluster of engines in the blockade runner rumbled to life. That got a few troopers' attention, and they turned to look back. The smaller Imperial shuttle was rising under Karé's command. A handful of stormtroopers broke off and ran for the shuttle, but they'd never make it before Karé got them off the ground. Even so, Wedge took the opportunity to lay down more fire, but he was already feeling dizzy, his good arm weak.

"Wedge . . ." Norra's voice held a warning. "No passing out."

"Wouldn't dream of it," he said. "But Norra, if I can't stay on my feet, I want you to . . ." He swallowed. "I want you to—"

"Don't even say it," she growled. "We're in this together. You stay, I stay. We make a run for it together or we don't go at all."

"But—"

"Done talking."

He smiled. "I love you."

"Good. Now stay alive."

It was all bravado. There were still two dozen stormtroopers between them and the shuttle. Hopeless.

Wedge thought about the last time he'd been captured by enemy forces. He'd been tortured and his body had never fully recovered. He'd been a younger man then, and he had still barely made it out alive. If he was captured now he had no doubt that the First Order would gleefully torture him to try to find the Resistance's whereabouts. He also had no doubts about whether he would make it this time. No, this was it, his last stand. He would rather die here with a blaster in his hand and Norra by his side than hope to survive the tender mercies of the First Order. Although . . . he looked over at Norra. What about her? Would he doom her to death, too? Maybe if he surrendered it would give her a chance to run. He hesitated . . .

And the wall to his left exploded.

The air filled with falling stone torn free from the interior wall of the building. Dust billowed around them, turning the world gray. Wedge coughed as the thick grime crawled into his lungs. Blinded, struggling to breathe, and his arm useless.

The sound of firing continued, but this was a big gun, not a stormtrooper's rifle, and Wedge realized, incredulously, that someone was firing from one of the starfighters in the hangar.

"What the?" He dragged himself up in time to see

the ship mow down the remaining stormtroopers like grain in the field.

"Poe better cut it out or he's going to bring this building down on us, too," Norra said as she came to his side, and while she had a point, all he could do was laugh.

"Do you think you can walk?"

Wedge nodded, and Norra got him to his feet.

"I did not see that coming," he admitted.

"Talk about it once we're on board," she said as they made their way down the now empty ramp. They hurried across the open hangar, expecting trouble, but the fighter hovered nearby, providing cover.

Snap was there to greet them as they reached the ramp of the blockade runner. His face clouded over as he took in Wedge's wound.

"My own fault," he said, jaw tight.

Snap nodded. "I'm just glad you're okay, Dad."

Something swelled in Wedge's chest. His heart, he guessed. *Dad.*

"I'm great, son. Just great." And he meant it.

CHAPTER 35

POE LED THE SHUTTLE out of the Corellian atmosphere, Suralinda flying rear guard. He grinned as he banked and broke into space. The First Order ship he'd lifted maneuvered like a dream. Lightweight, flexible. It put the borrowed ship he'd been flying to shame. But he'd still take his X-wing over this beauty any day.

His comm blinked. Not the one on the ship, but his handheld. He answered it.

"Looks like we've got pursuit," Suralinda said, voice bright.

"You sound happy about it," he said.

She laughed. "Aren't you? I want to see what this ship can do."

She had a point. "Our focus is to get the shuttle and that CR90 corvette out of here. Don't lose sight of the mission, Suralinda."

"Copy, Black Leader," she said, voice slightly mocking. "Breaking off to engage."

He thought about arguing with her, but what was the point? It was Suralinda.

Another call came in. It was from the shuttle.

"Did you see we've got company?" Karé asked, voice tight.

"Suralinda's on it. She'll draw them off and keep them busy until we can jump to lightspeed."

"There's a problem. We got a call from the *Falcon*."

Poe tensed. In the heat of their escape from Corellia, he had not forgotten that there was trouble on Ryloth, but there was little he could do to help, so he'd pushed it to the back of his mind. Now his worry came barreling back, and he asked, fear in his voice, "Everything all right?"

"Looks like the First Order found them."

His stomach dropped.

"Leia's all right," Karé added quickly. "Everyone on the *Falcon* made it. But we lost some, including Charth's sister and at least one of the Phantom Squadron."

He swallowed down some of the initial panic he'd felt. Leia was okay. But at least two lives lost, and one of them Charth's sister. Another likely a friend of Wedge and Norra.

"We can't go back to Ryloth, Poe," Karé said. "Where do we jump?"

"Pick a spot," he said. "As long as it's far from here and we know the First Order won't be there."

"They could be anywhere," she said. "How will we know?"

They wouldn't. They were on the run again, just like that. Nowhere safe. Nowhere they couldn't be found. Except . . .

"Karé, let me talk to Nifera."

A pause and then, "Hold on."

A few seconds passed before Nifera's voice came through. "Hello, Lorell."

"It's Poe. Poe Dameron."

He could almost hear her smile. "I know."

"We need somewhere safe to set down for a while. Not long. Just a meeting point to regroup, disseminate the list. A day at most."

Silence at first, and then, "And you think I can help you?"

"I think the Collective can help us."

"And why would they do that?"

"Because we just helped their benefactor escape certain death."

A soft laugh that he definitely heard this time. "Very well, Poe Dameron. I'll help you. After you make a generous donation to our cause."

"Yeah, about that . . . didn't you already take half our credits?"

"And now I aim to take the other half."

If he agreed, he was close to bankrupting the Resistance. But if he didn't, they wouldn't have a chance to spend those credits because they might all be dead.

"Take the money, lady," he said, jaw tight.

Another pause, and just when Poe was about to lose his patience again, Nifera was back.

"I've given your pilot coordinates to a safe house. She will transmit them to yourself and your other friends. I will let them know to expect us."

His shoulders loosened in relief. "Thank you."

"A pleasure doing business," she said, and then Karé was back.

"Did she give you coordinates?" he asked.

"Yeah. Sending out to Resistance channels now."

Poe cut the communication once he had the coordinates, too. He circled back around and waited until the shuttle, and then the blockade runner, blurred out, jumping to hyperspace.

He punched up Suralinda. "You ready?"

"Race you there!"

She accelerated and seconds later was gone.

Poe followed.

Poe pushed his way through the crowd, head down and hood drawn close to hide his face. He found the door, the lintel marked with the now familiar winding horned white serpent.

He glanced over his shoulder to see if anyone was watching him, but if they were, he couldn't spot them. He'd made this trip three times before, each time bringing in prisoners in small groups so they wouldn't attract as much attention.

He nodded to Finn, who stood watch in a slice of alleyway across the crowded road. Finn returned the nod. All clear.

Poe opened the door marked with the sign of the Collective and ushered in his last group of prisoners. He'd brought the weakest first, those most in need of medical care. This final group was relatively physically functional, if not quite whole in other ways.

Ransolm Casterfo, Leia's old friend, was the last

through the door. Seconds later Finn joined him, and they went through together.

The door opened into a deserted storage room, but Poe already knew this was a deception. He wound his way through the huge boxes piled to the ceiling, catching a glimpse of the Collective, shrouded all in white, who hid on top of the crates, tracking his path, blasters in hand.

Finally they reached a small side door where Zay, the young pilot from Inferno Squadron, was ushering the last of the prisoners through. She smiled when she saw him.

"Is that everyone?" she asked.

"Should be."

She let him and Finn duck through first. As she pulled the door closed, Poe saw two of the Collective appear to push crates in front of the door, hiding it as if it had never been there.

They entered a larger room, low-ceilinged and dark except for scattered yellow lights set high on the bare walls. Someone had set out long tables with food and drink. Nothing fancy, but the room had the feel of celebration about it. Muted, wary, but hopeful.

Poe and the others paused at the top of a small landing. Just below him, a handful of wide stairs led down into the main room, this one crowded with familiar faces and hushed conversation. He watched as Ransolm paused a few meters in front of him at the edge of the landing to look around, bewildered.

Leia approached Ransolm, a smile on her face as she climbed the steps.

The man seemed to shake, arms still at his sides, until Leia, very gently, as if aware he might break, embraced him.

"I thought you were dead," Poe heard her whisper.

"But you came for me anyway, my friend."

"I hoped," she said simply. They stood there a moment longer, together, before she broke away. She pressed a hand to his arm. "Come meet everyone," she said, ushering him into the room. Rose was there, and she took his hand, a warm smile of greeting on her face, and led him deeper into the room.

Leia watched them go before turning to Poe.

"General," he said.

"Commander."

Poe looked around. He saw that Leia and Rieekan had already turned the space into a sort of war room, a holomap of the galaxy spread out against one wall.

"Did Nifera give you the list?" he asked.

"Already disseminated," Leia confirmed. "Yendor and Orrimaarko are making assignments now. We'll find them all. Warn those who are in the First Order's sights, rescue those in danger, and recruit who we can."

"Yeah," he said, absently. A sudden wash of doubt, and Poe felt daunted by the task ahead of them, but Leia's voice brought him back, grounded him.

"One step at a time," she said, no doubt sensing his anxiety. "We're not taking on the entire First

Order tomorrow. We can't. But we can take one step, and that earns us another day to take another step."

"We can't do it alone."

"And we won't. We'll find people, we'll inspire them. Show them they aren't alone, show them what's worth fighting for. And we'll prepare and rebuild. This," she said, gesturing to take in the room, "is a beginning."

Poe took in all the faces, all the people who were now the Resistance. Nasz stood by the map, arms crossed, arguing something with Shriv. Yama hovered nearby, never far from the warlord. Black Squadron was spread around the room, all accounted for, as were Wedge and what remained of his hodgepodge Phantom Squadron, and C-3PO and R2-D2 and BB-8.

His heart swelled. He loved this, loved seeing them all together. But Leia was right. It still wasn't enough. And now, he had to break them up.

He stepped away from Leia, resting a hand briefly on her arm in gratitude as he passed. He planted his feet on the top step, surveying the room.

"We can't stay here," he said, projecting his voice over the assembly. Conversations faded as everyone turned to listen, faces wary. He cleared his throat, shaking off any lingering nerves. "If Ryloth showed us anything, it was that nowhere that the Resistance gathers is safe from the First Order."

Silence so thick Poe was sure he could hear his own heartbeat. He took a deep breath, exhaled, and continued.

"We can take joy in this victory," he assured them. "We made opportunity where there wasn't any"—his gaze cut briefly to Shriv—"we freed those who were unjustly imprisoned, and we've found those who will mold the future of the Resistance. We can be proud."

A round of applause that quickly died down when he raised his hand.

"But this is just a first step," he said with a nod of acknowledgment to Leia, "and we cannot rest."

"What do we do next? Where do we go?" someone shouted. Heads turned. It was the young pilot, Agoyo.

"Anywhere," Poe said. "Everywhere. Every corner of the galaxy where someone is fighting tyranny, where someone is standing up against injustice. Because the Resistance is not just in this room. It is not only the people on that list. In fact, it is not one person or one place. It is a million people, a thousand places, each one the Resistance.

"So, what do we do now? We scatter to every corner of the galaxy, taking our message with us. We help those already fighting the First Order, we make allies, we sow the spark of resistance. And when the time comes, we will be ready. We will rise up, and we will fight. And all of us, together, will burn the First Order to the ground."

More shouting and applause, and then he was surrounded, people slapping him on the back and laughing and calling his name in celebration. He soaked it all in, letting it wash his past away, allowing it to lift him to a better place. A future.

"Poe."

It was Wedge, his arm in a sling, and beside him Norra. "We're going, Poe," he said. "I know you and Leia were hoping we'd stay around and lead or whatever, but . . ." He shook his head. "I . . . we . . . belong out there. In the stars. I know that now."

"*We* know that now," Norra added, slipping her hand into her husband's. "And we can do good out there in the margins, like you said. Let people know a fight is coming."

"We're pilots, not generals," Wedge added. "You understand."

Poe nodded. He did understand. And it wasn't a complete surprise. "You'll keep in touch?"

"Snap will know how to reach me."

"Have you told him?"

"Told me what?" Snap asked as he took the stairs two at a time to join them.

"We're leaving, son," Norra said, her voice soft, patient.

Snap's face clouded. "What? But you just got here."

"I know," Wedge said, "and now we need to go."

"I'll go with you," Snap said hurriedly.

"I need you here, Black Squadron," Poe countered gently.

"But . . ." Snap looked at each of them, helplessly, scanning their faces for something. And whatever he saw there shuddered through his body as acceptance. "You always do this to me," he murmured before asking, "You sure you have to go?"

"We'll see you again," Wedge assured him.

"We promise," Norra added. She stepped forward and wrapped her son in a hug, arms tight around his big frame, before he could say no. But Poe didn't think he would have said no, anyway, that much was clear from the way he melted into his mother's embrace. Then Wedge was there, folding both mother and son into his arms and Poe stepped away to let the family say their goodbyes.

"Great speech," Finn said, bounding up the steps, a glass in each hand. He handed Poe a drink, something dark and unpleasantly thick. "You're getting pretty good at those."

"Thanks." Poe took a tentative sip. Awful. He set the mug down.

"So when do we leave?" Finn asked, eyes big over the edge of his glass as he drank.

Poe cocked an eyebrow. "You coming with?"

"I don't think you can stop me."

"Where are we going?" asked a familiar voice. Both men turned to find Rey, looking expectant.

Finn grinned. "I didn't want to ask."

Rey grinned back. "You didn't have to."

The two friends laughed, leaning in to touch shoulders in acknowledgment. Rey looked at Poe, eyes narrowed as if unsure. "You don't mind?"

Poe pressed a hand to his heart, giving Rey a small bow. "I'm honored."

She flushed, pleased, as he'd hoped she would be.

As he straightened, he caught Leia watching them, an expression he couldn't quite read on her face. He looked back, eyebrow raised. Ah, he recognized that look now. Satisfaction.

"She knows," Rey said, drawing his attention back.

"Knows what?" Finn asked.

"That the Resistance is in good hands," Poe said, quietly. "That we won't fail her."

"Because of the Force?" Finn asked, sounding slightly awed.

"I don't think Leia needs the Force to tell her that," Rey said.

"Ah! Right! She knows because she's got us."

Poe slung an arm around Finn's shoulders and pulled Rey in close on the opposite side.

"That's right," Poe said. "She's got us.

"Now let's go save the galaxy."

ACKNOWLEDGMENTS

Look, Mom! I wrote a Star War!

But I didn't do it alone. Thank you to the wonderful team that got me here.

To Tom, my patient and understanding editor, who always had a fix for my bad plot holes, a kind word for my ideas even when they were questionable (skywriting!), and approved when I said I wanted to try to get the gang all back together again.

To Jen, Matt, and Pablo of Lucasfilm who kept me on track and generously shared their vast and frankly intimidating knowledge of all things *Star Wars* with me.

To Elizabeth and everyone at Del Rey who read drafts and gave input and made me feel like maybe it was all going to be okay.

To my husband, Mike, and daughter, Maya, who watched the movies, games, animation, and everything else with me many, many times, who tolerated the past six months of insanity and me constantly yelling, "I can't do anything else because I'm writing a Star War," and who never hesitated to bring me coffee at 3 A.M., as if that was an entirely reasonable request.

To Sara, my superstar agent. Forget world domination. We're aiming for the galaxy now.

And thanks to everyone, especially the Indigenerds, who celebrated this awesomeness with me. I see you and I love you all.

Read on for an excerpt from

GALAXY'S EDGE: BLACK SPIRE

By Delilah S. Dawson

Published by Del Rey Books

CHAPTER ONE

THE LIFE OF A Resistance spy was all about excitement—or at least, that's why Vi Moradi signed up. That, and the chance to do some good and strike back at tyranny. As Vi stood outside the office of General Leia Organa, she was anxious to see what her next assignment would be. She was getting that old restless feeling and needed something to do, something real. On Major Kalonia's orders, she'd spent the past several weeks recuperating from her last mission, and she was itching for activity beyond debriefing pilots and gathering intel from their droids on enemy firepower and fighting prowess. They knew the First Order was out there and supposedly unbeatable; did they really need to keep reaffirming that through numbers? Vi liked being an underdog, but she didn't necessarily want to know the odds.

"Come in, Magpie."

Vi smiled at the way Leia always used one of her call signs and stepped inside the makeshift office, taking a seat on an old red crate. "Good to see you, General."

Every time Vi was in the presence of General Organa, once Princess Leia Organa of Alderaan, it felt a little like going home. Leia had a calm, steady presence, motherly but tough as nails, and no matter how dire things got, the older woman had a way of looking at each member of the Resistance as if they were the hero that could turn the tide against their enemy, the dreaded First Order that had risen from the Empire's ashes. Leia returned Vi's smile, her eyes twinkling.

"I have a mission for you," Leia said, her attention flicking from various holos to Vi and back. Leia's mouth fell into a familiar grim line, which told Vi she wasn't necessarily going to like her assignment. That was fine—she didn't particularly like how her last mission had gone, either. It wasn't her job to like it.

"As you know, we're massively outgunned. We don't know what the First Order is planning, but it's something big. Some kind of attack. I'm leaving immediately for Takodana to collect some valuable intel, so I wanted to meet with you personally and underline how very important your work will be."

"If you brought me in just to tell me it's important, it sounds like it might not be that important. I'm ready to work, General. Major Kalonia signed off. I'm back in top form."

Leia's gaze was unwavering. "I wouldn't blame

you if you just disappeared, after what happened to you on the *Absolution*. You were captured by the enemy, Vi. Tortured. Beaten. Shocked. Injured. I've read your med charts and your reports. Downplay it all you like, but an experience like that changes people. I should know."

Vi shook her head. "But I'm still me. So put me on a Star Destroyer and let me—"

"No." Leia cut her off, almost apologetic, and Vi's mouth snapped shut. "This assignment might sound like a vacation, but I assure you, it's of vast strategic importance. If you're ready."

Vi shifted on the crate, her back aching. Leia was right—she'd taken a beating on her last assignment, and although most of her wounds had healed, her body wasn't getting any younger. Leia had sent her to a forgotten planet called Parnassos to gather intel on the First Order's Captain Phasma, which was challenging enough. But on her way home, Vi had been captured by a different First Order officer, Captain Cardinal.

Instead of interrogating her through official channels or turning her over to Kylo Ren or General Hux, Cardinal had secretly taken her to a dank chamber in the ship's lower levels and tortured her for the information she'd collected on his rival in the First Order, Captain Phasma. In the end, Vi had managed to manipulate him into letting her go, and Cardinal had gone out to face Phasma in combat. Vi made it out of the enemy ship and back to the fleet, and for the last few weeks she'd struggled to process all that had happened to her and heal in body and mind. But despite what she'd told Kalonia and now Leia, was she really ready to go back to work?

Well, was anyone ever ready to move on from trauma?

It would never leave her, but she couldn't stay still any longer. It wasn't in her nature.

"I'm ready," she told Leia, putting the full force of conviction in her words.

"Good." Leia's smile returned. "Should the First Order succeed in their attack, or should they find us here on D'Qar, we need two things most of all: allies and places to hide. So I'm looking for suggestions on a place so out of the way that the First Order would never even think of it, a place where we could set up camp and put down roots. Specifically, we need an inhabited planet with an active port and resources, but not anything big, not anything the First Order would find advantageous."

"Castilon isn't safe anymore," Vi thought out loud. "Not Pantora. Nowhere in the Core or Mid Rim, or any place where we've had a base before. Definitely not Parnassos."

"Definitely not. Think, Magpie."

Vi raised an eyebrow; Leia was not in a patient mood. "Batuu, maybe? I've heard of it, but I've never been there. It's out on the edge of Wild Space. The main settlement is called Black Spire Outpost. It's rough. Primitive. Seedy. Exciting. Smugglers consider it a good place to hide or hop a ship that can't be tracked."

At that, the general nodded. "I knew I could

count on you. Batuu is perfect." She chuckled. "Han told me all about it."

Leaning forward, Vi gave her a suspicious look. "That can't be the only reason you called me in here—just to ask me a question. You have strategists for that."

"But I don't need strategists." Leia likewise leaned forward. "I need *you*, Magpie. I trust you. And what I need you to do is go to Black Spire Outpost on the planet Batuu, establish an outpost for the Resistance, and collect as much support as possible among the locals and visitors. We need bodies. We need friends. We need skills. We need ships and food and fuel. We need eyes and ears on the ground. We need a place we can go if everything falls apart, a place so far off the map that the First Order has forgotten it even exists. To them, Batuu will seem strategically useless. But to us, it's another spark of hope. I need you to cultivate that spark, to keep the fire burning."

Vi leaned back, letting her head fall to the side. "So why do I feel like you're promoting me out of harm's way? Protecting me? Maybe even coddling me?" She held Leia's gaze, never an easy task. "Use me, General. I have skills no one else has. I'm your best spy. So why are you sending me to what's basically nowhere?"

"Because nowhere is what might save us. You're not the only valuable person being sent out to nowhere." Leia gave her a significant look, blew out a sigh, and took on an air of urgency, as if Vi had already been excused. "That's your assignment. Take it or leave it. I'm needed on Takodana immediately. They're holding the ship for me, and I'm out of time to convince you. The great thing about the Resistance is that you always retain free will. I hope you'll trust me when I tell you that your work on Batuu is part of a larger plan. So do you trust me, Magpie?"

The general's eyebrows went up, her graying hair in a perfect crown. Yes, Vi did trust her. And Vi wasn't going to walk away, even though she knew it was always an option.

"I trust you, General," she finally said.

Leia nodded. "Good. Dismissed. Report to the hangar tomorrow morning. Lieutenant Connix will provide further details and a manifest of your cargo. You'll be assigned a droid to help with the heavy lifting and logistics. We're giving you the materials, and we need you to scout the ideal site, connect with the local population, recruit new bodies to join the cause, and establish communications so we can discuss next steps."

Vi stood. "I'll do my best, General."

The smile she gave Leia was resigned. Yes, she would do her duty. In this case, Vi didn't think she would like it, but she was a soldier, and she would do whatever it took to resist the First Order and keep the galaxy safe.

But as Vi headed for the door, the general said, "Oh, and Magpie? One more thing."

Vi couldn't help chuckling as she turned around. "Of course. There's always one more thing, isn't there?"

Leia stood, looking grim and regal and certain. Vi steeled herself for what she knew would be unwelcome news.

"I'm assigning you a partner for this mission, and again I need you to trust me."

Vi leaned against the door and crossed her arms. "Uh-oh. That doesn't bode well. You know I prefer to work alone. And if it was somebody I liked, you would've led with that."

"Perceptive as ever." Leia rolled her eyes as if to suggest Vi had caught her out. "Before you head for Batuu, I need you to make a quick stop on Cerea to pick up someone. Archex."

"Who's Archex?"

The general's gaze went dark, serious. "The man you knew as Captain Cardinal has chosen to return to his childhood name."

Cardinal.

Archex was Cardinal.

Vi went cold all over as images flipped through her mind—unwelcome ones. Cardinal pulling her from her ship, putting her in binders, strapping her into an interrogation chair he wasn't quite certain how to use. His face when she'd first convinced him to take off his shining red helmet. The conviction in his eyes, the unwavering faith in his calling. The way her vision went red each time he'd used that chair to shock her, pushing her further toward the edge of desolation, toward betraying all that she stood for.

She'd turned him against the First Order, sure—but just barely.

Cardinal had gone out to face his rival, Phasma, who'd nearly killed him. And then Vi did something unusual, something she still didn't quite understand: She'd saved him. Dragged Cardinal's dying carcass across the *Absolution,* stole a ship, and hightailed it back to D'Qar with her enemy and torturer by her side.

She'd seen something in Captain Cardinal, something she'd thought impossible: a good man who believed in the First Order with all his heart. And she'd used that good to convert him—if not into a Resistance fighter, then at least away from the First Order's lies.

She hadn't seen him since they'd landed on D'Qar and he'd been hurried to the medbay.

She hadn't wanted to.

"Archex," she said woodenly, dumbly. The name tasted like blood in her mouth, like the metallic burn left behind by his interrogation chair's repeated shocks.

But Leia went on as if she hadn't noticed Vi's discomfort. "I sent him to Cerea for . . . well, let's call it a restful retreat with gentle deprogramming while we monitored his recovery. He's as healed as he'll ever be and cleared for work. Although he hasn't fully committed to our cause and will continue to wear a monitor, he needs something to do. You two are more alike than you know."

Vi barked a bitter laugh. "I bet we are."

"Look, I need him with someone we can trust, someone *he* can trust. You were the first one who told me he might be worth saving, after all."

"Yes, I was. And I'm starting to regret it."

Vi still couldn't quite process what she was hearing, couldn't understand why Leia would do this. "Am I being punished for something?" she asked, voice rasping.

Leia swiftly moved around the desk and grasped Vi by the shoulders. "No. Of course not. I'm doing what I've always done: putting the best person on the job. You have the skills to command, to think on your feet. You're the one who turned Cardinal, who made that connection. I believe you can use that skill to help our cause. You're a great spy, Vi, but you're also a leader, and I know you're going to succeed. We need places like you're going to build on Batuu, and we need Archex, and as hard as it might be for you to hear, I think Archex needs you."

But what about me? Vi wanted to ask. *What about what I need?*

What she needed was a job that would bring back that old beloved zing of excitement, the thrill of going undercover, collecting intel, foiling bad guys, and returning a hero. Instead she was being sent to the far end of nowhere with her enemy, the man whose visage haunted her when she woke at night, screaming and covered in a sheen of sweat.

"Vi?"

Leia still held her shoulders, looking concerned. Vi shook off her misgivings, exhaled, and met the general's gaze.

She could do this. She *would* do this. For Leia, for the Resistance, she would do anything.

"Yes, General," she said. "I'll do my best."

Finally, Leia smiled that smile that made it seem like anything was possible.

"I know you will," she said. "That's why I chose you. Good luck on Batuu, Magpie. And may the Force be with you."

CHAPTER TWO

THE NEXT MORNING, BEFORE she was due in the hangar, Vi stopped in the medbay and asked for Major Kalonia. She'd seen a lot of the doctor since returning to D'Qar, and her wounds had healed as much as they ever would, inside and out. Today, however, she had a different reason for visiting.

"Trying to get out of this assignment?" Kalonia asked with her usual wry grin. The older human woman had smoothly bobbed dark hair threaded with gray and was known for her competence as a physician and her warm bedside manner. "As I told Leia, you're perfectly fit for your usual misadventures."

"It's not me I'm worried about," Vi told her. "It's Archex. I understand you treated him here when we returned from the *Absolution* and that you've been monitoring his recovery while he's been on Cerea?"

Kalonia tilted her head knowingly. "Discussing

the private concerns of my patients is generally considered a breach of protocol—"

Vi opened her mouth to interrupt, but Kalonia stopped her with a hand.

"But Leia and I suspected you would want answers. I don't blame you; if you're going to be stuck in a transport with him and then alone on a planet far from backup, you deserve to know what you're dealing with. Considering he's technically a political prisoner who hasn't yet formally joined the Resistance, we feel it's reasonable to share some information that will be relevant to your partnership."

Partnership. Vi snorted. "That's not the word I would use for it."

Kalonia shrugged. "Collaboration, then. Let me show you."

The physician led Vi over to a bank of screens and pulled up a holo. There was Cardinal as Vi had last seen him, still in his bright-red armor and black captain's cape as Kalonia, med droids, and other personnel swarmed around him under bright lights. He was on a gurney, his helmet off, unconscious. A worrisome amount of blood stained his armor, especially in the two places where Phasma had stabbed him with a poisoned blade she carried from her homeworld.

"When you brought him to us, he was in bad shape. Lost a lot of blood. The weapon introduced an organic compound we'd never seen before, and it took us a while to work up—well, not an antidote. We couldn't just cancel it out. But we were able to fight it. Still, one lung was punctured, and the wound in his leg was deep and festering. We did all we could, but for all our technology, as you know, medicine is still an imperfect, messy science."

Kalonia pulled up a new holo, this one showing Cardinal out of his armor and clad in the usual white medcenter gown, sitting up in a bed and connected to several machines by tubes. He looked so different without the bulky plating, smaller and more human, and Vi realized that this wasn't Captain Cardinal—it was the man who now went by the name Archex. His black hair had grown out a little, but his face was as she remembered it, his yellow-gold skin freckled from a childhood under the Jakku sun, and his creased brown eyes troubled. He wasn't smiling.

"At first, he was withdrawn and seemed . . . well, like he'd lost the will to live."

"He told me so," Vi murmured. "When I was pushing his gurney out of the *Absolution*. He said *let me die,* over and over."

"Yes, well, letting people die is not my job," Kalonia continued with a twitch of her lips. "So I did my best to help him through it. We see this sometimes, in war—soldiers become disillusioned. They lose faith. They don't know how to go on. And yet there's just something about him, isn't there? He's a survivor, but not the kind made cruel by the crucible that forged him. He didn't seem to want to live, and yet he approached rehabilitation like it was his job. He walked weeks before we thought he would. He exercised on his own time, even though I'd warned him that his lung wasn't ready for it."

She flicked the screen over to a video of Archex doing push-ups. Sweat beaded his brow, and he was clearly struggling. His arms and legs wobbled, and he toppled over, but he quickly got back up and continued. Vi watched him gasping for breath like he'd run a kilometer, his eyes grimly determined.

"He doesn't give up easy," she noted.

"He does not," Kalonia confirmed.

"But what about his psyche? Is he . . . broken?"

Kalonia clicked her tongue. "No more than you, or me, or Leia. So many of us came to the Resistance via tragedy. He's healing, but he has a long way to go. The program on Cerea is intended to give him the space and time he needs. When you're in the middle of things, on a base like this or one of our ships, you get caught up in the cycle. Everyone needs downtime to figure things out."

"But is he safe?"

"Let's not fool ourselves, Moradi. No one here is safe. But he's not violent. He's cogent and reasonable and even if he hasn't joined us, he's no longer aligned with the First Order. He's not going to attack you in your sleep, if that's what you're worried about. But like you, he might have nightmares for the rest of his life."

Vi sighed. "That's what I needed to know."

"I can heal bones. But I can't heal souls. You have to do that yourself."

Vi looked down, fidgeting. She'd been neglecting that, focusing instead on action. Maybe she'd find some healing herself on Batuu. Maybe life would move slowly and she'd, what? Commune with nature?

Sure, why not?

Well, because she'd run from Chaaktil, and she'd never stop running. As it turned out, there was always another fight.

"Work first, therapy later," she finally said. "I'll focus on healing when we've beat the First Order. So what about—"

"Attention, all hands," Leia's voice boomed through the intercom system. She sounded exhausted and sad, like she'd aged fifty years since the last time Vi had spoken with her, just yesterday. The general had to be well on her way to Takodana by now. The comm system crackled, and Vi held her breath, waiting for more. "To your stations. An unknown weapon has just . . . I don't even know how to say it. We believe . . . somehow . . . we are working to confirm this, but it seems the worst has come to pass. The Hosnian system appears to be gone. Yes, every planet. The entire New Republic government can only be assumed a casualty of this cataclysm." And then, as if an afterthought, "May the Force be with everyone who was lost. May it remain with us all."

It was as if a great hollowness entered Vi's chest. She'd been there—to Hosnian Prime and Hosnian and Cardota. Lived and slept and worked on their surfaces, felt their sun's warmth on her skin. And now they were just . . . gone? She struggled to breathe, thinking of everyone she knew who would count among the dead, recalling faces and names.

At least her brother was still on Pantora, she told herself; he'd once worked as an intern for the Senate. And in a flash she wondered: Was this how Leia had felt, so long ago, when she watched Alderaan explode, knowing exactly what had been lost?

"An entire system," Kalonia said, almost a question, as if she couldn't even comprehend it, either, because who could? "Billions of people . . ."

Vi put a hand on her arm. "Focus on the ones here, now. We're going to need you."

Kalonia nodded, and Vi watched her undergo the process that she'd seen so many of her compatriots undergo, that cycle of emotions she'd felt herself. Whatever doubts a person might have disintegrated in the face of necessity. If the First Order had a weapon like that, the answer wasn't to stop, go silent, wait, cry. The answer was to feel your will coalesce, to firm up your chin and focus on the future and what you could personally do to fight the enemy, to stop such a horror from happening again.

Her comm buzzed. "Magpie? Your mission to Batuu is on hold. You're needed in the hangar."

"I have to go," she said, and Kalonia nodded.

Vi ran.

The Resistance might need Batuu, but Batuu could wait.